CLOCKWORK MAGICIAN

The Two Monarchies Sequence: Book Four

W.R. GINGELL

This book is for everyone who was just as much of an unbearable smart aleck as I was when I was a kid.

❈   I   ❈

It definitely wasn't his fault. The clockwork was perfect—the clockwork was always perfect. Even the magic, as frustratingly old-fashioned as it necessarily was, was still perfect. He had bent it to his will, though he would have preferred to work solely with clockwork, because this was one thing that couldn't be achieved with clockwork alone. As much as Peter hated to admit it, all of his experiments with clockwork had brought him to the same conclusion: travelling through time was possible, but not by clockwork alone.

Four years ago he would have said it wasn't possible at all, but the application of some very uncomfortable magic had shown him otherwise, and he had eagerly taken up the challenge of reproducing that possibility. He had blended magic and clockwork for the last three years, looking for the perfect combination, and he had found it.

And the machine he had made, this perfect fusion of clockwork and magic, had worked for one glorious moment before everything went horribly wrong.

Worse than that, it had gone wrong in front of Miss Glenna Stoneheart—well, Stoneflange, but everyone called her Stoneheart.

Worst of all, she'd told him it would go wrong, and it *had*.

It was impossible: the clockwork was perfect. The magic was perfect.

Peter took off his glasses and polished them.

"You've got about two minutes to explain to me that things haven't gone as terribly wrong as I can tell they've gone," said Glenna Stoneflange. "And then I'm going to punch you in the nose."

"Don't you mean I've got two minutes to explain it, and *if* I don't, you'll punch me in the nose?" Peter asked, putting his glasses back on. "You can't punch me in the nose if I *do* explain it!"

"Don't tell me what I meant," Glenna said, with an ice-frosted flare of temper. "I'm going to punch you either way. I'm just giving you the chance to explain why you thought it was a good idea to kidnap me when I specifically told you *not* to."

That, considered Peter, was pretty rich. If there had been a mistake—and Peter still firmly refused to think of it as *his* mistake, though he admitted the possibility of *a* mistake—*if* there had been a mistake, it had been the inclusion of Miss Stoneflange in his plan. From the first, Peter hadn't meant to include Miss Stoneflange; hadn't, in fact, even known of such a person before he went to the University of Mechanics and Magic...

Perhaps that had been the mistake, going to the University of Mechanics and Magic. At the time, it had seemed better than sulking alone for another year, too far away from his former childhood friend to do any good but too close for comfort. At that distance it was impossible to accidentally run into her and casually begin talking again—just as impossible to make a special trip for the purposes of apologising.

He hadn't been the only one in the wrong, after all.

And it wasn't exactly that he'd spent the last year *sulking*. It had been more of an uncomfortable feeling—the feeling that, in some way, he had been wrong. Peter was unfamiliar with that feeling; it fit him as well as the far-too-large waistcoat he was at present wearing, pinned up at the back so that it didn't gape or hang so obviously. But there weren't any pins that could shore up a sneaking sense of shame, and Peter had preferred not to think about it. Instead, he had thought about the way Melchior had thrown him out of the house, and the way Annabel hadn't stopped it. Annabel was *his* friend, after all. They'd known each other for much longer than she and Melchior had known each other.

And Peter had always had the certainty that he was going to marry Annabel. She was annoying and sometimes slow, but they had agreed to marry when they were younger, and it hadn't occurred to Peter that she might one day change her mind if she met someone else. It was galling; and all the more galling because Melchior didn't possess even a tenth of the magical powers that Peter himself did.

Not that he would have used his abilities to fight back, of course. Magic was old fashioned and primitive, and Peter was better than that. But it did make it hard to fight back when he was thrown ignominiously from the house, his physical strength no match for the strength of a man roughly nine years his senior.

It wasn't as if he'd done anything dreadful, either. He had merely *asked*, politely, why exactly Annabel was going back on her word to marry him.

"That was when I was a child!" Annabel had said indignantly. "And you were the only male I knew!"

The discussion had only become more heated after that, with Peter goaded into wondering aloud if her change had anything to do with her new status as Queen heir, and had culminated in him being thrown out of the house by Melchior.

He had refused to use magic in that struggle partly because he didn't want to feel the need of it, and partly because he already felt slightly ashamed of himself for having said what he had said.

It was too late by then, of course, or so Peter told himself. Too late to bother trying to apologise—and Ann hadn't said anything when he was kicked out, so she should feel a bit badly, too, shouldn't she?

He couldn't go home, to be bothered by unanswerable questions about his disappearance from his mother or the casual violence of his stepfather, so Peter had gone back to the only place he could think to go—the cottage where he and Annabel had spent the last year or so before they went to Melchior. It was a pleasant place that managed to have doors that opened into open country and the city streets dependent on the will of the opener, courtesy of its owners. Those owners, Poly and Luck, were a couple of the strongest enchanters Peter had ever met. The doors weren't the house's only peculiarity, but Peter didn't like to encourage it by thinking about it more often than he had to. Cat-like, the cottage tended to show off its quirks the more the person being shown those quirks disliked being played with. Peter could hold his own against its tricks, but he preferred buildings to be somewhat more solid and less malicious. He and Annabel had already fought off a murderous castle, after all.

And so Peter had spent nearly a year away from Annabel with Poly and Luck, alternately sulking and regretting, and as the time lengthened it seemed less possible to go back and exchange some sort of apology. He wasn't even sure Melchior would have let him into the house to offer one.

Poly, the muted amusement in her eyes a very good sign that she thought he was being ridiculous, had eventually come into his room with an offer: school and board at the University of Mechanics and Magic, and the possibility of a sponsorship afterward, when he might be able to work his ideas and inventions into real life without thought of the real-life cost.

"You can come back here for the holidays, if you want," she had added.

"No, he can't," said Luck. "He's already been here. Five times. If he comes again the house will be confused."

"I've only been here twice," protested Peter. "Counting this time."

"If you ask me, the house knows exactly what's going on," Poly said, and added significantly, "More than some of us in the house, perhaps."

Luck grinned at that, surprising Peter all over again. In Peter's experience, the enchanter had a way of either ignoring or magically retaliating against anyone who implied that he was anything less than omniscient and omnipotent. It never ceased to surprise Peter that he accepted criticism from Poly at all, let alone with a good grace.

"Don't forget," had said Poly, turning her serious grey eyes back on Peter. "You can come back here any time. *Any* time, Peter."

That assurance made Peter feel slightly warmer and more cheerful when it came to standing in the blue receiving room of the University of Mechanics and Magic for the first time. He had come prepared to impress. His family bloodline was one heavily imbued with magic, and while he personally had all but foresworn the use of that magic, he knew his presence would cause something of a stir. He was also quite well aware that he would have to prove himself at once, or be looked down on for the rest of the year at least.

He had come to the school with his most impressive mechanical tickerbox in hand, though the slippery magical one was still squirming away in his pocket as well, making a nattering sort of sound that made him think, uneasily, that it was eating up the wasted seconds and minutes of time as well as whatever else was in its stomach cavity at the moment. That was nonsense, of course—the tickerboxes moved as if they were alive, on spindly legs that were connected to clockwork on the inside, and they even sometimes seemed to have their own personalities, but Peter knew it was just clockwork and the inevitable mechanical difficulties that manifest with such machines.

The time tickerbox was, admittedly, a little different. He'd had to imbue it with a certain amount of magic, for one thing. For another, it was the only one of his tickerboxes that he hadn't yet tested thoroughly. He had done some small tests, of course; using it to successfully propel a small carrot into next week, and then a field mouse into the next day—which turned out to be such a decided mess that he hadn't yet tested it on himself. There was no reason for it to be in his pocket except that he didn't like to leave this one in particular by itself for too long.

Like the others, the time tickerbox wasn't sentient—that would be ridiculous—but it did tend to eat unexpected things, storing them in its little stomach cavity to be burped out at inconvenient times. Peter hadn't yet been able to figure out why it did so, but he darkly suspected that the magic was affecting it in ways he hadn't yet been able to quantify.

And so the time tickerbox was in his pocket, buttoned securely and biding its time. Peter didn't have any real intention of bringing it out. Keeping it on him was more of an attempt to make sure it didn't go digging through his things to make itself extra appendages or develop new abilities that he had no leisure for testing.

Peter absently patted the pocket, and jumped a little when the door of the parlour burst open. A tall, broad-shouldered boy who looked as though his blonde curls should have been tidy but had walked just a bit too fast down the hall in a stiff breeze hurried into the room.

The boy looked him up and down in a not unfriendly manner. "So you're it," he said.

"I suppose so," said Peter, taken aback. It wasn't that he'd been expecting a welcoming party or anything of that sort, but he hadn't expected to be an *it* on his first day.

"We'd better get moving, then," said the boy. "I'm Thomas."

"What's the hurry?" asked Peter, and then, as Thomas went directly for the window instead of the door, "And where are we going?"

"Out the window," said Thomas. "Come along! I'll be showing you around: we're going to be sharing the same room, so I thought I might as well."

"Yes, but why the window?" protested Peter.

"Well, why not?" demanded the other boy. "Come *along*! Oh bother!"

More quietly this time, the door opened again.

"Ah, so here you are!" said a thin, elegant boy from the doorway. Behind him was a small group of other boys, each peering into the room with varying degrees of interest. "It's Peter Carlisle, isn't it? I'm Samuel. We've heard a lot about you. I'm interested in seeing how you do in school, with your pedigree."

Peter heard Thomas mutter something like, "Probably just like the rest of us mongrels."

Samuel sent him a polite, enquiring look, tilting his head back to display an elegant nose to best advantage. "In a hurry, Palmer? Don't let us keep you."

"Not right now," said Thomas. He seemed to have resigned himself to staying in the room. As Peter watched, he leaned his broad shoulders against the wall and shoved his hands into his pockets. "I was just about to show the new boy around. We're to share a room."

"Oh, there's no need for that!" Samuel said pleasantly. "Sir asked me to do it. I mean, unless you *insist*, of course!"

"That'd be a bit daft, wouldn't it?" said Thomas, with no less pleasantness.

Peter was left wondering what it was he wasn't understanding. Thomas' previous haste, compared with his current indifference, was something that would bear further investigation. There were undercurrents here that would bear investigation.

"Come along, then, Carlisle," said Samuel. "We might as well get a good look around before dinner."

Peter glanced over at Thomas, but the boy's face had closed into a kind of blankness that made Peter even more aware that there was something going on beneath the surface.

"Are you going?" Thomas asked, but it didn't seem like a question.

"I suppose so," said Peter, and followed Samuel out the door with a last, covert look over his shoulder.

"Don't mind Palmer," Samuel said cheerfully, when they were away from the room. "He doesn't like it when things don't go according to plan. I suppose he tried to hustle you out of the room before we could get there?"

"He didn't look like he was in a hurry back there," Peter said, unwilling to say too much when he didn't know the situation well enough. It had already occurred to him that if he and Thomas were sharing a room, it would be a bit uncomfortable to be on bad terms with him.

"Interesting," said Samuel, and led him toward the main front door.

For all that Thomas had tried to hustle Peter away before Samuel could get there, Peter found Samuel to be a good guide. He showed Peter the three-dimensional map of the school that was by the front door first; an artefact that Peter had seen on his way in but hadn't had the chance to stop and study as he would have liked to do. It ran by magic, to be sure, but although the vital spark was magic, there were a great many more moving parts that were mechanics instead of magics, much like Peter's tickerboxes.

Peter vaguely remembered the setup of the university

when he came away from the model—a main building that housed and provided food for the boys, and the second building that contained the studies, libraries, and classrooms—but his brain was fairly seething with ideas that the map setup had sparked within him, and left little space for anything else.

He didn't pay attention to the university around him again until Samuel led the way into a large, light-filled room and said, "This is our Library—study, really, but you can get any book you need for class here."

Books lined the walls that weren't given over to windows, and low, cushioned seats ran beneath the windows. Between rows of books, booths had been set back into the walls, equipped with a mix of seated desks and standing desks. Most of them were empty at this time, but Peter saw a red-haired girl stretched out in one of the seated areas, and an earnest, plump boy climbing into one of the others.

That surprised him: the mix of girls as well as boys around the room. He knew, of course, that the university was a co-ed institution, but he had expected *some* level of segregation, for study at least. From that interesting point, he quickly passed on to gazing at the mechanical models that had been put on display in glass cases above the books. Jointed, spindly, and made from a mix of metals and wooden parts, they reminded Peter irresistibly of his tickerboxes. He felt a resurgence of hope for what he might be able to accomplish here.

"Don't let the teachers or monitors catch you looking at those too much," advised Samuel. "They're guarded like the blazes and not for students' use: too expensive to let anyone get their grubby little hands on them."

That being true, Peter wondered why the red-headed girl in one of the desk hutches was fiddling with one of those models on the desk in front of her, even if she was tucked away from easy view of the door. Maybe she thought she would have time to hide it before a teacher walked far enough into the room to see her.

"Ah," said Samuel, with a satirical tilt of one eyebrow. "I see you've noticed Miss Stoneflange. Miss Stoneflange is of the opinion that rules do not apply to her. I would advise against getting too close to her if you don't wish for a scratched face."

"Or if you don't wish to be frozen," said one of the other boys who had accompanied them, feelingly. "Miss Stoneheart doesn't care for schoolboys."

"She can't be much older than us," protested Peter. "She only looks about eighteen!"

"She's seventeen," Samuel said. The satirical look hadn't vanished from his face; if anything, it had grown more pronounced by a curl of his lip. "The same age as myself. Not that you would know it by the way she treats us."

Peter took in the queenly set of Miss Stoneflange's chin despite the fact that she sat cross-legged in her booth with her shoes on the floor, her stockinged toes peeking out from the gathered mass of her skirts on the side closest to the booth opening, and frowned. She was barely a year older than he was, certainly: for her to be looking down on her schoolmates was a bit much.

Her way of sitting said that she didn't care what people thought of her so long as she could do whatever it was she was doing with her purloined model, but the set of the chin and the complete disregard for the group of boys that were very evidently observing her suggested that Miss Stoneflange thought herself far enough above her schoolmates as to actively discourage their company.

The fact that Peter himself would have warmly resented any interruption while he was working on something, he pushed to the back of his mind. I was obvious that Miss Stoneflange wasn't involved in anything like so important as his own research.

"She doesn't seem to be really doing anything, either," he said.

"Exactly so," agreed Samuel, smiling. "We're all very curious about why she gets such preferential treatment."

"She doesn't attend all the classes, either," said one of the other boys. "And when she does come to them, the teachers don't dare call on her for anything she doesn't want to do."

"I see," said Peter, feeling more and more uncomfortable. It wasn't his business what Miss Stoneflange did or didn't do, and he didn't think it was fair to be talking about her when she couldn't answer for herself. "What else is in this building?"

"You're not inclined to be stuffy, I hope?" said Samuel, his eyebrows rising. "All right, if you don't like the study, I'll show you the real library across the hall and we'll get you back to your room before dinner."

Peter followed, feeling as though he had been put down a notch or two, and caught the glances the other boys shot each other—the small, almost smug smiles. He was irritated enough at it to not pay much attention to the library as he was shown through it, wishing he had been able to get out the window with Thomas before Samuel came into the sitting room. He preceded the other boys out of the library, too, and nearly walked into Miss Stoneflange, who was exiting the study at the same time.

At his left shoulder, Samuel bowed slightly. "Miss Stoneflange."

She inclined her head very slightly but didn't stop to talk, which disappointed Peter. Miss Stoneflange, with her fiery hair and prodigious freckles, was somehow elegant and self-possessed in a way that made him wish he could have captured her attention for long enough to introduce himself. Of course, she probably already knew who he was: if Samuel was to be believed, they had been expecting and even looking forward to his arrival. Still, he would have liked a word or two with Miss Stoneflange.

"What was she working on in there?" Peter asked Samuel,

as Miss Stoneflange continued on down the hall with a light, decided step, looking neither to the right nor the left.

"Who knows?" said the boy who had been introduced as Tyrell. "You never do, with Miss Stoneflange, until right at the end of the term when projects are announced. Last time she had worked out a system for predicting which way a jury would vote based on the magical vibrations they gave off during a trial."

"Which is no doubt very useful if all of the jurors are magically inclined," said Samuel, "but rather less if they have no talent."

"I suppose that depends," Peter said. "Everyone gives off magical vibrations, even people who can't do magic. I've only ever met one person who didn't."

"Well, there are opinions on both sides, no doubt," Samuel said airily.

Peter opened his mouth to remark that there was no difference of opinion at all, just plain fact, but it struck him just in time that Samuel was probably just trying to hide his embarrassment at having said something incorrect without thinking it through.

"I'd like to know how she did that," he said instead. Perhaps he had been too quick to dismiss Miss Stoneflange's potential research.

Samuel looked amused. "Do ask Miss Stoneflange about it. I should very much like to see how you get on."

He sauntered down the hall while Peter was still trying to decide if the remark was permission or provocation, and the other boys followed his lead.

Some time later, Samuel took him back to the main manor and up to the second floor, where the hallways were carpeted and laced with anti-flammable, anti-stick, and anti-noise enchantments. Peter gazed around, his eyebrows rising a little as they all moved down one of the halls, and asked, "Is this the guest quarters?"

"No," said Samuel. "This is the first-year floor: they tend to be a bit overboard with magic and lacking in control when they first come here. I trust you don't have the same problems."

Surprised, Peter said, "Of course not. I've been in control of my magic since I was three."

"That's exactly why we wanted to meet you," said Samuel. "There's a lack of real talent here at the university. We like to make sure it's cultured if we can."

"Thanks," said Peter. He wasn't exactly sure if he wanted to be cultured by Samuel. He was quite talented enough to grow by himself if he had the necessary tools, and he didn't like the dynamic of the group that came with Samuel, either.

"This is you," Samuel said, stopping by one of the doors. His carrying voice didn't get any softer when he added, "I'm afraid you're stuck with that wet blanket, Palmer."

"He didn't seem to be too bad," Peter said uncomfortably. Thomas had, after all, been willing to climb out a window earlier, which didn't much suggest a wet blanket mentality.

"Oh well, I'm sure you'll get along," said Samuel lightly. "Just come to us whenever you want a bit of fresh air. We don't mind having a bit of fun at school, so long as it doesn't get too much on the masters' nerves."

"Thanks," said Peter again, and opened the door before Samuel could say anything more that would make him uncomfortable if anyone were to overhear it. "See you later."

He closed the door behind him, and saw Thomas across the room, perched in the window frame. By the look on the boy's face, Peter was fairly certain that he had heard Samuel's comments outside the door.

"There you are," the other boy said, with a distinct lack of enthusiasm. More pointedly, he added, "Enjoy your walk around the school and the fine company?"

Peter was about to reply pretty hotly that he hadn't chosen the company and didn't see why he was being sneered at, when it occurred to him that he hadn't actually enjoyed himself terribly much.

That realisation was followed by another which caused him to say, "I didn't really get to meet anyone but his group. I got the impression that there are a lot of people that Samuel doesn't get along with."

Thomas's brows rose. "Did you?" There was a moment of silence before the other boy grinned and added, "Good for you. I don't wish to be talking about other fellows behind their backs, but if you keep paying attention I suppose you'll figure things out for yourself. You might as well call me Tom, old man. By the by, your things are here. I had them put the trunk over by your bed."

"Thanks," said Peter, feeling unaccountably relieved.

It took him only fifteen minutes to throw his couple of pairs of shoes beneath the bed and his other things into the lopsided dresser, but by then Tom had stirred from his seat in the window and begun to dress himself.

Peter watched him for a few minutes before the other boy said, "If you've got dinner togs, you'd best start dressing. Supper is in fifteen minutes, and if you're late there's a good chance you'll be locked out, depending on who's monitoring the hall."

Peter did have dinner things: nothing fancy, and still a bit too big so that he would have room to grow, but they were dinner things. He scrambled into them without bothering to put his waistcoat on underneath, and resented the raised brow that the normally pleasant-faced Tom turned on him.

"What is it?" he asked.

"You don't want to put on your waistcoat, old man?"

"No one will see it anyway," Peter said, with a slight edge of impatience. And if they did, so what? Was a waistcoat necessary to eat dinner?

"If you're sure," said Tom, shrugging. "But they're a bit picky out there, and they have a habit of snickering at a fellow that gets annoying."

Peter understood a little better when he got to the dining hall. Both girls and boys lined the dining tables, talking and laughing, and most of the boys were dressed in their best clothes. Unlike Peter, those best clothes consisted of suits that fitted, shiny shoes, and waistcoats that both fit impeccably and were correctly buttoned.

He was aware of the snickers as he and Tom moved through the hall to find a seat at one of the long tables, and bitterly regretted that he hadn't listened to the other boy— who, to do him justice, ignored all the snickers.

"They're a bit traditionalist," was the only thing he said to Peter. "They tend not to take you seriously if you can't even dress yourself up to a certain standard. Silly, because some of the most brilliant fellows can't even tie a cravat, but there you are. Fellows like that get themselves valets if they want to be taken seriously here. Here we are!"

Peter, who in his blossoming embarrassment hadn't noticed that they'd come to a table with a few spaces empty, dropped into the seat next to Tom's. Tomorrow at dinner, he would make sure that no one could snicker at his clothing. Even if he had to patch it up with magic.

Tom good-naturedly helped him to food from some of the warming pans on the table, warned against others, then sat back with his own meal and ate with a heartiness that made Peter realise exactly how Tom had grown his impressively tall frame and broad shoulders.

He settled in to eat his own meal, hampered slightly by his too-large cuffs and more than ever aware of that fact, and as he became more comfortable, looked around at his dining companions.

Opposite him and one seat down to the left, was Miss Stoneflange, speaking with a Broman boy on her right, their voices low and earnest. They must have been discussing magic, because there was an effortless lick of magic glistening between the Broman boy's brown fingers that turned them golden on and off. Miss Stoneflange watched that flicker with fascinated eyes, which seemed nonsensical to Peter. Although the Broman boy was doing it effortlessly, it wasn't as though the magic itself was particularly strong.

He was still wondering about that when the boy on his left nudged him with an elbow, grinning. "Got your dad's togs, do you?" he asked.

"No," said Peter coldly, deciding to try and face it out by sheer cheek. "Why do you ask?"

"Because you look like the scarecrow in one of the hedgerows along the lane," said another one of the taller boys a few places down. "You're missing a button and a few inches in the shoulders, by the looks."

"The button's probably in the soup," said the boy directly across the table from Peter, grinning. He had inky hair and a rather blotched face, as though an inkwell had recently exploded in his face and he hadn't quite been able to clean himself properly. He looked, moreover, like he knew how to make mischief. "This is why fellows should make sure they're properly dressed before they come to dinner."

"They shouldn't come out with a face like yours, either, Leslie," said Tom, through a mouthful of beef. "But I don't see that stopping you."

Leslie crowed with laughter, surprising Peter. "Friend of yours, is he?"

"Dormmate," said Tom. "If it matters. My mother always taught me to be polite to everyone."

"Have a sausage, old man," Leslie said placatingly. "No need to get annoyed and bring your mother into it."

"I don't see why anything needs to be brought into it," Tom complained. "Don't see why fellows can't just eat when it's time to eat."

"All right, all right, have some mash. You'll feel better."

To Peter's relief, that put an end to snide remarks and snickers until the pudding came out, and with it, a couple of bowls of tangerines for each table.

The tangerines must have been an uncommon treat, because they were pounced on the moment they arrived, even before the pudding, and the bowls very quickly emptied. Nearest Peter, only one remained by the time he realised what was happening.

Peter reached for the tangerine at the same time as Miss Stoneflange, who immediately drew back. He let his hand drop and said, "You can have it."

"No thank you," said Miss Stoneflange. She didn't say it coldly, but she did say it without the faintest touch of emotion, and Peter felt chilled.

"It's all right," he said. "You have it this time. I'll have the last one next time."

"I don't do bargains," said Miss Stoneflange, and turned her attention away from him completely to the Broman boy by her side.

Peter, who hadn't meant to suggest anything of the sort, took the tangerine with a feeling of ill-usage and tried to peel it without the juice running down into his too-large cuffs. His temper wasn't helped by the fact that he was sure the other students were laughing at his somewhat clumsy attempts as much as his clothing.

"What's that in your pocket?" asked Leslie, from across the table. "You had it in there before, too, didn't you? When I saw you in the study?"

"It's one of my projects," said Peter. As his hand wavered briefly between the normal tickerbox and the time-eating one, he heard someone further down the table near Samuel snicker quietly and say something about *just like a country fair magician*. His jaw tensing, Peter plucked out the time-eating tickerbox. "I've been experimenting with time," he added airily.

Tom sat forward, leaning his head against his fist to stare sideways at Peter. "What do you mean, experimenting with time? It's not something you can really mete out in measurable quantities for batch lots, is it?"

"Neither is magic," Peter pointed out, and he thought he saw the smallest tilt of Miss Stoneflange's elegant head, as if she had turned her head a little to hear better. "But we still experiment with it."

Tom looked over the tickerbox as it tapped its way cautiously across Peter's dinner plate, avoiding the remains of a gravy puddle. "What sort of experiments can you do with that?"

"I've sent small things a few days into the future," said Peter, even more casually. "Just a field mouse and a carrot, that sort of thing."

"I say nonsense," said Leslie. "Can you prove it?"

Peter pointed at the tickerbox, which was pilfering a few sugar cubes from the sugar bowl. "I'll send those into tomorrow, if you like."

"That's boring," Leslie complained. "We'd have to wait until tomorrow or next week to find out!"

"And we'd have to make sure there were no shenanigans in case of a joke," pointed out another. "What about sending something back in time?

"That's even harder to prove," Peter objected.

The inky-haired boy grinned at him. "Not this time. I found something in that teapot yesterday—it came out when I poured my tea. If you try to send something back, I and the other fellows will know whether it's legitimate or not, because they saw what it was. *You* remember?"

"In your pocket still, is it, Les?"

Leslie winked and turned his grin on the table at large, girls and boys alike. "Looks like a lark, doesn't it?"

Peter shrugged. "All right," he said. At least it would be

obvious that he'd done no sleight of hand. "You fellows know I got here just today, I presume?"

"It's why I said yesterday," Leslie told him, dark eyes on the tickerbox, which, tiring of eating sugar cubes, trotted back to Peter and climbed his arm.

Its sharp, spindly legs snicked against his cuff, sending a button tickling down onto the tablecloth. That must have interested it, because it climbed back down and ate the button, much to the surprise of those around the table.

"Isn't it adorable?" said one of the girls. "Won't it have a stomachache, after all that sugar and now a button?"

"It doesn't keep things in there for long," said Peter. He opened the top of the tickerbox, where the few, tiny regulators hid away. They were as fiddly as they were tiny, and he had to be very careful about how he set them, otherwise he would risk sending the button into the previous month instead of the previous day. He desperately did not want anything to go wrong.

There would probably only be one chance to impress his classmates, and he wanted to do it thoroughly.

When he was sure he had set the regulators correctly, Peter closed up the tickerbox's workings and set it free. "Put the button in the teapot," he said.

Across the table, he thought he saw Leslie's brows go up briefly, but he was too focused on his tickerbox to be sure. That tickerbox, obedient to his commands, much to Peter's secret relief, crawled over to the teapot, retrieved the button from its stomach cavity, and poked it down the high spout of the teapot.

There should have been the sound of the button tumbling against the porcelain—perhaps even the sound of it plashing lightly into the leftover tea. Instead, there was a very heavy silence, and the movement of something that wasn't quite magic, but wasn't *not* magic either.

"Good heavens!" said Leslie, his brows making two sharp

triangles on his forehead. A murmur of excitement spread around the table.

Across the table, Miss Stoneflange looked up. She didn't look directly at him, but Peter knew she was paying attention, just like the Broman boy next to her, who had stopped talking mid-sentence.

"How did you do that?" asked the Broman boy, his brown eyes glowing with excitement.

"Fetch it out!" said the boy next to Leslie, elbowing him. "We all saw it yesterday!"

"Not so fast!" the Broman boy said, and leaned across the table for the teapot. He emptied all the tea into a spare teacup, but nothing else came out. Nor did anything else but soggy tea leaves plop onto the table when Leslie turned the teapot ruthlessly upside down and shook it.

"Well, well, well!" Leslie said, eyes sparkling. "I suppose that's my cue!"

He reached into his pocket and pulled out Peter's button, perfectly dry and present, still with a thread of Peter's shirt attached, dyed dark with the dregs of the tea.

Tom said in wonder, "Ain't magic grand? It's impossible, though, isn't it?"

"It's impossible," Peter agreed, his voice just a little louder. Miss Stoneflange still wouldn't look at him, but he was certain she was paying as much attention as everybody nearby. "But I worked out a way to do it. I've been experimenting recently, trying to make it stable enough for human use. That's what I'm hoping to work on while I'm here at the university."

Tom, his face serious and impressed at the same time, said, "If you present well enough to the headmaster, he'll probably give you your own workroom: they do that sometimes if it's for something dangerous but useful. They don't like people being hurt, but they don't want to discourage experimentation that could advance knowledge. I don't know of any other entry level boys who have been granted one, but I should think you've got a good chance."

"I should doubt it," said Miss Stoneflange, patting her lips with her napkin. Again, her voice was absolutely emotionless.

"Don't tell me you're not interested, Glenna!" said the Broman boy, turning his glowing eyes on her.

"I really think it best not to be interested," she said to him, and Peter saw the look that passed between them.

The Broman boy grinned ruefully and said, "Oh well, I suppose not. But it *is* a shame! Don't you think the headmaster would be interested in it? He's given out private rooms for less, after all."

"I should very much doubt the headmaster will grant any such concession for a first-year student," said Miss Stoneflange.

"Oh, are you still irked that you weren't given one for your own research?" asked a familiar, lightly mocking voice. Samuel, evidently on his way out of the dining hall, paused by Miss Stoneflange's chair and smiled down at her. "I was certain you would be given one—we were all terribly surprised that you weren't."

"Life is full of these surprises," said Miss Stoneflange. "Excuse me, gentlemen."

Samuel would have pulled out her chair for her, but Miss Stoneflange, as still as her name, didn't move by so much as a finger until the Broman boy stood, nudging Samuel out of the way with his chairback as he rose, and pulled it out for her.

Miss Stoneflange didn't take his arm, nor did the Broman boy try to offer it, but they walked out together, and Peter was quite certain they took the same direction when they were out of the dining hall, too.

"See you fellows tomorrow," said Samuel, and this time his slightly mocking smile was directed at Peter, who felt the sting of it keenly.

Why had Miss Stoneflange felt it necessary to try and

embarrass him in front of the other fellows? Why, having done so, had she swept out of the room with a boy who called her by her first name?

"Don't mind Miss Stoneflange," said Tom, who had been following his gaze. "She doesn't warm to people very easily."

"I noticed," Peter said, a little sourly. For just a little while, he had been delightfully aware of sharing with likeminded people the joy of his experimental ideas. Miss Stoneflange had not only been dismissive, she had dampened the whole air in his part of the room, and Samuel's extra touch of disinterestedness had sealed his fate.

"Come along," said Tom, in a conciliatory sort of way. "I'll show you around the places I was going to show you earlier. Bring the tickerbox: we can have a bit of a lark with it outside, I should think. Coming, Leslie?"

"Rather!" said Leslie, at once. "Unlike the usually very astute Miss Stoneflange, I think you've got a good chance at a room, and I'd like to see what you can do until then."

PETER HADN'T INTENDED TO GET INTO HIS THEORIES OR practise with an audience that consisted of a grand total of two other boys, but he was too eager to discuss and explain those theories to be too standoffish, and both Tom and Leslie were willing to plot and argue while sitting on the edge of the fountain behind the school until the sinking triad turned the evening dark around them and a passing master told them severely that they should be in either their common room or their own rooms.

"Well, that's torn it!" said Tom ruefully, standing. "They always think boys together is a sign of mischief. We're marked now!"

Peter had learned in the course of their discussion that Tom wasn't particularly brilliant when it came to extrapolating from incomplete ideas, but when it came to plain logic and small details he was dogged and persistent about accounting for absolutely everything. A good collaborator, thought Peter; though inclined to be annoying at times if you wished, as he himself and Leslie did wish, to make imaginative leaps into the unknown.

Leslie only grinned. "We'll give 'em something to worry about later in term," he said. "Let's go to the common room, anyway. We can take over one of the sofas."

That was fairly typical of him, too, if Peter's observations were any guide.

"I'll be working on this all year," he said. "There's plenty of time to talk about it later. More, if I can get one of those rooms."

That reminded him of the erstwhile Miss Stoneflange, who had the temerity to be exiting the main school building as they passed it, and when he and Tom finally returned to their room that night, he was still brooding on his wrongs.

"What is it she's so bothered about, anyway?" he asked Tom. He was still quite certain that Miss Stoneflange had been very interested in his tickerbox, and that she had merely been pretending not to be so. "Miss Stoneflange, I mean. Isn't she interested in the advancement of science?"

"I had a dog once," Tom said, which non-sequitur considerably astonished Peter. He splashed water over his face at the washstand, then wiped it with cheerful impreciseness. "Got it from my uncle. He said he was just going to drown it if I didn't take it—said it was useless, said it bit him and whatnot. Mother didn't much like my taking it, but it was a good size and had a nice face. The first time I picked it up, it bit me on the nose and wouldn't let go."

"What did you do?"

"Mostly I cried a lot," said Tom cheerfully, stepping aside so that Peter could wash. "The blasted thing wouldn't let go and it hurt awfully! Since it wouldn't let go, I just kept patting the thing like an idiot. After about five minutes it let go and just sort of cowered into my elbow. It didn't like to come out, so I sat there for another half hour with the blood dripping down my face."

"What did your mother do?"

Tom grinned. "Lucky for me, she didn't see. My uncle did —he came in when I was just deciding I ought to try to find something to tempt it out. Told me to stop acting like a girl and tried to grab the mutt off me. Said he knew that's what would happen. Anyway, I found out that he'd been stuffing it up into the chimney for fun to make it chase rats every time he picked it up."

Peter, who was quite sure that he would have been so embarrassed at being told to stop crying that he would have let the puppy go, asked, "What did you do?"

"Ran for it with the puppy, of course!" said Tom. "He would have drowned it."

"Didn't you care—" Peter stopped, tried to find a more politic way of saying it, and came up short. "Didn't you care that he'd seen you crying?"

"Why? I'd like to see him take about ten thousand needle-sharp teeth to the nose without *his* eyes watering a bit! Besides, why would I worry about what a man like that thinks about me?"

Peter thought about that for a moment, and in the midst of so doing, came to a realisation.

"Are you comparing Miss Stoneflange to a dog?" he asked, grinning.

"I should never dare," said Tom at once. "I'm just suggesting that sometimes people have a reason for how they react. And sometimes how people react has nothing to do with you."

"Easy for you to say!" Peter said. "She wouldn't even look at me!"

"You're not the best looking of chaps."

"Shut up!" said Peter, grinning, and threw his washcloth at

him. "Oh well, I can ask about a workroom tomorrow, I suppose."

"If you're up for it," Tom said, tossing the washcloth back at him. "But the headmaster is a much tougher proposition than Miss Stoneflange, so I suggest you give it a few weeks to work up your application and figure out how best to approach him."

❧   2   ❧

Peter met the headmaster the next day. He had come out fully prepared to make his case for a private workroom despite Tom's advice, but the right moment for doing so never quite seemed to arrive.

Peter was shown into the headmaster's office while the man was still engaged in perusing the contents of a file that was, if Peter wasn't mistaken, Peter's own file. It was quite thin, but his name was at the head of the paper topmost in the pile. It didn't seem as though the headmaster was about to look up any time soon, despite the silent wave of his fingers that Peter took as an invitation to seat himself, so he did seat himself, and took a few moments to look around the room.

The room was vast and ornate, with high ceilings chased with white mouldings around every edge—and, to Peter's glee, around the base of the chandeliers from which the newest of gas lamps hung. The wall behind the headmaster was likely lined with windows, for it was also lined with long curtains in four sections. Only one set of those curtains were open—the ones directly behind the desk—and to Peter's left, between desk and window, there was a massive sculpture that wouldn't have looked out of place in the gardens outside, but was certainly too large and ornate to be kept inside.

From behind that massive sculpture, Peter caught a glimpse of the front gates of the university through the window there. It wasn't until he also took in the rich surroundings of that window—the long, damask curtains that were caught up on one side and not on the other, and the matching padded window-seat—that he saw the stockinged toes that protruded just beyond the fringed edge of the loose curtain.

Peter had a sudden remembrance of Miss Stoneflange, sitting alone in her desk hutch with her shoes on the floor and her legs crossed underneath her with her stockinged toes peeping out.

He tried to crane his head around the sculpture just enough to see, but the exercise achieved very little: he didn't dare to be too obvious about it even while the headmaster's attention was directed down at the small packet of information that was spread on the table before him. If he squinted in just the right way, there might be a slight reddish tinge to the reflection of the window that he could see around the curtain, but that was all.

There was no way to be sure that it was Miss Stoneflange, but Peter was quite sure, rightly or wrongly, that it was indeed she. What she was doing in the headmaster's office hiding behind a curtain was quite another matter. It was also interesting that she felt comfortable enough to be shoeless and stretched out in the headmaster's office, regardless of guests. Perhaps he could ask Tom about it when he saw him next.

"Now," said the headmaster, startling Peter out of his thoughts. "Carlisle. Your record is somewhat impressive for your age. We were glad to hear you'd decided to come to us."

"Thank you, sir," said Peter. He was slightly confused, because there wasn't too much for the headmaster to know about him apart from his parentage, which was undeniably good when it came to magical bloodline but nothing that should count as an impressive record by itself.

Still, he couldn't help feeling slightly warm with pride: Poly had probably told them something about his achievements thus far as well as mentioning his parents.

"Your connections, too, are quite impressive," the headmaster said thoughtfully.

Peter didn't really have connections, unless you counted Poly and Luck—or, he belatedly realised, Annabel. So it was starting to get about that she was the next queen already, was it? He had the instinct to make sure Annabel knew as much, and was safe, but remembered a moment later that she had Melchior to look after her, and that Melchior undoubtedly already knew.

Peter made an assenting sort of noise, wondering exactly what use a tenuous connection to Annabel was. She had been —*was*—a good friend. Better than perhaps Peter deserved. But when it came to helping him with his research, she was absolutely no use at all. She was entirely without magic, but she commanded some of the most powerful magic in the Two Monarchies—and she *did* command it, regularly. She simply didn't use it in a way that was useful for experimentation or discovery: it was all protection and defence, with only the occasional offence.

"Now," added the headmaster, in what seemed to Peter to be a complete break of subject, "the games master tells me that you were out by the fountain with Palmer and Ffoukes last night."

"We were discussing mechanics of time travel, sir," he said, very glad of the opportunity to bring up his favourite subject and, hopefully, the subject of his own study and experimental space if the headmaster was interested enough in the idea.

Was it Peter's imagination, or did the curtain momentarily

bulge, as if a book had slipped from someone's grasp and been caught just before it fell?

"I see," said the headmaster. "Well, no doubt Palmer and Ffoukes are decent young lads, but I fancy you'll find them a little less talented and ambitious than yourself."

Peter couldn't help feeling pleased that his talent had made an impression (Poly *had* spoken for him, then!) but he also couldn't quite help protesting, "Ffoukes is very good at thinking outside expectations, sir, and although Palmer plods along, he makes sure a fellow doesn't miss basic things. They're quite useful."

"Perhaps so," said the headmaster, nodding gravely. "They're not inclined to be at all ambitious, however, and it doesn't do to tie yourself to companions who like to float along in life when you're trying to change the world. Attach yourself to young Samuel DeCourcy if you want to see what can really be done when it comes to mechanics of politics."

Peter nodded somewhat awkwardly. He hadn't very much cared for Samuel, and he was quite sure that Samuel didn't care much for him, either. He had the feeling that there could still be some sort of alliance between them, but as the head-master had said, it would be more of a political one. And since Peter wasn't yet sure exactly what it was Samuel would get from such an alliance, he wasn't eager to be used in such a fashion.

"I very much like the map at the front door, sir," he said, by way of changing the conversation. "It uses some of the same techniques I utilise in my own work—the magic spark, for example, and the use of natural principles instead of strictly magical ones."

"I understand very little of that," the headmaster said, waving a dismissive hand. "Like most here at the University of Mechanics and Magic, I've focused most of my efforts on the mechanics of magic itself. I leave the mechanics of the natural world to my daughter."

Peter's heart sank. He'd been hoping to find the head-master more open to mechanics in general, not just as they related to magic. It would be much harder to press the man for a private study if he didn't value anything outside of magic. "At any rate, I think it's quite a good little bit of work," he said. Perhaps there would be time later to convince the headmaster of his use to the university. It would help if he already had a tickerbox that worked for human travel as well as vegetable travel.

"If you wish to know more about it, make sure you speak with Miss Stoneflange," said the headmaster. "She was the one who designed the thing."

"Miss Stoneflange did that?" Peter was wholly astonished. "I didn't think she cared for that sort of thing!"

"Miss Stoneflange's interests are many and ranged," said the headmaster dryly. "As I mentioned, I have very little interest in mechanics that are not those of magic, but I do appreciate the use of people who can turn them to such good use. If that is your line of interest, I suggest speaking with her."

Why, then, wondered Peter, feeling more insulted than ever, had Miss Stoneflange been so utterly disinterested in his tickerbox last night? It was beginning to feel more like Miss Stoneflange had been deliberately insulting him rather than disinterested.

Perhaps Miss Stoneflange was one of those very sensitive girls, and he had offended her in some ridiculous way that she would no doubt inform him of later. Perhaps she had simply felt threatened by the tickerboxes; afraid that Peter would outdo her in the university.

He tried not to look too closely at the curtain as he said, "Well, if Miss Stoneflange is prepared to discuss her ideas with me, I'll be glad to talk with her. She's made quite a good start already."

"Very well," said the headmaster, and he seemed pleased.

"Then I'm sure you're eager to get on with exploring the university: I've your schedule here, along with the books you'll need this term. Look over the schedule with someone to make sure you know where you're going. Your classes are underlined in purple, and they each start exactly on time. Should you fail to make it to class on time, you won't be allowed in. See your floor monitor if you need anything relating to the bathrooms, and your study monitor if you need anything while in the library or study."

"Yes, sir," said Peter, aware that he was being dismissed.

He went back to his room, still digesting the conversation, his packet of schedules and books beneath one arm. Tom was there when he got back, smoking a thin cigar by the window to let out the smoke, and when Peter threw his packet on the bed, he put out the cigar and flicked it far into the open air.

"Let's see your schedule," he said, plucking it from the bed. He read it over, and his brows went up. "Now that's a bit odd. They've put you in the wrong classes: didn't you take a test last week?"

Peter frowned. "What, that little paper? It wasn't much of a test."

"How long did it take you to finish the perisher?"

"I don't know, perhaps fifteen minutes? It was all straight mechanical logic and a trick question or two."

Tom snorted. "That test takes most of us an hour or two to get done—we're always looking out for the trick questions. Maybe it's not a mistake. They've put you up a few years, anyway. You're with the fourth-year students for most of your classes: you're only with us first years in about two classes."

"At least I won't be bored, anyway," said Peter. He'd been worried he would have to work a bit harder to get into the upper classes. This was much better. "Does that mean I'm with Miss Stoneflange, then?"

"Not another fellow smitten with Miss Stoneflange!" Tom said. "*You* should be so lucky! You might overlap on a class or two, but that's all. She started third year herself in most subjects when she got here."

"I'm not smitten with her, I just wondered!" protested Peter. "Since she's allowed to do things the others aren't, and she's only a year older."

"I shouldn't interfere with Miss Stoneflange too much, if I were you," advised Tom. "She keeps herself busy and she doesn't like being bothered."

"I got that impression," Peter said. He was still wondering about Miss Stoneflange being in the headmaster's office. "I think she was in the headmaster's office, too. I know it sounds ridiculous, but—"

"Ridiculous, my eye!" said Tom, grinning. "She's there all the time. She's—oh hang it all, we're going to be late! Run, Carlisle! They won't let us in if we don't get to class on time. You're for Natural Magics and I'm for Interconnectedness; I'll show you where to go. Leg it!"

Tom wasn't in their room when Peter went back after classes finished for the day, which belatedly reminded him that the other boy had mentioned he was part of the rugby team and would be training that afternoon.

At something of a loss, Peter took himself off to the study, hoping to make use of one of the desks there to start work on his tickerboxes once again. One of the normal tickerboxes, of course: he didn't like the idea of people seeing him work on the time tickerbox while things could and did still go wrong.

When he got there, Miss Stoneflange was in the same desk hutch he'd seen her in first, and the others were taken as well. Rather disgruntled, Peter settled himself down on one of the reading benches that lined the library, and found that the Broman boy he'd seen talking with Miss Stoneflange last night was sitting on the seat one potted plant across from him.

"I see you've dived right into your work already," said a

familiar voice, as Peter spread out the supple piece of cloth he used to swaddle his tools over the seat beside him. Samuel sat down elegantly next to him, leaving just enough room for one of the three boys who drifted with him to sit also.

Peter tried not to sigh. Despite the headmaster's rather pointed recommendation, he didn't have any plan of making Samuel part of his circle. He would much rather have gotten to know the Broman boy on the seat next to his; at least that boy seemed to have some interest in Peter's tickerboxes, and enough understanding to keep up with him, if Peter wasn't mistaken.

Hoping to keep conversation to a minimum, Peter picked up the box he'd prepared for the outer shell of his newest tickerbox, checking the hinges and toggles on it automatically as he turned it over between his fingers, and kept his eyes stubbornly on that.

It helped a little, but it wasn't long before Samuel said lazily, "Everyone is so studious today! Look at this: Carlisle with his head down, putting legs on a box, Miss Stoneflange over there playing with something no doubt very interesting and important, and even Harry here with his nose in a book. It's only just the beginning of term, and everyone is so focused on their work!"

"Headmaster says we shouldn't discourage those who need to study from studying," said one of the boys with Samuel.

Peter didn't look directly at the boy, but he couldn't help looking up impatiently, and met the eyes of the Broman boy as he did so. The Broman boy was grinning, but when he caught Peter's eyes, he looked back down at his book.

"I'm trying to make a secondary tickerbox to complement one of the others," said Peter. "It's not terribly important, but that box keeps breaking apart the normal ones to augment itself to do things it shouldn't do, so I thought I should try to make it a friend."

"The University of Mechanics and Magic is certainly

blessed by its new intake!" Samuel said, loud and amused. "Clockwork friends for clockwork boxes! I look forward to seeing your end-of-year project, Carlisle!"

"At least I'm still working with magic," Peter retorted, a little too rashly. "That should be enough for the university, shouldn't it? Miss Stoneflange over there, whatever she's working on—she's not even using magic for it!"

He regretted it at once, because Samuel called out, "Miss Stonehear—oh, beg pardon, Miss Stoneflange! We're all very curious to know what you're making!"

Miss Stoneflange, utterly unmoved, ignored him. It was left to the Broman boy to say, "She's working on her end-of-year project. You know she doesn't like to be distracted by people when she's working—particularly when they're not saying anything."

"Out of favour today, Harry?" asked Tyrell, crossing one leg over the other. "It seems that you've been banished."

"Glenna's at a crucial stage in her planning," Harry said, dropping his eyes back to his book. He looked as though he wasn't particularly keen on talking with Samuel and his cohorts, either. "When she's making calculations with the models, she doesn't like to have to answer people."

"Isn't it all a bit useless, though?" Peter asked. As much as he approved of doing things without magic, he couldn't see the good of anything that Miss Stoneflange was doing with her model.

She wasn't using magic, nor was she doing anything except moving the extendable arms and legs by minute fractions, and writing down inexplicable numbers. Even if there had been magic to the equation, it would simply have flowed through the model and exited via any of the extended legs and arms that she was playing with. It looked more like a guidance system for splitting magic than anything remotely useful. Everyone knew that you achieved more when you combined magic to make a stronger entity: there was no use in diluting it by separating it out and letting it drain away.

Unless, of course, thought Peter, you were trying to make a system for minimising magical blowback; but most practitioners strong enough to need any such thing were also strong enough and canny enough to make their own wards to absorb any blowback.

Harry looked at Peter with an eyebrow lift that reminded him unpleasantly of the way that Melchior had often looked at him. "Her project isn't useless just because you can't see why she's doing it."

"No, it's useless because she's doing it without magic," said Samuel, laughing. "You know she's only here because of her family, don't you, Harry?"

Harry's generous lips pressed together, but seemed to tilt up at the edges. "Work on your own project, why don't you? We'll match them up at the end of the year, yours and Miss Stoneflange's—"

Peter, his interest piqued, wandered over and said to the apparently oblivious Miss Stoneflange, "I prefer to work without magic, too. What are you working on?"

"I don't prefer to work without magic," Miss Stoneflange said. "Go away, please. You're interfering with my workings."

"You aren't doing any workings," Peter said, with a touch of indignation. "And if you're not working without magic because you prefer to work without it, why are you working without it?"

"I really do wonder why people assume they have a right to my research," she said, a flush of annoyance lying lightly across the tops of her cheeks and the bridge of her nose.

It should have clashed very badly with her hair, but instead it made Miss Stoneflange look much warmer and more alive than her nickname and reputation would suggest.

Peter found himself saying, "I was just interested!"

This time, Miss Stoneflange didn't so much as look at him,

and Peter felt his temper fray. She still wasn't doing magic; she was still only playing with the jointed, moving model she must have gotten from one of the display cases—and how she'd gotten it was anyone's guess when they weren't allowed to be used and highly spelled into the bargain.

"You shouldn't be playing with that," he told her, rash in his pique.

Miss Stoneflange's copper eyebrow twitched up briefly, but she didn't look away from the model. Her fingers, slender and delicate, hovered over one of the extended arms of the model and tapped it lightly until it was set perhaps a millimetre further out than it had been.

"I don't have time to play with you," she said. "Go away."

Rather redder around the cheeks than Miss Stoneflange, Peter moved away and sat back down on his seat between Samuel and Harry.

Grinning, Samuel said, "She's a pleasant thing, isn't she, Miss Stoneflange! We all call her Stoneheart around here."

"Not all of us," said Harry, looking up from his book again. "But then, some of us don't go around bothering fourth year students when they're busy, either, I suppose."

"A fourth-year student isn't above a third year," Samuel said coldly.

"They're a year ahead," said Harry. "Literally a year ahead. I'm not suggesting it's a moral superiority."

"She's not even *doing* anything!" Peter muttered. Against his better judgement and his pride in not using magic unless necessary, he sent out a tendril of his own magic questing to see what it could see.

He sent it out carefully and quietly, and he was quite certain that none of the boys nearby saw it happen. He wasn't even sure that Miss Stoneflange saw it. If Peter had had to guess, he would have said that Miss Stoneflange didn't consciously react to his magic. Her right hand, lying at rest on the table, seemed to reach out a finger instinctively to caress the lingering magic, and Peter felt for a moment as if the library moved around him, or as if his heart had perhaps stopped.

In that brief moment of dazedness, Miss Stoneflange's fingers swiftly curled back into her palm, and she stood, looking directly at Peter.

"You," she said, her voice icy. "Stop it at once!"

"Third year students are allowed to do magic where they please, aren't they?" mildly asked Samuel, his eyes sharp and quick to catch the magic.

"That's right," Peter said. "You can't tell me where to do magic!"

He would have pulled his magic back to himself, but it was gone.

No, not gone: snatched—tangled—suddenly whipped into a frothy, sharp-edged chaos that Miss Stoneflange's model sucked in and then sent zinging across the room at the group on the seat. Books exploded above their heads as if struck by lightning, raining pages and fluttering edges of burnt paper, and students yelled and leapt for cover.

Harry alone didn't move. He'd gone back to his book, and if Peter wasn't mistaken, he even smiled slightly. That was annoying on several different levels that Peter didn't have time to analyse: Miss Stoneflange had left her booth and was even now sweeping across the room toward them.

She stopped in front of them for long enough to say, "I trust you're quite satisfied," before she continued on out of the library.

Peter frowned at the remains of the books scattered about their feet. "What was that all about?"

"Don't take it personally," advised Samuel. "She's always rude to us. Nearly all the male students here have tried to get her to talk to them, and she responds the same way to all of them."

"I don't mean that," Peter said, though that had been annoying. "I meant the books."

"That? That's what happens around here sometimes. Books explode, things burn up. Sometimes people get hurt. They've been trying to figure it out for years. No one can exactly blame Miss Stoneflange, of course."

"The only reason anyone puts up with her is because of her family," said Tyrell. "They run the university."

"Garbage," said Harry, shutting his book with a snap. "She was here before they adopted her. The family adopted her *because* she's talented."

"Why doesn't she do magic, then?"

Harry shrugged. "You'd have to ask her that yourself. It's not my story to tell."

"She wouldn't tell me if I asked."

"Exactly," Harry said, gathering his books together. "Neither will I."

Peter watched him leave the library in a bewildered combination of grudging respect and annoyance. He didn't particularly like being left with people like Samuel—perhaps because it felt as though he was being treated by Harry as though he was the same kind of person as Samuel—and he was still smarting from Miss Stoneflange's earlier, casual dismissal of him. On the other hand, Harry was perfectly right about keeping his own and Miss Stoneflange's private business to himself. The suggestion that Peter was somehow unworthy to know the whole was certainly galling, but Harry was every inch the gentleman toward Miss Stoneflange in acting so.

That made Peter ask, perhaps rashly, "What's between him and Miss Stoneflange?"

"Oh, you noticed that?" said Samuel. "They're quite the pair. I advise never saying a word against Miss Stoneflange in Harry's presence—but I suppose that's rather obvious."

"Rather," said Peter.

"I've gained the impression," Samuel added, "that Harry hopes to convince Miss Stoneflange that he's a good match. The family *is* dreadfully influential."

"I see," Peter said shortly, somewhat sorry that he'd asked. He hadn't particularly wanted to spend more time with Samuel, and it looked like the boy was settling in to stay. Still, it was nice to have his impression of Harry's actions verified. "She doesn't seem to favour him. Unless you count actually talking to him."

"Miss Stoneflange is too high in the instep to outwardly favour anyone: she certainly doesn't treat him with the same disrespect she levels at everyone else, however. And," added Samuel, lowering his voice, "she gets pretty good use out of the fellows who like her."

"It's not particularly safe, though," said Tyrell. "One of them is still in hospital, and one of them got sent down before he could talk too much. No one has seen him since. It must be pleasant to have a family powerful enough to cover up all your little…accidents."

"I suppose so," said Peter, regretting more than ever that he'd asked the question. He began to pack up his own things in the hope that Samuel and his friends would get the idea that he was going to go in and dress for dinner. Unfortunately, they seemed inclined to follow him out.

"Well," Samuel added smoothly, as they neared the door, "She certainly shouldn't be working nearby other people if she makes a mess like that."

It was regrettable that Miss Stoneflange should be walking back into the room just as he said it. Peter was quite sure that she had heard, because her eyes met his for a bare second, faintly amused, faintly satirical. Peter saw her lips curl in the same derisive smile she'd directed at Samuel earlier, and he edged his ear away from Samuel's far too talkative mouth, flushing.

The last he saw of her, Miss Stoneflange was reaching for

the model she'd left behind when she swept from the room. Peter didn't see any more after that because he was hurrying to get away before she could smile at him again.

Samuel kept pace with him to say affably, "Useful, isn't it?"

"What?" asked Peter, rather shortly. He felt that Samuel hadn't been only having jabs at Miss Stoneflange and Harry, but that he'd been jabbing at Peter as well. He could understand being antagonistic with Miss Stoneflange, but Samuel had only met Peter yesterday and there was no reason to dislike him quite so much just yet.

"Well, being the adopted daughter of the headmaster, of course! Did you not know that?"

"I didn't," Peter said, more slowly. Tyrell had said that her adopted family ran the university, but he had fancied they were rich and generous with donations. A few things made much more sense, now. It *had* been Miss Stoneflange behind the curtains earlier. She must have heard her adopted father suggesting that she and Peter get along: why was she so very rude, in that case? He had even expressed his willingness to discuss her very good interactive map!

"So interesting, isn't it?" began Samuel. "I suppose you—"

"How?" interrupted Peter, stopping in the hall.

Catching himself up, Samuel said, "No need to be short, Carlisle. You're not going to join the ranks of those fellows who are smitten with her, are you?"

"Of course not!" Peter said impatiently. "I just don't see what it's got to do with me who her family are, and what difference it makes anyway."

He did wonder, briefly, exactly why it was that Miss Stoneflange hadn't taken her adopted father's name, but it seemed like a very Miss Stoneflange thing to do, insomuch as he already knew her.

"It makes a difference to people who are on her family's side," interpolated Tyrell. "You don't have to be so snotty about it, Carlisle! We all understand the necessity of making good connections, after all!"

"Some are merely harder to make than others," said Samuel, gazing over Peter's shoulder back down the hall.

Peter turned his head to follow the other boy's eyes, and saw the last of Miss Stoneflange's skirts disappearing around the corner at the far end of the hall.

"We're going to be late for dinner if we don't change," he said, and started off toward the dormitories without further warning. Much to his relief, the other boys fell behind and didn't again try to catch up, and he was able to escape to his own room before they appeared behind him in the boys' dormitory hall.

"What's chasing you?" amiably enquired Tom, who was laying out on his bed in all his dirty, sweaty, post rugby glory. "It's not time for dinner yet, surely?"

"Close enough," said Peter. "Are you going down like that?"

"Heavens, no!" Tom swung his feet off the bed, scattering dirt and grass from the spikes of his rugby shoes. He took them off first, followed by his sweat-dampened shirt, then filled the wash basin and doused his head while Peter gloomily dressed himself.

Swiping the washcloth over his neck when he emerged, he added, "Look, old man; we've got to fix that dinner rig of yours. I don't have the fiddly sort of magic to fix it, but I know how to do the thing with pins and that sort of thing. Got a poor cousin who's a tailor—jolly fellow, great dabs with a needle, you know."

"Thanks," said Peter, genuinely grateful. It wasn't that he cared much about his clothes, but he very much disliked being looked down on. Whether it was Miss Stoneflange or Samuel, he was determined that from now on, no one should be able to look down on him.

❧ 3 ❧

The study of the Laws of the Interconnectedness of All Things had always been one of Peter's favourites when he studied alone, and if he had expected anything of the university, it would have been that he would enjoy it just as much there.

He was prepared to do so, especially since when he got to class the next day, the first person he saw was Miss Stoneflange, sitting at a desk in the back of the classroom with a straight back and her nose in the air.

So Interconnectedness was one of the classes where she hadn't quite attained to the fifth-year level, was it? Peter, feeling very pleased with himself, prepared to enjoy the class, and continued in that pleasant expectation until the master walked into the room.

It was obvious immediately from the very faint sigh that ran around the room, that this master was not the person they had all been expecting. It gave Peter to believe, moreover, that the change was not a welcome one.

"Is Doctor Harding unwell today?" asked Miss Stoneflange.

"Doctor Harding doesn't make me privy to his business,"

said the master, surprising Peter a great deal. There were a few titters around the room, Samuel's soft laugh amidst them. "Nor, if you do not already know, Miss Stoneflange, does he appear to make you privy to it."

Peter couldn't resist looking around to see how Miss Stoneflange had taken the put-down, and found in some disappointment that she was merely adjusting her ever-present mechanical model again, her chin set to its usual elegant degree. How she managed to get the model into the classroom without being called out on it was another of the mysteries that surrounded her.

"I see that we have once again welcomed children into our number," said the master. It took Peter a moment or two to realise that the master was talking about him, and by the time he turned around, the master was already saying, "But I fear we are not entertaining enough, if young Master Carlisle is already not paying attention."

"Sorry sir," said Peter. Perhaps this master was one of the ones that needed a firm personality to stand up to. "You don't have to worry about me. I can keep up with the others."

"Yes, I'm sure you think so," the master said. "Most of you who skip a year or two seem to have the same idea."

"Carlisle did very well on the test, I believe, sir," said Samuel.

Peter wished he knew why the boy said so. On the first day, he might have thought it was because Samuel was trying to make things easier for him; now that he'd seen the way the boy behaved himself around the school, he wasn't so sure. Today, he rather fancied it was because Samuel had some sort of perverse amusement in prickling the master to be as much irritated with Peter as he apparently already was with Miss Stoneflange.

"Is that so?" enquired the interim master.

"Indeed sir. I heard the headmaster speaking about it after dinner last night."

"You," said the interim master, tilting his chin at Peter. "Name the Three Laws of the Interconnectedness of All Things."

"There are four," Peter said in surprise. "Do you mean you want me to mention just three of the four?"

"I would advise against telling the master what you *think* he means," the man said coldly. "Name the Three Laws of the Interconnectedness of All Things."

"Yes, but which three did you want?"

Impatiently, the master said, "*All* of them. How many times must I repeat myself?"

"I can name three if you want," said Peter, with growing obstinacy. "But there are four in total. There weren't always, but there have been four since the start of last year."

"Perhaps someone else in the room can answer more appropriately." The master's eyes roamed the room, and stopped on Harry. "You. Proctor."

"Sorry sir," said Harry. "But there really are four. We covered them last week with another master. Not meaning to contradict you sir, but Carlisle is right."

"I see that some of you at least know how to address a teacher," said the interim master. His eyes came back to Peter, hard and cold. "Regardless of whether you feel yourself right or wrong, there is a correct way to address a master, Carlisle, and it seems as though you have yet to learn that way."

"Sorry sir," said Peter. "But isn't it more important to be right? If we're wrong about something as simple as the Four Laws of the Interconnectedness of All Things, we're going to make rather a mess when we practise."

"In the classroom, Carlisle," said the master, "Respect comes first. You will have time yet to excel in your studies. You are, after all, a *first*-year student."

"Yes, sir," Peter said, now unsure if the master had been setting a trap into which he had fallen, or if the man had genuinely not known about the Fourth Interconnectedness Law.

He was no closer to figuring it out by the end of the lesson. To his disappointment, the master didn't call on him to answer any further questions, either, and when he caught up with Harry out in the corridor, the other boy gave him a sympathetic grin.

"What do you want, Carlisle?" he asked, at odds with that grin. "If you need someone to show you to your next class, I've got the feeling you're asking the wrong person. You're above my touch, I fear."

"That—the master. Was he just testing me? Or did he really not know?"

"Of course he didn't know," said Harry. "He's not the real master and he has no idea. He was just trying to save face because he didn't know what to do when you corrected him."

"What sort of a master doesn't even know there are Four Laws of Interconnectedness? I should have—"

Harry grinned sardonically. "You already did enough."

"But—"

"It's not the best idea to antagonise the masters," warned the other boy. "They have ways of getting back at you without looking like they're doing it. I'd keep my head down if I were you, Carlisle."

"Miss Stoneflange didn't seem to be keeping her head down."

"Oh no," said Harry coolly. "She was keeping her head down. Nothing exploded, did it?"

He went on ahead by himself, leaving Peter to find his own next class in some perplexment.

The other classes went much more smoothly, though Peter didn't find anything to challenge him overly. He would have visited the headmaster to suggest that he go up to the next year in most of his classes, but remembered just in time that fifth year and sixth year students had much less free time than the third and fourth years, and that he could still use his spare time to work on his time tickerbox. That, after all, was his most pressing concern.

Still, Peter couldn't help his mind wandering after at least the chance of a room of his own in which to experiment; that was still something he ought to be seeking from the headmaster. That was something worth sticking his neck out for.

His mind agreeably engaged in exactly how he would utilise such a room, with its attendant resources, Peter didn't realise he'd walked past the corridor to the third form common room and on toward the further common rooms until he felt the magical protections on the walls cease. He stopped and recollected himself, almost tempted to continue going on to the fifth form common room instead of back to the third form one: there would be no one in the fifth form common room at this time of day. The fifth and sixth formers, male and female, all prided themselves on being dignifiedly on time for dinner, and dignifiedly well dressed for the same. It was likely that he would have a good forty-five minutes of uninterrupted time to work on his tickerbox in peace—unless he chose to arrive at dinner in a rush, in which case, he would have a whole hour free.

As Peter loitered at the division of protected and unprotected, a shadow with fluttering orange edges passed across the hall from the window and down the corridor that led to the fifth form common room, spicing the soft darkness of evening with magic that was both familiar and alien.

His interest piqued, Peter started forward again. The shadow was certainly no student: even the strongest magic user in the university—even Peter himself—did not possess magic so ridiculously strong. Nor did they possess the peculiar edge of warm amber that he had just seen.

Nor, for that matter, were students in the habit of passing through walls from the outside of the university, for the very good reason that there were exceedingly good protections on the outside to prevent that very thing. Peter had seen them on his first day, and he was quite sure that even he would have had difficulty in passing through them. The only people he could think of offhand who could do such a thing were Poly and Luck, and the magic he had just seen belonged to neither of them.

It was something that he didn't think he had seen before at all. And yet, it was achingly familiar.

So Peter followed. He followed carefully, quietly, and entirely without the use of magic to keep himself hidden. He was quite sure it would have been noticed immediately, and he felt that he would much rather remain unseen until he knew something more of the mysterious stranger who had so easily walked through a heavily fortified magic wall and had magic of a type he had never before seen.

More, he would very much like to know exactly what that stranger was up to.

Peter followed right to entrance of the corridor that led to the fifth form common room, then stole softly into that corridor. The stranger, nearly at the door at the further end of the corridor, was far more solid than he had seemed a moment or two earlier. Peter didn't know exactly when the stranger slowed his walk, but it was very obvious when he stopped altogether.

Aware that he had been noticed, Peter stopped by a door in the hallway—the broom closet, he rather thought—and briefly considered readying some kind of magical defence.

He was not given the chance to do so. The stranger, without turning around, unleashed a single, targeted pulse of hot magic that sent Peter flying through the air for one breathtaking moment, and straight through a wall into the broom cupboard he had just passed with a great splintering of wood, or perhaps time, or perhaps even matter.

When fully in command of a situation, if not his temper, Peter eschewed the use of magic except as a last resort. When casually hurled by a stranger into a nearby broom cupboard with the careless ease of a lion sending a cub tumbling with a flick of one paw, unable to so much as scramble to his feet from the shock of it all, his first response was a powerful, jagged aureole of magic that sliced through the wall and the shadows alike and glanced off something even more powerful further up the corridor.

Peter heard someone laugh, and that was strange and familiar, too. By the time he had struggled to his feet in the wreckage of what was left of the broom closet, he could hear only the mocking sound of footsteps in the distance. He would have tried to charge after the perpetrator, but the echo of those footsteps was just a bit off, and he wasn't sure if it was his glasses or the surrounding hall that was, for a moment longer again, not quite in the right place.

Peter blinked, and the fractured hall melted back together into one piece, but in that moment he lost all sound and feel of the interloper. He stumbled out of the timbers of the broom closet that were, due to the magics with which the walls had been imbued, sluggishly drawing themselves back together, and couldn't help walking the length of the corridor despite the fact that the interloper was long gone.

He also couldn't help opening the door to the fifth form common room to be really sure that the stranger hadn't hid himself there. Peter couldn't have said why he thought the stranger was male, nor exactly how he knew that the stranger wasn't in the room, the school, or even the same general area, but he was thorough enough to want to see as much with his own eyes.

Instead, his eyes fell directly upon Miss Stoneflange, the single occupant of the room. She was already looking toward the door when he caught sight of her, a flush on her cheeks that made her far less ice-like than usual, but when he met her eyes they immediately dropped back to the book she was holding.

Peter, glad to see anyone with whom he could discuss the oddness of the evening despite the fact that he shouldn't be where he was, asked without preamble, "Did you *feel* what happened out there?"

"I suppose the first-year children have been trying to do magic in the halls again," Miss Stoneflange said. Her voice was curt and her flush, which had deepened, began to fade. She turned a page and added, "Walking the corridors can be slightly fraught at the beginning of term."

"It wasn't a first-year student, I can tell you that much!" said Peter. "I had to fight jolly hard not to be thrown into the next corridor!"

"People who throw magic around in the corridors are likely to be chased down by the masters," she said. "That goes for defensive magic, too. Did you hurt anyone?"

"I know better than to hurt people," Peter said, and found that he had lifted his chin a little. It gave a very slight warmth to his chest to know that Miss Stoneflange was so well aware of the strength of his magic, even if he didn't choose to use it.

"You must have been rather startled," she said, going back to her book. "You made a bit of a splash out there. I shouldn't stay here very long, if I were you. The masters will be after you in a few minutes."

"If they are, they should be able to tell it was self-defence!" protested Peter. "The whole hall is soaked in his magic!"

That earned him a second look from Miss Stoneflange. "Him? It was a man?"

"I didn't see him clearly," Peter said. "But all the same, I'm quite sure."

"I see," said Miss Stoneflange. She was a little flushed again. "How very consistent of you!"

Peter opened and closed his mouth twice before he could settle on the question he most wanted to ask. At last, he asked her, "Are you laughing at me?"

"It's not as bad as that," she said, with what seemed to

Peter to be a deliberately pointed kind of bracingness. "I'm merely pointing out the fact that you always do seem very sure of yourself. I should also point out that you shouldn't be in here."

"I'm not hurting anyone," Peter said. "And there's no one else here."

"*I'm* here."

"Yes, but——"

Miss Stoneflange sighed a little. "I really was trying to be polite," she said. "But now I suppose I'll have to be very direct. Go away. I have an appointment and I don't wish to miss it."

"If you've got an appointment, shouldn't you be the one going? I didn't think any of the teachers visited the common rooms."

Miss Stoneflange's hand was at her waist, but Peter didn't realise until her eyes flicked downward that she was looking at the watch that hung there from a silver chain.

"They don't," she said. "And you shouldn't be here, either. This common room is for the fifth form students."

It struck Peter for the first time that Miss Stoneflange was looking more than usually elegant, though it took him some time longer to hazily suppose this must be because she was wearing something sparkling on her eyelids and had painted her lips with something else.

He opened his mouth to remark upon this, too, but Miss Stoneflange spoke before him. "You'd best be off, then, hadn't you?"

"What?"

"You can't be in here," she said. There was no malice to it; nor was there any warmth. Miss Stoneflange was merely stating facts. "It's the fifth form common room. Yours is back toward the stairs."

"All right, all right!" Peter said, with a touch of indignation. "There's no need to be so stiff about everything, you know."

"So everyone keeps telling me," said Miss Stoneflange, and turned her eyes back on her book. "Close the door behind you, won't you? You'll miss dinner if you're not careful."

"So will you!" Peter retorted, on his way out.

He kept a watch for her at the dinner table, but Miss Stoneflange didn't arrive for dinner at all. Nor, if Peter was very much mistaken, was Harry expecting her to do so. The other boy sat where Peter was used to him sitting, and applied himself rather quietly to his own dinner without looking around whenever someone walked behind him, as might have been expected were he actually waiting for his friend.

If he had thought Harry would answer the questions, Peter might have put himself to the trouble of asking why Miss Stoneflange had eschewed dinner—why, for that matter, she had been wearing what he was quite certain was lipstick and eye-paint—or why she was waiting for someone who wasn't a teacher in the empty fifth form common room. Since he didn't think he would get answers, Peter darkly mused on the questions in the privacy of his own mind, and very nearly missed both dessert and Tom's amiable remark that he would likely be out of their room earlier than usual the next morning due to early rugby practise.

Fortunately for Peter's appetite as well as his likelihood of getting up at the right time the next day without the usual expedient of someone to wake him, Tom was kind enough to repeat his remarks as well as help Peter to a decent serving of the pudding as it went past.

"You seem distracted, old man," he said. "I suppose your thinkbox is caught up with your experiments or something like that, but I'll be beating mine about on the practise field tomorrow well before dawn, so if you don't get yourself up in time for class by yourself, you'll be right out of favour with the masters."

"Good grief, yes," said Peter hastily. "I've got Interconnectedness first thing tomorrow morning, and the interim master already dislikes me."

"Strange fellow," Tom said, grinning. "There you are, then: better not to give him the chance to punish you if you don't have to."

It hadn't occurred to Peter that in the absence of Tom, someone might think it good to play some sort of prank on him. It hadn't occurred to him, in fact, that anyone else knew of Tom's absence until he opened the door, already in somewhat of a hurry, and nearly pitched headlong into a mud pit instead of stepping into a hallway.

Peter caught himself against the doorframe just in time to avoid a messy start to the morning, but the magic that had formed the particularly unexpected spell was so strong, and the enchantment itself so strong and sneaky that it took him a good fifteen minutes to safely disentangle it.

After that, it was a matter of sprinting through the corridors in a mad dash to avoid being late to the Interconnectedness class, darkly wondering who had managed to so thoroughly outwit the anti-magi protections in the halls. Peter wouldn't have minded so much being late to one of the other classes, on the chance that he would be locked out and have an entire class' worth of time to follow his own inclinations, but he didn't like the thought of being late to this particular class. It would look too much as though he were trying to avoid the master. As Tom had said last night, it also carried the danger of giving the interim master the opportunity to punish him, and Peter felt that he would much rather not give the man that chance.

Still, he only just arrived in time to avoid being locked out of the classroom, and Peter was quite sure it was disappointment on the interim master's face as the man said, "There you are, Carlisle. Next time, try not to run so fine to the time, won't you?"

"Yes, sir," said Peter. He would have gone to find an empty desk, but it didn't seem like the man was finished talking.

"Your partner won't look too kindly on you if you can't pull your weight for your end-of-term project," added the interim master.

"Partner, sir?"

"Ah, perhaps you're not aware of how a formal class in Interconnectedness works," said the interim master. "Allow me to explain before I introduce your partner to you."

Peter might not have been aware of how the university carried out its classes in Interconnectedness, but he was very aware of the malicious gleam in the master's eye, and of the barely concealed snickers around the classroom.

"Every term, the whole class is split into groups—partners, groups of three, five, ten—whatever seems good to the university at the time. The group, partners in this case, will complete a project together to present to the master at the end of term. The projects are judged and final grades awarded, but the couple with the highest scoring project will be given special privileges next term."

"Yes, sir," said Peter, since the master had paused and seemed to expect something of him.

"Partners were assigned just before you arrived," added the master. "No doubt you'll try to be on time for your partner's sake if not for your own from now on. Miss Stoneflange doesn't take well to her partners failing her."

Peter instinctively glanced toward Miss Stoneflange. She wasn't looking at him; she was writing something in the notebook she always seemed to have open in front of her, her other hand resting lightly on the wooden model in front of her. Of their other classmates, most seemed to be equally divided between watching avidly for Peter's reaction, and Miss Stoneflange's. He was left, once again, with the feeling that he didn't have quite all the information necessary for his current situation.

He said again, "Yes sir," and went to sit down at one of the empty desks. He would have sat down next to Miss Stoneflange in appreciation of their new partnership, but as usual, Miss Stoneflange was already entirely surrounded. It occurred to him that whatever the interim master meant by it, and whatever their classmates were expecting, the partnership couldn't have been better thought out. He was quite sure, after yesterday's classes, that Miss Stoneflange was the only one who could possibly keep up with him.

Peter had determined, after carefully mature thought through the lesson, that he would approach Miss Stoneflange in the most unexceptionable and flattering of ways to begin their partnership. If he had somehow offended her, he was sure that this would assuage any feelings of irritation. If Miss Stoneflange was not offended, it would no doubt cement their good relationship. She was obviously clever enough to keep up with Peter, as unusual as that was, and Peter had every intention of letting her know that fact in advance.

He found it difficult to say, therefore, exactly where everything fell apart.

Perhaps it was when he threaded his way through the other students who were making their way out to lunch, and stopped at Miss Stoneflange's desk. She was still, as usual, fiddling with one of the study models; had been so, if Peter wasn't mistaken, for the entire lesson.

She ignored him, though Peter was certain that she had seen him—couldn't, in fact, have missed seeing him—and it could have been when his temper slipped that everything began to go wrong.

It could also have been when Miss Stoneflange said,

without looking up, "Go away, please. I'm busy and I don't wish to be disturbed."

Peter's temper slipped a little more, but he drew in a deep breath to try and keep face before her at least *once*, and said, "The master said we're to be partners."

"I heard," Miss Stoneflange said.

Peter waited for her to say something else, but it seemed as though Miss Stoneflange, in her usual succinct way, had said all that she meant to say.

"I was very glad to hear it," said Peter, persevering with his plan regardless. "You're more likely to be able to keep up with me than any of the others, so I'm sure we'll get along well."

Miss Stoneflange seemed to sigh faintly. "How very complimentary, to be sure. Go away, please. I'm busy."

Non-plussed, Peter protested, "But when are we to sit down and discuss our end-of-term project?"

"There will be," said Miss Stoneflange, looking up at last, her eyes glittering with an emotion that Peter didn't understand, "a *very great deal* of time to discuss working together."

"Yes, but I only ever see you in the study and you won't ever talk while you're working there, either. How else are we supposed to discuss it?"

"I see that you don't quite understand the perniciousness of the interim master," said Miss Stoneflange. "We are not merely partners on our end-of-term project, we are to sit together during the class as well. We'll be partnered in class until the end of term. Whether or not we proceed to the next grade depends on how well we work together with our partners through the year."

"Well, that's all right, isn't it?" asked Peter, annoyed by her less-than-cordial tone against all his better resolutions. He now understood why Miss Stoneflange was still in a lower level of the Interconnectedness Class.

"Perhaps for you," Miss Stoneflange said. "It's not all I hoped for out of this class, I can promise you."

"I doubt you're likely to do better!" snapped Peter. "It's not like anyone thinks *you're* a joy to work with, and at least you'll have someone who knows what they're doing! Maybe this way you'll be able to get out of the Fourth Year Interconnectedness Class!"

There was a very small *snap* that made Peter's time ticker-box twitch in his pocket, and Miss Stoneflange said coolly, "Bother. That's another one broken."

The model on her desk, all tendrils of twine and jointed legs of wood, now had one broken leg.

"What are you doing, anyway?" asked Peter, interested despite himself. He took a deep breath to recover his temper once again, and said, "You can fix it and it'll still work: you just have to—"

"Thank you," said Miss Stoneflange. "I know of at least two ways to fix a wooden model of this kind."

"I can do it for you," offered Peter. After all, he had distracted her, and could be said to be partially to blame. "I forgot that it's hard for some practitioners to work when someone is talking to them."

"It can't be fixed for my use," Miss Stoneflange said, gathering together the model and its parts, along with all her school things. "Don't touch, thank you very much."

"I just told you I know how—"

"You can fix the model," she said, "but it won't be useful anymore. Not for what I want it for."

"Yes, but you *can*," argued Peter. "You just have to do a proper job of it. Look, give it to me if you can't do it. I'm offering!"

Miss Stoneflange stood, and said, with ice-edged words, "Go. *Away*."

"Yes, but if you just let me fix it, I can show you how you can still use—ow!"

The model exploded in a stinging shower of twine and splinters, prompting Peter to duck for cover beneath the desk.

Miss Stoneflange, who had merely shielded her face with her schoolbag, all but hurled that schoolbag down on the desk and snapped, "Oh for pity's sake!"

Peter, emerging from the underside of the desk, said rather shakily, "You can't blame me for that. What did you do?"

"It wasn't me," said Miss Stoneflange, prodding at the tangled mess that was left behind on her desk. The anger had gone from her face as quickly as it had come, and now she merely looked a little weary. "It's something that happens around here. Can you please go away?"

"I'll fix it," said Peter, resolute in proving his mettle. "Look, I'll show you how, and—"

Miss Stoneflange, without another word, left the classroom, the model, even her schoolbag, and swept from the room. Peter, left alone to indignantly gather up the pieces of the model and run a quick spell to collect the bits that had been flung across the room and into the ceiling by the force of the explosion. Whatever Miss Stoneflange said, he was going to fix it, and he would *show* her that he knew what he was talking about—that he was a worthy partner.

He would show her, in fact, that she was very lucky to have him as a partner at all.

In pursuance of that goal, Peter spent his lunch break that day in fixing the model. Wary of Miss Stoneflange's claims that it wouldn't work again anyway, he used as little magic as possible, and what he did use, he used only to encourage the natural fibres in the wood and twine to reform without adding anything magic-based to the model itself. Even if Miss Stoneflange had some odd aversion to working with other people's magic, there would be no residual magic to bother her; once it was fixed, he would be sure to draw out every last skerrick.

It took him his entire lunch break to fix the model, being as careful as he was. That done, Peter set himself to the task of finding the errant Miss Stoneflange, who turned out not to be in any of the classes she should have been in.

Peter asked Harry for her whereabouts when he found him in the halls, but Harry only gave him a significant look, and walked into his own classroom without answering.

It was just like life, Peter thought indignantly, as he watched Harry go with no better idea of where Miss Stoneflange was hiding herself, to continually saddle him with people who hated him for no reason. First it was his stepfather, then Rorkin, the magician who managed to ignore any question he didn't feel like answering if the questioner was Peter. After Rorkin was Melchior, once a cat, but now a constant wedge between Peter and his friend Annabel where he had no business being. Then had come Luck, an enchanter in whose house Peter and Annabel had spent some time, and who was even more slippery than Rorkin.

But worst of all had been Luck's wife, Poly.

Poly was worse because Peter didn't feel that she actively disliked him in the same way that Luck and Melchior did. In fact, he felt that she really quite liked him, but she would never take him seriously. More, in her quiet, stern way, she could wither the words on his lips as he opened his mouth to speak them—both figuratively and literally. Poly was an even more powerful enchanter than her husband, and although he thought very little of magic, Peter found that her quiet disapproval stung far worse than either the studied disregard of Luck, or Melchior's irritation.

What exactly had he done, now wondered Peter, to be always surrounded by unpleasant people? Harry and Miss Stoneflange were merely the latest of those, but the fact that Miss Stoneflange was undoubtedly the best looking of those made it very hard to bear.

Breaking one of his own rules, he found and followed her delicate trace of magic down the corridor, careful not to try and touch it whether physically or with his magic. If he touched it physically, Miss Stoneflange would know he was following her, and if he touched it with his magic, not only would she know he was following her, he was quite sure that delicate wire would burn through his magic with white-hot precisity. It didn't look very strong, but he knew that an almost incandescent appearance could hide very strong magic.

Peter found Miss Stoneflange not in her next class, but in the empty fifth year common room once again. He took in a deep breath and crossed the room, dropping her book bag on the seat next to her.

"Look," he said, sitting down. "If we're going to be working together, we might as well get on."

"I didn't want a little boy as a partner," Miss Stoneflange said. "I'm not going to be chummy with one, either. You pull your weight and I'll pull mine. There's no need for us to get along."

Peter, flushing, said, "I'm in your class instead of the younger one because I was too advanced for it."

"Good for you," said Miss Stoneflange.

"And *you're* in it," said Peter, unwilling to be wise, "because you're not up to all your other classes when it comes to Interconnectedness. So I *really* do think—!"

"I really think you aren't thinking at all," Miss Stoneflange said. "But I suppose it seems perfectly normal to you. I am not a year less in Interconnectedness because of any lack of understanding; I'm a year less because I know exactly how Interconnectedness works and it's far better for the Interconnectedness of All Things if I'm in this class and not the higher one."

Peter took off his glasses to polish them. "That doesn't make sense."

"Actually, I've just begun to doubt it myself, but it was working perfectly well until now."

"Why wasn't our normal master there?" asked Peter, since he wasn't sure that Miss Stoneflange wasn't, in a quiet and wholly non-understandable way, mocking him. "Doctor Harding, or whatever his name is? I haven't seen him since I got here."

"No one has seen hide nor hair of him since he got here," Miss Stoneflange said. "Some of us have been betting on whether he's not real, or if he's just a giant experiment in the interconnectedness of the teachers who have to take his classes for him until he starts doing it himself."

"Hopefully he gets over whatever he's got pretty quickly," opined Peter. "The interim master doesn't seem to like you much. What did you do to him?"

"Well," said Miss Stoneflange, beginning to gather her things again with great preciseness, "what exactly did you do to make him hate you so much?"

"I didn't do anything," Peter said. "He seems to have a bit of a beef with younger students, I suppose."

"I suppose that's close enough," said Miss Stoneflange. "Well, if you did nothing, I did even less than that. Pass me my pencil case, please."

It wasn't until she stuffed her things into the bag he'd brought her and stood that Peter realised she actually was preparing to leave. *Again.*

"Where are we going?" he demanded. He refused to be left behind like a little boy again.

"We're not going, *I'm* going," she said. "You can stay here, if you like. We're doing a project on Interconnectedness; we don't have to be physically connected to do so. We don't even have to be connected to the same space if we don't choose to be so."

"Wait!" protested Peter. "How are we supposed to decide on a project if you won't even sit down with me?"

"Come up with a few ideas," she said. "I'll come up with a few to balance it out. Then we'll decide which idea we want to use and go from there."

Peter returned to his own common room with the forgotten model, as well as something of a temper, and found it already full of boys who had just come out from lunch. Leslie threw a roll at him, and Peter took it, though he would have liked to have enjoyed his annoyance for a little while longer first. He dropped down on the sofa between Leslie and Harry, and caught the Broman boy's eyes.

"Didn't I tell you?" said Harry, grinning. "It wasn't a commendation to be partnered with Miss Stoneflange."

"Commendation?" Peter said indignantly. "It's a punishment!"

"Interim doesn't care to be cheeked," Harry told him. "What did you expect? Next time you'll know to keep your mouth shut."

"He was *wrong*."

"There's always going to be someone who's wrong," Leslie said, shrugging. "If you bother to tell everyone when they're wrong, you'll run out of energy pretty quickly. And then there are going to be a lot of people pretty happy about it when you get something wrong."

"I don't usually get things wrong," Peter grumbled, as Tom wandered into the common room and perched on the arm of the sofa they sat on. "Not when it comes to magic, anyway."

"You should do well in class then, old man," said Tom. He looked as though he was trying not to grin.

Harry snorted. "That's the irritating thing," he said. "He's doing *very* well."

"Bad form to arrive late, though," said Leslie, shaking his head. "A bit late to class this morning, weren't we, Carlisle?"

"Yes, I—" Peter stopped. "*You* did it?"

Leslie grinned. "Nice bit of work, eh? Get any mud on you?"

"If you've been booby-trapping my door again," said Tom, in dawning wrath, "I will make perishing sure you spend the night in the stables with the rats!"

"No need to be upset!" Leslie said cheerfully. "I didn't do

it myself—just appreciated it on my way down to class, as it were. Lovely bit of spell-casting; especially since the corridors are still protected there."

"Perhaps Miss Stoneflange didn't want you in class this morning, old boy?" suggested Tom, raising a brow. "Can't say I blame her, from what we've all heard."

"It wasn't Miss Stoneflange," Peter said shortly. Someone had done the job with very little magical residue left behind, using all the physical components of dirt and water in the mud to support an ecosystem that relied upon itself alone, but even that small amount didn't seem to be Miss Stoneflange's magic. "Besides, it wasn't like I wanted to be her partner!"

Tom's brown eyes glowed with amusement. "Oh, so that's what you're het up about! Not to worry, Carlisle! At least she'll be able to keep up with you!"

"That's what I said to her, but—"

"You—you *said* it to her?" Harry exchanged a look with black-eyed Leslie, who looked even more delighted than he had looked at mention of the mud.

Peter sighed. "Yes, but I don't think she appreciates it."

"Funny, that," said Leslie. "M'sister does the same thing. Condescend to her even a little bit, and she'll slap the ear right off your head."

"I wasn't—I wasn't condescending to her!"

Peter saw the second look that passed between the two boys, and even Tom looked faintly non-plussed. "I don't think you really know how condescension works, old boy."

"That must have been why she took it so badly," Peter said exasperatedly. "Are *all* girls as sensitive as Miss Stoneflange and Annabel?"

He hadn't meant to say Annabel's name aloud, because as much as she'd hurt his feelings, she wasn't in the same league as Miss Stoneflange for taking offence.

"Well, old man," said Leslie, very cheerfully, "I suppose that depends on whether they're the only two girls you know.

If they are, that's not much of a pool to generalise from. But just on a guess, I'd imagine that the more girls you get to know, you'll find that they're all pretty sensitive around you."

"Does that mean yes or no?" demanded Peter.

"It means that any girl interacting with you is probably going to be annoyed by you," Harry said. "I find that a man finds himself reflected back in the people around him. I have no problems with Miss Stoneflange."

"Neither do I," said Leslie. "Except for that time when someone put spirits in the end-of-term punch and I tried to kiss her, but that was my fault. She was pretty nice about it, too; only punched me."

"I don't really call punching someone being nice," remarked Peter.

"That's because you didn't have Leslie try to kiss you," Tom said, grinning. "I should think punching was the nicest thing that could be done to him."

Leslie aimed a short, sharp kick at Tom's shins and connected with enough force to make Tom yelp and Peter wince. That led to a scuffle that ended with the much thinner and smaller Leslie's head being captured and held within the circle of Tom's arm.

He wheezed, "She could have sent me to hospital; seen that happen to other chaps who tried something with her."

"That's because she likes you," Harry said.

"Puts up with me, you mean. Let me out, you dashed ape!"

Tom released him, still grinning. "There you have it, Carlisle."

"All right, all right," Peter said reluctantly. "So you think the problem is with me. All right. I'll be more careful with Miss Stoneflange. But I still think she could make it easier to work together."

"That's where you're wrong, old boy," said Tom. "I don't think Miss Stoneflange knows how to make things easier."

$\maltese$ 4 $\maltese$

Peter, unwilling to think that he was the one at fault, but grudgingly ready to cater to the vagaries of Miss Stoneflange if it meant they could begin working together at last, allowed two days to lapse before he tried to approach her on the matter again. He silently took his seat beside her in the Interconnectedness class both days, and as silently placed the impeccably mended model on her desk the first day, but since the model was still there the second day he couldn't congratulate himself that the gambit had been at all successful.

To Peter's frustration—and no doubt Miss Stoneflange's distinct satisfaction—nothing in their Interconnectedness class required them to directly interact until the third day. They simply sat together during class, and if Peter was very aware of Miss Stoneflange's every not-quite-right movement when it came to the work, Miss Stoneflange seemed utterly impervious to him—and to her own incorrect workings.

The not-quite-rightness of her workings made Peter itch to correct them, but to his surprise, each one of her spells came out exactly right. They simply did so in a way that made the hair stand up on the back of his neck in discomfort, and made him realise exactly why Miss Stoneflange was still in the third form Interconnectedness class. Interconnectedness didn't care about whether things came out right or not; it cared about the process being perfectly in line with everything around it. Still, if she could get so much right while doing the workings entirely incorrectly, Peter was quite sure her magic was easily a match for his own.

If he had thought she would accept his help, he would have tried to offer it, but she still hadn't even accepted the mended model, and Peter was more interested in cementing a useful working relationship with her than he was in showing off.

On the third day, there was a simple soft-wood model tree for every shared desk, and the interim master hadn't taken off his coat by the time everyone sat down. Peter reached over to pick up the tree that sat between himself and Miss Stoneflange, at a loss to know what either it or the still-coated master meant, and looked up to find that the interim master's eyes were on him.

Those eyes flicked away quickly, but when Peter looked consciously over at Miss Stoneflange to see if she'd noticed, she was smiling faintly. It was the same quietly mocking smile he had seen directed at himself more than once, and it irritated Peter to think that he could possibly be in the same category with Miss Stoneflange as the interim master apparently was.

Perhaps the interim master felt the sting of that smile as well: his own smile was quite cold as he addressed the classroom.

"I'm sure you'll all be desolated to know that there is another classroom requiring my attention this morning," he said. "That being the case, your classwork will be self-guided today. You'll work together with your partner to safely share magic: use whichever safety setup you wish, and whichever method of combination you choose, to combine your magic and cause your tree to grow and flower."

"Is Doctor Harding still sick, sir?" asked one of the boys in the back.

"So it would seem. Yes, Penrick?"

"Is it graded work, sir?"

"Naturally, Penrick."

"Yes sir. Then how will we be graded?"

"Your grade will obviously depend on how well you work together," said the master, and it seemed to Peter that the man's eyes rested on Miss Stoneflange and himself for longer than normal. "This is after all, an Interconnectedness Class. And of course, should you finish early, you'll have the added benefit of free time before your next class. Bring your projects to me before class tomorrow."

The added barb to that, thought Peter rather acerbically, being that if you *didn't* work well with your partner, you'd likely be working on the spell until the next day with no free time whatsoever. He was quite sure there was a malicious gleam to the master's eye as he left the classroom for his other class, and he was equally sure that the gleam was aimed directly at himself and Miss Stoneflange.

Miss Stoneflange, as unperturbed as ever, either didn't notice the gleam, or—more likely—didn't care about it. She merely reached to take the soft-wood model from Peter, her fingers cool and roughened at the tips, and set it in front of herself as a babble of noise broke out around the newly masterless classroom.

"Decide on a spell," she said to Peter. "I'll prepare the model."

Peter, fighting the inexplicable urge to protest her autocratic manner of giving him the exact choice he would normally have taken as a matter of course, watched her sketching out the wards and protections that the university demanded as a matter of classroom safety.

As usual, she was doing them completely wrong, and while Peter had held himself back over the past two days, this time he couldn't help the put-upon sigh that escaped.

"Why do you always do that?"

"Do what?" she murmured, intent on her work.

"Why do you always do the workings wrong?"

"They're not wrong; they're different."

"No, they're wrong. You're not following the diagrams."

"Interconnectedness isn't about following the diagrams," Miss Stoneflange said. "Don't touch, please! It's about things joining together correctly."

"Yes, but they *can't* join together correctly if you don't put the right connections in place! *Or* if part of the working expects to work in one way and part of it expects to work in another!"

"Then perhaps it's a good thing that Interconnectedness is all about communication," said Miss Stoneflange.

To Peter's irritation, she hadn't altered her workings to correct them.

"Just let me do it if you can't do it according to the book!" he protested. "I know you always get the results, but that isn't going to help in an Interconnectedness Class! If we don't get it right, the spell won't work—not with both of us adding magic."

"Luckily for us, we're capable of communication," Miss Stoneflange said. "This is me, communicating with you that you'll need to adjust your magic to allow for my workings. If you do so, I think you'll find that they'll be effective enough."

"That's not how it's meant to work," Peter said sulkily. She wasn't *wrong* exactly: merely prickly and difficult to work with. Doing things differently from the standard meant that he had to make allowances for it. And of course she had told him so, meaning that it was easy to do so, but Peter found he resented having to make allowances.

Still, it wasn't as though what she was asking was difficult, and it was ridiculous to protest against doing something that was so easy to do. He huffed another breath and leaned over her workings to watch them form. Of course Miss Stoneflange was feeding her magic into the spell differently, too; with her speed and lightness, the magic was a gossamer thread instead of a solid, clinging net to catch fall-out and contain the spell.

"If you slow down a bit, the magic will join together more solidly," he said. "Your magic is pretty strong, but even strong magic won't join together well if you don't give it time to attach."

"Exactly how long have you been at the university?" enquired Miss Stoneflange, without either pausing her work or slowing down in the slightest.

Flattered at the first sign of personal interest from her, Peter said, "Just since the start of the week."

"I see," said Miss Stoneflange, and sat back. This time, she looked at him properly, and Peter was left with the vaguely uncomfortable feeling that he wished she wouldn't do so. "Then why exactly would you think that your single week of learning give you leave to correct my technique after two years here?"

"They must have thought I was clever enough to keep up with you if they paired us together," Peter said sharply, his cheeks hot. Miss Stoneflange concentrating on her work was chilling; Miss Stoneflange paying attention was absolutely cutting.

"They didn't make you my partner because they thought you were up to the challenge," said Miss Stoneflange. "They did it because they were trying to take me down a peg. For your information, I have set up in an alternate—"

"—wrong," muttered Peter.

"I have set up in an alternate fashion, with an alternate distribution of power, because the standard setup will not work."

"It's the *standard* setup because it works for *all* kinds of magic," Peter told her. "It's why Interconnectedness has its own methods and bylaws. Everyone knows that."

"By all means, then," said Miss Stoneflange, plucking the soft-wood model from the centre of her workings and tossing it at him. "Redo it on your side of the desk. We'll start once you're done."

She sat back elegantly to watch him, and Peter, who had initially felt the dawning of victory, found that dawn clouded with suspicion.

"What have you done to the model?" he asked, turning it over in his hands.

"I've done nothing to it," she said impatiently. "You can see yourself that there's no magic whatsoever in anything here. If you're too scared to do the setup now, kindly keep your thoughts to yourself and begin whichever spell you've chosen with my workings."

"I can do it!" retorted Peter. "I'm not *scared*, I was just making sure you hadn't done anything to sabotage me."

"Out of all the partners I've had, I think you must be the worst," Miss Stoneflange said thoughtfully. "Most of them were at least at the same level as me before they started questioning me. And none of them ever found it necessary to question my honour. Congratulations are in order, I suppose."

"I didn't question your honour!"

"Is that so?" she enquired. "Then let me ask you: had one of the other boys suggested you'd done what you just suggested I've done, how would you react?"

"You're not a boy!" snapped Peter, quite pink with the knowledge that had any of the others said what he'd just said to Miss Stoneflange, he would have punched them.

"I see," she said, chilling him with her voice. "I hadn't noticed. Kind of you to draw attention to the no doubt very important distinction. Perhaps you could enlighten me as to exactly where that makes a difference?"

"It doesn't," said Peter reluctantly, after a galling moment. "I'm sorry. I shouldn't have said that to you."

"I don't have a problem with people speaking their minds," said Miss Stoneflange, and the thoughtful note was back in her voice. "But oh! I really do very often have a problem with their thoughts. Are you finished with the setup?"

Peter said, "Yes," rather tightly, drawing the last bold line of containment around the model. Miss Stoneflange was no doubt the most difficult girl he had ever had to deal with. Ann had never pulled him up on every little thing he said. Ann had never looked at him like he was a piece of dirt under her shoe —no, worse! As if he didn't matter at all.

"Then by all means go ahead," she said pleasantly. "You can draw on my magic whenever you choose."

"You want me to begin the spell?"

"You did the setup," she said. "Go ahead. I'm very interested to see how you get on."

With no other option, Peter did as he was told. The thread of Miss Stoneflange's magic was there just waiting to join his own, and when he joined it with his, it curled around his own thread willingly enough.

Flushed with a success that was entirely too easy for the elation it caused him, Peter took far too long to realise that although the magic had joined quickly and acceptably, the spell wasn't working.

"Dear me," said Miss Stoneflange. "It's not working."

"It—it—just give it another moment."

Miss Stoneflange, consulting the fob watch at her waist, gave him exactly another minute longer, one delicate brow raised. Then she snapped the tiny watch shut again and straightened.

"You're doing something!" Peter said angrily. "What did you do to the spell?"

"I think you'll find," Miss Stoneflange said coolly, "that the driving magic is all your own. Do check."

Peter didn't need to check: he had been reviewing the setup and the spell for the length of that entirely too short minute. He was as well aware as Miss Stoneflange that the driving magic of the spell was his own, and that beyond simply not working, it was a perfect setup.

He was also aware, in a particularly potent mix of frustration and shame, that he had insulted her once again. Perhaps that was why she was fiddling with the newest of those mechanical models that she shouldn't have and yet did have— so she didn't speak sharply back to him. If so, it would be the first time she hadn't snipped at him when she had the opportunity.

"It should—it should be working," he said. "Everything's perfect. The setup is perfect, the magic is perfectly joined—"

"For someone who supposedly knows all about the Interconnectedness of All Things," murmured Miss Stoneflange, adjusting one of the legs of her model, "you are surprisingly ignorant about what a perfect joining of magic entails."

"It's exactly in line with every textbook definition of joining magic!"

Miss Stoneflange's lips curved. "That, at least, is true."

"Then I don't see why you're sniffing at me—"

"Not sniffing," she said. "Merely pointing out that a textbook definition *isn't going to work* when you're working with me. May I now use my own setup?"

"I never said you *couldn't* use it," muttered Peter. There was no help for it. The spell wasn't working, and Miss Stoneflange had waited for longer than he would have waited were he in her shoes. "I just—"

"You just wanted to show how much better you knew," said Miss Stoneflange, nodding. "I perfectly understand. Are you ready?"

"Why doesn't the standard setup work with you?"

"It does, at times," she said. "And of course, it depends upon the class."

"How can it depend upon the class?" Peter said despairingly. He was inclined to think that Miss Stoneflange's magic was just as twisted as her personality, and had the same issues working nicely with anyone else. "That doesn't make sense!"

"I suppose it depends on how you look at the world," Miss Stoneflange said, with a curled lip. "Of course, if you look at it through the lens of straight logic, you won't be able to understand a more curly kind of logic."

"There's no such thing as curly logic," snapped Peter. "If it's curly, it's not logic."

"And that is why you don't properly understand about the Interconnectedness of All Things," Miss Stoneflange said. "I approach things in a less straightforward way than you do."

"And that's why your spells don't work properly!"

"I think you'll find," said Miss Stoneflange, with that faint smile once again, "that it really is working."

Peter looked down to a sight that was as galling as it was unbelievable. Threading around the soft-wood tree between them, sticky magic that didn't look quite like his magic or Miss Stoneflange's made a complete circle of the wards and glittered toward the tree.

"Not quite so much, I think," murmured Miss Stoneflange, pinching that thread of magic between her fingers and reducing it from a thread to a mere filament.

Peter watched in fascination, because unlike the two-toned magic that had formed when he did the setup in the standardised manner, a curving, clearly delineated twist of honey and toffee-apple, this magic had fused almost entirely and was something else entirely. The filament that Miss Stoneflange had extracted was too thin to have a real colour to it, and Peter didn't subscribe to the idea of magic having true colours, but there was a strength and a warmth to it that he had never before seen. As if his more yellow-toned magic now contained miniscule, shiny pieces of Miss Stoneflange's apple-red magic that reflected back through.

"Is that—how did you join it like that?"

"That," said Miss Stoneflange, her face warm with contentment for the first time that Peter had seen, "is very nearly real Interconnectedness. That's what happens when you let go of standardised commonalities and points of connection and see if you can connect in a real way. It's what happens when you can't connect in a standardised way and need to form your own connections."

"That makes no sense," Peter whispered, as the tree between them spurted leaves with the smallest flutter of greenery unfurling, fresh and healthy.

That greenery fluttered across the model, growing in depth as well as height, and soon there was a little tree before them that didn't look like the flat, leafy models around the rest of the classroom.

"The kind of interconnectedness they teach at schools and universities is only a copy of the real thing," Miss Stoneflange said, her own voice hushed.

Peter had the impression that the spell had gone much better than she expected, and her quiet delight in it was as fascinating to him as the spell itself was. How could a pair of eyes as sharp and cold as Miss Stoneflange's be so entrancingly bright?

"They can't help it," she added. "They don't know how to see it properly. Although, to be fair, I think they see part of it —it's just that they can't see all of it."

"I suppose," said Peter, a little ruefully, still caught in those eyes, "that you *can* see all of it."

"No," she said. "But I know there's more than I can see, and that's the important thing when it comes to really figuring out how things work. It helps when your connections to the world aren't the same as everyone else's; it makes you work harder."

She reached out to touch the tree, her spindly-legged model forgotten by her schoolbag, and a few of the carved branches seemed to grow in an attempt to follow her finger when she drew it back. Peter stretched out a finger to it instinctively, and it did the same with him.

He gazed across at Miss Stoneflange, and for the very first time he saw a real, warm smile on her face. The tree, as sensitive as Peter to that smile, burst out with a new crop of green leaves.

"Good grief!" he said, startled. "Do you think it's going to stop?"

"I certainly hope so," Miss Stoneflange said. "Dear me, I seem to have underestimated the combined power of our magic."

"I don't see how you could have used less," Peter remarked. She'd used the veriest thread of the stuff; much less than he would have used. "Good grief, if I'd done it, it probably would have grown right into the desk."

Peter wondered if he had imagined the amusement that flickered over Miss Stoneflange's face and then disappeared. She said, "More than likely."

He stared at the tree again and then back at Miss Stoneflange, who now sat very upright in her seat as if she were trying to distance herself from the soft-wood tree, her fingers running along the jointed arms of the model in front of her. To his disappointment, the warmth was gone from her face; her eyes were distant, and he couldn't tell if she was pleased or displeased with the work—or if perhaps that complicated emotion hiding behind her eyes was directed toward something else entirely.

How did one begin to understand another person when that person was so complicated as Miss Stoneflange? And how did one get close enough to be allowed to do so in the first place? More importantly, why did he so much want to do so?

Peter said without thinking, "Why is it so beautiful? Is it because I don't know how it works?"

For the barest fraction of a moment, Miss Stoneflange's

eyes flickered toward him, and Peter could have sworn he saw some softness—was it fondness? Regret?—in her eyes. Then she tilted her chin up sharply, breaking the brief connection, and began to clear her things from the desk and into her school bag.

"Wait!" said Peter, startled. There was more he wanted to ask Miss Stoneflange; more he wanted to discuss with her— more time he wanted to spend with her.

"The project is finished," said Miss Stoneflange, hefting the strap of her schoolbag over her shoulder. "The master said we could have free time now."

Feebly, Peter protested, "No, but—"

She paused for the briefest moment. "What?"

"We still need to discuss our end of term project!" Peter said, grasping at the one sure thing that certainly still needed to be discussed. "All the other partners have already decided on a project."

"I think not," Miss Stoneflange said decidedly, standing. "I've had quite enough for one day, thank you very much."

Helplessly, he watched her wind her way through the rest of the students and out of the classroom, while on the desk, the soft-wood tree sprouted one last, exuberant flourish of flowers and ceased to grow.

Peter studied it for quite some time after Miss Stoneflange was gone, but the only thing that he was quite certain of in the end was that there was a great deal he wanted to discuss with Miss Stoneflange when next he saw her.

MISS STONEFLANGE WASN'T IN ANY OF THE OTHER CLASSES they usually shared that afternoon, nor did Peter see her in the Interconnectedness class the next day. Since Miss Stoneflange did attend the other classes that weren't Interconnectedness, Peter was left with the conclusion that she wasn't sick so much as that she simply chose not to be in the class where she had to sit with him, and that was irritating.

As if he was likely to infect her with his presence, he thought rather indignantly. That was what it had felt like yesterday: that she had suddenly become aware that she was likely to be infected by something nasty if she remained with him.

Miss Stoneflange wasn't there the day after, either, and although he saw her yet again in each of the other classes they shared, she didn't so much as acknowledge his presence when he tried to approach her. She merely left the classroom without speaking, the legs of her new, smaller wooden model curling through her fingers like a thin, wooden hand, leaving Peter to what seemed like the increasingly mocking chatter of his classmates.

After the third day of such absence, Peter, too, abandoned the Interconnectedness class for the day, despite the buzz around the class that it would actually be attended by the mostly absent and as yet unseen Doctor Harding, and went in search of Miss Stoneflange.

It was unfair, he thought determinedly to himself, of her to expect him to do all the work of the project himself. It was unfair of her to expect them to have a successful project if she wasn't willing to work with him on it. That was all he was trying to do: make her attend to the project they both needed to do. That was all he would ask of her. That was all he wanted of her.

Miss Stoneflange was, as he had rather expected, in the fifth form common room once again when he found her. Peter threw his bag on the closest sofa and sat down beside her, irritatedly aware that she was ignoring him just as much as usual.

"Here you are," he said grimly. "Are you planning on skipping all of the Interconnectedness classes for the rest of term?"

"I haven't yet decided," said Miss Stoneflange, surprising him with her straight forwardness. "What do you want?"

"I *want*," Peter said, "to work on our project! I want to make sure that we don't both fail our class!"

Miss Stoneflange shot him a cool look. "I won't fail the class. I told you: I'm very well aware of how the Interconnectedness of All Things works, and it's much better for All Things if I stay away from class for a while."

"You mean if you stay away from me for a while," Peter said.

Miss Stoneflange, startling him a great deal more, said, "Well, yes, if you must know."

"You can't just ignore me for the rest of the term!"

"Certainly, I can."

"Yes, but *why*?"

"Because you're an awful little boy and I refuse to be made to work with you," she said. "Please go away."

"Our tree was the best one in the class," Peter told her, trying to ignore the insult. He had the feeling she had said it in order to annoy him, and he was trying very hard not to rise to the bait. "And I've seen the work you do—it's not far from the sort of thing that I do. If we both worked on it, we could do something the school has never seen before."

"I can do things the school has never seen before by myself," said Miss Stoneflange. "And there's certainly nothing stopping you. I don't see why we have to do it together."

Peter opened his mouth, but found himself with nothing to say. Truth be told, Miss Stoneflange was correct: there was no reason for either of them to collaborate, other than the fact that it was required by the school in this one instance. She was likewise correct that they didn't technically need to be together to work on the end of term project.

And yet, Peter remembered the tree project and it struck him that if he and Miss Stoneflange could separately do amazing things, together, they could be truly astounding.

"It's—it's just a matter of schoolwork," he said at last.

"I told you that we can do that. We don't have to do it together to do it, after all. I'm too busy at the moment to discuss ideas—look, do you think you could catch your little box before it knocks over my ink?"

"Sorry," said Peter, making a grab for his errant tickerbox. It was the time one, and how it had gotten out of his pocket and onto the table without him noticing, he had no idea. He took out the list of ideas that he had jotted down over the last few days, diagrammed and dot-pointed, and put it down on the seat next to her. "Look, at least check over these and pick one out," he said. "We can go from there; but you should at least do that."

Miss Stoneflange didn't look at him, but she reached out a slender hand and took the list without another word. That, Peter was quite well aware, would have to be enough for now.

Miss Stoneflange was not in the Interconnectedness class the next day, either. Peter, stifling a sigh, took an open seat by Harry at the back of the class just in time to avoid being shut out of the classroom. He felt the master's eyes on him the entire way to that seat, and wasn't surprised to see the man's eyes on him when he looked up.

"Carlisle. So pleased you've decided to join us for this lesson," said the interim master, his upper lip curled. "The headmaster would like to see you before lunch. Don't keep him waiting."

"Yes, sir," said Peter. The interim master must have taken the Interconnectedness class instead of Doctor Harding after all; no doubt he'd reported Peter's absence to the headmaster himself. It didn't seem likely that Miss Stoneflange would be in trouble as well, but Peter surprised himself by not feeling hard-done-by about that. There was no reason for Miss Stoneflange to suffer as well, after all.

"Now," said the interim master. "For those of you who deigned to attend yesterday's class and are happily possessed of partners; continue with your tandem spell-casting. Those without partners may make preliminary models of one of the options on the board and discuss between them and their seat-mate until they can work with their own partners. You may expect your grades on the tandem tree spellwork by the end of the class."

He retreated to his desk, which was still forested with tree models from the lesson a couple of days ago, rather to Peter's relief. It was uncomfortable to be spoken to so pointedly from the front of the class without actually being named.

Harry's eyes flicked in Peter's direction as the master sat down, and to Peter's surprise, he said softly, "Making more trouble for yourself, Carlisle?"

"Apparently so," Peter said beneath his breath.

"Well, perhaps it's easier to find trouble in this class," said Harry, and he was definitely grinning. "The interim master seems pretty intent on making life difficult for you."

"What about Miss Stoneflange?" Peter asked, in an undertone, with one eye to the interim master. "I should have thought he'd be too clever to make life difficult for her, but he doesn't hold back in class. Doesn't her father protect her?"

"That," said Harry slowly, "is something else entirely."

"Don't tell me," said Peter, trying not to sound as annoyed as he felt. "It's Miss Stoneflange's business and you aren't going to tell me."

"Not exactly," Harry said. "It's just not something people talk about here. I get the impression that Glenna won't be protected by the headmaster until she produces something worth protecting."

Peter frowned. "I've seen her work: it's obviously the best in the school. What more does he want?"

"I get the impression that he wanted more of an obedient

daughter," said Harry. "Not to mention advances of a rather different sort."

"What sort of advances?" asked Peter, with one eye to the interim master, who had risen from his desk and was stalking down between desks with no other purpose than to make the students aware that he was watching. "She makes useful and reliable machines that only have the slightest spark of magic to them. Her father would have to be mad to ask more than that."

The interim master, his eyes narrow, made sure to send a lingering glance at their notes as he passed their desk. Happily for Peter, Harry had already nudged his own page of notes between the two of them, and was helpfully pointing his pen at one of the notes there written. The master sniffed and moved on.

"You're a very confusing sort of fellow," said Harry unexpectedly, while the master passed down the other side of the class to return to the front of the class. "Why ever didn't you approach Glenna like this in the first place? It might have taken her a little while to open up, but she would at least have been interested in talking to you!"

"I did approach her like that!" Peter retorted, very nearly betraying his indignation by speaking too loudly. "We could have talked about her inventions or mine! At least she can understand me!"

"I really think you believe that," Harry said. Despite the words, his eyes were dancing. "What I mean is, why didn't you try to approach her by talking about the very real interest you have in her inventions instead of trying to push your own cleverness at her so she'd have to acknowledge you first?"

"If you're saying Miss Stoneflange would have been nicer to me if I'd flattered her instead of approaching her as an equal, I don't think that's a particularly good representation of her character," said Peter, who had noticed at least that about Miss Stoneflange, no matter how confusing the rest of her actions might be. She didn't seem to care about either the approbation or the disapproval of her peers, and she was particularly impatient with the sort of flattery that came from people like Samuel—which no doubt explained why Samuel disliked her so much. "She wouldn't have been any more interested in talking if I'd talked about how clever her school projection machine is!"

"Anybody would!" protested Harry. "I don't mean flattery, I mean real interest! And it's not to say she would have been your friend, but knowing Glenna and knowing the university, she would have been interested to talk to you about the benefits and drawbacks of magics in mechanics. Or the mechanics of magic, if it comes to that. Instead of that, you foisted your cleverness on her and expected her to be delighted."

Peter opened his mouth and closed it again. At last, he said, "Yes, but I'm younger than her. No one takes you seriously if you're younger than they are; you have to push a lot harder to be seen."

"Only with the sort of people who don't matter," Harry pointed out. "Careful, the master's looking at us again. Scribble something down on your paper, can't you? I've already decided what I'll be doing with my partner, so it's not much use discussing it with you."

Peter did as he was told; and, willing to discuss anything other than what they had just been discussing, said, "You said her father isn't really interested in Miss Stoneflange's inventions. What does he want from her, then?"

"Adopted father. Something with a bit more firepower, I expect," said Harry.

"Why should he? Did she make things like that when she was younger?"

"I suspect it's got something to do with who her father was said to be," Harry said. "And before you ask, no; I'm not going to explain that. There are enough rumours around the school as it is. Just…next time you talk with Glenna, perhaps you could *begin* with what you think of her inventions—and *not* in a way that makes it seem like you think they're *very good little things*. I try, but I can't keep up with the way she grasps things. I've a feeling you stand a better chance of being able to do so."

Peter made a rather dubious noise of assent: he didn't think Miss Stoneflange was ever in the mood to hear anything from him. It was silly to expect that to make a difference. Still, the conversation left him thoughtful for the remainder of the lesson, even if most of that thought was directed toward wondering who Miss Stoneflange's father actually was and why that was important, and Peter very nearly forgot to go and see Headmaster Tarrant at the end of the lesson.

Happily, he remembered on the way to the room he shared with Tom, which gave him a few minutes to tidy his hair and clothes before he went back out to the headmaster's office.

This time, Headmaster Tarrant wasn't writing, or doing any sort of work at all. In fact, he looked as though he had been waiting for Peter, which might have worried Peter more if the man hadn't looked so absolutely affable.

"Carlisle," he said, as Peter shut the door behind him. "There you are! Come in, sit down."

Peter did as he was told, cautious of the genial tone. If he wasn't mistaken, he had been called in to see the headmaster about the two Interconnectedness classes he had missed in the last week. Why exactly was the headmaster so cheerful—in fact, so downright welcoming?

"I'm told you've missed a few Interconnectedness classes over the last few days. I take it you were with my daughter?"

Peter choked just slightly. "Beg pardon, sir?"

"You were with Glenna, during the lesson yesterday, I believe."

Reluctantly, he admitted, "Well, I suppose so."

"Then I'm sure you were both studying," said the headmaster amiably.

Even less than before, did Peter trust that amiability. Not because he didn't think the man was pleased—it was obviously an unusual expression on the man's face, but it seemed genuine for all that—but because he didn't understand *why* the headmaster was so pleased about Peter potentially disrupting his adopted daughter's studies, when from all that Harry had told him earlier, the man expected great things from her.

"Yes, sir," he said. "We discussed our end of term project briefly and er, debriefed on the combined project we completed at the start of the week."

The headmaster said approvingly, "Well done. I told the interim master as much. My daughter was never one to waste time with nothings, and I very much doubt you skipped a class to witter it away, Carlisle."

Peter found himself with the rather bemused thought that no matter what answer he gave, it would be the right one. Willing to test that theory, he said in a carefully apologetic fashion, "I'm afraid we were in the fifth form common room, sir. I know it's not somewhere I'm supposed to be, but it was where I found Miss Stoneflange, who—"

"Perfectly understandable, perfectly natural," said the headmaster, nodding. "Where else could you converse comfortably? As I said earlier, I'm certain you were both studying, and we don't like to be too rigid here at the University of Mechanics and Magic. You and Glenna are partners, I believe?"

"Yes, sir."

"Then I don't see that there's anything to be overly concerned about. The interim master was slightly worried, but I told him you both wouldn't make a habit of it."

"If that's what you called me in here for, you don't have to worry about it, sir," Peter said. "I'll be careful to—"

"Not at all," the headmaster said. "Of course, one must

keep the interim master happy, but he doesn't have the run of the school, after all. I called you in here to give him some peace of mind and to ask you what you plan to do for the festivities at the end of the week?"

Peter was again startled into saying, "Beg pardon, sir?"

"Festivities, Carlisle," the headmaster said remonstratingly. "At beginning of term and end of term there is a general mixer in the auditorium. A buffet, dancing, conversation—past alumni are also occasionally in attendance, so it's a good chance for an up-and-coming young man to attract some attention to himself. Glenna is less than competent at such things; no doubt you could help her there."

"Help her, sir?"

"I've noticed my daughter does not usually attend dances," Headmaster Tarrant said. "When she does, she's often preoccupied and very rarely has a partner in attendance. I believe my daughter is somewhat intimidating, but I should hope she is not so to you."

"Not...not exactly, sir," said Peter. "Though I don't think she would go with me if I asked her."

"I'm sure you're too modest, Carlisle," said Headmaster Tarrant bracingly. "Very pretty girls are often too intimidating for fellows to ask out, after all, and they can very rarely surrender enough pride to ask someone themselves. I'm quite certain my daughter would be relieved if someone were to ask her to attend with them."

There didn't seem to be much to say to that beyond a cautious, "That's very kind of you, sir."

"Well, well, the best of us need a little help now and then," the headmaster said, more bracingly than ever. "Off you go, then, Carlisle. I'm sure you don't want to miss your next class."

Peter, somewhat befuddled, made his way to his next class, but he was no less befuddled by the time that class finished and it was time for lunch. It had really sounded as though the headmaster not only wanted him to ask Miss Stoneflange to the dance at the end of the week; it sounded as though he *expected* it. Peter was quite certain Miss Stoneflange would have something to say about that, were Peter foolish enough to actually ask. He was also quite certain that if it was something Headmaster Tarrant wanted him to do, he would need to think very carefully before he did so, lest he find himself meddling in things that he didn't want to be meddling in.

He found himself wondering if Miss Stoneflange knew her father was encouraging students to ask her to the dance, and in that way came to wonder, somewhat unpleasantly, if he was not the only boy the headmaster had so encouraged to do.

Peter was still wondering about that, a furrow digging its way between his brows, when classes finished for the day. He book himself off to the study hall just in time to secure one of the wall desks and spread his things out to work on one of the lesser tickerboxes. Instead of working on it, however, he frowned down at the components without making a move for quite some time. He wished he knew exactly why the headmaster was being so very friendly toward him.

Peter would have liked to have thought that it was on account of his own talents and abilities, but he was more inclined to think that in some way, he was meant to be useful.

Peter had just bestirred himself to actually work on his tickerbox when a movement at the entrance to his wall desk made him look up. Miss Stoneflange stood there on the first step, and as he watched, astonished that she should be the one approaching *him*, she removed his time tickerbox from her satchel.

"This is yours, I think," she said, stepping up to put it delicately on the desk. "He snuck into my bag somehow."

Peter stared at the tickerbox and then up at Miss Stoneflange. He could have sworn he had just felt it in his pocket; he had a habit of patting his front pocket absently to make sure it was always there.

"Sorry," he said. "I think it likes you."

One of Miss Stoneflange's brows rose, but it must have been amusement, because she sat down opposite him, perched on the very edge of the seat. "I've got an idea he's been trying to make himself a little companion, but I don't think he knows how. You might want to watch out for that: he seems very clever and determined."

"It's not trying to make a companion, it's trying to improve itself," Peter explained, trying not to speak too quickly, almost for fear of putting her to flight. "I programmed it to understand the mechanics of magic so it could always be improving itself."

"Interesting," said Miss Stoneflange, and for the first time, it didn't sound like an insult.

An unfamiliar warmth spread from Peter's chest and up through his cheeks, prickling heat along his neck. "It's the little touch of magic that does it," he said, trying not to hunch his shoulders against the prickle. Whatever was wrong with him? "If I add too much, it gets unreliable, but if there's not enough, the clockwork can't work."

"You need enough clockwork for it to run logically, and just enough magic to spark the impossible," she said, nodding. "It's about balance."

She reached out and picked up the tickerbox once again, and it chirped happily at her, curling its two front legs around her fingers.

"I noticed that you did something like it for your interactive map of the school," Peter said. "I liked that. It's the best thing I've seen here yet."

Miss Stoneflange's eyes dwelt on him for a moment or two, as though she was waiting for something else, but when Peter didn't speak again, she said, "I was happy with it at the time, but I fancy it needs a new iteration. I've learned a few more things since I made it, and I believe I could do a version entirely without magic, these days."

"I hope you let me see it when you do," Peter said seriously. "I've been trying to find a way to run a mechanical system entirely without magic myself, but it always seems to need a spark of some sort to start it off."

"I've been considering an outside starter," she said. "Something like what I already had in the map to get the thing going, but separate from the machine itself. Once the clockwork starts it doesn't stop, apart from outside interference and natural degradation."

"Dust," said Peter, nodding. "And sometimes if there's a storm, I've noticed that it puts the clockwork out by a decent amount."

"Exactly," she said. "But the starter would be something that could be reused—a key, of sorts. And it has the added benefit of making the machine customisable to the owner— and being a deterrent against would-be thieves."

Peter, blinking at the flood of ideas that her words prompted, asked in a faintly stunned way, "Have you patented the idea? I should, if I were you! What if someone else steals your idea?"

"If they come up with it before me, they're welcome to it," Miss Stoneflange said. "One way or another, the thing will be made, and I'm sure to make it in a different way to another person, after all."

"But what about Invention Rights, and royalties?" spluttered Peter. "Patronage, that sort of thing?"

"I've already had a taste of patronage," she said. "I find I don't care for it. As for money; well, I've got other skills as well."

"But what a waste!" Peter protested. "When you could be spending the time inventing!"

"There are different ways of giving to the world," said Miss Stoneflange. "And not all of them involve clockwork—or magic, if it comes to that."

"Well," began Peter, somewhat taken aback, "of course,

magic isn't the driving force in the world, but there's a great deal to be said for clockwork."

"I fancied you might think so," Miss Stoneflange said, and this time there was no mockery or derision to her faint smile. She shifted a little in her seat; the first movement to rise, Peter rather thought, and he hurried into speech again.

"What did you mean when you said you'd had a taste of patronage?"

Miss Stoneflange paused for a few moments, and Peter thought that she wouldn't answer him at all, but then one of her shoulders rose just slightly, as if she was shrugging to herself.

She said, "I suppose you could call my adopted father a form of patronage. He has some rather extensive expectations of me after I leave the University—before that, too, I believe."

"Yes, I got that idea when he called me into his office. He wasn't particularly concerned about me missing class, either."

That made Miss Stoneflange pause again, this time more thoughtfully. Peter watched her as she thought it over, her eyes distant, and wondered exactly what it was she was concerned about. She was certainly puzzled by something; it was likely she was as confused by her father's reaction as Peter had been.

"I think he wanted me to ask you to go to the dance at the end of the week with me," he added. He still didn't know why the headmaster had hinted as much.

"I shouldn't listen to Headmaster Tarrant too much, if I were you," said Miss Stoneflange. She set the tickerbox down very gently, but very decidedly, and it seemed to Peter that her eyes crystallised as she did so. "He has some very odd ideas and he's bound to have more ideas beneath those ideas if you know where to look for them."

"I wasn't planning on *asking* you," Peter said, with the vague idea of assuring her that he wasn't trying to do anything other than schoolwork.

"Thank you so much, I'm sure," said Miss Stoneflange,

but although her eyes didn't seem quite so icy now, she stood. "I did not plan on attending the dance, in any case."

"If that's the case, perhaps we can sit down and work on our project that evening," Peter suggested. Miss Stoneflange had certainly gone cold again, but she wasn't quite as icy as usual yet.

"No, I think not," said Miss Stoneflange. "I shall be far too busy, I'm afraid."

Peter protested, "But you just *said*—"

"I said I wasn't intending to go to the dance," she said. "I did not say it was because I had nothing better to do. If I didn't want to go to the dance with you, I certainly don't want to sit at close quarters with you for the better part of the evening."

"Are you meeting someone again?" asked Peter, annoyed with both himself and Miss Stoneflange. There was no reason for Miss Stoneflange to be getting so sniffy again; moreover, the suspicion that perhaps he had not been the only boy to be encouraged by the headmaster to ask his daughter to the dance still prickled at the back of his mind. "I don't see why you won't go to the dance with me."

"You said you weren't going to ask me," pointed out Miss Stoneflange. "So of course I can't go with you."

"You could ask me! Girls can ask boys to the dance, can't they?"

"That," said Miss Stoneflange, in a particularly icy voice, "is something that will never happen. I do not attend dances with little boys; nor do I *ask* them to dances."

"I'm only a year younger than you!" said Peter, stung by the injustice of it all. He had *assured* Miss Stoneflange that he wasn't intending to obey her father's no doubt loaded suggestion to ask her to the dance, so why was she still angry with him? "You can't call me a little boy!"

"Certainly I can," she said. "I can assure you that I am not in the slightest averse to asking a gentleman of my choice to school dances; however, the gentleman I would choose to ask is not yet here."

Peter felt the flush to his face as well as the acid bite of warmth between his ribs. "Does your father know you're meeting strange men?"

"They can't possibly be stranger than the boys he keeps sending to meet me," said Miss Stoneflange, and swept down the stairs and out of the library before Peter could think of a reply hot enough to do justice to the indignation he felt.

❦ 5 ❦

Peter fully intended not to attend the party. Now that he knew Miss Stoneflange wouldn't be attending— would, probably, be working on one of her projects— he wanted to use that time in seeking her out and prevailing upon her to do some work on their project together.

Unhappily for that plan, Peter caught sight of Miss Stoneflange from where he was reading on the windowsill while Tom dressed for the party. She was dressed up in what even Peter recognised as the finest of evening clothes, and she was walking in the direction of the auditorium, much to his indignation.

"Bother!" he said explosively, and threw the book onto his bed. To Tom's open amusement, he climbed down from the window and rapidly began to dress himself.

"Caught sight of Miss Stoneflange, did you, old man?"

"Yes," Peter said shortly. "She told me she wasn't going to the dance! Bother! Why is she making things so difficult?"

"I don't think Miss Stoneflange knows any other way," Tom said. "Careful, old man. Your collar will come off if you tug on it like that. You should have sent it down to be starched."

"It's too late for that now!" said Peter, even more impatiently. "Bother Miss Stoneflange! Now I've got to go to this party just to see if she's started working on her part of our project!"

"Do you know what I think?" enquired Tom, throwing himself onto his bed fully dressed to grin at Peter's machinations. "I think you were looking forward to having some time alone with Miss Stoneflange. *I* think it could wait until tomorrow but you're so far gone as to—ow! Watch it, old chap! I can still stuff you out the window in my evening togs, you know!"

"I know!" said Peter, grinning in spite of himself. He caught the book that Tom threw back at him. "Do shut up, Tom! I'm not trying to get along with Miss Stoneflange—she'd freeze me half to death if I tried!—I just want to sit down with her and work on this project."

"For you, that's as good as asking her to dance," remarked Tom. "If you just wanted to get the job done, you'd do it yourself and show her afterwards."

"It's a joint project!" Peter protested, somewhat jolted by the thought that he *had* been looking forward to working with Miss Stoneflange. Actually *with* her and not just presenting the project with her at the end of the term. He'd been looking forward to seeing how her mind worked. He already knew she was very clever; he would have liked to explore that cleverness a little. There was just no getting to grips with her. She wouldn't let anyone get to grips with her.

The only time it had looked like he was actually approaching some sort of understanding with her, in fact, she had immediately drawn back and gone icy again. Perhaps he really had offended her in some serious way, and not just in all the small things that seemed to annoy her so much about him. He couldn't for the life of him think how he'd done so, however.

"I suppose you'll keep telling yourself that," Tom said, still grinning. "Never seen such a chap! See you at the party, old man!"

And so Peter found himself at the beginning-of-term party with all of the usual irritants that were normal for his experiences for a party, and a few more annoyances above those. There was all the same chatter and noise that usually bothered him, not to mention the waste of time; moreover, he couldn't seem to find Miss Stoneflange no matter how much he searched for her in the crowd, and his best suit of clothes had had to be secured by music clips pilfered from the music rooms. Those clips were not, Peter had swiftly found, the most comfortable method whereby to secure his too-large shirt and suit jacket; nor were they the most secure. One of them slipped from the material halfway across the dancefloor and had to be charmed back through dancing feet with a whisper of magic he would much rather not have used. Still, rather that than crawl between those dancing feet in search of it.

He stuffed the clip in his pocket, resolving to fix his shirt again as soon as he could manage, and scanned the room once again for Miss Stoneflange. It wasn't until he had gone through the couple of rooms attached to the auditorium and come back again that he saw a gleam of red hair over by the far wall.

There was Miss Stoneflange, at last! She seemed to be filling up a plate from the buffet, while at the same time avoiding her adoptive father, and if Peter wasn't mistaken, she was planning on escaping with her plate as soon as it was full. He could see the way her eyes darted back and forth: he'd often seen Annabel doing the same when she was trying to find a convenient method of escape. Whatever else Miss Stoneflange had come to the party in search of, it had not been the company and the dances.

Peter started across the dance floor again, hampered by the dancers to such an extent that he at last abandoned that idea and skirted around the edge of them instead. The distance was longer, but by the gimlet look in the eyes of the young girl he had tried to push past, if he tried again, he was likely to get a corsage to the back of the head.

By the time he got to the same side of the dance floor as Miss Stoneflange, she was already sweeping past the punch table with her eyes on something across the room—the door to the next room, if Peter wasn't much mistaken. Peter resolutely tucked the excess of his shirt back into his pinned waistcoat, and intercepted her.

"Miss Stoneflange," he began, but she, with a look of barely concealed horror, said, "Absolutely not!" and hurried away before he could say anything more.

Determined to get the chance for more than two words, Peter started after her, but as he passed the punch bowl, the surface of the punch curved inward, then bulged out. Peter ducked with a yelp, just in time to avoid being drenched with punch. Everyone else within splashing range did the same, some with less felicity than Peter himself, and in the chaos of the moment, he lost sight of Miss Stoneflange. By the time he was free of the excitedly chattering crowd that drew around the buffet table to speculate on the cause of the incident, she was nowhere in sight. Peter caught sight of Harry lingering at the edge of the crowd, however, his faint smile observable only because of the sliver of white teeth gleaming between his darker lips.

Since he had the feeling that smile was directed at the general chaos instead of himself personally, Peter was able to approach the other boy without the usual annoyance his smiles evoked.

"Where did Miss Stoneflange go?" he asked Harry.

"I was under the impression that Glenna was trying to get away from you, not invite you along," Harry said. "I don't think she particularly wants you knowing where she's gone."

"What did I do *this* time?" demanded Peter, in exasperation. "I only spoke two words to her! *Literally.*"

"So have most of the other boys in the room tonight," Harry said. "I get the impression that she's being rather more annoyed than usual tonight. It is the start of term, after all. People tend to forget what was drummed into them last year."

"I suppose she spoke with you, as usual?"

"Danced with me, too," Harry said, and there it was again. That very small, privately amused smile.

"Why does she put up with you, then?" Peter asked, frowning.

"Because I'm not *trying* to get her to dance with me or smile at me or think I'm clever," said Harry. "I don't talk at her, either. You should try treating her like a person some time."

"I do treat her like a person!"

"You don't really treat anyone like a person. You treat them all like idiots."

"I can't help it if I'm more intelligent than most of the people here," Peter pointed out.

"Maybe not, but you can help being a self-important prat. Mentioning how you'd be *glad to speak to* someone about their *quite a good little bit of work* isn't the best way to do it, in my opinion, but that's just my impression as an outside observer."

"All right," said Peter, grinning in spite of himself. Had Harry been in the office during his interview, too, or had Miss Stoneflange mentioned it herself? He would dearly have liked to know which one it was. "But how else am I supposed to talk to people who think magic is the be-all and end-all of progress? At least Miss Stoneflange has grasped that much."

"It might help," said Harry, "if you remember that it's possible for you to be wrong. Even very clever people are, when they don't have all the information."

"Yes," Peter said, "but I always make sure I've got all the information before I do magic, at least."

"I find it's useful to apply that to people, too," the other boy said, with the barest of eyebrow raises.

"Are you going to tell me where Miss Stoneflange went, or not?" demanded Peter, aggravated by that eyebrow once again.

"I think not," said Harry. "Enjoy your evening, Carlisle! I'm going to dance—it is a party, after all!"

And Peter, indignant, was left by himself. Perhaps it was better, after all, he thought to himself, now that he'd had a moment to cool down from the annoyance of seeing Miss Stoneflange attend a party she had explicitly told him she was *not* going to attend, not to seek her out. He had his own work to do, and even if he'd come out to a rather useless party, at the very least he could find a quiet part of the auditorium and do some work on his tickerbox, which was, as always, in his pocket.

There was a promising sort of corner over behind the musicians, so Peter passed back down the room, stopping to look in passing at the shattered punch bowl. Interestingly enough, the magic that had been used to shatter it seemed familiar—or perhaps a mix of magic and something else that he wasn't quite sure was magic. Something sticky and tricky and unpleasant.

Peter reached out to pick up a piece of glass, and caught a familiar flutter of colour in the corner of his eye. He turned his head automatically, mind sparking into life, and caught sight of the tall, thin Caliphan who made a bright patch in the sea of black with his colourful robes. As he turned sideways to slip through the conversing Civetans, Peter caught a glimpse of a familiar hooked nose.

Rorkin?

Peter abandoned the punchbowl and charged across the dance floor to cut the Caliphan off before he reached the door. Explosive mutters and faint shrieks punctuated the music behind him, but he ignored them all, pressing onward until he wriggled through one last knot of people and found himself face to face with the Caliphan.

Bright brown eyes stared down at him, a touch to the wild side of normal, in a thin, brown face that looked younger than it actually was.

"*Finally*!" said Peter. "I've been looking for you!"

"It wasn't me!" said Rorkin at once. "The punch bowl was already unsteady and the surface tension should have held for the duration of the dance."

"I knew it! I knew I recognised the magic!"

"You can't have. I don't know you. I probably won't know you for another—" Rorkin fished out a pocket watch from one sleeve and consulted it— "five years. You look annoying. Go away."

"Wait!" Peter said indignantly, catching at the silken sleeve as Rorkin darted away again. "I have questions!"

"Exactly," said Rorkin. "Annoying."

"Wait!" cried Peter again. "I want to talk to you!"

"Can't talk! Not supposed to be seen but now I have been. You *can't* have my sleeve, I need it for putting things in."

"I'm not *trying* to take your sleeve, I just want to—"

But it was too late: Rorkin, in a slip of magic that wasn't just magic, moved sideways in space and perhaps even in time, freeing his sleeve, and darted from the room. Peter would have charged after him, but he felt the movement of the outer hall in the same kind of slip, and was made stunningly aware of two things.

One: Rorkin had certainly made a movement of his own accord and with his own magic, that had carried him to a different point in time as well as transporting him just a few inches away from Peter. That movement had been repeated in the next room, but with such finality that Peter was quite sure Rorkin was no longer in either the building or the same time.

Two: Peter was quite certain that he could replicate that movement—certain, moreover, that that replication would be the missing piece that would allow him to move a whole human through time instead of a button or a carrot.

He turned and dived back into the crowd of people, looking for Tom. If he had still been with Annabel, he would have explained it all to her, even though she wouldn't have understood it, but he no longer had that luxury. But if he wanted a sounding board, Tom was the best choice: besides being able to understand, he would point out anything obvious that Peter had missed.

Fortunately for him, Tom was in plain sight, head and shoulders above most of the other people in the room, and it was a quick dart across the room toward him. Tom saw him coming and watched with a somewhat amused curiosity until Peter stood before him, panting a little.

"I'm an idiot!" he said to Tom.

"All right, old chap," said Tom agreeably.

Ignoring the far too cheerful assent, Peter said, "I've been thinking of people as mass instead of parts."

"I don't particularly want to be moved piece by piece, thanks very much," Tom remarked. "I suppose you're talking about your time tickerbox?"

"What's this, Carlisle?" asked Leslie, from beside Tom. In his determination to get to Tom, Peter hadn't even seen the other boy. "Are you thinking of starting your own butchery?"

"No, I mean I should have been thinking of it like a moving mass of living things," he said breathlessly. "I knew I hadn't got it quite right because when I tried to move something breathing, it didn't come out alive. The carrot and the button were fine because they weren't living. It didn't matter if I didn't move all the parts in the right order, so long as they all went back in the right order, do you see?"

"Not really," said Tom. "But I suppose you'll explain. Look, let's get out of the way of this lot: they've been playing the same piece in my ear for the last half hour. I'll go deaf if I have to listen to it for much longer."

"It's because all the living bits that a human is made up of are alive in a different way to the bits that make up a carrot," said Peter, as he followed Tom, hardly aware of where they were going. "Well, not exactly differently, but they *connect* differently. So if you interrupt those connections from their positions, bad things happen. They have to *keep going* in exactly the same way to keep someone alive."

"Still not following, old man," said Tom.

"He means it doesn't matter if you have to take apart a carrot to move it, so long as you put all the bits back where you got them from. So if you've input all the right things, it's fine. But if you want to move a human, you have to worry about things like blood circulation and electrical impulses. If you don't—"

"People soup," said Peter, nodding. "Well, mouse soup, but it wasn't pleasant, and I've been trying to figure it out for a while now."

"So that's why you only tried it with inanimate things!" marvelled Leslie. "I'm glad Tom didn't let me pinch your tickerbox, then, Carlisle! I was going to try it out down by the lake with a couple of the boys."

"Sounds like it's a good thing you didn't," remarked Tom. "In here, Carlisle. No one uses this room because it's too close to the garden and it gets a bit cold."

Leslie grinned at him, and craned his head to see into the room. "Is this the room with fish in it?"

"Unless they moved them," said Tom, nodding.

"If they didn't, we will!" Leslie said, in great glee. "Look, Carlisle, do you think you can move one of these fish with your breakthrough? Just from the tanks on this side to the ones on the other, with a minute in between or something?"

Peter nodded. "As soon as I do a bit of reconfiguring. Everything will stay the same for mass; it's just the movement of everything I've got to consider. I think I can do it if I concentrate on moving the whole space instead of just the living thing. Give it a buffer, so to speak."

"Where are you doing your calculations?" asked Tom,

frowning. "Here you go, Carlisle. Sit down here. We'll use the card table—there are even a few notepads and pencils."

"I don't need them," Peter said, fluttering his hand at the notepads. "I do it all in my head."

"You'd better not when you're moving humans," remarked Leslie. "Not if you don't want to be known as the University Butcher for the rest of your natural."

"I don't make mistakes with my calculations," Peter said, with certainty. He had never had a problem with figures and calculations. It was part of what made his magic and mechanics alike so very prone to succeed. Paired with his problem-solving mind, it had led to him being very successful.

"Just the same," Tom protested, "if you want to be accredited, they'll need to see your calculations. The powers that be don't care to see results without figures, you know."

"I'll do it when I move the first human," Peter promised, his mind already full of complications, calculations, and possible pitfalls.

What he needed to do was allow for the movement of the water, along with the movement of all the other parts of the living fish, inside and outside. He hadn't thought to do that for the field mouse he'd moved, and what had arrived the next day was something quite other than what he'd expected. At the very least, he needed to allow for the smallest amount of water around the fish, just like he would need to allow for the smallest amount of air when it came to moving a human. It would stop him from getting anything dangerously wrong and would allow him to fine-tune for the first occasion when he would be able to calculate closely enough to safely move a human without the need for a buffer.

"Stand here, Tom. Make sure you keep an eye out for it when it arrives, all right? You'll have about a minute after it disappears, before you see it again. Mind the water, all right?"

"Perish it, *what* water?" protested Tom, but he stood where he was directed to stand agreeably enough.

"It's a fish, old chap!" said Leslie cheerfully. "Did you expect to have to watch out for sand?"

"I didn't expect to be watching a fish, I can tell you that!"

"Quiet, old chap; he's doing maths."

Peter grinned, because there was a kind of reverence to Leslie's voice, and even if he wasn't sure whether or not the boy was mocking him, he was quite sure of his numbers at least, and willing to wait to impress. Now it was just a matter of tracing the co-ordinates of the fish into the magics of the tickerbox so it could get some idea of the movement of it, and inputting new co-ordinates and a new time.

And after that, it was only a matter of tweaking the magic *ever* so slightly to mimic what he had seen Rorkin do earlier, by taking account of every moving part in the fish and the water.

It took him only a few minutes to make the calculations in his head: due to Miss Stoneflange's work, there was a pinpointing system in every building that could be accessed by anyone with enough magic to link to it. It was, Peter now discovered, an essential component to swift workings, and one that could and should be incorporated into the next version of the tickerbox. *If*, of course, he could prevail upon Miss Stoneflange to collaborate at all.

"Now," he said, shrugging off the irritation that thought caused. He released the tickerbox, and it toddled over to the further fish tank on its spindly legs. "Get ready."

"Thought it had to be touching something to move it," Leslie said, his eyes wide.

"I only do that for things that aren't alive," said Peter. "Everything else has to be entered into the thought processes; proximity is good, but it's not necessary."

"Shame," said Leslie. "Thought we were going to see it swim—oof! What was *that*?"

There was a small, sideways slip as the fish swam through time and space where a fish had no business swimming, then silence.

That silence stretched out while Leslie fumbled for his watch to mark the time and Tom looked frowningly from one tank to the other.

"Should be about time, Carlisle," said Leslie, just as there came a distinct splashing of water.

Tom said a very wet, very surprised, "Good heavens!" and frantically grappled with the slippery armful that had deposited itself in his arms while Leslie whooped with laughter.

"Quick! Carlisle, help me chuck the blasted thing in the tank!" panted Tom, trying desperately not to drop the fish. "Leslie, you little beast! Stop laughing and help me with this thing! It seems to think I'm trying to kill it!"

Peter grabbed for the slippery tail, swiftly discovering that the fish was both heavier and stronger than he had given it credit for—and perhaps more magical, as well—and he and Tom wrestled it into the tank together while Leslie leaned against the wall and laughed helplessly.

"Just you wait!" Tom told him, brushing scales and water droplets off his suitcoat. "Next time you're out playing rugger with the rest of us, I'll find a nice muddy hole for you!"

"Sorry about that," said Peter, while Leslie reminded Tom *sotto voce* that he never got on the rugby field if he could possibly avoid it. "It was meant to go into the tank. Good heavens! I didn't think it would be as heavy as that!"

"Oh well," said Tom good-naturedly. "At least I've got an excuse not to come out to another one of these blasted parties: m'togs are likely to smell like a fish-yard as soon as I get sweaty in the first dance."

That made all of them dissolve into laughter for no reason at all, but Leslie said, between giggles, "You've done it now, Carlisle! We're all going to be known as the fellows who were at school with you. Make sure you introduce us to all the important people, won't you?"

Someone applauded from behind them, and Peter already

had an annoyed idea of who it was before he turned his head, the laughter drawn from the air as thoroughly as though it had been evaporated.

"Very impressive, Carlisle!" said Samuel, crossing the room. Peter wondered gloomily if he had sprung from the womb in a V formation with other boys, or if it was a habit they had acquired through practise. "A few of us felt the ripples from your workings out there—they broke the secondary punch bowl, by the way. Between you and Miss Stoneflange, we seem to be doomed to do without any kind of alcohol tonight."

"We'd best run for it, then!" said Leslie cheerfully. "If you've broken the second punchbowl, I can think of at least two masters who'll be coming for you in no uncertain terms."

"Wait, we haven't finished yet!" protested Peter. "I need to refine my targeting and try again!"

"I'll say!" Tom retorted, grinning. "I can't wait around to be told I can't play rugby tomorrow as a punishment: quick, let's leg it out the windows before the masters find us!"

He and Leslie ran for the window, dragging the reluctant Peter by the collar, but once they were outside, Peter freed himself from their grasp.

"I'm for the dorms, old man," said Tom. "Back to the party, Leslie?"

"Rather! Even if the girls don't dance with you, they do with me. What are you for, Carlisle?"

"I want to do some more experimenting," Peter said, becoming mulish.

"Yes, but not right here, old man. Nip off into the garden if you need a few animals. I'll see you back in our room when you're finished, all right? I can't wait around if the masters are going to be looking for us."

He was gone before Peter could protest his need for assistants—or at the very least, onlookers—surprisingly light and fleet of foot for such a large boy. Peter hesitated where he was, caught between the sensible urge to follow Tom and the more exciting urge to continue his experimentation while everything was fresh in his mind.

"Still looking for Miss Stoneflange?" enquired Samuel from the window, as Peter hesitated. "I believe she's out in the garden."

"Thanks," said Peter, without stopping to wonder why the other boy had told him as much. He didn't realise that Samuel and the other boys were still following along behind him, either, until he stepped from the terrace and down into the garden. Then he saw the gentle shadows that fluttered on the grass at his feet, thrown by gaslight. "I can find my own way," he said, too impatient to try and be polite about it.

"And miss all the fun?" asked Samuel promptly. "I think not! Not now that you've made a breakthrough with your tickerbox. If you're going to show Miss Stoneflange, surely you can show it to us first?"

"I wasn't going to show Miss Stoneflange," said Peter, but he was aware as he said it that it was no longer true. He hadn't *planned* on showing it to Miss Stoneflange, but he couldn't deny that when Samuel mentioned her, his first, burning thought had been what good timing the knowledge had. "I just had something I wanted to talk to her about. It doesn't matter."

"Oh well, if that's the case, there are sure to be more animals in the garden," said Samuel. "I'm sure we could find a few between us!"

Peter threw a look over his shoulder, but both Tom and Leslie had disappeared: one back into the party, and the other toward the school. He rather regretted that he hadn't done so, too. Still, he wanted to do some further experimentation, and no matter who the onlookers were, it was still possible to do them. He could always go looking for Miss Stoneflange afterward. It wasn't outside the realms of possibility that she would sense the workings and come looking to see who was doing something so intricate, was it?

He would have done the same thing himself, had he sensed the kind of working that he was about to do.

"If we're going to be doing any more experimentation, we'd best get away from the windows," said Samuel, his eyes flicking warningly toward the glass panels, behind which couples danced and masters stalked.

"There's a folly up the path and behind the hedge," said the boy next to Samuel. "See how you go moving spiders from one end to the other or something."

Peter followed them, not entirely reluctantly, though he had a brief thought that if he followed either one of the other two fellows, he might have even now been planning another experiment with them. He didn't particularly care to be doing his experiments with Samuel and his minions.

Still, the important thing was getting another go at the targeting of his spell. The boys had mentioned spiders, but Peter was quite sure that he was ready for another kind of test now: the kind of test that saw him shifting through time and space himself. The targeting was an annoying little rough edge that needed to be smoothed out: the important thing that had been thoroughly established was that Peter could now move a living, breathing thing through time and space. Everything else could be fine-tuned.

Peter drew in a breath and passed around the hedge, and as he did so he caught sight of the single occupant of the folly ahead.

"How delightful!" said Samuel, his voice amused and just a little bit sharp-edged. "Look, it's Miss Stoneflange!"

Miss Stoneflange sat at the further end of the folly on a stone bench, her legs folded beneath her and her shoes neatly in front of her, with the model he had repaired in one hand and staring earnestly at the thing. One of the legs was broken again, though Peter was quite sure he'd fixed it. What had she been doing to the poor, hapless model *now*?

Miss Stoneflange didn't look up as they approached,

though Peter thought she sighed faintly. It irked him that he should have to be approaching her in the same job lot as Samuel and his friends, but the sigh irked him still more. As much as he disliked physically being in the same group as Samuel, did he resent being thought of as *being* in the same group.

"Good evening," Samuel said; the first of them to speak.

"I'd just begun to think so," said Miss Stoneflange, and her voice seemed weary. "It would certainly be pleasant not to be proved wrong."

Samuel laughed softly. "The other ladies are dancing," he said. "Shouldn't you be on the dance floor, too? I don't think there are enough ladies to go around."

"I think you'll find," said Miss Stoneflange, placing the model on her lap and turning her attention on Samuel, "that the other girls aren't here to be shared out like sweets. They're all much better at multitasking than I am, however, so you might as well try to get one of them to dance with you instead of me. Perhaps they'll take pity on you."

"Did I ask you to dance?"

"You came out merely to annoy me, then?" Miss Stoneflange asked. "In that case, go away. Take your little boot boys with you."

"You don't have to be rude!" Peter said indignantly. "We're partners, after all!"

"That's funny," Miss Stoneflange said. "I thought you were the ones being rude. What else do you call it when you interrupt someone else's work?"

Peter, stung, said rashly, "You're not even doing real work! Your model is broken and you're not practising magic."

"I thought you didn't think of magic as real work," pointed out Miss Stoneflange. "And I told you: just because we're partners, it doesn't mean we have to be chummy. Why don't you find friends your own age?"

"Look, we just came out here to do some magic," said Peter. "If you don't like it, you can go elsewhere."

"I don't see why I should," she said. "I was here first. Do your little experiments and go away."

"It's hardly a *little* experiment," Samuel argued. "Carlisle is practically ready to travel through time himself, which is bound to blow your end-of-year project right out of the water don't you think, Miss Stoneflange?"

"It certainly carries the possibility of explosion," she said. "But I don't fancy I'd be the one to suffer. Don't do that sort of thing around me: practising with animals is one thing, but doing it yourself certainly won't be allowed."

"You're always doing things you're not allowed to do," Peter said. "You've still got one of the models you're not supposed to have!"

"I'm not breaking a rule if it doesn't apply to me," she said.

"Just because your father is the headmaster of the university, it doesn't mean you're above the rules, Miss Stoneflange," said Samuel.

"It certainly has something to do with who I am, but not in the way that you think," Miss Stoneflange said. "If it worries you so very much, do report it to one of the masters. All of you. As quickly as possible."

"Why don't you report *him*?" muttered one of the other boys.

"Because I fancy my absence won't be at all pertinent to how badly that particular spell goes wrong," said Miss Stoneflange. She still hadn't put her shoes back on: had not even slipped her feet out from beneath her.

"The spell isn't going to go wrong," Peter said to her, with an undercurrent of irritation at her certainty. "I've already tested it, and it's already worked."

"Indeed," she said. "But that was inside, away from... everything. Out here is very different, and I think you'll find none of the masters would permit you to attempt what you're about to attempt."

"Let's see it, Carlisle," said Samuel. "Ignore Miss Stoneflange, do: she's a wet blanket about things like this, even if she's not a stickler for the rules in general."

"It's not against the rules," Peter pointed out.

"It's not against the rules because the university hasn't yet had to deal with boys trying to tinker with time," said Miss Stoneflange. "I do assure you that if it had entered their minds that one of you would do so, there would certainly be a mandate against it."

"Yes, but there isn't one now, and I've already moved a fish inside."

"Yes, but you haven't moved a fish out *here*," Miss Stoneflange said again. "I think you'll find that there is a considerable difference."

"There isn't any water out here, so I can't move a fish," said Peter, becoming stubborn. "But I'm out here and I can move *me*, so I don't see why it's any of your concern."

"It never is my concern," she said, and there was a rather bitter smile on her lips. "But it will certainly affect me and I think you'll find that you'll regret doing your magic here. It won't work well for you."

"It wouldn't affect you unless I took you with me," Peter said shortly, and moved to the other end of the folly. Truth be told, he would much rather have left the folly to Miss Stoneflange at this point. He didn't at all care for Samuel, or the boy's attitude toward Miss Stoneflange, but he was so much annoyed himself by her insistence that his tickerbox was doomed to failure that he was now determined she should see it for herself as it worked. Unlike their tree in the classroom, which had not worked even though he did things correctly, this time he was not relying upon Miss Stoneflange for any part of the magic, and it wasn't possible for it to go wrong. And unlike what he had said to her in anger on that previous occasion, he didn't suspect that she would try to make something go wrong with the magic just to prove him wrong.

Two of the boys lingered with Miss Stoneflange, talking and laughing to her impervious face, but Samuel joined Peter at the far end of the folly and sat elegantly on the seat beside him.

"Miss Stoneflange is certainly dubious about your abilities, Carlisle!" he said softly, laughing. "Wouldn't it be a lark if you took her with you! She couldn't be so high and mighty if she actually experienced it."

"I can't just take her with me," Peter protested.

"I thought you said it wasn't dangerous. I thought you said it was ready to go?"

"Well, yes," Peter said uncomfortably. "But it's better if I experiment on myself first, don't you think? It's a bit irresponsible for me to go around experimenting with other people."

"Can you not do it? Does that thing not have enough power to input the parameters for two people, or are the calculations too hard?"

"Of course I can do it!" Peter said. "Look, all I have to do is make sure I calculate our position in time correctly—I'm not bothering to try and move us from place to place, just time, so there's no need for anything complicated—and feed the information to the tickerbox through the regulators."

He showed it to Samuel as the spark of magic kicked the clockwork of the tickerbox into gear, and the very small watch that the tickerbox had eaten at some stage—was it Miss Stoneflange's watch?—emitted the tiniest of feathery chimes.

"It's going to shift both of you in time with nothing more than a flicker of magic?" Samuel's right brow went up. "I have to say, Carlisle, I expected something rather more powerful."

"The magic doesn't have to be powerful to make a powerful effect," Peter said shortly. "It just has to move the right things in the right ways. The clockwork does the rest."

"Very well, I concede," said Samuel at once. "I suppose

you know what you're doing, after all. We all felt the way the room moved when you tossed the fish through time. Give it a go, then!"

"This is the calculation for both me and Miss Stoneflange," Peter said, with the feeling of explaining himself over and over. "I'll have to redo it for my own trip."

"Don't be a wet dishrag, Carlisle! You see Miss Stoneflange over there looking so bored." Samuel threw a malicious look over at her, and said much louder, "She's simply waiting to be impressed! If you have the calculations to take both of you through time, by all means have at it!"

Miss Stoneflange said coldly, "I *beg* your pardon?"

"We were going to be nice if you left us the folly," said Samuel, strolling toward her. "But you insisted that you wanted to stay, so you might as well help Carlisle with his experiment."

"Certainly not. I refuse to be associated with this idiocy."

"It's not like it will hurt you," Peter told her indignantly, starting across the folly. He had no intention of taking Miss Stoneflange with him, of course, but it would certainly be nice to jolt her out of her complacency by making her think he was prepared to do so. "I've already made the calculations, anyway, so you might as well."

"I've already told you no."

Peter, irritated and increasingly stubborn to the point of ignoring the fact that he himself had already told Samuel that to involve Miss Stoneflange would not be proper, asked, "Why ever not? Look, I've already finished the calculations and the box knows exactly when to send us."

"Because I said *no*, you stupid little boy!"

"Don't be such a stick-in-the-mud, Miss Stoneflange," besought Samuel. "If you're nervous, play with your little model there. You're so fond of it, and I seem to remember a time when you defended yourself pretty well."

"I would point out that having to defend myself from a

group of boys is hardly an ideal situation," said Miss Stone-flange, her voice utterly icy. "But since that particular group of boys are all here again, it hardly seems worthwhile."

"Not all of them," said Samuel, and his eyes were very nearly as cold as Miss Stoneflange's.

"No," she said gently. "Perhaps you should remember that. *Stop* it, you silly little boy!"

Peter, stung by both the words and the look of cold dislike that she threw in his direction, said, "Stop calling me a little boy!"

"So high in the instep, our Miss Stoneflange!" said Samuel wonderingly. "I suppose you're ready, Carlisle? What are you waiting for?"

"It's done," Peter said, surprised that the other boy hadn't felt the hum as the tickerbox caught onto the direc-tives it had been given and began to turn over the idea in its clockwork.

Miss Stoneflange, who evidently *had* noticed it, said, "Stop it. You've got no idea what you're doing. You shouldn't be doing it by yourself, and you certainly won't be doing it with me."

"I know exactly what I'm doing!" snapped Peter. "I've calculated every variable and I know the risks!"

"You really don't, and you really haven't," she said. "If you attempt to kidnap me, you're going to regret it."

"You never think anyone but you can do things right!" shot back Peter. He wasn't going to take her with him; not really. But he still wanted her to think he really would, so he grabbed her by the wrist.

Samuel gave a hoot of approving laughter. "Let's see it, Peter!" he said. "Miss Stoneflange says you can't do it!"

"Don't," said Miss Stoneflange through her teeth, her face paper white. "Don't be an idiot!"

With a fizz of anger, Peter pressed the ignition button on the tickerbox. It could have been his anger that caused it, but it felt like there was a slight fizz in his finger where it touched the button, too.

Or maybe the buzz came from the fingers that wrapped around Miss Stoneflange's wrist.

Whichever way it happened, that spritz of power burred up through his limbs until his whole body buzzed right to the teeth.

Was this how the carrot had felt? wondered Peter, but he had no time in which to find the answer, or even to remember that carrots couldn't feel. Time became stretchy and touchable, and he saw, or felt, or sensed the tickerbox eating it all up in the brief moment before he passed out. Then even that moment was eaten, too, and there was darkness.

❧ 6 ❧

Peter wasn't sure if he lost consciousness so much as time. When he woke, the first thing he heard was the sound of the tickerbox chewing on something that shifted the world around him in tiny, ticking increments. Blue sky fractured above him—or perhaps his glasses had been broken, he wasn't entirely sure.

Peter opened his mouth to speak a spell that would fix the glasses, hoping devoutly that it was the glasses that were broken after all, but all that came out was a groan. He stayed where he was for another few minutes, gazing up at the broken sky while the tickerbox crawled over him, eating stray moments of time.

A girl's voice said the spell instead, and maybe Peter's mind was as broken as his glasses, because it sounded like she said it out of order. The glasses mended themselves in a glitter of reddish magic in spite of that, and Peter sat up in confusion, his memories nearly as shattered as his glasses had been.

Miss Stoneflange, sitting on the grass with her skirts arranged neatly around her and her stockinged toes peeking out beneath, watched him from a few feet away.

It struck Peter that this was the first magic he had ever

seen her do outside of the few workings he had seen her do in the Interconnectedness class. It also struck him that the magic she had done hadn't just fixed his glasses in the now they currently existed in, but had somehow sunk deep into them, knitting in pieces of the time his tickerbox hadn't eaten. Peter was quite sure that his glasses would never again shatter.

He meant to say something about the breath-taking thoroughness of her working, or the equally stunning strength of it, but when Peter opened his mouth he asked, "Did you say the spell back to front?" instead.

"Do you really think that's the important thing right now?" Miss Stoneflange asked in return.

Peter took off his glasses and polished them.

"You've got about two minutes to explain to me that things haven't gone as terribly wrong as I can tell they've gone," she said. "And then I'm going to punch you in the nose."

"Don't you mean I've got two minutes to explain it, and *if* I don't, you'll punch me in the nose?" Peter said, putting his glasses back on. "You can't punch me in the nose if I *do* explain it!"

"Don't tell me what I meant," Miss Stoneflange said, with an ice-frosted flare of temper. "I'm going to punch you either way. I'm just giving you the chance to explain why you thought it was a good idea to kidnap me when I specifically told you *not* to."

"I didn't kidnap you! I just moved us in time!"

"Perhaps that's what you intended," she said. "But I've been conscious a good deal longer than you have, and besides studying the remnants of time that your tickerbox hasn't eaten, I've had a bit of a look around."

"We should have gone into tomorrow," interrupted Peter. He was quite studiously ignoring the dreadfully complete wrongness of the world around him. "That's all."

"Well," said Miss Stoneflange, with devastatingly unwelcome logic, "unless your tickerbox shifted us spatially as well as chronologically, we've gone backwards instead of forwards."

Peter couldn't stop the question that tumbled over his lips, although he already knew the answer. "What do you mean?"

"The university isn't here. If you haven't catapulted us into the past by a good hundred years, you've thrown us a likewise startling amount of years into the future."

He had already felt that things had gone horribly wrong. There should have been no loss of consciousness, no floating pieces of time for the tickerbox to feed on. There shouldn't have been open grass around them, as Miss Stoneflange had pointed out, nor should the triad have been in quite the position it was in the sky.

"We're not in the future," he said, a bit thickly, climbing to his feet. His whole body felt odd and out of place and just a bit raw. "If we haven't moved spatially, we must have gone backwards a bit. I don't understand why it went wrong. Everything was set up and calibrated exactly. I made allowances for an extra person as well."

"Perhaps," said Miss Stoneflange chillingly. "But I very much doubt you made allowances for *which* extra person you would be bringing."

"I didn't make exact allowances because aside from positionally, it shouldn't matter which person it is," snapped Peter, but there was a very cold core to his being when he considered the deep and abiding magic he had just seen from Miss Stoneflange. "Even allowing for differences in magic level and concentration, nothing should have gone wrong!"

Miss Stoneflange took in a deep breath through her nose, eyes closed, and then opened them. "That may very well work with people who have mediocre to strong magic—"

"Oh, I suppose your magic is the strongest in the Two Monarchies!" scoffed Peter. He had heard just about enough of Miss Stoneflange's perfections over the last few days.

"Not at all," she retorted. "I thought you were convinced that was *your* title."

Peter shut his mouth.

"Perhaps you'll remember the way I set up my magic when we worked together," said Miss Stoneflange. There was no victory in her voice, just a certain ruthlessness. "I told you at the time that there was a reason for it. The way you set up things is no doubt suitable when dealing with someone with mediocre to strong magic, but it's utterly worthless when you apply it to someone whose magic is both ridiculously strong and jinxed."

Peter sat down again rather suddenly, feeling cold. "That's…that's not possible! Jinxes don't attach to people!"

"There's a reason I work with models to dissipate magic," she continued steadily. "And a reason why I avoid certain people, too."

A surge of frustration carried away the cold feeling in Peter's stomach. "Why don't you warn people about it!" he flung at her, his face hot with annoyance. Of all the things to keep to herself! No wonder his magic had gone wrong!

"*In general,*" said Miss Stoneflange, a banner of red across her own cheeks and her voice icily at odds with that warmth, "people *ask* before they have the rudeness to touch me. Or, for that matter, to forcibly include me in their experimentation."

"It's not as bad as that," protested Peter. He found himself again with that same, sick feeling he'd had when he was trying to decide whether or not to go and see Annabel—to apologise, or perhaps accept an apology. "I didn't—I didn't *know.*"

"Not knowing is the very *least* excuse you can possibly give!" snapped Miss Stoneflange. "You have a mouth and you seem to be perfectly conversant with using it when you choose. You chose not to ask questions and to show off. Not content with that, you got the magic completely wrong!"

"All right!" snarled Peter. "I got the magic wrong! It was my fault! Are you happy now?"

"No!" Miss Stoneflange flashed. "You used magic on me without my permission, *kidnapped* me, and now you've screamed an apology at me! How on earth is *any* of that supposed to make me happy? The fact that you were wrong in a detail or two is only the tip of the iceberg, you awful little boy!"

"If it *hadn't* gone wrong, it would have been fine. We would have been heroes to the university!"

"You really don't understand," said Miss Stoneflange, with ice-edged disdain. "I'd feel sorry for you if I wasn't so angry."

"There doesn't seem to be much point discussing it while we're both angry," said Peter, trying to match her in coldness. "I'll figure out how to take us both back to the university as soon as possible, Miss Stoneflange."

"I presume," Miss Stoneflange said, with equal coolness, "that you will need to know the current date before doing anything?"

"I was *getting* to that! We'll have to find a town nearby and ask someone. I can make allowances for your jinx, but I will need to know the exact date for my calculations."

"There's no need," said Miss Stoneflange. "I have a method of calculating the exact date based on the position of the triad and the combined levels of magic, unmagic, and antimagic in the air."

"Why do you have magic for calculating the exact date based on the position of the triad and the levels of magic matter in the atmosphere?" protested Peter, his emotions a tumble of irritation, respect, and helplessness that there could be someone as beautiful as Miss Stoneflange in mind and body, who was *so very frustrating* to deal with.

"I suppose you think you're the only person interested in the possibility of time travel," said Miss Stoneflange. "Kindly stop looking at me with your mouth open. It's irritating."

"I didn't think—you never *said*!"

"I fail to understand how my goals and interests are any of

your business. As odd as it may seem to you, there are people who go along perfectly well with their own experiments without them having any bearing on your own."

"I didn't *say* that! I said that—oh never mind! I'll check on my tickerbox while you get the date, then!"

He turned his shoulder away from the prickling presence that was Miss Stoneflange, wondering how he could have ever missed the utter wrongness of her magic that should have tipped him off to the fact that she was jinxed in some way. He had not often seen her do magic, but now that he looked back on everything, it was blindingly obvious. No doubt she had been using the models to dissipate the bad effects of the jinx before they could hurt other people.

If she had only *told* him!

If she had only said something instead of sealing everything behind lips of marble!

If only…

If only Peter hadn't allowed Samuel to irk him and goad him into doing something so unforgiveable!

Peter swallowed, feeling sick, and hunched over his tickerbox. The ignition button rattled a little when he moved the box, and there was very little movement from the tickerbox's legs. There was no reason for him to feel so very bad about that, of course: it was just a machine, and it didn't have any feelings. But it was hard not to feel bad about it despite that, and when Peter opened it to look at the regulators inside, he suffered another sting of remorse. One of the regulators had melted altogether, and the others looked distinctly misshapen.

Peter's stomach sank. With fingers that trembled, he leveraged the box apart completely to get to the clockwork. The uppermost half was a little sooted up, but that wasn't the worst of it: the worst was the smallest secondary engine that had probably caused the soot. It hadn't so much exploded as it had peeled itself apart into curls of metal and very tiny, melted trails of the same.

Peter touched it cautiously: the remains weren't still hot, but when he drew his finger away it was coated with a kind of slick residue that shouldn't have been possible. It wasn't exactly time and it wasn't exactly magic—nor was it exactly jinx. It was almost, he thought, antimagic.

"I think your jinx left some residue," he said over his shoulder, forgetting he was annoyed with Miss Stoneflange. "That's not really possible."

"People mention that fairly often," said Miss Stoneflange. "I find that it's not a very useful observation."

"No, I suppose not," he admitted. "Has it always done that?"

Miss Stoneflange's voice said coolly, "Not in general. Your magic is quite spectacular, which gave the jinx quite a lot to feed on, and that seems to have given your tickerbox something of a shock. I'm also inclined to think the tickerbox might be suffering indigestion from all the time it ate. It was nipping about pretty sharply before you woke up."

"I hardly used any magic at all," protested Peter, gazing down at the mess of tickerbox in some despair. It was no good trying to fix it right now: he would need parts that he could make without magic, hand ground and plain-smelted. Nothing from a mage's forge. "It was just a little bit to spark the possibility and input the right co-ordinates."

"Yes, but you added me to the mix," said Miss Stoneflange. "And due to the rather tricky effects of being interconnected in that manner, you gave my jinx access to your magic. The jinx does so love to amplify and push back magic at things, and I fancy it pushed enough magic into the tickerbox to turn things rather sideways."

"More than enough!" said Peter gloomily.

"I suppose you mean by that, that it's no use my having found out our exact location in time?" she asked.

Her voice was quite mild, and Peter found himself relieved. Miss Stoneflange might be ragingly angry with him, but she had certainly not lost her head, and it didn't seem as though she were about to panic, either.

"I'm afraid so," he said. "The co-ordinates won't do us much good until I can fix the tickerbox. It's barely moving now, which isn't surprising: this particular secondary engine is vital."

"I see," she said, and he caught a flutter of movement in the corner of his eye as she stood up. "Then I rather think that our ways part here."

"What do you mean?" asked Peter, startled. He scrambled to his feet beside her but managed to stop himself from grabbing her arm when she began to walk away briskly. He jogged after her. "What do you mean, Miss Stoneflange? We should be sticking together!"

"I fail to see why that should be so," she said, without pausing. "You didn't ask me what the result of my co-ordinate check was, by the way. Don't you think you should?"

"I suppose we're just a little bit further away from the university than we thought we were," Peter said, nettled. If Miss Stoneflange was walking away from him, no doubt she had learned that she had been wrong initially in her estimation of their position, and simply didn't want to admit as much. She must feel fairly safe to be walking away; if they had been thrown back into the past or into the future by any great margin, she would have been a lot less certain, he was sure.

"I suppose you could express it like that," she said. "I don't think I would, but no doubt I'm the odd one."

Peter hated that sarcastic voice more than anything. Impatiently, he said, "What are you talking about? I suppose we just slipped a bit sideways because of your jinx and you're trying to walk back to the university."

Miss Stoneflange gave a short, humourless laugh. "That would be an achievement indeed! By my calculations, were you to try to walk to the university, it would take roughly three hundred and twenty-four years."

Peter stumbled over a sudden hillock. "What?"

"By my calculations, we're something like three hundred and twenty years in the past. I stopped before getting the exact date when I saw the damage to your little box's baby engine, but I think you'll find that's accurate enough for now."

"It's a *secondary engine*," said Peter in shock, because it didn't seem possible to comprehend anything Glenna had said outside the one wrong thing.

"Yes, I'm sure that's a very important distinction," Miss Stoneflange said. She hadn't yet stopped walking, not even to allow for Peter's stumble. "Why don't you stay here and try to fix it? There's no need for us to be going around together, after all."

"What can you do by yourself?" protested Peter, but there was a very cold part of him that wondered what *he* could do by himself. The cold feeling made him angry, and he said, "You can't get back without me, at any rate!"

"I suppose I'll just have to shift as best as I can for myself," said Miss Stoneflange lightly. "I'm sure I can find someone to help if I really can't manage by myself, after all. I have a friend who is rather powerful, if it comes to that."

"And how exactly do you think you'll find your friend?" Peter said. "Do be sensible, Miss Stoneflange! If we're really three hundred or more years into the past—"

He saw the fleeting smile that came and went on her face.

"I don't see what you've got to smile about!" he said angrily. "I'm trying to be sensible here!"

"I was just thinking," said Miss Stoneflange, stopping and turning to face him so suddenly that he nearly walked into her. "That you never really seem to change. Stop following me, please."

Peter, cold and confused and rather shocked, stood where he was and watched her walk away. There was nothing he could do to stop her. He had already once imposed his magic on her, and the results of that had been disastrous. He couldn't talk her out of it: he had never been good at talking. Ann had told him so, as had Poly and—

Poly.

Poly and Luck.

"No!" said Peter, his mind blazing suddenly into life. He started after Miss Stoneflange once again. "Wait! Miss Stoneflange, I know where we can go! They—well, *he*—can probably help us."

Miss Stoneflange stopped.

Peter, panting, ran the last few steps toward her and said, "I know someone. They can help. At least go that far with me: I got you into this, and I'll get you out of it, I swear!"

She thought about it for far longer than Peter was comfortable with before she said, "I don't particularly want to go anywhere with you, but if you think you know someone who can help, I'll follow you that far. And you can stop calling me *Miss Stoneflange* all the time, thank you. If we're going to be walking together for a while, it's bound to be annoying."

It wasn't the most promising of moments, but Peter felt unexpectedly cheered. The worst might have happened: he might have made a colossal mistake through lack of knowledge, catapulting himself and Miss Stoneflange into the worst kind of trouble, and he might have done serious damage to his little time tickerbox—he might, moreover, have lost any shreds of respect he had had in Miss Stoneflange's estimation—but at that moment he felt as though there was a slight reprieve from the darkness.

"By the way," said Glenna. "Who is it you know old enough to be still around in our time *and* here, about three hundred years ago? Don't tell me those particular rumours were true!"

Peter felt a little more cheerful. "There were rumours about me?"

He'd hoped as much from the way the headmaster treated him, but from subsequent lacklustre reactions around the school he hadn't been as hopeful of those rumours as he might otherwise have been. And thinking of the headmaster…missed classes were one thing, but Peter was quite certain the same lackadaisical attitude wouldn't persist when it came to him dragging the headmaster's daughter through time. It wasn't as though it were a harmless little jaunt—unless he could bring them both back safely with very little difference in time, that was.

"They said you know the Enchanter Luck," said Glenna. "I didn't believe it, actually. Luck doesn't care for people who are as irritating as he is; he likes to be the most annoying person in the room at any one time."

Shrugging off the uncomplimentary nature of her explanation, Peter said, "I do know him. Not that well, but well enough to be able to call on him. He'll have the parts I need, at least."

"Then I suppose it's as good a place as any to start," said Glenna. "We'll have to have food, at the very least."

"I could try to shift us there so we don't have to walk," suggested Peter.

"I don't think that's a very good idea," Glenna said. "You very inconveniently kidnapped me without notice, and I don't have one of the models on me. The jinx would be delighted, but I don't particularly want to be shifted right into the middle of a house."

"I don't shift right into other people's houses anyway," said Peter, somewhat stiffly. "It's rude, and I have better aim than that."

"I'm sure you do, but when I say *right into the middle of the house*, I mean that being conjoined with one of the walls or the floorboards isn't my idea of felicitous interconnectedness."

"All right, all right!" Peter snapped. "You don't have to keep reminding me about your jinx! I can make allowances for it now that I know about it."

"Perhaps," said Glenna. "But I find I don't really trust you at the moment, so you'll have to excuse me if I don't immediately jump at the offer of allowing your magic to affect me again."

Peter would have said, "I wouldn't have done it without asking you," but it didn't seem likely that Glenna would believe him. He wasn't sure if he would have believed it were their positions reversed.

Instead, he said, "The house itself won't be there yet, anyway. He built it for Poly when they first got there."

"I think you'll find it's moved itself back to accommodate its owner," Glenna said. "Things are much more likely to pass through borders of time and space than people are."

"That's what I found out!" exclaimed Peter. "Actually it was how I—"

"Yes," Glenna said. "That's how we ended up here. I'm aware."

"That wasn't what I was going to say," Peter muttered. All the same, it had been the logical conclusion of that discovery.

"At any rate, I think you'll find the house is still right where it always is," she said, surprising him by not following up on the complaint that she was quite justified to make.

"I suppose so," he said. The house tended to move around a bit, but its general area was usually the same. With Luck, it was more important to find the patch of space where his house wandered: that particular patch of reality was self-contained and bigger on the inside, and the house didn't tend to wander outside its borders.

"Then we're in luck," Glenna said. "Because somehow or other, you've managed to slip us sideways a little bit. If I were to guess, I'd say it's because the pull from that particular part of the country is pretty strong."

"How do you know?" demanded Peter, looking around. "I didn't get a chance to do a working to find out exactly where we are."

"I recognise that particular copse," said Glenna.

"You *can't* recognise it," said Peter, despite the fact that it really did look like the copse of trees that was on the university side of Luck's little pocket of space. "It wouldn't be there yet."

"I'm fairly certain that Luck's magic leaches into the surrounding land and has done so for quite some time," she said. "And it's a rather recognisable copse. Look at the magic."

To put off the inevitability of having to admit that she could be right, Peter asked, "Do you know Luck, then?"

"Not exactly. He used to be my next-door neighbour—"

Peter burned to open his mouth in protest that Luck had never had neighbours: the bigger-on-the-inside bubble that housed both Luck and Luck's magic was as close to air-tight and magic-tight as anything so big and complex could be. It was nonsense to imagine that there was any way to live alongside that sort of magic in any meaningful way; it certainly couldn't happen in the physical way that most people were said to be next door neighbours.

He would have said it, in fact, if Glenna hadn't been watching him with one brow raised.

"What?" he asked defensively, instead.

"I beg your pardon," she said. "I fancied that you wanted to let me know how impossible that is."

"Well," said Peter, before he could stop himself. "I was curious about how you managed to look over the fence, so to speak. It doesn't exist alongside houses properly."

"That's correct," Glenna said. "But when you're a child with far too much magic and a way of it going very wrong at the slightest notice, you find that impossible things are usually possible. Not just possible, but rather uncomfortable. At any rate, he was always prodding at my magic and I was always prodding at his walls until he came back to the city with the Sleeping Princess and made the exclusion so strong that I couldn't get in."

"I'm surprised he let you play for that long," said Peter.

"Yes, I suppose so," Glenna said. "He was irritating, but he was someone who understood, at least. I went to the university after that, and Headmaster Tarrant seemed to… well, for a while, I thought he really did want a daughter. After I found out he was only really interested in trying to get me to make things for him, I tried to get back to the house, but Luck wasn't much interested in playing by then."

"I think Poly and Onepiece keep him pretty busy," said Peter, but the first thing in his thoughts was that he finally understood why Glenna hadn't taken her adopted father's name. He hadn't taken his stepfather's name, either.

"The stream stopped playing with me, too," Glenna said.

"It's a stupid stream, anyway," he said, aware of the sadness in her voice. "It's always hiding from me. Actually, the house hides from me, too; I just assumed it was all part of Luck's irritating personality."

"I wouldn't have thought so."

Peter looked suspiciously at her, but although she looked faintly amused, Glenna didn't seem to be sarcastic, so he said only, "It won't hurt to look and see if it's the right place."

"It is," said Glenna, and continued on.

To Peter's mixed annoyance and relief, Glenna proved to be entirely correct. Once they were past the copse of trees that shouldn't have been where they were, there was a distinct bulging of reality where several other things that shouldn't have been where they were decided they would really quite like to be, anyway.

"Good heavens," said Glenna. "I keep forgetting how strong Luck's magic is when it's not right in front of me."

"It's not like ours isn't as strong as his," Peter pointed out. He'd seen enough of Glenna's magic to know that it rivalled —perhaps even slightly outstripped—his own, and he had always been quite certain that he would have been able to contend with Luck if the necessity arose.

Glenna shrugged one shoulder. "Not just yet, I should think."

"Magic doesn't grow or get stronger," Peter told her, looking around for some sign of the way in to Luck's Inverse Pocket of space. "It just becomes more familiar and you use more of it as you learn how to utilise it."

"No doubt you know best," said Glenna in an amiable sort of way that immediately made Peter suspicious that she was aware of something that he wasn't. "Are we going through the door, or should we stand here longer?"

"I can't find the door," Peter admitted. "It likes to hide from me, and since we're in the past, it might not recognise me at all."

Coolly, she said, "I've already found it; I thought you'd seen it as well. I'll open it, then, shall I?"

"Oh. I suppose so."

Peter cleared his throat, trying vainly to see what Glenna seemed to have connected with so easily, and an invisible door cracked open in front of him, suddenly and disorientingly.

"Interesting," Glenna said, her fingers running gently up the invisible door. "I think he left the back door open for me."

Peter frowned. "Why would he leave the back door open for you?"

"Just what I was wondering," said Glenna slowly.

"He doesn't even know you yet."

"That's not exactly what I mean," Glenna said, even more slowly. "He's set it to recognise my jinx."

"That's—"

"Impossible," she said, nodding. "I know. But here we are. He seems to have used it as a key. Shall we?"

Peter followed her through the yawning gap between greenery and house that seemed to be trying to decide whether the floor ought to be grass or floorboards. It had settled on a happy medium of green-tinted floorboards with a slightly rough appearance by the time Peter and Glenna had both stepped into the house, much to Peter's relief. He didn't like grass for floor, and the house was generally quite well aware of that.

The room into which they walked seemed to be the main room; not dissimilar to what Peter was used to, but it also had a few bookcases that were deeper than they appeared and didn't exist in the version of the house that he knew. Neither did the kitchen open directly from the main room in the house he knew.

In fact, from what Poly had told him, this house was at least as similar to the house in the village as it was to Luck's house that was based in the Capital. Perhaps that was how Luck's inverse pocket was dealing with the fact that the house didn't yet really exist.

Peter couldn't help looking around the room somewhat convulsively for any sign of Luck. At the best of times, Luck tolerated him: now that Peter was in the past, where Luck couldn't be expected to recognise him, he was rather less certain of any welcome that didn't include Poly.

"It's all right," Glenna said. "Luck's not home. I'd be able to feel it if his magic was anywhere nearby. He's probably out interrupting some poor animal's hibernation in Broma or something."

Peter couldn't help snorting. It was extremely likely that was exactly what Luck was doing. "All right," he said. "I'll look for what I need here, then. Where are you going?"

"Exploring," said Glenna, pausing at the door. "I've always wanted to get into here."

"I suppose you wanted to be out interrupting defenceless animals during hibernation in Broma," said Peter. "And you're just annoyed that Luck decided to settle down and get married instead of taking on an assistant or something."

"I would have been a partner," she said, but Peter saw the

self-mocking smile on her lips. "But as you say, Luck got married instead. So I might as well explore the place while I'm here, at least. Call when you've found what you need, or if you need help."

"I'll call when I've finished," Peter said, lifting his chin ever so slightly without intending to do so.

"Of course," said Glenna over her shoulder, as she went through the doorway. "I should have guessed as much."

Left alone, Peter began to make his way through Luck's workroom methodically. Luck had a great deal of interests, up to and including clockwork, and it was very likely that Peter would find everything he needed if he searched long enough. Unfortunately, Luck also tended to hide things in odd places and store things in slightly-out-of-synch patches of reality, and the smaller those things were, the likelier they were to be hidden away in a pocket of altered reality.

Still, Peter eventually found a few thin sheets of treated metal that were, if he was not mistaken, slightly ahead of their current time, and some spare cogs of assorted diameter and shaft size that were maker-marked with a familiar, stylized *M*.

"You don't exist yet," he said to them, frowning. Peter used Marcus Montashe cogs whenever he could, and he was quite well aware that the manufacturer wouldn't exist for another couple hundred years. It was all very well to say that Luck's house would tend to work itself backward in time, but for there to be so much around the house that didn't yet exist in the outside world was surely odd?

But perhaps there was something good about it, after all. If Luck's house was around when it shouldn't be, and there were bits of the world that didn't yet exist in the house, then there was a reasonable chance that Peter's old room—and, by extension, a great deal of his work supplies—might also be present, too.

Grinning victoriously, Peter left the main room without stopping to consider how much the house liked to play tricks on him, and dashed down the perpetually shifting hallway in search of his room. He was just direct and quick enough to tumble into his room before the kaleidoscoping hallway could set him wrong, which made him feel even more triumphantly exuberant.

Still grinning, he ransacked his workbench and pigeon-holes. There wasn't as much there as there should have been, but his second-best set of tools had been slotted into one of the pigeon-holes, wrapped tightly in their oiled-leather cover, and those would certainly be useful. They weren't quite as light or new as his best ones, but they numbered among them two of the smallest screwdrivers that were currently available, and he would find both of those screwdrivers delightfully useful in fixing the engine that had exploded.

He put them on the top of his dresser and went through the rest of his drawers, ignoring his untidy and distinctly harried reflection in the mirror. If that's what he looked like, no wonder Glenna was always treating him like a little kid instead of a collaborator. Still, there wasn't too much else to be found in the drawers that he couldn't find elsewhere, so Peter bundled the few cogs, connectors, and replacement regulators that he needed into a paper bag and stuffed them into his pocket.

A movement of red and white in the mirror caught his attention as he took up his tools again, and Peter found himself looking at the reflection of Miss Stoneflange in the doorway. Not Miss Stoneflange—Glenna. But it was hard to think of her as Glenna right now when she was looking state-lier and more untouchable than usual. Peter caught her eye and turned his head to call her into the room and see if there was anything she thought they ought to take with them, but as he turned, there was a ripple of fabric by the door and Glenna vanished down the hall.

"Wait!" Peter said, snatching up the leather-wrapped tools. "Glenna, wait! The hall doesn't stay where it's meant to stay!"

Perhaps she didn't hear him; perhaps she didn't want to hear him. By the time Peter tumbled out the door, he caught only the tiniest flicker of her skirt at the end of the hall, white instead of the light blue he'd thought it was until now. Maybe Luck's house was playing with colours as well as time and place.

Still, the hall stayed in the right place as he followed Glenna; and when he got to the end of it, it still led to the kitchen as it ought to have done.

There in the kitchen, to his annoyance, was Glenna. He fancied he caught the sound of another voice as he came through the door, but although Glenna jumped a little when she caught sight of him, there was no one else in the room.

"I was *calling* you!" Peter said, in exasperation. "Why didn't you stop?"

Glenna raised a brow. "What are you talking about? I've been in here since I left you in the main room."

"I just *saw*—wait." Peter stopped, his brow furrowing. "Who were you talking to? Is Luck here after all?"

"Luck isn't here." Glenna stood, and her cheeks were just flushed enough to make it possible that she could have been darting down the hall just moments before him. "And I wasn't playing about in the hallways, either."

Peter didn't exactly suspect her of lying. But she *was* flushed, and he had certainly just seen hair of a familiar red hue—but then, who had Glenna just been speaking with? She wasn't the sort of girl to talk to herself.

He opened his mouth to pursue the matter but Glenna asked abruptly, "Did you get the things we need to fix the tickerbox?"

"Yes," said Peter, remembering his first worry. "But I thought I would have to make do with what Luck had in the house: I didn't expect him to have the exact things I needed."

"Perhaps I'm misunderstanding," said Glenna. "Isn't that a good thing?"

"I suppose so," Peter said reluctantly, bringing out his paper bag. "But when I say he had the exact things I needed, I mean that he had the exact things I would have used—well, the exact things I *do* use."

Glenna stared at him for a moment, then took the paper bag from him and peered inside. When she looked at him again, her eyes were very wide.

"Montashe parts?"

"Exactly. They were in my room."

"In your—oh dear."

Slightly startled, Peter protested, "It doesn't have to be so bad! The house is here, after all!"

"Yes, but it's *Luck*'s house," said Glenna. "And I'm rather sure that he has a way of coding things into the universe. It's just a little more worrisome when things that shouldn't yet be around are in the house, too."

Peter stopped himself arguing that it *needn't necessarily be worrisome* purely on the basis that Glenna was arguing for the opposite, by reminding himself that he'd had the same thought himself.

Instead, he said reluctantly, "Yes, I wondered about it as well. But it could still be nothing."

"It could be," Glenna said. "But I can't help feeling that other things being here when they shouldn't be is a symptom of something rather bad. Perhaps we should leave as soon as we can."

"There's no need to stay now that I've got everything I need, anyway," said Peter, feeling more stubborn than ever. "But it might be easier to put it together here in Luck's house than sitting down under a tree somewhere."

"I don't think that's a good idea," said Glenna. "I'd feel much more comfortable trying to fix your tickerbox outside, where whatever odd thing is happening with things being in a time they shouldn't be in, won't affect the magic in odd ways."

"Fine," said Peter. "But if we're talking about magic being

affected in odd ways, shouldn't you be trying to find something you can use as a dispersal after the tickerbox is fixed?"

Glenna stood. "That is something that unfortunately can't be helped. The models were made from a specific kind of treated wood, and they weren't able to stop the worst of the effects. If I take precautions and you make an effort not to be as annoying as usual, we'll manage well enough between us."

Peter was indignant enough to be unable to reply as Glenna swept back out of the room. Even more annoyingly, he had to hurry to catch up with her in order to avoid being lost again: Luck's house might still dislike him, but it had no such issue with Glenna. It was irritatingly reminiscent of chasing the phantom of her that he'd seen earlier, except that he was quite sure the more solid Glenna was capable of giving him a decided tongue-lashing if he tried to prolong their time in Luck's house by so much as another minute.

By the time he caught up with her, she was on the point of stepping out of the inverse pocket and back into the world outside. Peter followed her once more, and felt the familiarly peculiar way in which the world settled around him as it did every time he left Luck's house. It wasn't as though it was a different dimension, but then again, it was very close to being so.

He lost sight of Glenna briefly as she stepped back into the outside world, but when Peter hurriedly stepped after her, she was right where she ought to have been, this time without the rather worrisome kind of blurriness that had covered her exit.

Glenna raised a brow at him, and Peter came to the realisation that he had been staring at her.

"I thought I lost you," he said. "The door was blurry when you went through."

"Interesting," said Glenna, and took a step toward the door.

At least, she *tried* to take a step toward the door. Instead of moving forward, that step saw her shunted back gently until she was exactly where she had started. Her lips twitched, surprising Peter, and she took another experimental step forward.

Again, something unseen and effortless moved her back from the door.

"Goodness," said Glenna, with a gleam of amusement in her eyes. "That does seem to be rather final."

"What on earth?" Peter shoved sharply at the door with a goodly amount of power, and it threw him back more robustly than he was prepared for. He caught himself up, trying for a little dignity, and asked, "What did we do, do you think?"

"Perhaps they have someone in there that they don't want us to meet," Glenna said, thoughtfully.

"It's probably just Luck being difficult, as usual," muttered Peter. "He must have figured out that someone got in and doesn't want it happening again. Cheek, that! Poly said I could come in *any* time."

"She probably wasn't prepared for you to take it *quite* so literally," pointed out Glenna, settling herself in the grass in a puff of skirts that were once more pale blue.

"No, I think she was prepared for exactly how literally I took it," Peter said, rather grimly. "As a matter of fact, I'm pretty sure she keeps contact with Ro—with a few people who are always dodging about and playing with time, so I wouldn't be surprised if she was planning for something like this."

"I suppose it was rather lucky to find the things we needed to fix the tickerbox," agreed Glenna. "Still, if we're not being let back in now, there must be a reason for it. Whether it's because they don't want us in there or because we're supposed to be out here, we'd best keep trying to get ourselves back to our own future. I'll get the exact chronological co-ordinates we need and you fix the tickerbox. The sooner we're back at the university, the better."

Peter left her to find the co-ordinates and set to work fixing the tickerbox. He couldn't rebuild the secondary engine exactly as it had been when he first made the tickerbox, but Peter had learned quite a bit since that time, and he rather thought he could rebuild it better this time. At any rate, he could infuse it with a bit more magic to smooth things along. It was no good making it a point of pride to include as little magic as possible while he was out in the field, after all.

By the time he had finished putting together the new secondary engine and slotted it in where the old one had been, the triad was low in the sky with the first sun already dipping down below the horizon, and Glenna was lying on her back in the grass, playing games with a very fat bumble bee.

Peter closed the tickerbox with something of a sense of relief, and gathered a tiny pinch of magic together to spark it into running again. He was too late: the tickerbox snapped back into action almost before he shut it, and the pinch of magic stayed at the end of Peter's fingers until the tickerbox nipped across and ate it. Peter saw the spark of it sing along the internal magics and cogworks, then fizzle out somewhere deep in the works.

"Bother!" he muttered beneath his breath. What had gone wrong *now*?

He ignored an aside from Glenna, asking why he didn't have some sort of diagnostic imaging connected with the tickerbox's insides, and drew out the slender network of magic that lived inside the clockwork to examine it. Just where the targeting attached to the clockwork was where the magic had fizzled and died; a small tangle of wires that should have been orderly and attached to particular points of the magic. One or two of them were missing, though it didn't seem as though they had exploded or melted, like the secondary engine. It was more as though they had never existed. The wafting ends of magic to which they should have been attached were floating free.

Peter shut his eyes briefly. What an unfortunate consequence! If he had considered the possibility back in Luck's house—if he had been able to fix the tickerbox back inside the house—he would have had the chance to test the tickerbox and gather more supplies. He had been so busy trying to fix the secondary engine that he hadn't considered the possibility that there was more damage that might need fixing.

The tickerbox chirped at him, and Glenna looked across. "Oh, are you finished?"

"I didn't get all the things I needed to repair the tickerbox," he said. *Now* he was for it. He could only imagine how much delight Glenna would take in raking him over the coals for failing at one of the most important tasks he had set himself. Still, he had to tell her. "The targeting system is half unhinged, so even if we have all the co-ordinates we need for where we are, we'll still have trouble getting back to exactly the right time. I didn't notice it when I was looking at the secondary engine."

"I see," said Glenna, and came to sit beside him, crossing her legs beneath her. She was frowning, but that frown, much to Peter's surprise, didn't seem to be directed at him. "Is it supplies you need?"

"Yes: specially treated wire that hasn't been invented yet. I need it to make a connection between the magic nervous system and the clockwork so that we can target the right co-ordinates. I'm not sure I could even replicate the wire: it's not my area of expertise. It's the connection that allows me to relay *time* into the co-ordinates from the magic section to the clockwork. Everything else can go through the clockwork, but time needs to go through a magical synapse to connect properly."

"Then we'll have to find a way to shore up the gap in another way."

"What—what sort of way?" asked Peter, thrown off balance by Glenna's lack of anger.

"Well, if we can't target based on time *directly*, perhaps we can target based on particular physical constants: the school has a few stones that were set up at exactly *this* or *that* time, and Headmaster Tarrant has a habit of making sure those stones are special in some way. Do you think you could target a physical—"

"Not a stone!" said Peter, interrupting in the eager blossoming of an idea. "A person—two people! I'd have to have some idea of the physical makeup of the stones to target them, but I have our exact physical makeup already in the tickerbox. All I have to do is program it to find us again and connect the two instances of ourselves!"

"I suppose that would work, as well," nodded Glenna. "And if it's seamless enough, we might even be back at just the right time to avoid causing a panic at the school."

That, of course, was no part of Peter's plan, but he was sure he could program the tickerbox well enough to allow *just* enough difference between the two instances of themselves as to make it obvious that he and Glenna had in fact, moved through time as well as space.

"Just a moment," he said to her. "I've got to program it in while I'm thinking of it. The hardware is all there; it's just the spark that needs to be rewired—oh, and maybe one of the dials. And the ignition button isn't connecting properly, so I'll need to push in a bit of magic to get it started instead."

"You mean you're rejigging the magic," she said, nodding.

Peter let that go by, since Glenna had, after all, not snapped at him when she could have. There wasn't really enough magic in the tickerbox to be considered as any kind of rigging; it was, as he had always said, a mere spark. That, and a few connections. There was more of it now, of course, but the clockwork was still what did the bulk of the work.

Much to his relief, Glenna didn't seem to be inclined to try to talk to him while he was working: if he was right, she was even doing a working herself, though he didn't care to pay enough attention to find out what that magic was. Probably something odd and backward to make sure things didn't go wrong with her jinxed magic this time.

At any rate, by the time Peter had finished threading the delicate web of magic back through the slowly winding cogs of the tickerbox, Glenna had been sitting still for quite some time. When he closed the tickerbox once again, she sat up a little straighter and held out one hand.

"Now," she said, in a wary sort of fashion that put Peter's back up a little, "before we do anything, I'd like you to explain exactly what you've done here. I can see enough to guess, but I want to make sure nothing goes wrong this time."

The tickerbox, to Peter's further ire, scrambled across his arm and made a small, spindly leap for Glenna's outstretched hand.

"I've programmed it to search time and space for us, and input a lack of us into its thought processes that bypasses the present instance of us. Technically, it's not targeting because I'm not technically trying to steer by it."

"Then, in theory, we should be dragged back toward ourselves in the future to satisfy the box's lack of us."

"Exactly," said Peter. "It just like the principle of magic abhorring a vacuum—"

"Yes, I'm aware of the Base Laws of Magic," Glenna interrupted. "I was more concerned about being drawn toward another version of ourselves in another time."

"I told you, I've already *thought* about that. I've programmed an exclusion to the instance of us that exists in this little bit of time so that it won't interfere with the magic or confuse the clockwork."

"What about other instances of ourselves in other times?"

"Why would there be other instances of us in other times!" protested Peter. As far as he could see, Glenna was just being obstructionist.

Glenna smiled humourlessly. "There shouldn't even be *this* instance of ourselves in the past. I'd very much rather take the necessary precautions than end up in one place at the same time with an older instance of myself. I've got the feeling that it wouldn't end well for either version of myself."

Peter drew in a breath through his nose, and let it out very slowly. "All right," he said, in his most calm, adult voice. "If it will make you happy, I'll add in an exclusion clause for any other instances of ourselves, too."

It was nonsense, of course, but if that's what it would take to make her stop snipping at him, he would do it. There was no harm in being extra thorough, after all; in fact, if Tom had suggested something of the sort back at the university, Peter would have good-naturedly gone along with it without more than a token protest at the extra work. But Glenna was *so* sure of herself; *so* determined to be listened to all the time, that it irritated him to have to listen to her.

"Thank you," said Glenna, deceptively cool. "That was all I wanted to make sure of."

"All right," said Peter, fighting to keep his temper. "Now that we've got that sorted out, how does your jinx work? Tell me as precisely as you can: I haven't worked with one before and Poly tells me they're all different. I'll need to know how to work with it before I can make sure I program the tickerbox correctly."

Glenna looked at him wonderingly. "You still think you're the one who's going to be doing the magic, don't you?"

"It's my tickerbox!" Peter said. "Why shouldn't I? I don't want other people fiddling with it. Once we've decided the best way to go about things, I'll input everything myself."

"No, I think not," she said decidedly. "We'll do it together, thank you very much. If you try to do it without consulting me I think you'll find that the results will be quite unpleasant for both of us."

"I suppose your jinx is as sensitive as you are!" Peter shot at her.

"Significantly more," said Glenna, with an entirely humourless smile. "And beside all that, I still don't trust you."

"Fine!" Peter said bad-temperedly. "I'll enter the coordinates and then we'll ignite it in the same way we did the working for our Interconnectedness Class! Both of us working together."

Glenna nodded. "Certainly. I certainly hope you'll allow me to do the safety workings in my own fashion this time."

"Yes of course! Now that I know it's because you need to do it, why wouldn't I!"

"Oh, I see," said Glenna, settling back into her puff of skirts to trace a backward pattern in the dirt with one long finger. "Everyone should tell you everything about themselves and explain why they need to do things before you'll allow them to deviate from what *you* think is right."

"I didn't say that!"

"You quite often don't have to come right out and say things when your actions spring from your thoughts," Glenna said, still sketching. "It's quite an effective way of communicating your thoughts, believe me."

Sulkily, Peter said, "Oh, believe what you want to believe, then! Are you finished?"

She nodded, and lifted her hand away from the dirt. "You should join me here in the centre of the circle. And I don't have a model this time, so if things go wrong, they'll go rather strenuously wrong."

"I suppose you're trying to tell me not to irritate you," Peter said, rather shortly. He didn't see why he was the only one who wasn't allowed to be irritating.

"Not exactly," she said, rising as he joined her in the circle. "It's more of a general warning. You've already seen how strong my magic is; it will be quite dangerous for you if things go wrong."

"It'll be dangerous for you as well," objected Peter. "I'm

not the only one who'll be in danger. You'll just have to control yourself as best you can."

"I won't be in danger," said Glenna, with a rather tight smile. "I may be made uncomfortable, but I won't be in danger. You stand a very high chance of both being made uncomfortable *and* being bodily injured. Please make sure your magic stays within the bounds of the setup."

"I've used an Interconnectedness setup before! I know how to colour within the lines."

Very coldly and calmly, she said, "You may remember that last time we worked together—"

"Yes, but *I know now*!" Peter snapped. "I don't make the same mistake twice!"

He didn't like the faint smile that appeared and vanished in an instant.

"Very well," said Glenna. "Then suppose we begin? I take it you've finished with your exceptions?"

"Yes!"

No need to tell her that he had only input the two different exceptions: she had been far quicker with her wards than he anticipated, and Peter was stubbornly determined to be at least as good as she was. He wanted to be able to hold his head up. And there was no *point* to the other exceptions.

"Then here we go," said Glenna.

This time, Peter distinctly felt his magic being drawn out and joined; and when it joined with Glenna's he felt that, too. Strong and hearty and full, it coursed through them both through their clasped hands, though Peter wasn't aware of having reached for Glenna's hand. The tickerbox started and scrabbled on his shoulder, and then time opened, or perhaps just scattered into particles before them, edged with the stickiness of a colour of magic that wasn't Glenna's toffee-apple red or his own bright yellow. He saw it for the briefest moment, and was searingly annoyed because magic didn't *have* true colours, so why should he be able to see it so clearly now?

The tickerbox nattered wildly at him, separating time or maybe Peter and Glenna into little bits and pieces that should have meant he couldn't hear, or see, or sense, or even *be* in any meaningful way. Peter felt the warm firmness of Glenna's hand around his even though it was impossible; and that hand tightened for one brief moment.

Then something huge and powerful and distinctly orange slapped everything sideways.

A scream tore from Peter's throat, while Glenna's short shriek sounded sharp in his ears, but the pain was only for the briefest moment before they hit something hard and solid and definitely not magical.

Then there was just a ringing sound, and darkness, until Peter woke with the impression of fractured blue sky above and dirt beneath him once again. The first thing he saw when he could focus on anything was a nose: large and brown and hooked. Above that was the vague impression of two eyes that were offputtingly piercing despite a lack of clarity due to being without his glasses.

"You're an extremely irritating boy," said Rorkin.

7

Beside him, Glenna sighed and sat up. "I suppose this is another one of your friends."

"Not exactly," Peter said irritably, feeling for his glasses. He found them, but had to wipe the fingerprints away from the glass before he could put them on. One day, he'd have to formulate a spell to fix that sort of thing.

"That's what I meant," Glenna said dryly, gazing at the buildings behind which they had arrived. "Is this a stables? We appear to have shifted in positionally as well as chronologically once again, and I'm rather certain we haven't gone in the direction we planned on."

They were, Peter belatedly realised, certainly behind a stables. The ground beneath them was no longer grassy, either; cobbled and hard, it had left some bruises that he would no doubt be finding later. Somewhere at the front of the particular building they were behind, he heard the sound of hooves, loud and sharp, and the building beside that was piled high with hay on two levels.

"You went backwards," said Rorkin. "Very backwards. Well, not very backwards, but very *not* forward, and that's nearly the same."

"I rather fancy we hit the stable wall, too," said Glenna thoughtfully, rubbing her nose. To Peter, she said, "Thank you for that, by the way. I suppose I can be thankful not to have broken my nose."

Rorkin said, "That would have been a pity; I like your nose. So regal! So freckled!"

To Peter's utter astonishment, Glenna gurgled with laughter. "Thank you! Who are you, by the way?"

"Always your servant," he said at once, his thin face lighting up. "You're my favourite person to keep meeting."

"Wait until I tell Annabel," Peter said sourly, wincing as a sore spot above his brow made itself felt. He didn't see why Rorkin had to fawn over Glenna.

He looked around him once again, ignoring them both. The stables must have belonged to what he fancied was an inn further down ahead of them. Positionally, they seemed to have arrived roughly at the centre of a city which loomed over the stables at the back and spread out on a gentle downward incline toward the front of the inn.

"Annabel is my second favourite person," said Rorkin to Glenna, while Peter took in the world around them. "Nice little thing, but too clever for comfort. I only get to meet her twice. That's why she's my second favourite person."

"That doesn't make sense," said Peter, reluctantly turning his eyes away from the rooftops that surrounded them. "As usual. Miss—Glenna, Rorkin is a wizard. I keep meeting him in bad situations."

"I suppose you think it's all fun and games for me," said Rorkin, *sotto voce*. "Came out far too early and I didn't even have time to find my best socks. Look at 'em: substandard and not even remotely likely to assist me in dancing."

"You're not a wizard," Glenna said, still looking at Rorkin. "But I think you're familiar."

Was it Peter's imagination, or did Rorkin suddenly look shifty?

"I do know you," said Glenna, her eyes narrowing. "*And* you've gone all shifty."

"You're still my favourite person to meet," said Rorkin, and disappeared.

"What on *earth* was that all about?" Glenna said. "Who was he and how did he know where we are when we don't even know where we are?"

"I don't know," said Peter. "But when he appears, there's trouble."

"Yes, I could tell that. Specifically, what sort of trouble?"

"I don't know—crown and country stuff? Oh…" Peter trailed away. "And time-related troubles."

"Wonderful!" said Glenna, with thinly veiled sarcasm. "Then I suppose we've still not been saved from your dreadful lapse of judgement. Did you make the allowances I told you to make?"

"I don't see why you're looking for problems! We probably just shifted sideways as well as forward in time."

"Your wizard friend said we'd moved *backwards* in time."

"Yes, but he's also popping in and out of reality with no shoes on and part of his breakfast in his beard!" protested Peter.

"Your tickerbox," Glenna said gently, "is eating time again. Did you notice? Once again: did you make the allowances I told you to make?"

Peter scrambled to his feet and said in frustration, "Why would there be another instance of ourselves in another period of time? Why should I make stupid allowances that would take power and accuracy away from what I was trying to do?"

"I would suggest that the possibility of other instances of us might have something to do with the fact that you keep ignoring my input and doing whatever you feel is best," she said. "Never mind, I can already see that we've not gone back to the future. You completely ignored my warning, didn't you?"

"I didn't completely ignore it!" Peter said defensively. "I just didn't see why we should do something that would take away from the power of the working when it wasn't necessary."

"Pft!" said Rorkin's voice in his ear, an unexpected explosion of dismissive air that made Peter jump. "Of all the people to think non-compete clauses in time travel aren't necessary!"

Peter twitched himself away in annoyance, hunching his shoulder up to his ear. "Don't do that! Where did you go?"

"I think you mean *when* did I go," said Rorkin, his beady eyes bright. "Or perhaps *when* did I make a different *when*, but that's not the point. The point is that you're an irritating boy and I don't want to be chasing you up and down the timeline. Not that there *is* an up and down, exactly."

"I suppose these are yours," Glenna said. To Peter's utter astonishment, she held up a pair of woolly socks. "They appeared just before you did. I assumed you must have left them for yourself."

Rorkin beamed at her and took the socks. "I did! Would you like to know when I left them?"

"About five minutes before we got here, I should think," said Glenna. "Which means that you know exactly when we are, which we would also like to know."

"You already know," said Rorkin, putting his socks on with great glee. He seemed to grow more solid as he did so, but that didn't stop a shifty expression from spreading across his face. "No, I mean you *can* know. You can figure it out for yourself. I can't: I just follow my nose."

Glenna looked at him curiously, as did Peter. Peter asked, "How do you know about Glenna's method for finding out current time based on her natural surroundings?"

"Oops!" said Rorkin, and disappeared again.

"Peter," Glenna said, in a voice that was even icier than before, "would you like to know *when* we are? Because I can tell you."

Peter would have given a great deal to be able to tell her that he was perfectly sure they had arrived at exactly the time he meant them to arrive, but he couldn't. The stables they had arrived behind weren't New Civetan style, for a start—at best they were an *Old* Civetan style that had not been seen in New Civet for a couple of hundred years. And that meant that he and Glenna must have travelled in space as well as time, because any remaining ancient stables nearby the university should have been in the Parrasian style. Nor did these stables appear to be old by any stretch of the imagination.

"I can't tell when," he said, doggedly. "But I can tell we're not in the right place, all right?"

"Yes, the stables are a bit too ye olde Civetan, aren't they? If I had to guess, I'd say we've travelled a good hundred miles or so in a decidedly southern direction. And if I'm not mistaken, that monstrous shadow further up on the hill is the old Civetan castle."

"I can *fix* it," said Peter, with a rough edge to his voice. He had somehow managed to block the castle out of his mind as he looked around: it was quite obvious now that Glenna pointed it out. "I made the mistake, so I'll fix it!"

"Would you like to guess what time we've arrived at?" asked Glenna.

Bitterly, Peter said, "I suppose it's the worst possible time we could have arrived."

"Not quite. By my calculations, we're here just a few days after the attack on the Sleeping Princess, and perhaps just before the affair of the enchanted battlefield."

"I suppose you're going to blame that on me as well."

"No, but I will point out that since we've been dragged here instead of into the future, that an instance of ourselves must have been hanging about in this time at some point," said Glenna, growing less cool and more annoyed.

"You can't *prove* that!" snapped Peter.

"And now we've got an enchanter who shows up during times of civil unrest and incidents of time trouble dogging our footsteps," continued Glenna, a faint flush of annoyance making its way across her cheeks. "Which no doubt means things are about to become significantly worse."

"I don't see why they would get significantly worse," said Peter, a little sullenly. "They're bad enough as it is; I don't think Rorkin's going to make them much worse. He might even help a bit."

"Let's hope so," she said. "At the very least, he's an enchanter, and unlike us, he seems to have absolutely no trouble travelling through time without the aid of a tickerbox."

"That's because I don't get attached to things," said Rorkin from behind them, the snap of his passage through time and space somehow occurring just a little *after* his voice fell on their ears. "You should never get attached to things when it comes to time. It doesn't work out well."

To Peter, listening in irritation, it was nonsense. He only said, "Look, do you *have* to keep popping in and out like that? We need your help."

It was greatly to his surprise, therefore, that Glenna patted Rorkin on the shoulder in a consoling sort of way and said in the gentlest voice he had yet heard from her, "The connections are still there. It just takes a while to find them again."

"Some of them aren't there yet," said Rorkin. "That's why you're my favourite person to meet."

"At least you can leave socks around the place for yourself," Glenna said, and wiggled another pair of rolled socks in Rorkin's general direction.

"Where are you *getting* those?" demanded Peter in exasperation.

"They're all over the place," said Glenna, shrugging one shoulder. "You just have to look. Didn't you see me pick them up?"

"No!" Peter said in annoyance. "I was too busy wondering when Rorkin was going to pop up behind us again!"

Just as he said it, Rorkin flickered briefly, disappeared, and appeared again.

"Oh, there you are," Rorkin said. "Are you popping in and out, or is that me?"

"It's you," said Peter. "Do you have to keep doing that?"

"Better put your socks on," Glenna said. "It made you a bit more solid before. Do you think it will help if you hold onto me?"

Rorkin took the socks and put them on with two very well-aimed lunges toward his big feet, then seized Glenna's hand with both of his like a bashful boy and said, "*Much* better!"

"She didn't say you could hold her hand!" objected Peter, annoyed by this and that, but especially annoyed by Rorkin's far too satisfied expression. "Look, if you're going to keep appearing and disappearing, the least you could do is whatever it is you do to time travel and take us with you so that we can go back to our own time."

"Can't do that," said Rorkin, in what seemed to Peter to be a suspiciously guilty way. He might even have edged behind Glenna by a fraction of an inch. "Can't take things with me. Wouldn't take you if I could, actually."

"Rorkin," said Glenna gently. "Exactly why do you keep coming back to us, then?"

"Exactly!" Peter said. "If you're not going to help us get back to our own time—"

"Ah," Rorkin said. "That's the problem. Time. That's what I'm here to tell you."

"*What* is what you're here to tell us?" Peter said impatiently. "You've been bobbing in and out and haven't told us *anything*."

"I'm here to tell you that you'd better hurry up if you want to fix the *giant hole* you made in time and reality," Rorkin said promptly. "It's messy and has too many loose threads and Mordion already got out even though he isn't imprisoned yet, which is *very inconvenient.*"

"What?"

"You're supposed to clean up your own messes," said Rorkin. "I'm pretty sure it's a general rule. Why else would someone be running up and down through time and space?"

"What giant hole?" demanded Peter. "You're the one who was playing with time when I said it wasn't possible—*you're* the one who sent the royal castle back through three years! If there's a hole in time and space, you're probably the one who did it!"

"Rorkin," said Glenna sweetly, "what Peter means to say is, What is the problem we need to fix; why, and how? And is it connected with why we don't seem to be able to get back to our own time?"

"It's a hole, and it's there because Peter put it there—"

"That's *not*—"

"We don't need to fight about whose fault it is!" Glenna said, turning on Peter in exasperation. "So can you kindly be quiet about it!"

"Why is it all right for him to say it's my fault but not all right for me to say it could be his?"

"Because I didn't make a dreadful hole in time and reality," said Rorkin, and stuck his tongue out.

Glenna made a very small choking noise that was only the second real laugh Peter had heard from her. It struck him again as highly unfair that she should be so comfortable and pleasant with Rorkin when she was so cold and snappish with him.

Of Rorkin, she asked, "This hole in time and reality— does it have something to do with the fact that there seem to be several instances of Peter and me running around in different parts of time?"

"Indirectly," said Rorkin, his brown eyes sparkling. "But it isn't so much the fact that there are multiple instances of you running around so much as the fact that you *are* running around in time. It was the first incursion that tore a hole: the rest of them aren't important so long as you don't meddle too much. Or at least, so long as you meddle just enough."

"And you want us to fix up the hole?"

Rorkin beamed at her again. "Exactly! I knew I should have talked to you first!"

"How exactly are we supposed to patch up the hole?" asked Peter, trying not to sound impatient. If it was, after all, his fault that something had apparently gone wrong with time, he didn't really have the right to be angry. "And if we made a hole by dodging through time, how is it possible that you've been doing it without making holes?"

"We started at the same time; just at different points," said Rorkin, turning his eyes on Peter.

"Look, if we've made a hole in time or the fabric of the universe by breaking through time, shouldn't it fix things if we go back to where we began? I'll just program the tickerbox again and put more conditions in to make sure we go to the right set of ourselves this time!"

"Your time won't let you back in," Rorkin said. "Even conditionally."

His eyes were serious, now, and that worried Peter a great deal. He very rarely saw Rorkin entirely serious.

"What do you mean, our time won't let us back in?"

"It's more that it doesn't recognise you at the moment," said Rorkin. "The hole pulled a few things sideways and deleted a few things, and your presence at the university was one of the things that changed."

"Did my presence there change, too?" asked Glenna, a sudden edge to her voice.

Rorkin grinned, sharp and bright. "You always understand so quickly! I like working with you."

"What are you both talking about?" demanded Peter, annoyed to hear the surly note in his voice. "Why should it matter if Glenna isn't at the university?"

"Well, why should it matter if *you're* not there?" Glenna said, but Peter almost thought he heard her sigh. "Sometimes it's not how big or important something is—"

"It's how it connects with all the other things," said Rorkin, nodding. "Interconnectedness! Such a pernickety thing, isn't it?"

"If we patch up the hole, will we be able to get back to our own time?" asked Glenna. "I've the feeling there might be a few instances of us around the place that we haven't met with yet; but if those aren't the problem—"

"They're the opposite of a problem," Rorkin said cheerfully. "We don't want to meddle with those. Very bad idea to meddle with other instances of yourself. We're lucky there's two of you: we can always make sure one of you deals with the other if we happen to run into each other."

"Yes," said Glenna, glaring at Peter. "I've got the feeling that the instance of us that drew us to this particular time made very sure they didn't meet up with us by knocking us sideways into the stables."

"Very sensible," Rorkin said approvingly, making Glenna laugh again. "Yes: fix the hole, and you can theoretically get back to your future. Well. That's what I told myself, so unless I'm lying to myself, fixing the problem of the hole fixes all the problems."

"Do you often lie to yourself?" Peter asked sourly. Glenna was far nicer to Rorkin than she was to him, which was completely unfair.

"Only when necessary," said Rorkin. "Or when I'm getting back at myself for something."

"And why exactly," Glenna said, as though she were trying hard to be stern, but was fighting back a smile, "are *you* running through time and space?"

Rorkin beamed at her. "I still like you the best," he said.

"Why are you always so nice to him?" Peter demanded. He was aware that his voice was pitched a bit higher than usual in indignation, and that annoyed him more. "It's at *least* as much his fault as mine, because he's the one who showed me how to do the thing in the first place! And he's at *least* as annoying as me!"

"He's nothing like as annoying as you," Glenna said. "And I don't suppose he can really help what you learn from him; you're far too clever for your own good. Rorkin, what *exactly* is it that's gone wrong, and how do we try to fix it?"

"It's a hole," said Rorkin. "So it needs to be sewn up."

"Yes, but is it a knitting type hole, or a cutting type hole, or—"

"Knitting," Rorkin said at once.

"So we need to catch some stitches," said Peter, trying very hard not to lose his temper. "All right. What stitches exactly?"

"For a start, Mordion."

"*What?*" said Peter and Glenna at the same time.

"I'm sure you already know about him," said Rorkin, in surprise. "Why are you startled?"

"I'm startled because I *do* know about him!" Peter snapped. "I helped Annabel get rid of him back in the future. Why is he still causing trouble back here?"

"Because you made a huge h—"

"If you say it's because I made a huge hole in time and reality just *once* more—!" began Peter, in exasperation.

"Well," Rorkin retorted. "You can't say that you—"

"Rorkin," Glenna said. "How exactly is Mordion caught up in all this?"

"Well," said Rorkin again. "I'm not exactly sure. That's

the problem. I know there's something odd happening with the timeline, and I don't know if it's already happened or if it's going to happen, but it involves Mordion and Poly and quite a lot of people marching or not marching as the case may be."

"Mordion already did all that," Peter said, feeling more relieved than he had in quite some time. "Poly told me about it. It's how she became the Sleeping Princess."

Rorkin's eyes grew serious. "Yes, but he seems to have gotten an idea of that future. And he's been trying to find his way into a new future instead of going through the history that was already laid out for him."

"How did he manage to get a sight of the future?" asked Glenna.

"He accessed a very strong source of power at the same time that you both broke into the timeline."

"He couldn't have done it at the same *time*—"

"All right, clever clogs, I know that," said Rorkin. "But in terms of very big incursions into time and reality, there were two very big ones, and they sort of joined together enough for him to see exactly what was going to happen to him."

"Interconnectedness is not always a benefit," murmured Glenna. "So Mordion saw what was going to happen to him and didn't like it, so he's altered the past, which is altering the future?"

"Exactly," said Rorkin. "And now everything is unravelling and things are getting messy. The future is a different future at the moment, and until we can fix that, things are going to keep unravelling."

Peter caught Glenna's eyes, and it seemed to him for just a moment that she looked as guilty as he felt he must look.

She asked, "Do we know where—or when—we need to go to fix it?"

"Not a clue!" said Rorkin promptly. "I thought it was

something that was set in stone: you'd just *be* where you were supposed to be while reality tries to reset itself."

"Wait a moment," Peter said, frowning. "Then how did you know where to find us?"

Rorkin blinked at him. "It was a happy accident."

"You ran away from me at the party!"

"That was a less happy accident."

"Rorkin," said Glenna sternly. "You're getting shifty again."

Rorkin coughed a little. "Perhaps someone gave me a hint about how to find you."

"Yes," Glenna said. "I rather fancied so."

"*Who* told—" began Peter.

"I lost track of you at the Inversion Pocket," added Rorkin, interrupting him. "That was a bit of a worry. Luck's place has a habit of running into the past and future, and if you'd wandered off into the future and found yourselves again…"

"Do you mean to say that if we'd stayed in the house a bit longer, it would have eventually taken us back to our own present?" demanded Peter, glaring at Glenna. For all her continued bleats of everything being *his* fault, she was the one who had pushed them out of the house when by staying, they could have made their way comfortably back to their present.

A touch of annoyed pink bloomed in Glenna's cheeks.

"Yes, but it wouldn't have done you any good," said Rorkin. "I just *told* you. You would have gone back to the wrong future, and you wouldn't have fixed the *giant hole*—"

"Yes, yes!" said Peter testily. "The giant hole I made in time and reality!"

"Exactly," Rorkin said. "Unless you stayed in the house for the next three hundred years. That would have fixed the hole quite nicely."

"Would it?" asked Glenna, her tone light and amused despite the quizzical lift of her brow.

Rorkin grinned a startlingly white-toothed grin at her. "It *would*, so there!"

"But?" she asked.

"It would have made another, more difficult hole. Well, several. A bit like moths in a sock drawer. Holes everywhere!"

Peter frowned. "Wait. That suggests that we're essential to not just the future, but to our own historic timeline as well, and that's nonsense!"

"Isn't he humble!" marvelled Rorkin. "Yes, you're very important. *You.*"

"I hope you're not going to say that *I'm* especially important," said Glenna, laughing. "I'm quite well aware of my part in history, thank you very much!"

"I don't think you are," said Rorkin loftily. "Well, I wouldn't exactly say you're especially important. Not *more* than him, at least. I think we're all agreed that you have the most difficult job, though."

"Who is *all?*" demanded Peter.

At the same time, Glenna said in amusement, "And what exactly is the most difficult job, Rorkin?"

"You have to put up with *him*," said Rorkin, tipping his chin at Peter.

"If you're both just going to stand there and make fun of me, I might as well get to work on trying to retarget the ticker-box," Peter said shortly.

"We can't go back to the future anyway," Glenna said. She still looked amused. "Not yet."

"Yes, but if we're going to be fixing slipped stitches or whatever it is that we're fixing, we'll need a more focused and versatile targeting system anyway. Not to mention the ignition button still needs fixing, and—"

"All right," said Glenna. "You work on that. I have some questions for Rorkin."

That was also annoying, though Peter couldn't have specified why. He patted his pockets for the tools he'd brought with him from Luck's house, and suffered a sharp shock when he found that they were gone.

"Hey!" he said, rather indignantly. "Glenna, did you take my tools?"

Glenna sent him a cool look. "Do you suppose I know how to pick pockets?"

"Well—"

"Or am I supposed to have ransacked them while you were unconscious for the sheer joy of annoying you?"

"No, but where are my tools, then?"

"The same place my shoes went, I suppose," said Glenna, lifting her skirts just a little to display her dirty, stockinged feet. "I did find some at Luck's place that were the right size. We might need to take another look at your tickerbox before we attempt another shift. From the last shift, it seems to have a problem shifting anything that wasn't originally on us."

The tickerbox, crawling out from Peter's pocket and onto his shoulder, nattered at him.

"That is…interesting," said Peter. "Because the cogs are all still there: the ones I fixed it with."

"My hair stays cut when I shift, too," Rorkin offered. "Things about my actual, physical self that change always stay changed."

"Ah, so you'll keep aging, then," Glenna said thoughtfully. "I was wondering about that. What a shame that shoes aren't included in physical changes! I suppose I'll be in the same frock for quite some time, then."

"I can adjust that," Peter muttered. "It's just because I programmed the tickerbox to the particular physical attributes of us; I've imbedded the ability to recognise growth, but I didn't think to allow for changes of clothing. I'll have to see what I can do about that."

"Later, perhaps," said Glenna. There was a faint amusement in her eyes. "If I endure no worse than the same dress and a lack of shoes before we get back to our own time, I shall count myself fortunate, I dare say. It's not our chief concern right now."

"Fluffy socks should be everyone's concern," Rorkin said below his breath. "If no precedent is made, how will those suffering ever——"

"I'm very sorry about your sufferings, Rorkin," Glenna said. "But perhaps we can work on that problem after we've fixed the hole that is currently unravelling reality?"

Rorkin sighed rather wistfully. "I suppose so. Make sure you don't forget."

"If I do, you'll have to come back and remind me," she said. "Now; Peter——"

"You don't have to tell me what to do," Peter said crossly. "I'm already looking at the tickerbox. I shall need things to fix it. And before you tell me, I'm *going* to make sure that I make allowances for any other versions of us that might still be in time, so you don't need to nag!"

"Very kind of you," said Glenna, rather shortly.

"Even if," Peter continued, unable to stop himself, "it's almost certain that there won't be any other versions of us to watch out for. Now that I know there's the possibility——"

"The possibility is, of course, why I insisted upon you taking into account any other instances of us in the first place."

"I don't see why there should be other instances of us in history!" argued Peter, well aware that he was in the wrong but somehow unable to stop himself. "Not more than the ones we've had trouble with already! And I *know* you're going to say that that's why there *are* other instances of us in other times——"

"I have already said so," Glenna interrupted. "It seems such a waste of time to say it again. Rorkin already said we don't need to concern ourselves with them except to make sure we don't meet, and the other pair of us already seem to be pretty well aware of that. I'm more worried about other problems."

"What problems?" demanded Peter, though he was quite certain he would regret it.

"The problem we have with you thinking that no one but yourself knows what they're talking about, and refusing to consider their concerns before acting. I'm surprised there aren't running instances of us in every time, at this rate!"

"*I* didn't put other instances of us through time!"

Rorkin coughed. "Technically, it's because he keeps doing stupid things while trying to fix his mistakes."

"And technically," said Glenna, in an amiable sort of way, "this particular problem is because he didn't listen—again."

"I'm *right here*," said Peter.

"We know," said Glenna. "Isn't that rather the problem? You're far too much *here*."

"It was an instance of you as well," Peter muttered. "Or the tickerbox wouldn't have taken us here exactly: I programmed it for the both of us together. It seems like I can't get away from you."

"That," said Glenna, with a particularly cold smile, "is not precisely my fault, is it?"

She seemed cool and collected, and not particularly angry, but when Peter jabbed a spark of annoyed magic at the tickerbox to jumpstart it back into some kind of useful internal motion, a huge flare of jinx ignited it into something more approximate to an explosion that threw him clear across the courtyard and into the water-trough on the other side.

Flailing and spluttering on mossy water, Peter surfaced to the hooting laughter of Rorkin. He struggled out of the trough, and as he slopped grimly back toward Glenna and Rorkin again, someone called out in surprise from the front of the stables. The surprise in the voice was clear, but it might as well have been in another language for all the sense he could make out of it.

"Ah, I forgot about that," said Glenna as he approached. She didn't apologise, which was bad enough, but her single offering was, "I'll have to make us both a bit of a translation spell. I forgot it would be old Civetish they're speaking here. I've studied Pre-Battlefield Parrasian, but I didn't get to old Civetish when I was studying as a child."

"You *threw me* into a *water trough!*"

"They said that your lady-friend seems annoyed with you," said Rorkin helpfully.

Glenna sniffed.

"You threw me into a water trough!" snapped Peter once again.

"I did nothing of the kind," said Glenna. "And in fact, I've already warned you that you'll be mad uncomfortable if you do magic around me, willy-nilly."

"You can't keep exploding magic at me every time I annoy you!"

"If you're allowed to be a plague on society, I don't see why I shouldn't be allowed to be a plague to you," Glenna snapped. "If you *will* insist on being as offensive and annoying as possible, you must suffer the consequences of that choice!"

"How is *your* temper *my* fault?" Peter demanded, in disbelief.

"I see that you don't yet fully understand!" snapped Glenna. "When you choose to use magic after annoying me, the jinx latches onto it and pushes it back outward."

"Do you mean to say I've got to stop annoying a *jinx?*" Peter demanded. "That's ridiculous!"

She raised one brow. "More or less ridiculous than you flying into a water trough whenever you try to do magic after annoying me?"

"I don't see why I should have to worry about what I say every two seconds!"

"Every two seconds isn't necessary," she said, with a cold smile. "But I really do advise being more careful when you're just about to do magic. After all, if I have to try and reign in the extreme irritation of being constantly in your presence to give your magic the best chance to work, the least you could do is make it easier for me."

"It's not my fault if you get annoyed at everything I say to you!" retorted Peter. "Maybe you should try to fix your temper! Why you haven't ever tried to control your jinx, I don't know!"

"It's absolutely no use trying to control a jinx," said Glenna, and her smile was once more ice-cold. "Your strength is turned against you and used to hurt you—or others. The only thing I *can* do is control my temper as long as possible and try to mitigate the damage where I can."

"It's not exactly your temper, though, is it?" said Rorkin, a little bit slyly.

"That's close enough for now," Glenna told him. Her voice sounded very school-marmy again.

"You don't look like you're losing your temper," Peter said sulkily. "You look like Miss Stoneheart again."

"Unfortunately for the both of us," said Glenna, her eyes icy blue, "the jinx is not concerned with whether or not I express my temper—it feeds on the actual emotion."

"Oh," Peter said. "Well, but you didn't have to throw me into the water trough!"

"I think you're still misunderstanding. I don't *do* anything. The jinx takes your magic, your strength, and twists it into an explosion of magic. If you want to do something while you're annoying me, I really do recommend doing something with as little magic as possible."

"Or point it at anything other than us," suggested Rorkin.

"Perhaps," Glenna said, "it would be best if I worked on a translation spell to allow us to speak to the people here. I'm sure Peter wants to work on the targeting system of his ticker-box, and Rorkin—"

"I didn't do it!" Rorkin said at once. "It was Peter, and he—"

Peter gritted his teeth.

"Yes, yes, Peter made a hole in time and reality. But perhaps you could do a little explaining while we work on our respective tasks," Glenna suggested.

"It's very simple," said Rorkin. "You have to catch up your stitches, starting with Mordion. Everything unravels from him."

"Yes, we understand that, but I'm talking about another explanation," said Glenna.

Peter couldn't help smiling a bit as he sat back down with his tickerbox, not unpleasantly cool in the warm afternoon after his sudden ducking. It didn't sound as though Rorkin was going to get away with the kind of fudging that he had gotten away with when it came to Annabel. Glenna obviously had some idea of what the wizard had been up to, and while Peter didn't know exactly how she knew it, he was pleased to see her gimlet eye on someone else for a change.

"Don't know what you're talking about," said Rorkin promptly. "I'm very good at explaining. Explain things all the time."

"You were pretending to be Doctor Harding at the university, weren't you?" asked Glenna. Her tone was mildly disapproving, which struck Peter as grossly unfair considering the not very great difference of Rorkin's misdeeds in comparison to his own and the very different responses that Glenna had to both.

"Perhaps I wasn't pretending," said Rorkin, but even his elbows stuck out in a shifty sort of way. "Perhaps I'm pretending to be Rorkin now. Perhaps I really am Doctor Harding."

"You've been pretending for a lot longer than a few weeks, then," Peter muttered. "You're Rorkin whenever I meet you."

"I prefer not to meet you whenever possible," said Rorkin unexpectedly. "You're so sharp you could cut yourself."

"Glenna's sharp, too!" Peter said exasperatedly. "I'm not the only one pulling you up on the ridiculous things you say!"

"Yes, but I like her a lot better," explained Rorkin. "And her magic is pretty and inside out."

"You *would* like that," said Peter. *Inside out* was a very kind way to describe Glenna's jinxed magic.

"I thought so," said Glenna, without regarding how off-topic the conversation had gone. "Well, one way or another, Rorkin or Doctor Harding, I knew there was somebody influencing the Interconnectedness in the university to hide something."

"I knew you knew!" crowed Rorkin, to Peter's combined astonishment and confusion.

"What *are* you talking about?" he asked, looking from Glenna to Rorkin and back again. "Interconnectedness has nothing to do with Rorkin sneaking into the university or you finding him out! It's about doing things in a wide-spectrumed and standardised way that meets as many commonalities as possible in as many systems as possible! All it does is provide common points in every facet of the world that you can use to maximise your chances of a desired outcome in magic."

"Poppycock!" said Rorkin at once.

Peter glared at him. "The Interconnectedness of All Things is exactly what I've just described! It's how we can make a fusion of magic and clockwork and time, for pity's sake!"

"It's really not," Glenna said, sighing. "If that were so, magic would work perfectly every time and you could be sure of your outcome so long as you do the right thing at the right time."

"But you *can!*" protested Peter.

"Thought you went the university," said Rorkin, peering

into Peter's face with all the subtlety of a hawk staring down its prey. "Did you skip classes?"

Before Peter could reply to that, rather heatedly, Rorkin turned his disconcertingly sharp gaze back on Glenna and said accusatorily, "You missed *just* the right class. Him, too."

"You're welcome," said Glenna. "Don't take it as a compliment or a favour, though. I had other reasons for skipping that class and I was trying to catch you, not help you."

"I won't take it personally," Rorkin beamed, his bright face a direct contradiction to his words.

Peter, who hadn't been able to follow the conversation at all but refused to admit as much to them, said impatiently, "I assume you haven't always wanted to run an Interconnected-ness of All Things class, so why were you playing silly beggars at the university?"

"Because it's better for the Interconnectedness of All Things if I'm not connected with certain ones at certain times," said Rorkin promptly.

Peter turned his accusing look on Glenna. "That's what you said."

"Yes," she agreed. "But if you're about to suggest what I think you're about to suggest, allow *me* to make a suggestion."

Aware of the martial gleam in her eye, Peter said sulkily, "I suppose you're going to tell me to keep my mouth shut."

"Keeping your mouth shut is always a good suggestion," said Rorkin. "I do it all the time."

"I was only going to ask——"

"If we were in cahoots?" prompted Glenna, when Peter stopped, struck with the blistering thought that he had been about to insult her intentions and actions yet again. "Yes, that's why I was about to offer a suggestion of my own."

Peter flushed. "I didn't say it!"

"No," she said thoughtfully. "I'm really very impressed. Rorkin——"

"Can't say anything else!" he said hastily. "Better for the Interconnectedness of All Things!"

"Yes," Glenna said, a little suspiciously. "That's a very useful excuse."

"*So* useful!" Rorkin said enthusiastically. "Shall I give you a translation spell? A warming blanket? I've got about five minutes before something happens, and I'm supposed to be there when it happens. Actually, a couple of me are supposed to be there, so we have to co-ordinate it very well."

"Aren't you going to stay with us?" asked Glenna. "I thought you were here to help us."

Peter fancied that there was a touch of wistfulness to her voice.

"Oh no!" said Rorkin. "I'm expected elsewhere and if I don't turn up then, it will mean big trouble."

"More trouble than *this*?" Peter asked, somewhat disbelieving. If things were as bad as Rorkin would have them believe, what could be more important? "What's more important than trying to fix a hole that's made a new future?"

"Didn't say it was more important," Rorkin said at once. "I said it would mean big trouble if I didn't go. It's a very small, unimportant thing, and if it doesn't happen, there will be Big Trouble."

"I think you're already rather more Interconnected with All Things than is strictly healthy," said Glenna, thoughtfully considering the wizard.

Rorkin looked bashful. "Anyway," he said. "I can't come with you because I'm otherwise occupied, and even if I could come with you, my help would probably only make the hole worse."

"I suppose you're still trying to fix your own hole," Glenna said, patting the hand she held with her other hand.

Rorkin shot her a lean, narrow look. "How did you guess?"

"You're wandering through time yourself," Peter said,

rather grumpily. "Of course you've made a hole! If we have, you *must* have."

"Anyway," said Rorkin. "I still have a royal castle to spell while tiptoeing around all the pitfalls and other versions of myself, so if you'll excuse me—"

"Wait!" Peter said, but it was too late. Rorkin had gone. To Glenna, Peter protested, "If the future is where he's going, what's the point? He said the future is different now!"

"I've got the feeling he isn't going as far forward as that," said Glenna, her eyes thoughtful. "I rather think he's only going as far forward as he can before the royal Parrasian castle is destroyed."

"I don't see how that's more important than helping us here," Peter said. Reluctantly, he added, "Oh well, I suppose that if Mordion's seen something of the future, he could know about the castle and how he'll be trapped in there eventually. Maybe that's what he's trying to change, and Rorkin is trying to stop it."

"In which case, it could be good to have someone working from our side of things," said Glenna, nodding. "Very well. We can't stay in the stables all day. I rather think we need to see if we can make it into the castle proper to see how things stand. If my grasp of history is good, the Sleeping Princess being put to sleep should precipitate the enchanted army very soon."

"Poly," said Peter, without thinking.

"I beg your pardon?"

"Her name is Poly." Peter stopped himself just before he told Glenna that Poly wasn't a princess either. It was true, but it wasn't common knowledge, and it was far better for the political situation in New Civet if people still thought she was a Civetan Princess from the elder days.

Of course, that had been true when he left the future not long ago. It may not be true now. It might not ever be possible, in fact, for Glenna to ever tell anyone else what she potentially learned.

So, with a tug of regret that reminded him exactly whose fault that was, Peter added, "She's not a princess, either."

"Yes, but she's called the Sleeping Princess, and I don't have a personal connection," said Glenna. She didn't sound very surprised; nor did she sound particularly cordial, and Peter wondered what he had done to annoy her now. "I happen to know someone who talks about her quite a lot."

Peter frowned. "Who's talking about her?"

"Never you mind," said Glenna, a little sharply. "Look, I've made us a translating spell that should help with the language problem, and Rorkin seems to have put a temporary something on us that will keep us from being too noticeable unless you do something like the bit of magic and flying you did earlier, so——"

"Oh, so that's what that is," Peter said. He hadn't noticed Rorkin doing it, but he had certainly sensed it afterward; a cobwebby net of magic that had no colour or even real substance, connected not to himself and Glenna, but to the space around that which they occupied. "Quite clever, isn't it? He hasn't tried to pin anything to us, so it shouldn't attract attention from anyone who's a bit too noticing about things like that."

"I thought so," said Glenna, touching the magic very lightly with one finger. "If you didn't know, you'd think it was just atmospheric magic. That being the case, I wonder if we'll have trouble trying to purchase food? No, I'm sure he would have made it so we can interact if we wish to do so."

Peter looked at her in surprise, then at the suns-lit stables around them. "Food? It's not even lunch time!"

"No," said Glenna. "But even if the triad's out here, it feels like it's time to sleep, and I haven't eaten since the start of the party. I realise it might only have been a few hours since we left our time, but it was late then, I'm horribly hungry, and I shall need to sleep very shortly."

"We can't stop to sleep and eat!" Peter protested. "We need to be fixing the problem with Mordion!"

"I'm sure we'll be able to fix the problem with more alacrity after we've eaten and slept," said Glenna. "I do assure you that I am *far* less amiable when I've not had an appropriate amount of sleep."

"All right," Peter said, after a brief, awful thought of how badly things could go with a sleep-deprived Glenna. "But how are we going to buy food, even if we can be seen? I don't have the right kind of money for this time, and I'm pretty sure there's already standardised magic in markets preventing the alteration of other coin to match the country's coin."

There was silence for a moment or two, and when Peter glanced enquiringly over at Glenna, he was surprised to see that she was blushing faintly.

"I have some coins from roughly this time," she said, after another moment or two. "In fact, I'm beginning to suspect that they're from exactly this time."

Peter stared at her as she pulled out a small pouch from one of her pockets. It jingled faintly; the definite sound of coins clinking against each other.

"You had that in your pocket?" he asked incredulously.

"Yes," she said. "I was advised to always keep them on me; a sort of lucky charm, he said."

"He? Do you mean Rorkin?"

"No," said Glenna. "Another acquaintance. Never mind; at least we can buy food."

"If people can see us when we talk to them," Peter said crankily. He didn't like the fact that Glenna wasn't telling him everything, but he didn't see how he could change that, given her sharp tongue. He wasn't eager for another tongue-lashing. "All right, we'll buy food and sleep for a while. But tonight or tomorrow, we need to try and find out what we can about Mordion."

"Agreed," said Glenna. If he wasn't mistaken, she was relieved not to have to answer any more questions. "And later on, I'll have a look at that tickerbox of yours to see if I can't add something helpful to it. I have a few ideas about it."

She swept across the stableyard her stockinged feet, as regal as ever, leaving Peter to trot after her with various renditions of *no one touches my tickerbox but me* running through his mind—none of which he quite dared to say.

Perhaps, he found himself thinking at last, that was also something that could wait until they had eaten and slept.

❧ 8 ❧

The smallest sun had already sunk when Peter and Glenna woke from sleep in the hayloft. There was little enough left of the food they had purchased from the inn out the front, and it vanished quickly. They hadn't dared buy too much with how little coin they had, nor had they used any of that coin for board when there was a perfectly good supply of straw nearby.

Left to himself, Peter would probably even have tried to scrounge supplies from the stableyard and cobbled together a solution to fix the tickerbox for good, but Glenna had other ideas.

In pursuance of those ideas, she marched him across the city after dark until they found the largest University of Magic that the city had to offer, then just as coolly marched them both into the place. She also managed, with the barest minimum of conversation, to dispossess two stammering, blushing young men of their table and ensconce herself and Peter in it.

Peter found himself very nearly as speechless as the two young men, and much less pleased about it, but he couldn't deny that Glenna had brought them both into the perfect position. Not only did this particular university have what amounted to a buffet in the study hall, it apparently had no problems with the students availing themselves of that food at the same time as they were about their studies. Students all around the hall were engaged in study of the practical as well as theoretical sort, and crumbs of food were as plenteous as the crumbs of magic.

Glenna as high-handedly provided herself with food as she had with a place to sit down, leaving Peter as speechless as before, and explained kindly, "They'll only throw us out if they think we don't belong. If we act like we belong, they'll think we belong."

"All right," said Peter, "but if we get thrown out, I'm going to pretend I don't know you."

"Certainly," Glenna said, with the same inflexion that she might have said *there, there.* "Do you think you could have a look on the odds-and-ends table over there? I rather fancy they have a bit of treated silver over there, and even if it's not the same as treated iron, it's——"

"Yes, I know," said Peter testily. "It's a precursor to the stuff I use in our own time. It won't hold up as well as the treated iron, though."

"I know," Glenna said. There was a faint line between her brows. "It's such a shame that we can't take anything extra with us! It will last us a trip or two before it burns out, I think. But after that——"

"There shouldn't be more than a trip or two needed," Peter said. He felt vaguely affronted. "I'm not going to make mistakes this time when I move us! We should only need to make a move once or twice, unless the stitch we need to catch with Mordion is in another time. After that, it's just a matter of getting home."

"Yes," said Glenna slowly.

Peter had the feeling that she was trying to be kind in her own way, and that stung a little, too.

"I suppose you're thinking about the other instances of us in time and reality," he said, trying to sound dignified. "But we only know that there's another one roughly when we arrived, which would seem to suggest that it's right here we need to be for Mordion. The extra instances around now are probably because we're trying to fix the problem!"

"We can work on that supposition while we're just trying to decide what to do next," said Glenna. "But do you think we could work on the supposition that there are multiple instances of us in time and reality when it comes to actually shifting, this time?"

"Of course," said Peter. He would have preferred that his voice didn't sound quite so stiff, but it was very hard to bear the justified warning. "Look, I don't think it has to be you doing the work on the tickerbox. I know how to fix the targeting myself."

"I know," Glenna had said, without giving up the ticker-box. "But I've been doing magic-assisted work for the last ten years, and we did decide that my work was likely to be the most precise, after all."

They *had* decided that on the way, though Peter wasn't quite sure how. He had found himself agreeing to a lot of incontrovertible statements that had somehow led, with a dreadful inevitability, to the fact that Glenna was the properest person to be doing repairs on the targeting system.

And so Peter found himself still watching hours later, with all the anxiety of a new parent, while Glenna constructed a complex and beautiful framework of magic around his tickerbox—which seemed perfectly happy to trot around on the inside of that framework and prod at the prettiest bits of it while Glenna worked.

Rather to his annoyance, the tickerbox showed no sign of trying either to fight or run when Glenna opened it to access the inner workings and replace the threads of magic-laced wire that connected the physical workings with the possibility of magic. Instead, it went perfectly still just as it did when he worked on its engine, curling its legs in on themselves.

"We'll have to watch that," said Glenna, nodding at the small pile of glittering magic the tickerbox had already assembled in one corner of its enclosure. "It took those from the workings I did. Obviously I'll fix it up before I start using the structure, but it does seem to have a habit of eating things it shouldn't eat."

"I know," Peter said. "I think it's trying to improve itself. It was trying to build itself another secondary engine a little while ago."

He found that Glenna was looking across at him with one brow up, and added defensively, "It's true!"

"I don't doubt it," she said, and went back to her working. "I was simply surprised that Headmaster Tarrant hadn't tried to take you aside and set you in the right way."

"He did," said Peter. "He also tried to get me to make friends with you."

"Yes," Glenna said, with a faint smile. "I remember."

"Is that—" Peter started, and stopped again.

"Is that why I was so reluctant to talk with you? Only partially. I know that Headmaster Tarrant is very fond of using people to connect himself with other people. I had one or two other reasons as well, but I will admit that I very much dislike it when people push me toward things for their own convenience."

"Oh," said Peter. He wasn't sure if he felt soothed or not. Fortunately, he was distracted from that not entirely comfortable statement by the fact that Glenna had finished everything that she had to do by hand, and was about to begin work with the structure she had put into place earlier.

He watched anxiously as she set magic coursing through the setup. He would have been willing to work with her at the University of Mechanics and Magic, but even in that time, he didn't see why working with her meant that she should be allowed to meddle with his previous handiwork.

"Do you think you could stop hovering?" asked Glenna. "You're getting in my light."

Peter restrained himself from retorting and sat down again. From where he was, he could clearly see what she was doing: the fact that she was pouring even more magic into his tickerbox left him extremely uncomfortable. The fact that the way she was doing it meant that the magic was merely a workman and a structure around the actual work being done fascinated and annoyed him in equal measure. If he had begun to experiment with magic-built yet magic-less clockwork, Glenna had very nearly mastered it.

The feeling was very akin to having a favoured toy taken from him. Peter didn't like that feeling, but he liked even less the fact that, having recognised it for what it was, he knew he was capable of feeling such a puerile annoyance.

"I *will* try to squeeze as much of the magic out as possible before I give it back," said Glenna, without looking at him. "So you can stop looking so worried."

Peter looked out the window instead, trying not to fiddle. The streets of Civet were far busier than he would have expected at this time of night—more so because he had expected, with his knowledge of what must already have happened, that Civet would be preparing to march on Parras with the help of an enchanted army. If he had expected anything, it would have been that life would have ceased its natural flow, but most of the people outside seemed to be doing something that included food, the university not excepted: walking with food, setting up a cart with food, studying with food beside them, playing games with food.

"Maybe they don't know what's about to happen," he muttered to himself.

"I fancy the royal family kept it very much quiet," said Glenna, surprising him by attending to what he was saying. "I should, if I were about to suck the magic out of an enchantress and use it to enhance an army."

Peter turned back to watch her, and saw the structure she had put in place drawing out magic from the tickerbox swiftly and effectively. Mere glimmers remained when Glenna said, "I'm afraid that's all I can draw out without rendering the connections between clockwork and magic ineffective."

Peter didn't like to say it was better than he had ever managed to do with the tickerbox, so he only said, "That's enough, thanks."

"Very well," she said, and drew a hand over the top of her structure.

Peter opened his mouth to protest that he wanted to look more at the structure, but it was too late: it collapsed in a spun-sugar pile of thatch, and scattered in Glenna's general direction. She gathered the pieces toward herself as if she were sweeping up crumbs, and they disappeared beneath her hands.

When she was finished, she dusted off her hands, and leaned forward to observe the unmoving tickerbox. It had not moved since it curled its legs in on themselves, and now didn't so much as twitch.

"Hm," said Glenna, entirely unembarrassed. "I may have over-estimated my own skills with your mechanics. I did think that should work."

"Let it settle for a while," Peter said, taken aback at the ease with which Glenna could admit that she might have made a mistake. "The tickerbox is a bit funny about new things added if it's not the one who adds them. It takes it a while to get along with the new pieces."

"I see," she said thoughtfully. "I suppose if someone gave me an extra leg I might take a while to learn how to walk again. I thought it might be the extra little bit I added."

Peter felt the hairs stand up on the back of his neck. "*What extra little bit?*"

"There's no need to panic," said Glenna, rather amused. "It's just a diagnostic. You're always having to open it up to see what's wrong, so I've put in something like what I did for the school: a representation of the whole. You should be able to track changes in the box."

"Oh," Peter said, shifting in his seat. There was very little he could say about that: it was something he would have done himself, if he'd known how to do it. Again, he found himself forced to say, "Thanks."

Glenna set the tickerbox in the centre of the table and Peter saw the endmost sections of its legs twitch, a familiar and hopeful sign. Glenna must have seen it, too, because she sat back, satisfied.

"Once we're able to target times again, what should we do, do you think?"

Peter, surprised and rather pleased to be asked, opened his mouth to say what he thought, and realised belatedly that he had no more idea than Glenna. "I don't know," he said.

She grinned at him. "Neither do I. It's all very well for Rorkin to tell us that we need to be picking up stitches or whatever it is, but I don't really know *how* we're supposed to do that. There was obviously another instance of us already around this time, and it would be comforting to think that they've already done something about Mordion, but it sounds like that sort of thing isn't working very well at the moment."

"I suppose so," said Peter gloomily, but he felt a little bit cheered by Glenna's smile, despite that. "What do we do first, then? Find Mordion?"

"I think so," said Glenna. "We need to know exactly what he's up to. The Sleeping Princess, too, I suppose: if there's anywhere that something has gone wrong, it would have to be with what he's doing with her. She's his power source, after all."

"Yes," Peter slowly. He hadn't really thought about it seriously up until now, but now that he was in the right time, it occurred to him that he could possibly prevent what happened to Poly in the past.

"Don't even think about it," Glenna advised him.

Guiltily, Peter asked, "Don't think about what?"

"You're thinking that it would be nice to stop what happened to her, aren't you? You can't, though."

"I know," said Peter. "It's supposed to be in the timeline, and a lot of things are attached to it. But—"

"That's not exactly what I meant," she said, tilting her head to watch the tickerbox as it cautiously stretched and retracted its legs. "I meant that she probably wouldn't thank you for stopping her meeting Luck, no matter what she went through to get there."

"Not to mention Onepiece," agreed Peter. Onepiece might be ridiculously overpowered and far more trouble than he was worth, but Peter knew Poly didn't think so. "All right. But how are we supposed to know where what he *was* planning and what he *is* planning now diverge from each other? That's the exact bit of time we need to find."

"That's what I mean, too," said Glenna. "He learns everything while he's in the process of stealing her magic, doesn't he? That's the big incursion Rorkin was talking about. So we need to go to that exact time if we want to separate what he was doing from what he's doing now."

Peter shifted his shoulders uneasily. It was odd and uncomfortable to think that while he and Glenna were sitting here fixing his tickerbox, Mordion was somewhere in the castle nearby, stealing after Poly with that noiseless, catlike tread of his, waiting to do his mischief.

It made a kind of sour taste cling to the back of his mouth.

"What do you think he's doing right now?" he asked Glenna.

Glenna looked up from the tickerbox at him, and then

past him. Her face went quite blank. "Wandering through the university, it seems."

"What?" Peter twisted in his seat, but Glenna's hand, seizing his collar, stopped him in the action.

"Don't look!" she hissed at him. "And *don't* do that with your magic! It's so noticeable!"

"We're supposed to be investigating him!" said Peter beneath his breath, but he drew back the questing magic he had instinctively formed before it could advance too far toward Mordion.

"Yes, but he'll be looking for us. He's already seen something of the future and we don't know how much of it he saw."

"All right," Peter said. "That's fair. He could know our faces already."

"Well, yes, but I was thinking more that he'd be especially likely to recognise our magic," she said. "What a good thing we have Rorkin's spell! We'll have to be careful how we approach him."

"And it's probably best if we don't approach him right now," agreed Peter. "All right, you can let go, Glenna. I'm not going to turn around."

She released him, and Peter was left with a rather cold feeling where her hand had warmed. He hadn't ever thought of himself as a coward before, but that cold feeling didn't restrict itself to his collar: he had had to deal with Mordion before, and he had not been the one to overcome the man. If he had been alone, he was quite certain he wouldn't have survived that encounter. It made him less certain of himself this time.

Mindful of Glenna's warning, Peter didn't turn around, but he did catch a glimpse of Mordion out of the corner of his eye as the man moved toward one of the other entrances. Like Samuel back at the University of Mechanics and Magic, he seemed to have collected a coterie as he walked, and that coterie followed him as he left the hall without a backward look.

Glenna, who had sat up very straight and picked up the tickerbox between her hands when Mordion first appeared, relaxed very slightly.

"I don't think he saw us," said Peter cautiously. "Should we—do you think we should try to follow him?"

Glenna hesitated before she said: "I don't think we should count on him not having seen us just yet. Mordion is…very tricky."

"I know," Peter said, trying not to sound stiff about it. "I've already fought him once. Well, mostly it was my friend who fought him."

"The Queen Heir," she said, nodding. "Yes, I heard about that. One day you'll have to tell me about it. I'm curious to know a few things that they didn't tell me about."

So there *had* been talk about him before he got to the university! Not that it really mattered now, but Peter couldn't stop himself from asking, "Did you ask them about me?"

Glenna put the tickerbox down very carefully in the middle of the table and said after a very small pause, "A friend of mine mentioned that you might be coming to the university and told me to keep an eye out for you. He knew I was interested in Mordion and in time travel, so he thought we might have something in common."

"Wait," said Peter, because he had just realised something other than the almost-too-distracting fact that Glenna had, in fact, been asking about him before he arrived at the university. "You're talking like you know Mordion, too."

"Every child in the Two Monarchies knows about Mordion," said Glenna quietly.

"Yes, but you're talking about him like you *know* him," Peter said. He looked at her more closely, and came to the conclusion that she was, as she had earlier said about Rorkin, looking distinctly shifty. "You do, don't you?"

"You and the Queen Heir aren't the only ones who fought with him and survived," Glenna said, even more quietly. "Nor is the Sleeping Princess. Once I did, too."

"You—*when?*" asked Peter blankly. "Poly and Luck ran him out of the Capital about seven or eight years ago in our own time, and you told me you were Luck's next-door neighbour before that, so you can't have seen him in the Capital."

"My mother is from the Capital," Glenna said. "And it was when I was just a baby. I suppose you could say that he's my father."

"What?" asked Peter stupidly.

"Oh, not biologically," said Glenna. "Though he might as well have been. He's the reason my magic is jinxed."

Peter very narrowly stopped himself from saying that it was impossible either for a baby to face Mordion, or for anyone's magic to be jinxed because of someone else, and found that Glenna was watching him with that faint smile again.

"Have a pastry," she said, pushing one across the table at him. "That must have been very hard for you."

Peter laughed before he was aware that he had. "How did that happen?" he asked instead. "I've never heard of someone being jinxed because of a person before—although I didn't know it was possible for a jinx to actually adhere to a person, either, so… I wouldn't have thought that a baby could face Mordion, though. I remember exactly what it took to—well, what it's going to take to imprison him in the castle, and I don't see how a baby could do that."

"Mordion bit off more than he could chew," said Glenna. There was still a humorous quirk to her mouth, but her eyes were distant and sad. "He was trying to gather a bit of power in the same way he did with the Sleeping Princess, but he didn't know my mother was pregnant. He didn't know the magic he was looking for was mine and not my mother's, either. He might not even have known it was antimagic instead of magic that I had."

"He's not originally a very strong magic user," Peter said, nodding. "He wouldn't have been able to differentiate."

"The process was enough to kill my mother," Glenna said. "But at least it meant Mordion didn't get his hands on my antimagic."

Peter didn't know quite what to say, so he said, "I suppose you got the jinx because your mother was trying to protect you."

"No," said Glenna; but at Peter's confusion, she added, "She was trying to protect me, but that isn't why my magic has a jinx attached. It attached to me because Mordion was trying to take magic he thought was my mother's when it was mine, and because baby me was trying to protect my mother. That's why I said I've fought him before. It made an odd sort of connection that didn't fit anywhere and turned quite a few things inside out, the antimagic included."

"That's what Poly said a jinx is like, too," said Peter. "But wait, if your mother was still pregnant with you, how did you survive?"

"There was a decent midwife nearby," Glenna said. "He was also a pretty good magic user, too, so he managed to detangle me from my mother before I followed her."

She paused for a moment before she offered: "It's the reason I became interested in time travel. When I was younger, I wanted to go back to the time before my mother was attacked and try to stop it from happening."

It hadn't occurred to Peter that someone could be interested in time travel in order to change something rather than just for the sake of it. He said, "Wouldn't that make a hole as big as the one I've already made? I mean, with it being Mordion and everything."

"Yes, so I was led to believe," she said. "I met someone last year, when I first started really experimenting—"

"Rorkin?"

"No," she said. "*Must* you keep interrupting? If you don't want to know, I'll just stop talking about it."

"No!" said Peter hastily. He had begun to be very interested indeed. "Sorry. Please go on."

"They told me that it would be much better if I didn't try to change things that had to do with Mordion, since it was possible it could affect the entire history of the Two Monarchies. I was made to understand that a lot of things, the welfare of the Sleeping Princess included, rested on things remaining exactly as they are."

"Did they tell you that you couldn't fix your own jinx?" Peter asked indignantly, angry on her behalf. "What rot! There must be ways of doing it that don't cause huge holes in time and reality, especially now that we've already gone back. We can't do worse than we've already done, anyway."

"I've been wondering about that," murmured Glenna.

"I suppose you think I'm going to do something worse," said Peter, still indignant, but for different reasons now. "Well, for your information—"

"I'm more worried about the both of us doing something awful," Glenna said mildly. "We don't interact particularly well, and the mix of your ridiculously strong magic and my jinx creates rather a potent chance for things to go very wrong."

"Oh," said Peter, taken aback. "Well. We can at least ask a few questions around the castle and university, anyway. We don't have to rush into doing any magic just yet. Why don't we try to follow Mordion and see what he's up to?"

"I'm sure we'll be able to find him later," said Glenna. "Right now I rather want to do a few more checks on the ambient particles in the air. Rorkin said it was easy for me to test and find out what time we're in, but the readings I took when we first got here are slightly different from the readings I took just before we came into the university tonight."

"It's probably just all the magic that's being done around here," Peter said. "They're playing with magic all the time, by the looks of this place. I shouldn't be surprised if they were experimenting with natural antimagic and unmagic, too. It's bound to throw off your calculations."

He stopped to try and fairly consider Glenna's point of view, and added, "I mean, it should be easy enough to find Mordion again, considering how popular he seems to be around the place, but I'm not sure we need to be fussing with the particles in the air at this point."

"Normally, I'd agree," said Glenna. There was a crease between her brows, and unusually, she chewed on her lip. "And it *could* be something to do with the atmosphere around here, but I did make allowances. Besides that, we've already gone wrong more than once when it comes to the targeting of the tickerbox, and Mordion is far trickier than people tend to think."

"Yes, but he doesn't know we're *here*," said Peter. "He saw his future, that's all—maybe our faces at the most. Rorkin said it was the working he did with Poly's magic that gave him an insight to the two of us, but that would only have shown what we did in the future, now where we are now."

"Yes," she said. "But I do think we ought to check everything before we go doing anything we might regret later."

"All right," said Peter. She might be right, after all, and even if she wasn't, he didn't particularly want a repeat of what had happened earlier in the stableyard. Better to humour her right now. "Then I'll see if I can program the tickerbox the way we'll need to program it if we have to go anywhere else, and you see what you can find out about Mordion. The fellows around here seem happier to talk to you than they are to talk to me."

Glenna surprised him by grinning. "That's because you're a bit too young to look interesting to them," she said. "No one likes a young upstart who's far too clever."

"And I suppose everyone likes a pretty girl who is far too clever," he retorted, grinning back at her.

"That," said Glenna, laughing, "depends very greatly on the person! I'll see what I can find out. Do you need anything else from the parts table before I go?"

"I'll get them myself, if I do," Peter said hastily. He would very much rather be engaged with the tickerbox than in watching Glenna charm half the young men in the room. She'd already set the room by the ears just by the mere fact of her presence, and he didn't find that a particularly enjoyable thing to watch.

He set himself to work on the tickerbox's secondary engine once again while she wandered around the room, and kept his head down, ignoring the sudden buzz of noise to the hall. He heard Glenna laugh a few times, and ignored that, too.

He had almost forgotten everything else in the soothing familiarity of working on his tickerbox by the time Glenna wafted back toward the table at which he was working. She leaned over the table to allow her gaze to linger on the nearly complete engine, and gave the smallest of nods.

"It's nearly done," Peter said, turning his eyes back on his work with the faintly irritated knowledge that he had felt gratified by her approval. "What did that lot have to say?"

"They say he's been pretty close with the royal family over the last few months," Glenna said, sliding back into the seat across from him. "Even living there and being called into meetings that would normally only be for royalty and advisors. Everyone's very impressed with his cleverness and pretty much everyone thinks he's up to something right now. Most of them seem to be excited to see what it is, but there's a few who aren't so sure, if I'm right."

"We're going for the castle, then?"

"If he's living there now, we'd probably better. The enchanted army is due to be marching any day now—we think." Glenna stopped, and Peter saw that she was chewing her lip again. "Peter, the readings are still off and I don't know why. There's something odd here that we need to be sure of before we do any targeting."

"What time do your readings say we're at now?"

"Here and now, they suggest we've arrived just before the princess is cursed."

"Well then!" Peter said, rather surprised. "I'd call that a good thing. We were surprised about how normal life looked out there: you must have taken wrong readings at first."

"I don't think so."

"And it means that Mordion wouldn't recognise us, anyway!" Peter added, brightening. "Because he hasn't seen us yet!"

"Yes, but if my first readings were correct and we get the targeting wrong next time we use the tickerbox—"

"We don't need to worry about targeting just yet, anyway," said Peter. "Right now, we just want to make sure we're ready to do something when Mordion starts his working."

"Yes, but—" Glenna stopped, and sighed faintly. "All right, we'll need to think about that when we get to the right time, anyway. Have you thought about what we're going to do to stop him seeing the future?"

"I thought we could do some sort of working around what he's doing with Poly to stop him getting a look at the future."

"Yes, the fact that he can see it seems to be the biggest problem," she said, frowning. "But we might have to try disconnecting the two incidents rather than just trying to block him seeing the other incident. The connection is the important thing."

"Look, I know that you're good at seeing Interconnectedness of All Things," said Peter, though he was still highly sceptical about that, "but are you confident enough to try and interfere with a hole in time and reality?"

Glenna's lips twitched. "I'm not terribly inclined to link

confidence and skill when it comes to theories of Interconnectedness," she said. "But in all honesty, I'm not looking forward to it. We know we don't have just a single chance to fix it—we've got the tickerbox, after all—but I do think it will become significantly harder to fix once Mordion knows we're here. We're really fortunate right now: he doesn't seem to have seen us. We should try to use that advantage."

"I'm not saying we shouldn't use it: I just think we're better off trying something that's less complicated. And something with more research backing it, actually."

"Whose research?" asked Glenna, but she was smiling still. "All right, it looks like we're going to have to talk about it a bit more before we decide what we're going to do. We should at least make sure we're both agreed before we do anything. We already know we can make a decent, powerful bit of magic when we work together, so that shouldn't be a problem."

"All right," agreed Peter. "Then we'll go track down Mordion first, and make sure we know where we need to be at the right time."

The tickerbox, as though it approved of the idea, twitched its front legs and made a small chirp.

"Hm," said Glenna suspiciously. "It does come around more quickly after you've been working on it. How impolite. Very well; we'll start with the castle tomorrow. For tonight, I'll take a few more readings. I've a feeling that when things begin moving, they'll move quite fast, and I'd like to be ready."

"I THOUGHT IT WOULD BE MUCH HARDER TO GET INTO THE castle," Peter said the next day, frowning. There had been more guards as they approached the higher streets from which entrance could be gained to the castle surrounds, but none of them had tried to stop him and Glenna, despite the fact that Rorkin's spell had worn off sometime during the night.

Nor had the ones at the gates made a move to ask them

for identification, as they did for one or two other would-be entrants, and despite the powerful magic that Glenna had done earlier to make them understandable and able to understand, he couldn't sense any sort of alarm going off as that magic was noticed.

Peter felt, in fact, uneasy and twitchy, as if something was going to go wrong suddenly but he didn't know what. He added, "I know they were still experimenting with magic at this stage, but I did think they would have had enough trouble with magic and enemies that they'd have some pretty good wards on the castle."

"They do," Glenna said. "Really clever ones, too; they're in the stones, nice and deep, and dreadfully hard to see."

Peter formed a small, testing prong of magic to send out and explore, but Glenna elbowed him as they passed from the outer courtyard and into the first inner courtyard.

"Don't do that! I've got us hidden for now, but if you go sending out that sort of thing, they'll certainly notice!"

"*You've* got us hidden?"

"Yes," she said. "It's built into the translation spell. I told you this morning: it's not so much a translation spell as it is a perception and depth spell. It affects more than the language, and it affects perception of us as well as our perception."

Glenna had talked about it, but she had also talked about the particles in the air, and after a while Peter had stopped listening because it seemed as though she was talking to herself.

Now, he hunched his shoulders. "Is that why it feels so odd and itchy?"

She threw him a look that was as much amusement as it was surprise. "Oh, you can feel that? It's not the spell itself; you're feeling what the jinx feels like. Pleasant, isn't it?"

"Not very," Peter said, shortly.

"Have you been feeling it all along?"

"No; just now when we got into the castle. It must be because the castle tickled it up a bit."

"Interesting. Harry never felt it, even when the spell was being taxed." She seemed to think about that for a moment or two before she shrugged and added, "But then, I suppose his magic isn't as strong as yours, either."

"Why were you friends with him, if he wasn't a very strong magic user? He wouldn't be much use to you, would he?"

"I don't pick my friends based on their use," Glenna said, with a rather chilling note to her voice. "Oh, and while I'm still thinking of it, the spell won't keep us hidden as well as Rorkin's did. It's working hard enough just to make people think we belong here and make us able to understand the language. Try not to do anything to make people watch us, all right?"

"Of course not," Peter said, a little bit stiffly. "I'm not stupid, you know!"

"I know," said Glenna, sighing faintly. "That's what makes things so difficult."

Peter was about to respond to that, fairly crossly, when he saw a familiar figure in a grey dress, her hair chopped short and uneven, sweeping down one of the covered walkways across the courtyard from himself and Glenna.

"Poly!" he said, with a sharp, jagged pain of longing. They had arrived in time! They had arrived in time, but he still wouldn't be able to help Poly. "There she is! No, *this* way, Glenna!"

He would have liked to charge across the courtyard to intercept her on the walkway, but he had just pooh-poohed the notion that he would do any such thing to Glenna. Instead, he pulled Glenna after him, perpendicular to the achingly familiar figure of Poly as she walked.

"All right, I'm coming!" Glenna said. "You can't rush us here and there without making us noticeable!"

"I'm just walking," argued Peter, though he slowed his step a little. Poly walked very quickly, just like he was used to, with a business-like bounce to her step, and he didn't want to run the chance of losing her. "Hurry up, Glenna! She went up that walkway—I think she's going deeper into the castle."

He didn't wait to see that she was following him as he turned onto the section of covered walkway that Poly had also turned onto. She was not too far ahead, but she wasn't slowing down, either, and if she turned down any of the other walkways, it would be far too easy to lose her.

As he stepped up his pace once again, Peter felt a strong, slender hand close around his forearm.

"Wait," said Glenna jerkily. "There's something gone wrong with the particles in the air."

"What?" he asked in a low voice, trying very hard not to sound impatient. They would lose Poly if they didn't hurry. "Is it something that'll affect us?"

"No," she said. "But it shouldn't be happening and it's making me feel…odd."

"Then keep holding onto my arm and let's keep going," he said. "We don't want to lose her."

"All right," Glenna said. "But we'd best be careful. My jinx is very happy and that's never a good sign."

Sometimes, Peter thought, trying to be understanding, sometimes Glenna was just a bit too sensitive for her own good. It was likely that she was a stronger magic user than he was, but the downside of that was her sensitivity to things other people might not notice. It was a good thing they'd stayed together, if she was likely to be overcome by things like that.

He moved Glenna's hand to tuck into the crook of his arm where it would be easiest to support her, and kept going after Poly. She had been out buying something, he was quite sure: there were a couple of bulges in her front apron pocket, and he had heard the very faint jingle of coin across the courtyard earlier.

He tried to walk just a little bit more quickly, and began to gain on her, Glenna a determined but dragging influence on his right arm. As they drew near, there was a flutter of deep blue and someone who had been waiting between the colonnades intercepted Poly.

Peter found himself whirled away behind one of the columns by Glenna, who did so with surprising strength, if imperfect balance. Narrowly avoiding a tangle of skirts and legs that would have seen them sprawling on the flagstones outside the general walkway, Peter sagged against the marble and tried to convince himself that he was too much of a gentleman to tell Glenna that her elbow was making an uncomfortable point somewhere in the region of his stomach and that her hair was in his mouth.

Glenna whispered in his ear, "Put your arms around me, idiot!"

"What?" said Peter, trying very hard not to cough on the far-too-sudden breath he'd taken in.

"There's a pageboy staring at us!" she hissed.

"I'm fairly sure that'll just make him stare more," he protested, but did as he was told. The pageboy grinned and pretended to look away, and Peter felt his face grow warm.

Glenna's voice said crossly in his ear, "Yes, but at least then there's a reason for us to be hiding behind part the colonnade!"

"Oh! Right!"

"Now, lean back *just* a little more," she instructed encouragingly. "I want to see Mordion. If I can see him, I'm pretty sure we'll be able to hear him."

Peter, who was swiftly finding that Glenna in his arms was just as overwhelming as Glenna glaring at him from across a desk, but in a wholly different way, said weakly, "What?"

before he quite grasped what she said, and then leaned back too suddenly in an effort to catch up.

"Good heavens," said Glenna, staggering a little as she gripped his collar. "You were so steady just a few minutes ago!"

"You're heavier than I expected," Peter said, without thinking about it. It wasn't so much that Glenna was heavy—she was simply very real right now, and the effort of holding her had made not just his face but his neck hot and, he was quite certain, very red.

There was a sputter of laughter around his ear that made Peter swallow rather hard, and Glenna said softly, "I really do wonder if you make an effort to be offensive or if you just can't help it. Oh bother! They're moving!"

They managed to disentangle themselves from skirts and column without worse incident than Peter stepping on Glenna's shoeless foot, and followed the stiffly uncomfortable Poly, whose hand Mordion had put on his own arm.

Peter saw her pull away a moment later, and that made him very happy. He still remembered the way Mordion had called Annabel *darling* all the time; the edge of contempt and dismissal underpinning it.

At the same time, Glenna said a deeply satisfied, "*Good.* What a pity we can't hit him!"

She was still leaning on Peter's arm for balance, so the energy with which she said it made Peter grin.

Mordion, watching Poly walk away, called over a page. Peter heard the page address him as *Grand Mage* and tried not to snort: whatever else he was, Mordion wasn't a real mage. Any real power he had in the past or present or future had always been stolen from someone else.

He didn't see what Mordion gave to the page: it was small and not remotely magical, as far as Peter could tell. Then Mordion strolled away through an archway through which Peter could see the shadowed greenery of a courtyard garden.

"Should we follow him, or the page?" he asked Glenna, who was beginning to look a little more steady on her feet.

"The page," she said, without hesitation. "He was giving him something to take back to his quarters, I think. And if he's not going to be there, we might as well have a look around while he's not."

Either the particles in the air had steadied once more, or Glenna had simply become used to them, because she started after the page without waiting for him, her step nearly as business-like as normal, and Peter followed after. They tracked the page up several winding sets of stairs and fairly deep into the castle, though they were still outside what Peter would have thought of as the nobles' quarters, until at last the boy entered a room on the north-facing side of the castle.

He was in there only a moment or two before he slipped out again, and as he passed them to go back down the corridor, Peter saw the frown on Glenna's face that mirrored his own.

"No lock," she said softly, when the page was out of hearing and they stood before the door.

"No, but there's a bit of magic on the handle," Peter said, ducking his head to look at the spell. He gazed at it for a few moments before he whistled in surprise. "Oh, that's interesting! It looks like he doesn't care about who gets into his rooms so long as he knows who it was. That's the only magical security I can see."

"Me too," said Glenna, after a moment. She added, decidedly, "We'll have to do something about that, then. I'd much rather he didn't know we were here."

Peter grinned. "That's easy to do."

He set the tickerbox on the handle with its spindly legs, and the door opened by a small crack. Peter pushed it open further with his shoe, avoiding brushing the handle as he passed into the room, and Glenna did the same, careful to hold her skirts close to her legs as she entered.

They found themselves in a large bedroom suite with a few grand pieces of wooden furniture for clothing and two windows; pleasant and light-filled, it was furnished and decorated richly. This was a suite for someone of reasonably great importance.

"It must be his quarters," said Peter, looking around. "We'd best take a look around: we'll probably need to get in here at some stage if we're to stop him seeing things he shouldn't see."

Two doors led from the main room on either side of the room: one to some sort of ablutions chamber, that was laughably primitive to Peter's critical eye, and another to a room even larger than the main one. This room was well warded and abundantly provided for in spells of every kind: things that would be useful to someone who didn't really have much magic of his own and was meting out what he had stolen from others to last until he could get more.

Toward the back of the room was a single chair, and that was warded, too; perhaps more strongly than the room itself.

"This is the room," Peter said, with the feeling that the air had suddenly become colder. "Poly says they found her in the princess' room, but this was the room she told me about: it's warded up to the ceiling."

"That was useful of her," said Glenna.

It was nothing that Peter hadn't already thought to himself, but he fancied there was a slightly sarcastic—or perhaps merely sharp—note to her voice.

"Yes, it jolly well was!" he said. "She must have been trying to tell me enough without telling me too much."

"This is the room, but when is the time?" asked Glenna. "And *why* is it different in here?"

Peter frowned and gazed around the room. It looked the same as it had looked when they first entered; there was also no difference that he could feel between being in this room and being out in the halls, apart from a certain warmth that could be explained by the fact that there was a window in this room.

"What are you talking about?"

"It's changed again," said Glenna, with a helpless note to her voice that Peter had never yet heard. "The content of the particle mass in the air has changed *again.*"

"It's a good thing we already know when we are, then," Peter said, trying not to be impatient. "Glenna, we already know that things are unravelling from the future; you can't be sure that all of your tests will be helpful anymore."

"That would only apply if the changes were coming from the past," she said. "And it's unlikely to affect natural laws, either. The future might well be in flux, but it'll be happening according to the natural laws already in place."

"All right, well, maybe you're not interpreting the results correctly."

"I am," she said shortly. "It's not at all complicated. The levels of free magic, antimagic, and unmagic are both seasonal and cumulative, and while they can affect weather systems, they're not affected by weather systems. At this stage of the year and at this distance from the beginning of all things, there are certain things I would expect to see. I would *not* expect to see that level change enough from hour to hour to suggest that it's a completely different week. *Or* from room to room."

"What time does this room seem to be?"

"The same as when we first arrived here: a few days after the attack on the Sleeping Princess."

"All right," he said, "but we just saw Poly down in the courtyards, and I can hear music and see everyone still going about their lives. It's *got* to be your readings being wrong!"

"There is certainly something wrong," said Glenna, frowning.

"All right, but there's meant to be something wrong! We're here to fix it!"

Peter saw her open her mouth, then close it again, and bitterly resented those unspoken words.

"I *know*," he said. "We're not here to fix the problem, the problem needs to be fixed because we're *here*."

"I didn't say that," she said. "We'd better leave before Mordion comes back, anyway. We can talk about what we're going to do to stop him after we get out of the castle. I don't like talking too much about it here in his room."

Peter would have liked to argue with that, but it made sense to leave while Mordion still didn't know they were around, as much as he would have liked to study the room in more detail. He had the feeling that Glenna had a lot more yet to say on the subject.

❀ 9 ❀

"I'll do some readings of the particle content of the air in a minute or two if you're happy to go and get us some lunch," Glenna said, when they were safely back in their hayloft.

Peter would have preferred to stay in the open air, but there were a few too many curious stablehands around the place for comfort.

"It's more like afternoon tea at this stage," he opined. He thought it pretty bad form of Glenna to be so very concerned with food when the world was falling apart. Still, his own stomach was growling, and at least if he went to get food he wouldn't have to listen to her muttering about the particles in the air. "All right, if you're just going to be doing tests, I might as well."

He would rather be doing anything than sitting around in the hay while Glenna did tests.

In view of that preference, Peter allowed himself to wander a bit in search of food, and even to ask someone what the date was. It earned him a strange look, and an even stranger answer that reminded him that the calendar had changed not ninety years after this particular time, and that he had no idea how to convert that date into anything approaching understandability.

Then, with a good half-hour of strolling behind him, and the last sun of the triad nearly overhead in the sky as a splendidly warm late afternoon, he reluctantly returned to the stables to find Glenna still in the hayloft.

"Oh good!" she said, when she saw him. "I was beginning to think someone had robbed you. I have good news and bad news. Give me some of that bread and cheese and I'll tell you about it."

Peter sat down warily. "What's the good news?"

"The particle content of the air appears to have settled again."

"All right," he said cautiously. "Then what's the bad news?"

"It's settled back to the same point it was at when we arrived—which suggested several days after the attack on the sleeping princess—so we still don't know exactly when we are."

Peter groaned. "I thought we'd finished discussing this," he said.

"No, you just went for a walk," said Glenna.

"Then I suppose it's good that we already know when we are when it comes to the historical timeline," Peter said pointedly. He was trying very hard not to remember the soft tickle of Glenna's hair at his collar earlier in the castle, or the warmth of her arm against his. Greatly to his surprise, it was a difficult enterprise when he could see her right across from him. "We shouldn't need to wander too far away to fix up the hole."

"I'm not so sure," Glenna said, linking her fingers in her lap. "I don't know if it's because time is damaged or if it's something else, but this morning in the castle, from time to time, we appeared to be just a day before the attack on the sleeping princess, and this afternoon my results would have it that we're roughly three days after it. I'd like to do a full-length test to make sure exactly when it is we've arrived before we go too much further with stopping whatever it is that Mordion is up to."

"We *know* we can't be in the time after the attack!" Peter said. He was rather tired of discussing Glenna's current bother when everything they had seen this morning pointed to the certainty that the attack on Poly had not yet happened. "The army hasn't marched on Parras yet. Everyone is still out there doing their jobs! And judging from where we saw Poly this morning, we should be just in time to do something about Mordion, but we can't do it if we sit here doing test after test."

"I don't want to do test after test; just one big test. It might take a little longer, but it will be worth it to make sure that we haven't arrived too late to do anything right here."

Peter tried very hard not to sigh. "We *saw* Poly earlier! She hasn't even been attacked yet!"

"I know," Glenna said. She looked as though she was trying very hard to be polite, and Peter found that he resented that. It suggested that he was being unreasonable and difficult, and he was quite certain he was being neither. "But there's something off with the anti-magic and unmagic particles in this particular bit of time that I really should look at before we try to do anything against Mordion. I feel as though time isn't quite right here. At the very least, we need to be sure that we're not playing into Mordion's games before we act."

"He doesn't even know we're here," Peter said. "You said he didn't see us."

"I did," she said. "But I'd like to make sure of a few things before we do anything. There are some other qualities I can check if I have the time."

"If we wait too long—"

"I *know*. But it will only take a day to do the full test. If we get this wrong, it'll be far worse than losing a day, I'm certain."

"I don't see how you can be certain about that," Peter said exasperatedly. "If we do something wrong, well, we've still got the tickerbox! We can target another time or two more before we have to worry about the wires burning out, and we can get the wire we need if we don't stray too far from here."

"You could say the same thing about waiting a day," Glenna pointed out. "Look, just let me run my tests this evening; we'll be able to check on them late tonight."

"By then it might be too late!"

"But that's what we're really after, isn't it?" asked Glenna. "Not Mordion-before-he-does-something-out-of-order, but Mordion-once-he-does-something-different. It's loose threads and dropped stitches that we need to be finding and fixing up."

"It's *better*," said Peter crossly, wishing he didn't feel quite so hot in the face, "to fix problems *before* they happen."

Crisply, Glenna said, "You can't fix something that hasn't yet happened. That's nonsense, even with time travel. You can try to prevent it, but since it needs to happen before it can be fixed—! And I *do* think that we came here for a particular reason, which brings me back to the point that we need to be quite a lot surer about *when* we are before we try to fix what we did."

"All right, fine!" Peter said in exasperation, giving up on eating at all. "You do your tests and your checks! I'm going for a walk!"

"Just make sure you don't walk toward the castle," Glenna said, with one brow slightly raised.

"Of course not!" snapped Peter, who had in fact been going to do that very thing. "I'm not planning on leaving you here, if that's what you're afraid of!"

"No," she said, with a rather bittersweet smile. "I don't think you could do that if you wanted to. Make sure you don't get seen, all right?"

"I'm not *stupid*," said Peter, and marched as best he could down the hayloft ladder.

TECHNICALLY SPEAKING, IT WASN'T TOWARD THE CASTLE BUT the university that he went. The university and the castle might be joined, but they weren't one building, and if Peter went toward the university Glenna couldn't protest that he had done what he said he wouldn't do.

There was also a chance that Mordion would be in the university again, and Peter very much wanted to be prepared to observe him if possible. Despite the bee in Glenna's bonnet, it was clear that they had arrived just before the attack on Poly, and he was determined that if he were given the opportunity to investigate Mordion further, he would take it, no matter where it led and no matter what Glenna said.

As he approached the grand building, however, Peter spied a blue-vested figure exiting the university with an unhurried, familiar step. Mordion, passing easily between strolling pedestrians and avoiding the nastier parts of the cobbled roads, unhurriedly made his way down the street toward Peter.

Peter, drawing in a deep breath, forced himself to keep walking toward the university. There was nothing to worry about, after all: Glenna's spell was still perfectly functional, and unless Mordion really did know about them already, there wasn't a chance he would be able to see Peter unless Peter called attention to himself by talking to him.

The certain knowledge didn't make it any easier for Peter to keep walking, and when Mordion passed him without so much as a twitch of discomfort, it was a great relief. Peter allowed himself the luxury of taking in a few, calming breaths before he turned quietly and followed the man, careful to move just as unhurriedly as Mordion. Despite the fact that he was certain the man didn't yet know about them, he was as well aware as Glenna that Mordion was sharper than a newly-whet knife.

It was something of a trek through the city; Peter followed Mordion for a good hour before the man entered a small establishment with a mix of sweets and feathered decorations in the windows. By then, Mordion seemed to be limping, which made Peter grin a little. Mordion didn't have enough of his own magic to comfortably shift, and he wouldn't waste the last reserves of what he had gained from someone else by shifting when he could walk. Neither, if he was up to no good, would he care to take any kind of transport with a driver who could swear to where he had been.

Peter lingered on the street for some time after Mordion entered the shop, still wary of being noticed. He didn't want to ruin things by a lack of cautiousness now, and he could see through the windows that Mordion still stood by the store's counter with the neatly pressed clerk.

While Peter waited, a second man entered the shop, the door swinging wide and slow behind him. As if he'd received a signal, the clerk disappeared, leaving Mordion to nod at the second man and follow him into a small booth at the side of the shop. As they did, Peter felt a surge of magic flare into life on the doorframe. There was a seal on it when he glanced at it; strong magic that had been activated from somewhere inside. As soon as the door shut, he wouldn't be able to get in without blowing the spell to smithereens.

Peter darted forward and caught the door before it quite closed, slipping through in an instant and leaving it to shut naturally behind him again. To his relief, there was no sign of Mordion or the second man; they had disappeared into their booth and wouldn't have seen him enter even if they had been able to see through Glenna's workings.

He felt the seal on the door take up as he moved carefully

into the shop. Mordion and his companion shifted and settled in their booth, covering any sound that Peter himself made as he crossed the room, and as he took a position within the clerk's little boxed-in counter, Peter felt that he couldn't have asked for a better place in which to eavesdrop.

As Peter settled cautiously on a box behind the counter, Mordion, his voice gently mocking, asked, "Is this location far enough from the castle for you? Or should we, perhaps, have left the city entirely? I shouldn't like to ruin your enjoyment in this affair, after all."

"Some of the items you required," said the other man frostily, "are *illegal*. It wasn't fitting to supply them in the castle."

"Nothing is illegal to the crown," Mordion said. "They are above the law."

So the man was a royal envoy? Mordion's contact with the royal family?

"While *technically* that may be true—"

"The Family prefers that no one should be aware they are doing such things," agreed Mordion.

"You must understand that the Royal Family has nothing to do with this, officially."

"It will be rather hard to pull it off if they're not," Mordion said. "As I have already informed their majesties, this endeavour will require me setting things to spellpaper if they wish to have any control whatsoever over the power it produces."

There was a vague shuffling that Peter took to signify that the envoy was shifting uncomfortably. At last, the man said, "*Officially* the Royal Family is only concerned with acquiring a certain resource. How that resource is obtained is none of their affair. They will put their blood to any spellpaper that is required."

A chill spread down Peter's neck. He was sure they were

speaking of Poly—of the use they meant to make of her magic.

"I trust that you'll clear my wing of the castle in readiness for the process," Mordion said. His voice was mild, but Peter's ears pricked up.

So it *had* been as obvious as he had thought it must be! Even for a time when magic wasn't as widely used as his own time, any naturally magically inclined person would have sensed that something was wrong with the workings Mordion had done—*would* do. Too many questions being asked about the kind of magic about to be done in Mordion's rooms wasn't the sort of interest Mordion would like to encourage.

"Of course," said the royal envoy. "The Family doesn't wish anyone to be privy to the…the kind of thing that goes on when something of this sort happens."

"I'm less concerned about that and more concerned about someone using a portion of the power for themselves," said Mordion. "There will be enough of it coming out that it will be hard to monitor all of it; if someone senses that and decides to use it as a power source for their own ends, we'll lose power."

"Can't you stop that sort of thing?"

There was a silken movement; Mordion shrugging his shoulders, Peter rather thought. "I'm no enchanter," he said. "I can harness it and use it, but my sensing abilities aren't the best. I prefer to take no chances with such a powerful source."

That, thought Peter, rather triumphantly, was *bound* to come in useful. How delightful to have his suspicions confirmed to handily!

"I'll make sure every precaution is taken," said the envoy. "As I'm sure you understand, you can hardly be more concerned about the situation than the Family is."

"The Family has very little to worry about," Mordion said. There was a note of impatience to his voice. "All the difficulty is mine, as is all the peril. If something should go wrong while I'm harnessing this power, there will be very little I can do; the royal family certainly won't suffer any damage because of it."

It couldn't be anything else other than Poly, could it? Or had Mordion chosen other people for their power before Poly? He had to make sure he had all the facts, this time. It wouldn't do to make another mistake.

"It's the girl's birthday tomorrow," said Mordion. "I'll make the attempt this evening: when I return with these last few ingredients, as a matter of fact. I'd rather get to her before something as chancy as a birthday. Her magic is sleeping quite heavily and I don't want to run the chance of it waking up before we're ready to handle an enchantress as powerful and young Mistress Polyhymnia."

Peter, who had stiffened, felt a fizz of satisfaction. There! He knew they'd arrived in time! This evening was the last chance he would have to fix the hole before Mordion actually became aware of the hole they'd made. What a jolly good thing! They'd arrived just in time to stop Mordion from becoming aware of them.

The question was, how was he to do the thing? Whatever he did, it would certainly have to be done now; there was too much risk in trying to come back via the tickerbox once the Mordion in this time became aware of them. Nor would it be advisable to use the tickerbox to get into the suite while Mordion was doing his workings. Getting through the wards on the room once they started up would likely take up enough energy to burn through the wires he had just replaced, leaving him with no way of leaving again if things went badly wrong.

Delicately, the envoy said, "The Family has seen fit to inform me that if you should need assistance when it comes to a useful setup—"

Peter grinned. As if Mordion would want someone else's input when he was trying to raise all that power for himself!

Peter would be very much surprised if Mordion allowed anyone else in the rooms with him when he began the work.

"I've set up the room already," said Mordion, interrupting both the envoy and Peter's thoughts. "There's no need to concern yourself with that part of it. All you need to do is send someone to put the girl in there. She should be well and truly unconscious by now."

"You haven't left your rooms unguarded and unlocked?" the envoy said, in horror. "If somebody should go in there—!"

"If somebody were to go in there I would know," Mordion told him calmly. "I have some very specific magic in place to inform me when my perimeter is breached. The setup itself should tell a would-be prowler nothing useful, and for my part, I find it very much more useful to know who is interested in me than I do to keep them out of my suite."

"Surely stopping it from happening is more important than knowing who did it?"

"Not at all," said Mordion, and his voice was again amused. "Do you have anything else for me, or may we conclude this regrettably clandestine meeting?"

"I—well, I had supposed that—" The envoy trailed away and then said, rather stiffly, "I suppose not. I trust you know better than to shift directly from here to the castle?"

"I've no intention of wasting my strength," said Mordion. Then, surprising Peter with his openness, he added, "I've little enough energy left for this working; if the Family prefers things to be done so hastily, I'll save my strength for the important things. I'll purchase and make use of a shifting spell once I'm far enough away to allay your concern of being seen with me."

That brought on another series of throat-clearings and shufflings from the envoy, whose discomfort Mordion ignored. Peter, his mind whirring with as much speed as the cogs in his tickerbox, ignored the man, too, only ducking his head when Mordion rose and sauntered back toward the front door.

The seal on the front door shattered, sparks of magic flying, and Peter just barely stopped himself from jumping. The envoy, unprepared for such a sudden explosion of magic, wasn't so disciplined in his reaction, and both jumped and swore.

Relishing the distraction, Peter shifted himself without recourse to the tickerbox. In general, he preferred not to use magic when he could rely upon clockwork to do the same thing, but speed was of the essence, and he didn't want to run the risk of destroying the repairs he had made on the tickerbox by an overzealous excess of magic to ignite it into action. He still hadn't been able to replace that troublesome ignition button.

He found himself in the high street just before the castle entrance, and breathed a sigh of relief. Too close to the castle and he could have triggered their wards, too far and he wouldn't get to Mordion's rooms in time to do anything about the plan that was afoot.

There was no time to fetch Glenna, Peter told himself, sweeping through the gates. There was barely time to get to Mordion's chambers before the envoy had Poly sent around— or before Mordion himself got there again. Peter walked swiftly through the colonnades where denizens of the court clustered, ran through the hallways that were unpopulated, and arrived at last, breathless, at Mordion's door. He could already hear raised voices further down the hallways: the royal envoy clearing the area, no doubt.

Peter made the tickerbox open the door for him once again, and walked swiftly through the suite, casting a half-superstitious look around as he walked. Despite the sunshine that had gone with him until he entered the castle again, the sky outside the window showed a suddenly gloomy aspect that chilled him. He *almost* expected to see Mordion somewhere in the rooms even though he had left the man somewhere in the city.

There was no one there, of course, but that didn't stop the unpleasant crawling sensation that Peter felt down his back as he passed across the main room and into the work room. It wasn't merely the fact that this was Mordion's workroom and that Peter knew the man would be back soon, it was how very much the room had changed since he was first in here. If this morning the room had been warded to the roof and beyond, this evening there was a specificity to the wards themselves and the spells they surrounded that made Peter very much aware that this was a room in which somebody was about to be held against their will and stripped of their power. The chair alone was laced with four different kinds of containment, from physical restraints to muscular inhibitors, and the entire suite was glossy around him with containment magic meant to reflect any loose magic back into the rooms. It wouldn't keep everything in the room, but it would certainly make it easier to collect when it came out.

Peter only allowed himself a quick look around the suite. There was little enough time before Mordion would arrive himself, and Peter would first need to solve the matter of where to hide. It would be madness to try and hide himself with any kind of spell that he had done himself—he might as well set up a Find Me message in his own handwriting—and it was undoubtedly just as mad to try and hide without doing anything magical to camouflage his presence. He knew enough of Mordion to know that the man would do certain checks before he began work on something so dangerous as what he was about to do.

But if Peter remembered correctly, amongst all of the spells and magical curios that cluttered Mordion's workspace, there were at least three masking spells: a very early kind of Don't See embedded in a ring, a cape that was imbued with Look Away in every thread, and a Don't See/Don't Hear combination in a pair of boots.

None of them were particularly noticeable with the naked

eye, but the cape hung from a hook beside Mordion's desk, and was partially hidden by the cloak stand that had hanging from it various feathered and magicked cloaks that might, thought Peter, looking at them critically, help someone glide safely down a flight of stairs but would be no good at all if they fell out of a window.

If he sat down with his back against the desk to keep the cape in its original position and hid himself beneath it, it was very unlikely that Mordion would ever find him. So long as nothing was out of place, even if Mordion did find his eyes gliding over that particular spot, he wouldn't find it odd. Peter, on the other hand, would have a very good view of all the proceedings. It occurred to him that he wasn't particularly going to enjoy that particular aspect of things, but the sting of that thought was slightly ameliorated by the knowledge that his actions would help to fix not only Poly's situation, but the entire future of his own world.

A warm burr of satisfaction sat in his chest. Finally they were coming to grips with the problem! But below the satisfaction was a certain churning of his stomach that made Peter feel uneasy as he crouched beside Mordion's desk. He hadn't anticipated any sort of physical weakness when it came to the point where he had to do something. He could only hope that he wouldn't disgrace himself when Mordion and Poly entered the room.

As it was, his stomach lurched when he heard the sound of voices filtering through from the next room, and someone opened and closed the door. It was too early. He hadn't anticipated not even being able to set up his spell before Mordion entered and began his work.

Much to his relief, it was only another royal envoy, carrying an unconscious Poly. The man put her carefully in the chair Peter had seen earlier, activating a trickle of magic that fastened her wrists and ankles to the wood, and left as quickly as he had arrived.

Peter, cold with haste and worry, prepared himself to thread a working around both the room and Poly, with Poly's own sleeping magic. All he needed to do was put a seal over this particular patch of time so that Mordion couldn't see beyond it when he accessed Poly's magic; a sort of magical reflective surface that could expand as required without being noticeable. He would have to sit through Poly's attack, and that realisation made his stomach lurch again, but at least he could stop something worse from happening. He could fix the hole he had made.

More than that, he would be sensible and thoughtful. He would make a back-up plan for himself—and, more importantly, for Glenna—that took into account *every* known variable that he had. He remembered briefly Glenna's insistence that they might not be in the time they thought they were in, and found himself smiling. She might be incorrect when it came to that, but it had given him a very good idea for a back-up plan.

If he pre-programed the tickerbox with a series of cycling, randomised possible time jumps within the suite, one to be randomly chosen and initiated at ignition, even if something went wrong and Mordion *did* happen to find him in this time, it wouldn't help the man. Peter would have been shifted back into that time before Mordion saw him, and so long as he shifted inside the wards, he wouldn't alert the earlier Mordion to his presence. So long as he also calibrated that shift to put him in one of the other rooms, all Peter had to do was wait for the outpouring of power that was Poly's magic bursting out, and use that as the ignition to shift both himself and Glenna back into their own future without using any of his own magic at all. Whether or not Mordion knew what Peter's magic looked like, he wouldn't notice Poly's magic being used in the excess that would be pouring out at the time. Nor would there be any firm time for him to catch onto if he *did* happen to catch the slightest glimpse of Peter: if the time was randomised, even Peter wouldn't know what it was before he shifted.

He was less than happy with how prepared the tickerbox was, but as he would have told Glenna were she in earshot, it was now or never. The tickerbox was as ready as he could make it, and the weakness with that damaged ignition button would be more than made up for by using Poly's magic instead.

Of course, the plan carried with it the distinct peril of alerting Glenna, and thereby, her jinx, to what was happening, but that couldn't be helped. It was only a safeguard, after all; he didn't plan on using it—though he did plan on using the power from the magic done in this room to ignite the shift that would send himself and Glenna back to the future as unnoticeably as possible. Peter wasn't keen to make another hole of the same kind he had already made by misjudging how very fragile this time already was.

First, however, Peter had to construct a spell around the entire room to prevent Mordion from seeing things he shouldn't see, and he was aware that he was going to find it a disagreeable exercise. It would have been less so if he could have used his own magic, but Mordion would be very aware of strange magic within the room, and the only other source of magic in the room was Poly.

He drew magic out of Poly slowly and carefully, sick in a distant, wobbly kind of way that was worse than the fear he felt at the certain coming of Mordion. He pushed the feeling away, and found himself sniffing away hot tears. He felt that he was very little different than Mordion at that moment, but there was nothing else he could do.

There wasn't much power he could take without waking Poly to a knowledge of her power, either, or without letting Mordion know that there was more than a leakage of magic about the room. Fortunately, that little was enough for the lightweight spell he needed to do. The intricacy and inherent fragility of the spell that hid it from notice would also enable it to stretch as required.

Much to Peter's relief, the spell worked itself out beautifully. He was quite confident in his ability, but here in the coldness of the room with a captive Poly just out of reach, it seemed possible that things could go horribly wrong, despite his expertise.

The spell done and nestling in every corner of the room in tiny, glittering particles, Peter heaved a sigh of relief and turned his mind to programming the tickerbox. It had been rattling a little since they went spiralling into the past: it had eaten Glenna's fob watch at some stage, and now Peter found himself grateful for its kleptomaniac ways. He could, of course, rig a purely magical system of timer for sending Glenna home, but the less magic there was about the place in general, the better, given what was about to take place in the room.

A little feverishly now, his ears straining to hear the least shuffle of noise from the main room, Peter opened the tickerbox and felt in his pockets for the last of the wire that remained there. He would have to be quick; but this time, he would also need to be *right*.

This time, Peter wasn't going to make a mistake. This time, he was going to think about how his actions affected everyone he was responsible for. He had considered all angles from a mature and dispassionate point of view, without allowing himself to be overrun by his emotions. He had thought in the best interests of Glenna. He hadn't let anyone distract him from fixing the problem.

This time, in fact, he hadn't thought only about himself.

He had considered every eventuality, and had planned accordingly.

He would even take extra precautions: the timer attachment he had added to the tickerbox should do it. Glenna was already in the tickerbox's pre-set recognitions; all he had to do was plug in that version of her to a timer that would send her back to the future fifteen minutes after any randomised ignition. Then, if anything happened to him after he stopped Mordion, she would still be sent to safety, no matter what happened to him.

At any rate, Glenna would get back home, even if Peter didn't.

He had a rather good idea that she wouldn't appreciate being sent back and forth like a piece of mail, so perhaps it was a good thing he hadn't been able to bring her with him. He was trying to keep her safe, after all. She would appreciate it when she realised that he had kept for himself all the risk of things going wrong and had given to her the benefit of being safe. He had, after all been responsible for her being here in the past in the first place. There was no reason why she should have to encounter the peril of Mordion again.

And, of course, there was the fact that Glenna's jinx was far more likely to impact Poly's magic in the worst possible way if she were here to experience the negative emotions that his plan was likely to bring out.

Peter pushed that thought away rather hastily. The lingering feeling that Glenna would undoubtedly be very annoyed with him wasn't one he wanted to allow to grow. It wasn't as if he had any other choice at this point; he was here, and Glenna was in the stables, and everything was happening *right now*.

His fingers were cold as he attached the timepiece to the insides of the tickerbox, smoothing over the connection with a touch of magic that he could draw out at the end. The tickerbox itself he imbued with randomised times in the near past, in a constantly moving series, one of which would be applied to the shift to the main room of Mordion's suite if Peter should be seen. Glenna's watch, he imbued with the necessity of counting down those fifteen minutes after a randomised shift was initiated. When it finished counting down, if Peter wasn't there to stop it, it would send her home.

Then he drew as much of the magic out of the tickerbox as he could, setting the clockwork into motion again with a fizz of power.

There. It was done.

The tickerbox crawled down from his shoulder and onto his knee with prickling legs, and that brought out an unpleasantly shivery sensation all down his back. Peter didn't mean to wring his hands as he waited, the tickerbox ready and poised on his knee with its front legs tapping sharply against his legs. When he found that he was doing it, he shoved his hands in his pockets instead, and tried to stop his eyes from wandering over to the helpless Poly. He couldn't see all of her, just her skirts and the top part of her head where it slumped forward nearly to her knees, her unevenly cut hair spilling on her lap, but it took a lot of determination not to get up and free her. He had already made a hole in time and reality: he might argue about how much of it was his fault, but he didn't doubt Rorkin when the wizard spoke of the extent of the damage, and although his knowledge was almost entirely theoretical at this point, he was quite as well aware as Glenna was how badly he could ruin things by interfering in major timeline events.

He was almost relieved when he heard the turning of the doorhandle and Mordion's footsteps in the main room. It was a sick kind of relief, and it didn't make the odd little quivers down his spine quite stop, but it helped him ignore them.

It was time. It was time to fix the mistakes he had made.

Mordion didn't seem to be worried about time; he strolled into the room quite casually, the gleam of spellpaper in one hand catching Peter's eyes as he circled behind Poly.

That was the contract, then, thought Peter, rather sickly. He would cut Poly's hand open to get a blood seal as soon as Poly woke.

As he thought it, Poly sat up straight with a caught breath that Peter heard, even if he couldn't see her face. She didn't ask why she was confined to a chair, or what Mordion was doing, though Peter was certain she knew he was there behind her chair: she seemed to take it as something normal to be so treated.

"Useful things, spellpapers," said Mordion, as if he were explaining, circling back around to face her. He seemed to be enjoying himself, as if he expected her to understand and appreciate what he was doing. "They have the benefit of turning legally binding contracts into magically binding ones."

Poly said, her voice thin but unwavering, "That's very interesting. But what's the point of binding me into a legal contract, let alone a magical one? I haven't got anything of value."

"Now, that's where you're mistaken. You're very valuable to me. Try not to move, won't you? I'd hate to cut off a finger by mistake."

Peter saw a single finger twitch in the hand that was closest to him, but the only thing he heard from Poly was a small gasp as Mordion slit her palm and pressed the spellpaper to the blood.

Peter found his eyes wet and hot, and blinked away the tears as Mordion said, "Thank you, darling."

It hadn't occurred to him that it would be so hard to be present and not able to do anything without making bigger problems.

"I don't have magic," said Poly, as Peter briefly pressed his face against the cloth of his shirt. "You're wasting your time."

"Young enchantresses are always the best," said Mordion exultantly. "Magic bottled so tightly inside that most of them think they haven't got any. That's unfortunate for you, darling, but it's very helpful to me. I don't need it to be active, you see. I can draw it out of you like marrow from a bone whether it's active or not. And this little paper makes it all legal. You're an asset to the crown, Poly."

Peter put his hands over his ears. It didn't stop him being able to feel magic stirring around the room, powerful, new, and very raw, but he couldn't bear to listen to Poly's voice like that any longer. So quiet and resolute. So very alone.

Mordion said something, and laughed, and Peter's lip curled when he realised that the man was actually drawing out what amounted to a thin rope of Poly's magic while the rest of it poured out, fast and furious and much too powerful to capture in one fell swoop.

And above and around the swell of it, Peter's containment grew and flexed.

Perhaps the conscious, half-frightened look that he gave it to make sure it was still holding took his attention away for too long. Perhaps Mordion was simply more noticing than Peter had expected. Because as Peter's eyes dropped from the spell and back to the blue-garbed figure, Mordion said, quite clearly, "Aha!" and looked directly at him.

Peter wasn't sure if the whole room around him flickered, or if it was simply the shock of being seen that made everything waver. Without a doubt, those dark blue eyes, cruel and amused, pinioned him.

"There you are!" said Mordion. "Stop it at once and *come here.*"

Peter snatched at Poly's magic and shoved it into the tickerbox, igniting the shift as Mordion's magic-sharpened words darted at him, and the whole world around him drew sideways. Somewhere far away, in the stables where Glenna was running her tests, Peter distinctly sensed the jinx sit up and pay attention, but he was already safe and whole in the main room of Mordion's suite. He heard Mordion laugh, and then felt the beginning of the outpouring of Poly's magic, a massive torrent that couldn't hope to be contained and buoyed with it Peter's certainty that he had gone back just far enough.

But if Mordion had no idea how to contain all that power, Peter found that he had vastly underestimated it as well. Power was all around him: too much to field, too much to contain; too much to even comprehend. He didn't think he had ever appreciated how very powerful Poly was, now that he was in the middle of her wakening magic, hardly able to breathe in the crushing weight of it all and somehow dragged toward it at the same time.

He couldn't help the steps he took toward the door of Mordion's workroom, dragged toward that power without being able to stop himself, just to see it. He managed to stop himself just before the doorway, his eyes wide and entranced at the movement of all that magic. Around it, in the thinnest of egg-shell barriers, was the working he had done before; still holding, still shielding. And in the centre of the room, Mordion swayed on his feet, his fingers white where they clung to a chairback and his eyes closed, blind and deaf to everything but the power he had usurped.

Peter's body felt almost too heavy to move, but Poly's magic was there to be used, and the jump was already pre-programmed and ready to go. It was now or never: time to fix what he had broken, and take Glenna back to the future with im.

He took of Poly's magic one last time, and pushed it into the tickerbox, igniting a final shift.

They were safe! Peter was safe: Glenna was safe. Poly wasn't safe now, but she would be, in time. The containment spell he had made was holding, and he had prevented Mordion from glimpsing the future.

The tickerbox, its clockwork beating with all the reverberating quality of the inside of a clock tower, ticked into life, burrowing into the magic that was all around, and the world shifted around Peter again. But instead of snatching him from where he was and Glenna from where *she* was and tossing them both back into the future that should have been waiting for them, safe and whole, it drew them both through layers of castle and reality and flung them together somewhere dark and cold and wet underfoot. Glenna caught herself against him, her eyes dark with pain, and as she did so, a million teeth seemed to sink into Peter, drawing a hoarse cry from him.

"*What did you do?*" Glenna said, her face absolutely white.

"I fixed—I fixed it," Peter gasped. The tickerbox was chewing, chewing, the clockwork gonging impossibly loudly around them, but this time it felt as though it was chewing on moments of his life instead of the leftover time that should have been scattered about. "I fixed the hole. I stopped Mordion from seeing us and I used the power as a springboard to send us home!"

Glenna, her voice razor-edged, asked, "What *exactly* did you do?"

"I—"

Impossible to tell her that he had attached her to the tickerbox like a parcel while he worked against Mordion, when he had told her he would wait for her. Impossible to tell her that he had used what Mordion had unknowingly told him against the man.

"We should be going back to our own time," he panted.

That was where he had set the timer for, after all. Now that the pain was fading, he could already feel the hopeless entropy of it all; he knew the whole thing was going wrong again, but he couldn't for the life of him think *why*. He had stopped Mordion from seeing them, and everything had gone exactly as planned. He had even acted before the jinx had a chance to come in and ruin everything.

"We're going to faint again in a few moments," said Glenna, and there was an iciness to her voice that chilled him more than the cool breeze that was slipping right through his shirt, "but when we come around, we're going to have a discussion about you starting up spells on me without the common politeness of *asking*."

"Oh," said Peter, light-headed and not exactly sure what he was saying. "I thought you were going to say that you'd punch me."

"That," Glenna said, her voice a mere whisper now as it was dragged somewhere into the future or the past, "goes without saying."

$\text{\Large ❧ }$ **10** $\text{\Large ❧}$

Peter woke to the dreadful sound of the tickerbox nattering away at time and the fabric of reality. That would have been bad enough, but the tiny filaments of reality that floated past his nose when he opened his eyes didn't seem quite right. That they were there at all was bad enough; he was quite certain they shouldn't look like they did.

Tatty around the edges—or perhaps burnt around the edges—they fluttered and separated on the breeze. Somewhere nearby was a heavy, solid kind of feeling that wasn't physical, and Peter knew that somehow everything had gone wrong yet again.

It took him far too long to realise that the light by which he could see the filaments of reality wasn't a candle or magic light, but a window in the Civetan University of Magic: a window by which he and Glenna had sat down at one stage to fix the tickerbox.

That tickerbox was now nibbling chronological increments in his pocket, its legs sharp and too busy.

Peter blinked his eyes stickily at the light and then at the jinx-infused, straight-backed incarnation of silence beside him, and managed to make his mouth move enough to ask blearily, "What happened?"

"We've been thrown forward by a few days to a week," said Glenna shortly, her face at first blurry and then clearing as Peter blinked again. "I did check to see if we could get back a few days into the past, but it's like there's a bubble around that particular section of time. Mordion has made *very sure* we can't get in there now."

"But…but I fixed it!" Peter mumbled. He would have sat up but he couldn't quite get his body moving properly. His mouth seemed to be the only part of him that was capable of functioning normally, and he wasn't quite sure about that, either. "I stopped him from seeing it. He can't know about us."

Glenna shrugged, and it seemed to Peter that her face closed off. "Of course you know best," she said.

Peter struggled to sit up, indignant at the very pointed sarcasm, and overbalanced to the other side. He caught himself against the window and sat up while Glenna watched him with a particularly grim expression. That look was more than usually uncomfortable, so Peter turned his attention to the room around him; then, taking in the eerie quietness of it, to the equally empty street outside.

"Where is everyone?" he asked. He could still see the middle sun of the triad and half of the first over the roof of the facades across the street, so the street ought to be in the throes of the mid-afternoon business.

Instead, a solitary horse plodded steadily along the street, drawing a cart behind it. It stopped at each house and then moved on again, but there was no driver to direct it.

"That's the milk cart," said Glenna, following his eyes. "The horse seems to have been at the job some time."

"Where are the people?"

"Halfway to the Parrasian Capital by now, I suppose," said

Glenna. "I didn't see them go; we've arrived a few days late for that, I should think."

"What about—what about the Frozen Battlefield?" asked Peter, stumbling over his words. "Someone stops it. They never make it past the Frozen Battlefield."

"I don't know," Glenna said, icy cold. "Because we *arrived a few days late*. And now we can't get into that particular section of time."

"That can't be possible," said Peter, but he could feel sweat springing up on his brow because none of what they had done since he snatched Glenna from the university party until now had been previously thought to be possible. "How could he have done that? I'd swear he didn't even know about time travel until—until—"

He stopped and swallowed, because the fact that Mordion hadn't known about the possibility of time travel until he became aware of it due to Peter was still a bitter thing.

"He is a *very quick* learner," said Glenna. Her smile was bitter, too. "I've been intercepting the messages that have been sent in Parras and the news isn't good. The royal castle is gone and they're already asking terms of surrender from Civet. No matter what we do now, we can't change that."

"We knew that was going to happen," Peter said, but his voice sounded stifled. It was one thing to know it as history: it was entirely another thing to know it as a direct result of his own actions.

"Yes," said Glenna. "But there's been no word of anything to do with the Frozen Battlefield, and that should have happened in the couple of days before we got here, too."

"How are you getting into the message lines?"

"They don't know about the way that magic bounces off water," said Glenna. "Not yet, at any rate. So I've been—"

"Checking water sources in the area," Peter said, nodding. He felt very sick, but he wasn't sure if it was a residual effect of whatever had gone wrong this time, or because he knew that he had done something so dreadfully bad that it couldn't be forgiven this time. He threw a quick glance at Glenna, but she was gazing out the window. He said hesitantly, "Aren't you—aren't you going to say you're going to punch me?"

"What's the use?" said Glenna wearily. "I don't think it's possible to fix you, actually. I've certainly no intention of trying when you're not capable of listening to anyone other than yourself."

"I didn't mean for it to go wrong! I was just trying to fix things! I even had a plan to send you home if something happened to me!"

Quietly, Glenna said, "I didn't ask you to send me back. I didn't ask you to save me. I asked you to make sure you spoke to me before you did anything with the tickerbox that affected me again."

"Yes, but—"

"Speaking of the tickerbox," she added. "Why don't you have a look at it? I'm sure you'll find it very interesting. Try using the diagnostic element I added earlier."

"Wait!" said Peter, as she stood. "Where are you going?"

"I really don't want to look at you right now," said Glenna. "I'm going for a walk. I'll be back in the stables later tonight."

Proffering a rag of comfort, Peter protested, "We can sleep anywhere we want; the people are all gone."

"Have a look around the university after you're done looking at the tickerbox," said Glenna. "You'll see why I'm not too keen on the idea. Whatever Mordion did with the princess' magic, it didn't affect everyone."

"What do you mean?" asked Peter, but she was already walking away, picking her way across the floor in her stockinged feet. Those stockings had been black and brown and grass-stained before, but now they seemed to be rusty red, and behind her, Glenna left a sticky, quickly vanishing trail of the same, sticky red.

It wasn't until Peter looked around the room that he realised what that sticky red was.

It wasn't that the room was filled with bodies; there were just a few here and there. But it was a shock to see bodies at *all*. What Peter had taken to be just another part of the general disorder around the study hall was in fact blood, and a lot of it. The bodies from which that blood had come hadn't been moved or arranged in any way. They simply lay where they had fallen around the room, though some appeared to have been walked over.

They hadn't been killed in the same way, either: one had been bludgeoned with the closest cake stand, another stabbed with several knives that still protruded from the places they had pierced, some of the knives driven all the way through; still another body looked as though it had been trampled to death.

Now, far too late, did Peter understand the smell that lingered just beneath the scent of books and food. He had distantly thought it was part of the food preservation spell failing—and perhaps it was. Perhaps the food preservation spell had been keeping off the worst of the smell of the bodies from permeating the air, and now that there was no one around to maintain the spell, it was falling apart, allowing the corruption of the bodies as well as the food to begin.

Peter thought for a horrible few moments that he might throw up where he stood, and as he swayed by the table, he saw the single, still-moving point in the room. He focused on that point: Glenna's back as she continued across the hall.

Panting, he called out, "Glenna!"

She paused by the door, stiff, but somehow swaying, and Peter knew in a dizzy kind of relief that she was waiting for him. She certainly hated him, but she wasn't going to leave him here alone with the bloody, fleshy reminders of death lying so casually throughout the study hall.

He ran across the hall toward her, catching her arm with

both of his hands, and though Glenna pushed off one of those hands, she did so only to wrap her own fingers around it.

"There's no one in the stables," she said. "I already looked. It doesn't smell in there, either; well, nothing but manure, anyway. You can take a look at your tickerbox while I try to see what I can do about the bubble that Mordion seems to have put over time and reality beside us."

"You said that before," said Peter, trying very hard not to look at the two bodies that had been trampled in the hall. "But I don't know what you—"

He stopped, but Glenna continued to pull him through the hallway, picking her way through the mess in her stockinged feet.

"Could—shouldn't we get you some more shoes?" he asked quietly.

"No," she said shortly. "I'm not going up there again. I'll take off the stockings once we get to the stables."

"Next time we shift, it'll fix that," he told her, but his voice quivered.

"Yes, I suppose so," Glenna said. "But there's something odd about the tickerbox, or maybe just the way it's connected to us. You should check on that."

There was no anger to her voice; no ice, either. It worried Peter, that complete expressionlessness. He had relied on Glenna, if not for warmth, at least for unshaking, unmelting, unbreaking ice.

"I'll have a look at the tickerbox," he promised her. "Whatever went wrong, I'm sure I can fix it. I'll make sure we can get out of this time again."

Someone pinched his arm, hard, and Peter had said an indignant, "Ow!" before he remembered that Glenna had every reason to want to pinch him. But at the same time, Glenna gasped a little and said, "I really think you ought to look at your tickerbox *right now*."

Peter pulled the tickerbox out of his pocket, and it scrabbled to get away, as if eager to keep munching on the scattered increments of time that still seemed to cling to himself and Glenna. He fished the tickerbox out by one leg anyway, and it did an impatient, midair dance with the other legs as it tried to get away. And still something pinched at Peter's arm, tugging, *tugging*. Almost as if they were about to shift, except he hadn't put in any co-ordinates or even input himself and Glenna into the tickerbox—not since setting everything up in Mordion's chambers, that was.

"Why has the tickerbox latched onto me again?" Glenna asked. "I made sure to disentangle myself some time ago while you were unconscious."

"I don't know," said Peter, clawing at his shoulder. Why, for that matter, did it feel as though someone had him by the shoulder and was dragging him backwards? None of the other shifts had felt like this—none until the last one, that was.

And that last one had been a pre-programmed jump. What if Glenna's jinx *had* caught up with him in time? He had thought it hadn't, but if it *had*, would it have been twisty enough to alter the way he had connected the timer to the tickerbox?

Glenna reached over and seized the tickerbox. "What did you do to it? Why is my watch attached to it? Why is it counting back minutes?"

"I didn't—I set a timer. It was for sending you home if things went wrong. I set it for nearly this time, just in case Mordion caught me or something went wrong with the spell."

"What about the secondary engines?"

"Ow!" said Peter, trying to pull back against the invisible tug against him. "The one we fixed is still fine: I can feel it still working like it should. I might have pushed a bit too much of Poly's magic into it. I think—I think your jinx might have been fast enough to latch onto the timer I set, though. I think it's preparing us to jump through time again."

"What time is it set for?"

Peter, desperately trying to draw out the diagnostic schematic Glenna had added to the tickerbox, said rather feverishly, "There is no time selected. I'd put in randomised times to send myself to in case Mordion saw me, but they were attached to another condition. The jinx has—I think the jinx has fused those functions and now the tickerbox is scrolling through randomised times and setting off a shift whenever it counts down."

"Without a time co-ordinate as an ending point?"

"Yes," Peter said bitterly.

"You'd better hurry and input one, then," said Glenna, through her teeth. "Because I fancy you've got about ten seconds to fix it before it kicks us through time and reality without a tethering point at the other end, and I'd very much rather not find out what that means in practical terms."

Peter stifled another yelp as the tickerbox tried to draw them out of time, and punched in a new time that wasn't so far removed from the now they were already in. "I fixed everything! This shouldn't be happening!"

"We're being moved again," Glenna said, her voice not quite even. "And I hope you've picked a time that we're not likely to meet ourselves, because I don't think the tickerbox cares about what you think you have or haven't done."

This time, neither of them lost consciousness. Peter wasn't sure if that was due to the fact that it was such a small shift— he moved them a mere five minutes when it came to time—or the fact that when the world settled around them after a moment or two of blackness, Rorkin was staring at them.

"A castle," said Glenna, looking around. "That's something. The Parrasian castle, I believe. And it seems as though my stockings are back to normal, so that's nice."

She looked at Rorkin while Peter was still trying to fathom how they could be so far away from where they'd started when he hadn't programmed any kind of spatial movement, and asked unexpectedly, "Did you pull us here?"

"Sorry," said Rorkin, shrugging apologetically. It was a sharp, hunched shrug that made him look like a shabby, anthropomorphised hawk on a bad feather day. "There's a fair bit of unravelled time around out there at the moment, and you nearly ended up in one of the bigger bits. Managed to reel you in, but you shouldn't really be skipping around merrily like that while the world's unravelling."

"I wouldn't have said *merrily*," Glenna said. "But then, I wouldn't have shut myself into a castle and taken it out of the current time and reality, either. Are you yourself, or are you a younger yourself?"

Rorkin's head jutted forward to observe her piercingly. "I like you," he said.

"Yes, you've said that," she said. "I like you, too."

"How lovely!" he said enthusiastically. "You'll be my favourite. Not like *him*."

Peter glared at him.

"Made a big mess of it, didn't you?" said Rorkin. "I told you Mordion was tricky. I told you he was trouble."

"No, you didn't," Peter said flatly. "You hardly told us anything."

"We already knew he was dangerous," Glenna interrupted. "What we don't know is exactly what went wrong when Peter tried to fix it. As far as I can tell, there's a section of time that's separated from the others in Mordion's suite."

"So you can't get back in, either," Rorkin said, rather gloomily.

Peter found that his forehead felt rather damp. "We'll just go back to the future—*before* we left, Rorkin! I haven't forgotten that we can't get back to the exact time—and try to stop ourselves from there. Then we won't need to be worried about Mordion seeing us at all."

"It's no good trying that," said Rorkin sadly. "Already tried it. Now it's not a hole in time——"

"I told you!" Peter, triumphant in his relief. "I fixed the hole! The army is marching just as it was always meant to, and the Battlefield is still——"

"——it's more of an unravelled future," Rorkin finished, ignoring him. "That's why you didn't go back to your time when you tried to springboard off all of that Poly power—don't think I didn't see you try! The future's not there anymore. There's just a thread from your now, unreeling into something black and nasty. I can only knit socks; you can't expect me to knit time as well. I'm already working hard to stop this castle from falling apart."

Peter swayed a little and propped himself up against a nearby closet with one hand. "What?"

"Someone caught onto your little—what was it, containment spell?—after all the Poly power exploded; stole all the marrow out of it and made a tidy little barrier that hardened around a particular section of time instead. I can't crack it."

"Yes, but Mordion didn't *know* enough to——"

"And now there's an army on the march."

"We already know about the army," said Glenna, rather grimly. "What we don't know is why it isn't stopping."

"Oh," said Rorkin. "Well, neither do I. Don't know anything about armies, especially not enchanted armies. You should have thought of that before you let Mordion loose with them: much worse than a regular army, and much harder to stop."

Indignantly now, Peter said, "You can't blame the army on me! I might have been to blame for getting us into this mess and for…and for—actually, exactly what is it I'm supposed to have done this time? Even if what I did didn't work, you can't say I've made things worse!"

"Can too," said Rorkin at once.

Glenna, for once, was utterly silent, but the contempt she

looked at him was more than enough. Peter couldn't help stammering as he asked, "What—what is it that I did *now*? M-made it worse *how*? We already couldn't get back to the future, and once we fix the hole, that'll be fixed, too! We can try again!"

"Well, it should have stopped by now, shouldn't it?" said Rorkin. "That enchanted army. It's no use pretending; I should have been able to bring the castle out of hiding by now, but it's all maniacally happy people and Civetan Knights keeping out of the way out there."

"Glenna said, that, but—"

"And you can't get back to the future, can you? No. Neither can I. Because there's no future to go back to."

"All right," said Peter, trying to think the thing through logically. There must be still some residual effect from how they'd shifted, because he felt sick to his stomach and his mind didn't seem to be able to work like it ought to work. "How far into the future can we safely go?"

"It depends," Rorkin said cautiously.

"On what?"

"It depends on where you go."

"What do you mean, it depends on *where*?" Peter asked, rather giddily. He felt as though his mind was the only part of him that could properly move. "I thought you said that time was unravelling? Are Poly and Luck still in their little bubble?"

"They're bound to be at some stage," Rorkin said. "They're always in there. If you can get to them, you might be able to do some good, but I wouldn't count on it."

"We'll get there," Glenna said. "At the very least, we should be able to get parts there to fix the tickerbox *again*."

"It might do," said Rorkin, but he didn't seem convinced. "But you don't seem to have had much success so far, have you? You," he said, turning that hawk-like look on Peter, "have made a very pretty mess of things this time."

Peter, who passionately wished to continue arguing, found

that the ground had been completely cut from beneath him. He had known it all this time, but hadn't been able to do anything but argue in the vain hope that he could somehow convince himself as well as the other two. A dreadful warmth built up behind his eyes, and a choking feeling in his throat.

There was nothing he could do but apologise.

But even if he apologised, it couldn't fix things. Worse than needing to apologise was the awful thought that he had done something so dreadfully wrong *again*; that he had done it while being so absolutely sure that he was doing the right thing. So sure he was doing the thing that was right, and noble, and self-sacrificing.

So smugly, self-righteously sure of himself.

No wonder Glenna looked at him the way she did.

He opened his mouth to say something—anything—that would have lessened the dreadful weight that rested on his chest, but they all heard the footsteps approaching along the corridor outside the room they were in, and Rorkin stiffened at once.

"Into the cupboard with you both!" he said.

"I *beg* your pardon?" said Glenna, in astonishment.

"Into the cupboard!" he said again. "Sorry, sorry! You're still my favourite, but you'll have to be my favourite while being in the cupboard. This dialogue is very important!"

Peter would have protested, but talking was still too difficult, and between Rorkin and Glenna he was bundled into the cupboard before he could compose himself enough to talk. There in the dark with only the light of the keyhole and the cracks around the edges of the doors, Peter heard muffled voices.

One of them, blunt and matter of fact, pierced the door with its familiarity, and Peter's heart jumped. It was impossible, but it was Annabel's voice!

Peter made a brief, impulsive move forward, but stopped himself. He would have dearly liked to go out and talk to

Annabel, but he was quite sure the Annabel he heard out there was an Annabel he had known roughly three years ago. It was no good hugging her—no good trying to tell her what an idiot he had been and ask for her forgiveness in the same way that he would like to ask Glenna's.

He would have to wait until the time they finally managed to work everything out and they got back into the right time. He inched himself back against the wall, heart heavy, and looked over at Glenna in the darkness of the closet.

She had settled on one side of the closet, her eyes shut and her head leaning against the wooden panels at the back as though she had simply run out of energy like the tickerbox had once tended to do before he made it its own energy source.

"I suppose it's not as bad as it could be," he said, in a low voice, trying to make her feel better. "We might be shifting through time in randomised increments, but at least we can still decide what time we want to go to. The secondary engine that regulates time and interval is still up and running. So long as I keep looking at the watch to know how long we've got, it should be fine."

"Oh, perfectly fine," said Glenna, with a humourless smile that was lit by the crack of light from the cupboard door.

"Aren't you…" Peter stopped, and tried again. "Aren't you going to say something? You always say something. I won't answer back if you want to make a cutting remark, or something like that."

"What's the use?" Glenna asked wearily, turning her face away. "It doesn't make a difference to you, and it only makes the jinx worse. Leave me alone."

Peter tried to pick out her face properly, but all he could be sure of was the white curve of her jaw in the muddling darkness. "I was trying to protect you. You'd already faced him once and nearly died, and I didn't think there was time to get to you and explain things, so—"

"I didn't ask you to protect me," she said. "I asked you to listen to me. I asked you to wait on making a decision until we'd talked it over because I was quite sure you didn't have all the information."

"But I was *trying*—"

"Do you think you could shut up now?" asked Glenna. "They'll hear us. I don't feel particularly protected—in fact, I feel like the only protection I need is from you."

"I won't—I didn't mean to hurt you."

"I know. It just didn't occur to you that discussing an integral decision with me before you hooked me up to your tickerbox again was something that you ought to do."

"There wasn't time to talk it over," Peter said, though he no longer felt like he quite believed that. "I thought it might make up for everything if I could just get you all the way back to your present: that's why I linked you to the tickerbox again."

"I suppose it didn't occur to you to ask what *I* thought before deciding that for me."

"But I was trying to *protect* you!"

"That hardly makes up for the fact that you didn't leave that choice—or, in fact, any other—with me," Glenna said. "Do you think we could stop talking about this now? If we talk about it for too much longer I really do feel like I'm going to hit you, and they'll certainly hear it out there."

"All right," said Peter, but he couldn't be angry when he said it, because no matter what Glenna did or said, it really couldn't make up for whatever it was he had just done to the both of them. He still didn't know exactly what it was he *had* done. To the heavy, jinx-burdened area of the darkness beside him, he said, "I'll fix this. I promise."

"No, thank you," she said. "If you have to promise something—if you think you can stop yourself—do please try not to use any more magic on me without informing me first."

"I wouldn't—I mean I won't. I promise."

"That's nice," Glenna said, and there was that weariness to her voice again. "Do you think you could look at your tickerbox? I feel as though I'm about to be pulled sideways again."

Peter fished the tickerbox out of his pocket, but it was almost scaldingly hot, and he dropped it. He swore before he could stop himself, then slapped a hand over his mouth.

Glenna gave him a warning thump in the side and grabbed the tickerbox herself. The tiniest, softest tendril of light wrapped around it and illuminated the fob watch.

"Two minutes left, I should think," she said. "Quicker than last time. I wonder if that's going to continue to decrease?"

Peter was loath to say that he didn't know. Instead, he said, "I wonder why it's getting hotter, these days?"

"The wires, I expect," Glenna said. "I've had a few experiments explode from sheer friction heat; some melting, too. I try to make sure I build in some form of coolant for anything that's likely to have that trouble."

"I pushed too much of Poly's magic into to ignite the shift," Peter said. That was another thing he hadn't accounted for: if he had waited to ask Glenna, no doubt they could have come up with something together that wouldn't have melted the tickerbox in on itself like the power of Poly's magic had done. From a quick look at the diagnostic, he already suspected that the tickerbox's physical insides were a mess of melted wires and perhaps melted magics.

Whatever he had done this time, it hadn't just affected the Frozen Battlefield, it had affected their ability to be able to do something about fixing it, too.

Worse, in that quickly unravelling future somewhere out of reach, Poly and Luck were sure to be paying for it, along with everyone else from the future.

"Poly," he said, rather numbly.

"Yes," said Glenna. Peter would have given a great deal to

hear the usual ice in her voice, but there was still nothing there; no ice or fire, no emotion whatsoever. "We should try to get back into the house if we can. It's as good a place to start as any, at least. I fancy we'll find we can't get to Rorkin once we leave here, even if we try, and we're going to need some help. Now that the princess and the Battlefield is out of play, we have nothing to knit with, so to speak."

"It will put us out of time, too," he added. "Being in Luck's house, I mean. I know that's not exactly right, but—"

"It's a good plan," she said. "We need all the advantage we can get, and if we can try to edge out of the normal flow of time and reality, it'll give us a chance to stop and think, and try to fix the tickerbox before it tries to throw us into another time."

"Do you think you can find them again?" he asked her. "I don't think I can."

"Perhaps," said Glenna, but she took the tickerbox when he handed it to her. "I'd try to input our current location, but I don't think the tickerbox would be able to recognise it, and I rather think it will move us on regardless."

Peter sat in silence as she entered the coordinates. He would very much have liked to point out to her exactly how much he was trusting her at the moment—how very hard he was trying to show that he valued her input—but it occurred to him how that might seem from her perspective and stopped himself.

For that reason, when Peter took back the tickerbox he only said, "Thank you".

"We'll see how it goes," Glenna said, rather worryingly. "Ow!"

Peter, who had already felt the tug of the tickerbox, had a brief moment to wonder *when* exactly Glenna had sent them before they arrived. Instead of the hard wooden base of the closet, grass softened beneath them, velvet dark and gold-edged in the last light of the smallest sun.

If they hadn't already been sitting, Peter rather thought Glenna would have sat down. He could actually feel the jinx moving around her in tangled, seeking coils; her face was utterly weary as she gazed around them.

He asked, "Where did you put us?"

"As close to Luck's place as I could get us. The other ones were there this morning."

"You mean the younger versions of us?"

"Yes. I wanted to make sure we didn't accidentally run into each other. What does the watch say now?"

"It's set on the hour, now," Peter said, calling up the diagnostic. "But it's not moving. I'll have to see if I can access the —yes, there it is. There's a stack of hours behind it: it's given us ten hours this time."

"I suppose there's that," said Glenna, as though to herself. "Is the random shifting something you can stop, do you think?"

Peter cleared his throat. He had been very much hoping that Glenna wouldn't ask him that question until he could give her a solution to go along with the bad news.

"I don't—I'm not sure," he said. "The wires are a mess, and the magic seems to have found a shortcut that bypasses most of the mechanics to go straight to the timer. It looks like it's going to keep throwing us into a shift until we can fix it. I can—I can see the next two times, though."

"Wonderful," she said, smiling rather bitterly down at the grass. "What are the increments?"

"After the next shift, there will be one the next hour. After that, the next one gives us a couple of hours."

"Well, I suppose we know it's not decreasing, at any rate," said Glenna. "We'll have to see if we can fix that before long. At least we can still choose our times."

"Yes," said Peter quietly, although he wouldn't have brought that up again himself. "The last sun is nearly gone.

We should try to sleep while we can. We'll try to find the way in to Poly and Luck tomorrow."

Glenna didn't reply, but she did curl up on her side with her feet drawn up under her skirts, her profile to the last fading rays of the smallest sun. She didn't move from that position until the suns had disappeared and the air grew cool around them; Peter had the impression that she had been waiting for it because she rolled back over onto her back and gazed up at the starry sky.

Into the darkness, Peter said quietly, "I didn't mean for it to go like this."

"People usually don't," she said, and sighed. "I don't think you really appreciate how much I dislike you."

"I know," said Peter, and if it seemed like Glenna welcomed the dark, he found he appreciated it, too. There was a certain tight, hotness to his eyes and an unpleasant warmth to his chest that bespoke tears, and he was certainly too old to be crying because someone didn't like him. He had never cared whether or not someone liked him; opinion and companionship had never before seemed either necessary or desirable.

"Who knows?" said Glenna, and there was a thread of mockery to her voice. "Perhaps I've been too hard on you. I thought it might help if I pulled you up every time you were a horrible little brat, but I don't think it's done the jinx any good. It certainly hasn't done you any good."

"It wasn't your fault," Peter said, his voice just slightly snubby with hot tears. "None of it was your fault. Go to sleep; we'll see what we can do about everything in the morning."

He might have told Glenna to go to sleep, but Peter was certain it was quite some time before she did so, and it was certainly a long time before he did so himself.

Two of the suns were in the sky by the time they woke; Peter in a panic and Glenna with a kind of sluggish disinterest that worried him. The last two shifts had taken a toll physically, and he had been exhausted last night, himself.

"One hour," he said to her as she sat up. "Before we shift, I mean."

She nodded, but didn't say anything, just climbed to her feet and started off in the direction of the rising suns. Peter followed her, his tickerbox already in his hand. He would have liked to stop and look at it for a while in hopes of being able to do something helpful, but with only one hour until they shifted again, he wanted to get safely into Luck's house again.

This time, when they got closer to the house, Peter found that he could tell. He couldn't help saying to Glenna, "It's easier this time. I can tell where we are."

"Yes," said Glenna. "They've put out something like a welcome mat. Very strange. The door's over there, nice and easy to see, and I'd be willing to wager that it's not locked this time, either."

"You think it's a trap?" he asked.

"No," said Glenna. "I think we're being invited in. I'll bet Luck has figured out what's going on. If we've made as big of a mess of it as Rorkin thinks, he'll have bundled the princess and the little dog to safety as quickly as he could."

"And Rorkin will probably have told them to expect us," agreed Peter. There was still a listlessness to Glenna, but it was obvious that her mental processes were working as well as ever. "Oh well, I suppose it will be easier to get help if they know what's gone wrong, too."

"Yes, and Luck's much less likely to attack us if he's expecting us," said Glenna, as she opened the door.

Peter had a brief, rather panicked thought that Luck might still immobilise first and ask questions later, but Glenna had already stepped through the door, and all he could do was follow her.

He found himself in a kitchen that was almost tear-inducingly familiar, with the smell of scones wafting in the air and a homey patchwork of magic, anti-magic, and unmagic rising from a chair to greet them.

"You're just in time," said Poly, her dark hair roiling around her as it always did, fraught with magic and spells and random feathers. A few tendrils reached forward to greet Peter, as familiar as the warm smile and the round glasses on Poly's face. "I was just about to take the scones out of the oven."

Peter thought he had never been so glad to see someone, and in that relief, he did something he hadn't done in several years: he threw his arms around her and hugged her.

"I'm sure it can't be as bad as that," she said bracingly, patting him on the back. "Careful! Don't get too close to the stove: reality has been unravelling over there, and you never know what your hand will turn into if you touch it."

Peter gazed at her sickly and then at the blurry section of wall behind the stove that should have been solid. "It's gotten in here as well?"

"When reality unravels, not even Luck and I can stop it," said Poly. "Let's talk about it after we've eaten. Sit down, Glenna."

Glenna's gaze focused sharply at her, but Peter had the impression that she had been watching Poly for some time. "How do you know my name?"

"We're…acquainted," said Poly.

"No, we're not," said Glenna. "And I'd very much rather start work on fixing the world that's falling apart out there instead of eating scones, thank you very much. We only came in here because we thought you could help us with that."

"I'm so sorry," said Poly apologetically, carefully extracting scones from the partially real oven. "But I don't think that's going to be possible."

"Do you mean it's not possible or do you mean that you don't choose to help?" asked Glenna, still very stiff. Peter hadn't expected her to be so stand-offish with Poly; at the very least he had expected them to bond over their shared exasperation with him. "I can see that you're an enchantress from here, and I'm quite certain that you've got an antimagic arm, too, however that happened."

"I mean that Luck and I can't leave the inverse pocket," said Poly. "Not without unravelling, I mean. We retreated in here because the inverse pocket was the only safe place in our particular present time, but we weren't the only versions of ourselves to think of that, so it's less stable than it could be. You'll be safe in here for a little while, but unless you fix the problem that you're here to fix, even this pocket of safety won't last forever."

"We already knew that," Glenna said. "We only came in because we thought you might be able to help us. If you can't, we'll just—"

"Ah, that reminds me," said Poly. "There's a visitor for you, Glenna: he's been waiting for a little while now. He came from a rather different present."

Glenna's eyes became luminous, and it struck Peter again how very quiet and listless she had been until she came into the house with him. "*He*? Where is he?"

"What visitor?" demanded Peter, startled and worried in equal measure. "How did he know we'd be here?"

"Well, how did Rorkin know where we were earlier?" Glenna pointed out. "Where's my friend? I've been waiting for him."

"In the garden," Poly told her. "He said he'd be waiting by the stream, but it *does* like to play tricks on him, so you could find him anywhere out there. Be careful of anything that's a bit too blurred for comfort."

"I'll come with you," said Peter decisively. He didn't know who this mysterious visitor was, but anyone who knew enough to find himself and Glenna at this moment was not someone to be trusted without careful thought.

"No," said Glenna, without looking at him.

At the same time, Poly said, "Oh, I don't think so. You can help me sort through these playthings for Onepiece, instead. I just grabbed the first things to hand when everything started going wrong and I'm quite sure he shouldn't be playing with some of them."

"You don't need my help with those little things," protested Peter, instinctively starting after Glenna, who exited by the door Poly opened for her without waiting for him. It was the door that they had entered by, but now that Poly had opened it again, it led into the back yard instead of the outside world. "What if he's dangerous?"

Poly shut the door and said, as if she were very amused, "He's not dangerous to Glenna."

That annoyed Peter a great deal. What annoyed him more, however, was the fact that through the kitchen window, he could see Glenna very clearly, though he saw only the back of the stranger. That wasn't the annoying thing, however: the annoying thing was that he could see her kissing the stranger on the cheek.

"How did he know she was going to be here?" he complained to Poly, who smiled faintly. "*We* didn't even know we'd be here! It took Rorkin a bit to find us, too, and he's *Rorkin* for pity's sake!"

"Oh, so you have been working with Rorkin!" said Poly. "I was hoping he'd caught up with you both. Did he mention that he needed your help?"

"He said we'd made a hole in time and reality—or that we were going to make one. He didn't seem to be very sure about exactly what it was we needed to fix, but he was pretty certain about the fact that we needed to fix it."

"Yes, he does get a bit confused," Poly said forgivingly. "I suppose that's what comes of living half in time and half out of it. You never know quite when you are."

"I think he was pretending to be a master at the university, too," Peter added. "He made perishing sure I didn't see him before we—before I made a—made a mistake."

He looked up, and found that Poly was gazing rather thoughtfully at him. It was one of the looks that he didn't like on her. It was a look that his mother would have given him if she'd cared enough to make sure that he turned into a decent person or at the very least a competent magic user.

"I did something really awful," he said, in a rush. All the sickness and suppressed shame bubbled to the surface, heating his face. "I was so sure I could do it—take myself into the future, that is. And Glenna just *laughed* at me so I lost my temper and tried to take her with me. She told me to stop but I knew I was right so I just pressed the button and everything went wrong."

Poly nodded silently, the air heavy with things not said. Peter was grateful for that, but he was also aware that he didn't deserve it, so he said one of the things himself.

"Actually, I suppose it went wrong a lot earlier than that," he said. "I let one of the other boys get under my skin, and then I let Glenna get under my skin. And if I'd been paying attention before that instead of trying to show off, I might have realised that there was more to Glenna than meets the eye instead of just telling her she was doing things wrong. I could—I could probably even have figured out that it was a jinx if I'd been paying attention."

"Sometimes it's easy to remember why I love you," said Poly, passing him a scone. "Sit down, darling: you don't really have to sort those things out. Onepiece will sort them out later."

It should have made him feel better, but Peter knew a certain heaviness that suggested to him how little he deserved either Poly's love or understanding. He cleared his throat and asked, "How do you—I mean, Annabel and I haven't been here yet, have we? You haven't even got that scar on the back of your hand yet. How do you remember me?"

"I know you quite well from here and there," Poly said, smiling. "Remember that you're not the only one who has had…experience when it comes to time."

Peter thought he could just about understand that. "Do we…do we keep running into you?"

"In a way, I suppose," she said, and her smile became a little pained. "I'll be something of a motif in your life for a while."

"And you're not going to tell me why, I suppose," said Peter. Poly might not have the scattered unintelligibility of Rorkin, or the deliberate obstructiveness of Luck, but when she didn't want to reveal something, she was much akin to a very polite door closing in someone's face.

Poly looked at him apologetically. "Not right now, I think. If it helps, you seem to figure it out for yourselves quite quickly; we'll meet again later on, and you seemed to be pretty well aware of it then."

"My later on, then," said Peter, and his voice sounded

grim to his own ears. "Poly, I've made such a mess of this! I don't think I can get us back to the right time; I can't even stop the tickerbox moving us whenever it wants to move us, now. If I could just get Glenna free, it wouldn't matter so much; I've already done so much wrong by her that I couldn't fix that if I tried. And now—and now it's the whole world unravelling and that's my fault, too."

"Well, yes," said Poly. "But just because it's your fault doesn't mean you're the only one who can fix it. In fact, it would be foolhardy to try and fix it by yourself."

"Yes," said Peter. "That's why we came here."

"Mm," Poly agreed slowly. "But I mean more that you'll need to work with Glenna if you want to fix this. I don't think it's something either of you can do alone. Luck and I certainly won't be able to follow you back out there; the only benefit of being in here is that you have a little time to think. You won't be able to fix it from in here."

Peter, reminded of one of the more important potential benefits of being in Luck's house, made a grab for his ticker-box. It tried to elude him again, but he dragged it out regard-less and flicked open the casing to look at Glenna's watch. Just as he had hoped, it was no longer ticking—had stopped moving altogether—with just fifty minutes left before the next shift.

A faint hope stirred in him for the first time since he had woken to find that most of Parras was on the march and the future was unravelling. At least here he had the time to mend the tickerbox as much as possible, and perhaps make a plan to stop Mordion and bring the timeline back to where it ought to have been.

"Good boy," said Poly approvingly. "Here: have some scones. Luck always works best if he has scones to eat while he's trying to make things."

Peter took the scones gratefully and set them beside the tickerbox for easy reach. Luck had never encouraged Peter to join him in his own experimentation, but Poly had always at least made sure they both had something to eat while they were working on their separate projects. Thinking about the last few days with Glenna, Peter now had a much better idea of why Luck had never been eager to work with him: Peter must have been even more annoying to Luck than Luck was to the rest of the world.

Poly settled herself by the fire and allowed him to work in silence, though she seemed to be knitting, and Peter didn't remember her ever knitting before. Her presence was a comfort, despite that slight discrepancy. From the kitchen table he could still see Glenna through the window, too. He had been trying not to look, with the kind of stubborn conviction that if he didn't look, it wasn't happening, but whenever he looked up from the tickerbox his eyes went there automatically.

Glenna showed no signs of coming in, either: she walked with her hands linked around the man's arm, and that annoyed Peter so much that he put his tickerbox down with a bit more force than he'd meant to, and demanded of Poly, "Who *is* that, anyway?"

Poly paused her knitting, and for just a moment, Peter wasn't sure whether she was close to laughing or crying. "He's my father," she said. "He comes to see me sometimes. This time he came to see Glenna, though."

"But—" Peter stopped. Poly must be joking: from the little he could see of the man with Glenna, he was possibly in his late twenties, but certainly no older. "He doesn't look old enough to be your father—and he's not acting like *anyone's* father! Why was he letting Glenna kiss him? Why did he put his arms around her?"

"Because he's very fond of her, I suppose," said Poly, and this time it was certainly laughter making her eyes sparkle. So she *was* joking?

He tried not to be sniffy about that when he asked, "Then

if you three are trapped in here, and he's your father, why isn't he trying to do something to help?"

"He is," said Poly. "It's just that he's not helping right in this moment. He has another function."

"That's what Rorkin said just before he disappeared last time," Peter said, somewhat crankily. "I don't see why people can't just be more straightforward."

"That," said Poly, very gently, "is because time has already been made a mess of, and we have to be very careful with what we say."

Regret and shame burned a hole through Peter's chest. "I'm sorry. Oh Poly, I'm sorry!"

"I know," she said. "But it's so much easier to be sorry after the damage is done than it is to be thoughtful at the time. Do you think you'll be able to do anything with the tickerbox?"

"Something," he said, discouraged. "But nothing useful, I think. The wires have completely melted into the magic, and the magic has fused itself to the box; I can't separate them."

"Can you separate yourselves from the tickerbox?"

"Yes, but what's the good in doing that? It's the only way we can get back home—it's the only way we can fix this problem. If I had another one I could program us out of the tickerbox and into the new one, but it took me *years* to get this one just right. I couldn't do that in time."

"No," said Poly thoughtfully, casting on a few stitches. "I rather think that there's going to be less time than we thought at first. A few things haven't gone just as we'd hoped."

"Yes," Peter said, watching her knitting. "Is that why you're knitting new walls over the unravelling parts?"

"Exactly," she said. "Rorkin thought it might help."

"That was useful of him," said Peter. He still felt a little grim about Rorkin.

"Where was he when you last saw him, by the way?"

"Stuck in a castle somewhere," he said.

"A castle?" Poly raised her eyebrows at him.

"Of course it's *that* castle!" he said grumpily. "What else would it be? I even heard Annabel talking to him. Rorkin knew very well what he was about."

"Rorkin usually does, in a manner of speaking," said Poly. "Apart from a couple of people I can think of, he's the only one in the Two Monarchies who really knows how things are supposed to go when it comes to the Mordion timeline."

"That's why he was at the University of Mechanics and Magic," Peter said, even more grimly.

"Yes, so I was led to believe."

"He knew before it happened," Peter said, indignation and frustration driving heat to his cheeks. "He *knew* it was going to happen, Poly!"

"I'm sure he did."

"Then why didn't he stop it?"

"Are you saying you would have stopped if Rorkin told you to stop? Or are you saying that he's responsible for your actions?"

"I'm not—I'm—neither! But he didn't try to warn me, or speak to me—all he did was run away when I tried to speak to him!"

"Yes," said Poly. "I got the impression that he's trying very hard not to ruin things that are supposed to happen while stopping things that shouldn't have happened. Things were already complicated enough with Mordion; he's worried about ruining the very delicate balance there."

"Anyway, I wish he'd tried to say something," muttered Peter. He knew it wasn't exactly fair to be blaming Rorkin when he himself was the one who'd done wrong, but it seemed not quite fair not to mention it, either. Rorkin always seemed to get away with doing slippery things and vanishing before anyone could figure out what he was up to or where he was going.

"I know," said Poly. "Have another scone. I think Luck's coming and you know how he is."

Peter took the second scone just as the door to the kitchen opened. Familiar golden magic swept into the room around Luck as he entered, highlighting his dark, riotous hair, and made luminous particles in his green eyes. He must have been working on one of his inventions in the other room, because he was in his shirtsleeves and waistcoat, which had a vast, black stain that could have been oil but probably wasn't.

"There you are, Poly," said Luck. "The stream's gone wandering again and—oh, it's you again."

"I'm glad to see there's someone else the stream likes to play games with," Peter said, rather bad-temperedly. "I was beginning to think I was the only one it hated."

"You are," said Luck, after staring at him for a few moments. "Huh. You're still in one piece. Good."

Peter stared back at him, frowning slightly, because he rather fancied Luck's eyes were more gold than they were the usual green. In addition to that, his magic seemed to have infused itself into the walls and fixtures around the room; Peter had been so caught up with Poly that he hadn't noticed until now, and now that he did notice, it seemed very obvious.

"If you're going to start unravelling reality, the least you could do is not scowl at me in my own kitchen," said Luck, conversationally.

Peter knew very well that Luck was simply diverting attention from what he was up to, but it had always been hard for him to get Luck to give him straight answers, so he turned to Poly.

"Is he connected to the house?"

"Something like that," Poly said. She looked distinctly worried.

"It's rude to make remarks about people's houses," Luck said reproachfully to her. "You told me so last week."

"That was when you asked Margaret if her new wallpaper

was a particularly virulent kind of mould," Poly said. "A completely different thing."

"Has he *bound* himself to the inverse pocket?" asked Peter, appalled.

"See!" said Luck. "Rude!"

"I'm not being rude, I'm concerned!"

Luck opened his mouth to make another remark, but caught Poly's eyes and instead said beneath his breath something to the effect that it *was* rude to bring up things he was trying to be heroic and silent about.

Aloud, he said, "Are those my scones?"

"This one's mine," Peter told him. "Poly kept some for you."

"It's my house," Luck said. "Actually. So *all* the scones are mine. You get scones only on sufferance because you're still in one piece."

"There are more in the oven," Poly told him, kissing his cheek and causing a starburst of green and gold magic that scattered particles every which way.

Peter sniffed slightly, but looked away from them and toward the outside door. He still felt a bit raw, and it was something of a salve to see Glenna walking back toward the house alone. At least she hadn't invited him back into the house, even if Poly and Luck *did* know the man.

If there was a suggestion of movement around the room as she came toward the house again, there was an absolute riot when Glenna came through the door. The stove door rattled, the scone trays on top of it sidling toward the door, and several of the cups and saucers in the cupboards wedged opened their doors and made a run for it across the kitchen floor.

Mischievous magic roiled across the floor, sending flowers shooting up to the knee, and set the painted figures on a milk-jug dancing across the porcelain surface.

"Good heavens!" said Luck, clutching his magic to himself

as if it were his only covering. "Don't do that! I'm not travelling today and I refuse to be sick when there are scones to eat."

Glenna patted her pockets rather feverishly, and pulled out a little wooden model that she certainly hadn't had before she left the house. As soon as the disordered magic curled around it and sank in, something twitched a little bit sidewise.

"Very useful!" said Luck, peering at the arms and legs of the model. "Did you make this?"

"Yes," Glenna said. "Just now. Someone broke the other one I had."

"It wasn't me," Luck said at once. "I've never seen you before."

"Yes, you have, darling," Poly told him. "This is Glenna."

"Is it?" Luck said.

Despite his vague tone, Peter was fairly certain that Luck knew exactly who both he and Glenna were, which was surprising given the fact that Peter and Annabel wouldn't officially meet Luck for another few years. Peter was less sure why Poly knew them, but he'd been sure enough that she would, to come here in the first place.

"We haven't met before," Glenna said, adjusting one of the wooden arms. "Not face to face, at any rate. There's no reason for him to remember me. Oh, there we go."

The room cleared and the pots and pans settled back down in their places, though one of the cups continued in its escape attempt.

"What on earth!" protested Peter, scooping up the cup as it toddled past his chair. "What's going on? I thought you said your jinx made magic go wrong when you're annoyed!"

"It does," Glenna said, becoming rather pink.

"What did I do *now*?"

"You didn't do anything," she said, with great certainty. "It's got nothing to do with you at all."

"Actually," said Luck, "I'm pretty sure—"

"Your jinx is connected to your emotions?" hastily said Poly, elbowing him squarely in the stain on his waistcoat. "Good grief! I've never seen that before! How inconvenient!"

"If he was annoying you, you should have come in before," Peter muttered. "It's not like you don't let people know when they're annoying you. I don't see why you're more polite to—actually, who *is* he?"

"He wasn't annoying me," said Glenna, pinker than before, "and it's none of your business who he is. He's an old friend of mine, and that's all you need to know."

"He's old, all right," Peter said, disgruntled. "He looks like he's twenty-five at least. What were you talking about all that time? And why were you kissing him on the cheek, actually? Does the university know you're meeting an—"

"I really don't think it's any business of the university what I do and who I meet," said Glenna. "And it's not yours, either."

"Actually," said Luck, "that's probably not—Poly, if you elbow me again—!"

"Have another scone," Poly said.

"You're trying to shut me up again, aren't you?"

"Darling, I thought we decided—"

"*I* am darling," said a small, snubby voice. "Dad is dad."

The restless, jinx-touched magic around the house must have awakened Onepiece's interest. Now in his boy form instead of his puppy form, he trotted over to Poly and climbed into her lap.

"I'm bigger than you are," Luck told the tiny interloper. "And if we're judging purely on concentration as a measure of who has the most right to be called darling—"

"*Which* we are not," prompted Poly, with a reproachful look.

"—which apparently we're not, I have the most right based purely on mass."

"Pish," said Onepiece, with devastating simplicity.

"I could try to take a look at your jinx if you like," suggested Poly. "It would be tricky since you're a person and not a thing, but I've unravelled one before."

"I don't think so," Glenna said. "It's already quite unstable, and I've got the feeling that—"

"Yes," said Poly, as though she was agreeing. "Peter and I are quite similar, aren't we?"

"Quite," Glenna agreed.

"There's no need to say it like it's an insult!" protested Peter. "I'm a strong magic user, even if I don't choose to use my talents, and—oh."

"Yes," said Glenna. "The jinx and strong magic aren't the best together."

"What did Poly mean, the jinx is attached to your emotions? I thought it was just triggered by annoyance."

Glenna became stiff again. "It is. It's also triggered by other emotions."

"Good as well as bad, I take it," Poly said, a little dryly.

"Yes. It's worse if the emotions are negative, but it interferes with the good ones as well."

"That's very unfortunate."

"It's very interesting," began Luck. "And—"

"She's not here for you to experiment on," Peter said, before Luck could continue. He was very familiar with Luck. "So forget about it. If anyone's going to try to help out, it's Poly."

"I'm quite capable of deciding who to ask if I feel like I need help, thank you very much," said Glenna, even stiffer than before. "I'm also quite used to making allowances for the jinx, so there's no need to trouble anyone."

"All right," said Poly, still friendly. "Let me know if you change your mind."

"I said I don't need help!" Glenna said fiercely. The cup over by the door made a dash for freedom, closely followed by a spoon, and Glenna stood up. Tightly, she added, "I'd like to wash now, if that's all right with all of you. I haven't had the chance since last shift."

"Onepiece, show Miss Stoneflange the bathroom," Poly prompted the little boy, allowing him to slip to the floor again. "We're *not* playing right now."

"No one plays," said Onepiece sadly, but he took Glenna by the hand anyway.

Peter went back to his tickerbox, though he felt like there was little enough he could do to fix it, and he felt something in the room grow a little tighter and safer as Poly began knitting again. He didn't notice when Luck left—there was still too much of the man left in the room—but by the time he came to close his tickerbox again, it was apparent that Glenna still hadn't returned, though Onepiece had trotted happily back.

"You might think about washing, yourself," Poly said, without looking up from her knitting. It was difficult to differentiate between her knitting and her hair, and that worried Peter rather a lot. He had a feeling that Poly was just as dangerously connected to the inverse pocket as Luck was. "No, Onepiece, Peter can find the bathroom himself. You'd better sit with me for now, I think."

Doubtfully, Peter asked, "Is it important to wash right now?"

"That's entirely up to you," Poly said amiably. "But Glenna hasn't come back yet, either. I wouldn't like her to get lost in the house."

The house seemed to like Glenna a great deal more than it did Peter, but Peter didn't say that. He put the tickerbox back in his pocket and went in search of Glenna anyway. It wasn't until he was walking down the hallway in search of her that it occurred to Peter to wonder exactly what Glenna had been feeling while she was walking with the stranger to cause her to put the room into such disorder when she entered it again.

More importantly, how did she know the man, and why had she kissed him?

Perhaps he was a friend of her father's? Only Glenna had been very clear about how much she disliked Headmaster Tarrant—more, she'd been very clear that he wasn't her real father. He didn't see her getting along well with any of the people that got along well with Headmaster Tarrant, either.

And that reminded him: he had been pulled into Headmaster Tarrant's office when he and Glenna had both skipped Interconnectedness—the day when she said she had been meeting someone. Had it been the same someone then?

And if so, *how* was the man continuing to find her? Was it the mysterious kind of Interconnectedness that Glenna was always talking about? And if so, what business did she have being Interconnected to another fellow when she, magic and all, was already Interconnected with Peter to such an extent?

The bathroom door was open when Peter came to it, and he was almost bad-tempered enough to walk in without knocking. With an effort he made himself stop, and having stopped, to knock on the open door.

"You can come in," called Glenna's voice. "I've finished washing."

"If you're finished washing, what are you doing?"

"Come in and have a look," she said. "The walls are purled and the floor is knitted."

"Yes, Poly's trying to keep the house together," said Peter, stepping cautiously through the door. The main rooms in the house were usually grass, but the floor here certainly felt more like wool than grass at the moment.

Glenna stood by the bathtub, peering down into the plug hole.

"Don't tell me," said Peter, remembering something of the haunting, empty blackness of the castle's insides several years ago. "It's black and it won't stop moving?"

"Yes," she said. "Rather disturbing."

They looked down at it in silence for a moment before

Peter said rather tentatively, "Your friend seems to have no problems finding you."

"Yes," said Glenna, straightening. "That's never been a problem for him."

"Who is he?" Peter asked her. "He's the one who was in the university that time, wasn't he? The one that threw me into a broom cupboard. You were waiting for him, weren't you?"

Glenna laughed, and for the first time, she sounded really amused. Peter wasn't sure whether to be offended or enchanted, but there was nothing mean about her laughter, after all.

Still, his voice was slightly stiff when he asked, "What's funny?"

"You, not recognising the magic," Glenna said. "Goodness! I didn't expect that!"

"Whose magic was it, then?"

She shook her head decisively, and started toward the door. "No, I think not. I don't particularly want you to know about him. It's bad enough that you saw him; he told me you might, but I'd hoped you wouldn't."

"Did he tell you why he threw me into the broom cupboard?" demanded Peter, following her into the hallway. "He hasn't ever met me! What did I do to annoy *him*?"

"It wasn't because you annoyed him, exactly," said Glenna. Amusement still glowed in her eyes, but she looked thoughtful, too. "I rather fancy it's because you were annoying me."

"It's not his business if I *was*!" Peter protested. "What's it got to do with him?"

The amusement utterly vanished from her face. Quietly, she said, "He told me that, too. The last time we met."

"Well?" demanded Peter.

"I said he told me, not that I was going to tell you."

"Oh well, if you're going to be *snippy* about it—!" he said, somewhat indignantly. "I don't see why everything has to be such a secret with you!"

"Well, I don't see why everything has to be shared with you, if it comes to that," said Glenna, her nose elevating just slightly. "All right, if you must have it, he's my fiancé."

It should have annoyed him even more that she was laughing at him again, but it occurred to him that Glenna had regained something of her usual life and vinegar, and even if that had been because of the stranger, he still welcomed it.

"All right," he said, more good-naturedly. "Tell me about it later when you feel like it. Are you coming back to the kitchen?"

"I think we'd better," said Glenna, closing the bathroom door behind them. "The whole house is shrinking. That's why he sent me back in: the garden has probably disappeared by now as well. The kitchen might be the safest place for us all now."

When they got back to the kitchen, Luck was gone, yet not quite gone. Peter, who had sensed the Luckness of the room while Luck himself was present, found that he could sense the Luckness of the room even more now that the man was gone.

"What did you do to Luck?" Glenna asked bluntly, looking around. "I can sense him here, but I can't see him."

Poly gazed at her for a moment before she said, "He's shoring up the inverse pocket."

"Why would you let him do that?" Glenna's voice was shocked. "If he's part of the inverse pocket while reality is unravelling—"

"I know," said Poly quietly. "But it would be cruel not to let him do what he can to protect us."

"But he already rescued you! He rescued you, and looked after you, and now you're going to let him die for you?"

"It's not like that," Peter said, taken aback. "You don't understand, Glenna! Luck's not a grand hero or a—"

"I'm aware of that, thank you very much," said Glenna.

"He's just about as awful as you, I should think. But he was a friend of mine and I don't like to see him taken advantage of."

"It was the only way he could bear to do it," Poly said, still knitting. "I have been…rather bitter about it myself."

"Is that why you're knitting?" asked Peter.

"Yes," she said. "It stops me wanting to hit him. It also seems to be shoring up the inside of the pocket quite nicely, and Luck has promised—well, never mind that. Onepiece, if you're not going to stop wriggling, you can go and fetch Luck again. There's something he wanted to show Peter."

"Does he know how we can fix the unravelling time?"

"No," said Poly. "But he seems to think he can show you the extent of the problem, and that's very nearly as helpful."

$\mathbf{\$}$ 1 2 $\mathbf{\$}$

"This is it," said Luck. "Obviously not exactly *it*, but this is what it would look like if you could see it."

"How did you do this?" asked Glenna in astonishment.

In front of them, on the kitchen table, was a constantly-moving, multifaceted representation of the Two Monarchies —no, Peter realised as he looked it over, a representation of the *timeline* of the Two Monarchies.

"It's beautiful!" he said. The information was all magic-based, of course; fed by information-gathering spells and maintained by the same—but the visual projection was all clockwork and light particles and tactile machinery. "How did you do this? I haven't even started experimenting in light-source representations! It's the perfect example of clockwork put to its best use!"

"It's a marvel of Interconnectedness," Glenna retorted. "Look at that! It's collated all the incidents from a week before the attack on the Sleeping Princess until two weeks after, and tracks the changes to the timeline as they happen."

She looked at Luck in awe and said, "You've even *colour coded* it."

"That was Poly," said Luck. "I can sense the connections but she's the one that sees 'em."

"We arranged it to pick up on the things that are different from how they ought to be," said Poly, still busily knitting. "But now that everything's unravelling, it's not as accurate as it could be, and things are changing all the time."

"This bit," said Luck, pointing vaguely at the purple-tinted section that looked like a very large water-droplet suspended in the air, "is the bit of time that's been sealed up. Familiar type of workings, too, by the looks."

Peter went red. "That's because Mordion took the spell I was using to stop him from seeing the future and turned it into something else."

"If you'll look a bit closer," said Poly, "it's not just one time caught up in there, either."

Peter looked closer at the section and saw the pinching there, like a bad job of mending had been done and left as it was. Seen as a physical representation, he could tell that part of the timeline caught in the spell was from a couple of days before the attack on Poly, and part of it from the day of the attack. Both of those had been combined with the time that they had first arrived: a few days after the attack.

"That must be why the particle mass in the air kept changing," he said to Glenna. "Mordion patched different pieces of time together to make us think we were safe. I'm—well, I'm sorry I didn't listen to you."

He didn't hear her sigh, but there was slightly less tension to her shoulders than there had been a moment before. "All right," she said. "I forgive you. It was a really clever way of doing things, pinching them together. I suppose he did it with the princess' magic."

"That's right," said Poly. She sent a rather amused look in Glenna's direction and said, "You don't have to keep calling me *princess*, you know. I'm not actually a princess. You can call me Poly."

"Thank you," Glenna said, but she said it somewhat stiffly. "I assume he caught you just as your magic manifested itself: I didn't think it was possible to do something like this with magic."

"Not with magic alone," said Poly, slightly apologetically. "But you see, I've got quite large resources of unmagic, too, and Mordion was always very good at figuring out how to make best use of all his resources."

Peter, frowning, considered the small ball of tangled times. "Do you think he sealed it up because he was hoping we'd get caught in there, or because he didn't want us to be able to get back into it and try to alter things again?"

"A little of both, I imagine," said Poly. "It would have amused him to see you trapped on the inside and Glenna trapped on the outside, and the tickerbox divided between the two of you. It's a good thing you shifted out when you did, or this would have been a much more tickly problem."

Peter nearly muttered that at least he had done *something* right, but fortunately, it occurred to him in time that it was churlish to make everyone else try to feel sorry for him when he was, in fact, entirely to blame for the entire situation.

Instead, he cleared his throat, meeting Poly's eyes across the table. She shot him the same amused glance she'd earlier turned on Glenna, and he wondered briefly if his unsaid response was something that could be visible somewhere like the representation on the table in front of him. Unsaid this time, but perhaps said in another set of circumstances. That thought opened another bright, interesting thought about prediction models that Peter hastily told himself he had no time yet to follow.

He cleared his throat again and said, "So we'd need to figure out how to get into that section again if we want to fix the hole—somehow get rid of all the linking points of connection instead of just trying to hide them, this time."

"I don't think we do, though," said Glenna, who had been

gazing at the representation for quite some time in silence. She pointed at the other purple dots all around the representation. "Those are all the fallout items from the purple event. The orange section here is where the Frozen Battlefield should have been—where and *when*—and the fallout items from that still have a bit of an orange tinge to them. It's like everything is trying to fix itself, and all the connections are still there; we just need to draw them back and connect them."

Peter stared at her in surprise. "You don't want to try and fix this bit? You're the one who said we should try to sever the connections in the first place! If we'd done it then, it would have solved the problem."

"*If* we'd done it then," agreed Glenna. "But we didn't, and now it's sealed up. Besides that, there's this bit we should be worried about."

Peter had already seen the bit she was looking at: two black-edged orange dots together that seemed to leave a faint, black trace on every other event in the representation.

"Is that—is that us?"

"Unfortunately," said Luck, far too cheerfully. "Let me wind back the clockwork and show you how things progressed."

He did so, and the representation fluttered for a brief second before it flickered back into constant life.

"Watch," said Luck. "Here you are, playing with Mordion. There you go, spinning away into unravelled time—there's Rorkin fishing you out in a wrong time. There you go again, looking for us."

"Oh," said Peter. With each jump of the tickerbox, the representation had shrunk. When Luck had first wound it back, it had filled the room; it proceeded to unravel at the edges for each jump of the tickerbox until it was the size of the table. And those little black-edged dots, once almost completely orange, burned from the outside in.

"For every jump we make, we're unravelling the timeline even more," he said. "How can we—how can we hope to win? I can't stop the tickerbox jumping from time to time, even if I can detach us from it, that leaves us no way of getting to the right time to fix things before everything unravels."

"The jumping isn't the problem," said Luck. "Well, that's not quite right. It is the problem now, but it's only a problem because time and reality were already destabilised. Once it's stabilised again, jumping will be the opposite of a problem."

Disgruntled, Peter said, "That only partly makes sense. Do you mean that if we manage to shove Mordion back into the course he's meant to be on, we can safely jump without altering the timeline?"

Luck gazed at him for some time. "Oh no, you'll alter it. But there are things you're allowed to alter."

"What Luck means," said Poly, jabbing her husband in the side with one of her knitting needles, "is that if you can bring the timeline back to where it ought to be, you can jump through time as often as you choose without making another hole. It was only the original jump that caused problems because it linked you to Mordion."

"All right," said Glenna, rather pale. "Can this thing extrapolate?"

Luck blinked solemnly at her. "It can, but I don't think you'll like it."

Peter closed his eyes briefly, then opened them again because Onepiece was poking at him with one of Poly's spare knitting needles. "No sleep," the boy said. "Even Onepiece, which is *me*, is not allowed to sleep."

"You already tried it," he said, wresting the needle from Onepiece. "All right, then; how bad was it?"

"The consensus was five more jumps until the end of the world," said Luck, still abominably cheerful. "Before everything disappears completely, anyway. But that was before you jumped here, and the world will be in trouble long before everything finally disappears."

"Safely, two jumps, I should think," Poly said. "We'll be gone by then, but I like to think that we'll be able to come back once you've fixed things."

Peter dreaded looking at her, but when he did, ashamedly, she seemed just as cheerful as Luck. She didn't stop knitting, either, though she did smile at him just as she had always done.

"If we've only got two jumps, we'll need to know exactly where we're going when we leave," said Glenna. "And we'll need to be sure that what we do will work. If Mordion knows we got away, he'll be expecting us to try at that bubble of sealed time again."

"We need to attack from a front he's not expecting," agreed Peter, slowly.

Luck nodded. "He's bound it up because he thinks that's his weak point. It's not: it's every other point between then and the Frozen Battlefield."

"But if we shift to the Frozen Battlefield, he'll know to expect trouble, won't he?"

"That's the good thing about the Frozen Battlefield," said Luck. "The good thing about it not happening, I mean; it isn't really fixed in place yet."

"You can see it on the representation," Poly told them helpfully. "It's those patches of orange: the possibility of the Battlefield being there. They're not as bright as they once were."

"Moveable things, battlefields," said Luck, and stood up.

Poly looked up at once, though she didn't stop knitting. "Do you have to go?"

"My coat hems are unravelling," said Luck, by way of answer, and when he passed by Peter, Peter saw that his coat hem really was unravelling—or was, perhaps, just a little less there. "I'd better go out and check on that."

"Will you come back?" asked Poly. Her hands were busy, but her face was turned up to look at him, and Peter saw the sorrow there.

"It'll only be bad news if I do," Luck said, and kissed her.

He kissed her for a long enough time, in fact, that Peter looked away and Onepiece apparently found it necessary to poke the enchanter in the leg with a knitting needle.

"Ow," mumbled Luck, and released Poly. "Bad dog."

"Shouldn't go, then," Onepiece said sulkily.

"Oh, it was a stab of love, was it?" said Luck, his eyes very green for a moment. "All right. Stay close to your mother."

"Was going to *anyway*."

Luck said to Peter, "I suppose I'll see you again later if everything goes well. Don't expect me to show you how I made that thing; it was at least half Poly. And don't stay here too long; it's not healthy."

"I'm perfectly capable of figuring it out for myself now that I've seen it," Peter said, to Luck's departing back, forgetting that he had very lately had quite a bit of proof that he was by no means as adept at figuring things out as he had thought. He remembered that rather quickly, and said hastily, "Never mind. We'll want to get to the Frozen Battlefield, then; one of the possible places that he doesn't expect, I suppose, but what then? No one knows exactly what happened."

"Ah," said Poly. "There's one thing we do know: you two are the ones who are responsible for the Battlefield."

"I don't see how you can know that," Glenna said, rather stiffly. Like Peter, she knew the *what* if not the *how* of the Enchanted Battlefield; hundreds of people lost their lives on that particular field, embalmed in a mixture of magic and lost time that would one day, three hundred years later, simply disintegrate.

"Poly knows what she's talking about," he said softly to Glenna. "She got to see the other side of it before it collapsed. All of the magic that was in it came to her."

"Convenient for her," said Glenna, and she didn't say it quite under her breath.

Peter, rather belatedly, realised exactly what it was in Glenna's voice; what had been there since they came into the inverse pocket with Poly and Luck, in fact.

It was jealousy.

The thought startled and slightly unbalanced him. He was so used to Glenna being cold on the outside at least that it hadn't occurred to him before now that she could feel such an emotion, the jinx notwithstanding. He would have liked to have thought that the jealousy was because of his own connection with Poly, but he was quite sure that it had more to do with the fact that Glenna had once had a friend of a kind, in Luck, and when Poly appeared, she had lost that friend. Peter knew that feeling well enough himself: he had experienced it when Annabel and Melchior began to grow closer, and he had reacted with far less restraint than Glenna had done.

Peter was quite sure that Poly was smiling over on her side of the room, so he didn't look at her. He didn't know what the smile meant and he rather thought it might be laughing at him in some way, which might well be deserved but still felt raw and a little bit unpleasant.

He had picked up his tickerbox with the rather hopeless thought that he needed to do *something* with it while he still could, when Glenna said, sharp and sudden, "Get up, Peter."

Peter of a few days ago might have sat where he was and demanded to know why he was supposed to move; Peter today hesitated a moment in sheer surprise, then got up, instinctively moving toward Glenna. Today's Peter, therefore, lost only a cuff to a deep, burning nothingness that had crept up over the kitchen table without him noticing it, instead of a whole arm.

Onepiece shrieked and darted under both Poly's hair and her knitting, which were beginning to look suspiciously alike, clinging to her waist. Poly's hair furled out, gossamer and impossibly long, threading around them along the walls and ceiling like a cocoon.

"Better get into the middle of the room," she said.

They did as they were told, hand in hand, and Peter wasn't sure if he was the one comforting Glenna, or if she was the one comforting him.

"What about the door?" Glenna asked, as that, too, disappeared beneath a covering of hair. "Won't we need to get out that way?"

"Doors are never a problem around here," said Poly, smiling reassuringly.

As if to prove her right, the hair cocooning them parted the next moment to allow Luck to tumble back into what was left of the room.

"Luck?" Peter said, and his voice sounded very small to his own ears. Perhaps it was just the acoustics of the room now that it was hair lined. "Why are you back here already?"

He already knew the answer. Luck had done all that he could, and now that it was too late to do anything else, he had come back to be with Poly.

"Oh dear," said Poly, putting aside her knitting with great precisety. "It looks as though things are getting worse more quickly than we expected."

"What's happening?"

"Huh," Luck said, gazing at the blackened edges of the floor that crept beneath Poly's layer of hair. "The bubble is bursting. Careful, Poly! It's going for the stove. I refuse to be without scones."

"I have to go back," said Peter. "As soon as possible."

"I'm afraid so," Poly said. "I hoped we could keep you for a little longer; give you more of an idea what you need to do, but I'm afraid I know very little about what happened after I was put to sleep."

He asked Poly, "Can you keep one more person safely in here?"

"We're both going," said Glenna, and in their cocoon of hair, things of metal and china and magic began to tremble.

Peter drew in a deep breath. It was obvious that she was already annoyed—or even perhaps frightened—and he knew she wouldn't like what he was about to tell her. That meant that the jinx was also going to be unhappy.

"I have to go by myself," he told her. His voice came out even and reasonable, and that pleased him. "I'm the one who made the trouble to start with, and I'm the one who made it worse. I've already put you in enough danger."

"I'm fully aware of how much danger I'll be in," Glenna said. "And this time I can make the decision for myself. We'll go together."

The coils of hair twisted and curled nearby, but Peter pressed on. "I *can't* take you with me. Glenna, I've already done so much that I need to fix! If you're here with Poly and Luck, at least you'll be able to get back to your own time again if something happens to me. With the three of you, you should be able to last quite a while."

"Peter," said Glenna, in a particularly icy voice that by no means betrayed the anger the rest of the room so clearly displayed, "if you dare to try and make a decision for me just *once* more—!"

Perhaps the room moved around him. Perhaps it was simply the force of Glenna's emotions moving the room but held in check in her appearance; perhaps it was the remembrance of her saying *I don't think it's possible to fix you, actually.*

"Right," Peter said, feeling sick. He'd told himself that he would listen to Glenna, and he'd already forgotten. Even if he wanted to keep Glenna safe, it wasn't fair to take that decision away from her, too. He'd already taken away so many decisions from her. He didn't dare to do it; not because Glenna was too fearsome, but because he didn't think he could bear the way she would shut him out absolutely if he did it. She had as much of a right to put herself into danger as he did, even if she didn't have the responsibility. And she was right: it was her own decision to make.

"I'm sorry," he said. "I won't—I'm trying, all right?"

"I know," said Glenna. She smiled at him, but there was a tinge of bitterness to it, and Peter would dearly have loved to know why. "It will take both of us to do something about this," she added; and around the room, things began to settle down again. "Besides, last time we tried to fix things separately, and that didn't work terribly well."

"You mean the last time *I* tried to fix things," said Peter, and there was bitterness to his own smile, too. "You don't have to spare my feelings."

"I could have spoken up a bit louder," Glenna said. "I decided to sulk and let you go off on your own without trying to do anything about it. It wasn't as though I didn't know you'd try to do something. I suppose I wanted to be able to jeer when you got it wrong again; at any rate, I'm just as much to blame as you are."

"I'm very much in favour of the both of you coming to a better understanding," Poly said. "But I'm afraid that we're getting rather short on time. You need to get out now: if the inverse pocket collapses with you in here, that's it for the rest of the world as well."

"Come with us," Peter said. "I'll—I'll find a way to program you into the tickerbox so that you can travel with us too."

"It's too late," said Luck, lifting one arm. The sleeve of his overcoat was in tatters, but they weren't tatters of material; they were tatters of reality. "I only came back in because it's all over now. Thought I'd rather spend the rest of the time here with Poly before we disintegrate."

"Poly can come, then," Peter said.

"Not possible, I'm afraid," said Poly. "Nor Onepiece, either. We can't exist outside of the house anymore: history is too far gone without us."

"You know where the Battlefield should be," said Luck. "And the good thing about the Battlefield is that it wasn't where everyone started out, so at least there's that."

"What does that even *mean*?" asked Peter in despair.

"*Out!*" said Poly, pushing them toward the door. "You've only got one or two more shifts before you unravel altogether: make sure you use them well."

Glenna took the first step, but Peter had hold of her hand and he stumbled after her onto sun-warmed grass. He looked back for a last glance at Poly, and for a very brief moment he saw Luck, tatters and all, with his arms around Poly and Onepiece, and the vast, magic-laced whorl of Poly's hair surrounding them.

It was just for a moment, and when he blinked, they were gone.

Only Luck's voice wafted after them in an answer to Peter's question, eerily calm, "Well, it means that it doesn't have to be exactly where it was. Or even where it should have been."

Very distantly, they heard Onepiece said, "Pish," and the echo of Poly's voice saying, "I love you."

Then the house, and the inverse pocket, and everything that had pointed to Luck and Poly vanished altogether.

Left alone in the bright sunlight of the countryside with a bare fifty minutes left before they would be shifted on again to a place they couldn't yet determine, Peter and Glenna looked at each other.

Glenna said rather faintly, "Do you have *any idea at all* what he was talking about?"

"I was hoping you would," Peter said. It was too hard to think that there was no Poly and Luck left in the world: he much preferred to think that the inverse pocket had merely detached from this part of the world and was waiting, in a much smaller form, for when he and Glenna stitched the world back together. He blinked away the heated tears and said to her, "I was hoping it might make sense in an Interconnectedness kind of way."

Glenna wrapped her arms around herself as if she was cold despite the warmth of the triad. "Well, I suppose it does. All the points were connected, you know; all the ones that should have been at the Battlefield; but they're not definitely connected to any one place, did you notice? There was a possibility for a few different places. If Mordion thinks it should be in one particular spot, I don't see why we can't pick another one and channel the Battlefield there, even if we don't know what causes it to happen."

"We know that we're the ones that do it, though," said Peter, sniffing one last time to clear the moisture from his eyes and nose. "So I suppose we'll just plan it out like we would do if we were working together instead of how we *think* we would have done it. And instead of me just trying to do it on my own."

"All right, then," she said. "But what is our way?"

"I don't know," said Peter. He had been busy for so long in thinking of ways that *he* could fix the problem, that *he* could allow for what he'd seen as Glenna's shortcomings, that he hadn't really thought about how they could work together.

Now, with a little over forty minutes before the tickerbox would usher them into their penultimate shift, he wished he had thought about it long ago.

"All right," he said. "We know that you see connections really well, and we'll probably need that. I can try to program the tickerbox to—"

He stopped, wild possibilities flying through his mind, and

he and Glenna both said at the same time, in astonishment, "Bring the Battlefield to us!"

Exultantly, Glenna said, "They're all interconnected with us; we won't even need their separate identities input into the tickerbox! We can just use the connection."

"And it will still count as one shift, no matter how many people we're bringing."

"And if we get a critical mass of people coming over, it's likely to provide its own pulling power once it's started, even if it's difficult to begin with."

"And—" Peter stopped, the bright joyfulness of knowing exactly what they needed to do tempered by the sudden realisation of the most likely consequence of those actions. "That will bring Mordion to us, too."

"That's what we want, isn't it?" Glenna said, but her face was pale. "He's the one we've got to stop. We make sure we pick the right place, we make sure we're properly prepared—"

"We're going to need to have a containment spell ready so they can't move," said Peter. "And it'll have to be *strong*. If we're fighting against Poly's magic, it'll fight back; it won't just wait to be contained."

"It'll have to be clever as well as strong, and it'll need to be adaptive."

"Or," said Peter, bright with possibilities, "absorptive!"

"Yes. But what about Mordion? We can trap him, too; use the critical mass of all the trapped people to keep him there, but we know he escapes later."

"He's supposed to escape later," Peter said. "That was always in the timeline. But—do you suppose it's going to matter that he still knows about us?"

"That's been the problem since we started, hasn't it? He knows about us and he's not supposed to know about us. We'll have to do something about that, but even memory blockers fade if given enough time, and a lot of time is exactly what he'll have."

"Three hundred years or so," agreed Peter gloomily. "I wish—I wish I'd come back to get you in the first place! Then we would have severed the connections that made him able to see instead of me just trying to stop him from seeing them."

There was a brief silence before Glenna said. "It's already done; it's no good thinking about it all the time. If you're sorry, well, I'm not going to hold it against you."

Peter had to wait for a few, desperately blinking moments until he could say, somewhat snubbily, "That's rather good of you."

"I still regret not hitting you, of course," she said, looking away. "All right, if it comes right down to it, perhaps we can use the containment spell to help with the memory blocking, but—oh! No, but what if we tried it again? Disconnecting instead of blocking?"

Peter stared at her. "You're really beautiful, you know that?" he said reverently.

For a brief moment, a very astonished Glenna stared back at him, her cheeks flushed. Then she cleared her throat and said, "You're the one who mentioned it! It just occurred to me that we might be able to make it work this time."

"No one has ever tried to disconnect memories before," Peter said, grinning. "We'll be making history and no one will ever know."

"*If* it works," she said, but her eyes were already very distant, and Peter knew she was running the idea through her mind, looking for weaknesses and possibilities. "And that's the point, after all, isn't it—making history without anyone knowing about it?"

"I suppose so," said Peter, with just a touch of gloom. "Do you think you can really do it?"

"It's all connections," she said, nodding. "Interconnectedness affects everything, inside and out. If I can find the right connections, I'm sure I can separate them entirely. He might not even know there's a part missing if I do it well enough."

"What about the Old Civetans? Are we only stopping them, or should we try to disconnect them, too? See if we can save them?"

"We should try to disconnect them," she said decidedly. "I know we're not supposed to have done it in the future we know—or at least that we don't succeed, but—"

"No," said Peter. "I agree. If we're doing it our way, then we try to save them. I don't care how it turns out in the end; if we don't at least try to do it so we can save them as well, we'll have failed again."

He looked down at the tickerbox again, unable to help himself, and saw that Glenna was doing the same.

"We're going to have to decide where to go, too," she said. "Quickly. We're going to need a bit of time to set up there. Will Mordion know about the different possibilities, do you think?"

"He hasn't had access to Luck's timeline representation," Peter said. "And he doesn't seem to know about possibilities, only the things that definitely happened in the future that's gone."

"Very well. So if we pick another place that the Battlefield didn't originally happen at, he might not guess what's happening."

"Does it matter if he does? Once we've got him, I mean?" asked Peter. He still remembered the quietness of Poly's voice; she had known herself trapped and helpless, had known what was about to happen to her. He very much wanted Mordion to know exactly where he was, and to know exactly what was about to happen to him. "If we have him, he can't do anything about it. All his stolen power is bound up in the army now, and he didn't even get a tenth of what there was to get from Poly. We can hold him."

Glenna met his gaze; she nodded shortly. "All right," she said. "We'll do it that way. We'll either have him or not, no matter where we are. And who knows, it might help things along if we trap him in the place we should have trapped him; it might help put things back onto the right track with less problems."

Silence fell for a brief moment; the calm before the storm, thought Peter, rather fatalistically. He broke it to say, "We should go now."

"We don't want to waste a tickerbox shift on getting there," she said, and she sounded just a little bit breathless.

"No. But if you trust me to shift us both without using the tickerbox, just magic alone, I can get us there safely. *Then* we can use the next shift to bring the Battlefield to us."

Glenna nodded decisively. "Do it. I can't do shifts at short notice without a lot of setup, but I can promise you that the jinx won't interfere this time."

"Yes," said Peter. He hesitated, but he wanted her to know that he *did* understand; that he *was* trying. He added, "It'll probably help that I'm not talking over you and ignoring everything you say."

"That certainly helps," she said. "But I still wouldn't let you shift me if I didn't trust you."

Peter shifted them both while he was still feeling warm and content and as if not quite *everything* was awful. Perhaps the jinx liked that, or perhaps Glenna really did trust him as much as she said she did. At any rate, nothing awful happened and they arrived exactly where they were meant to arrive.

Peter, looking around, felt a strange sense of familiarity that was edged with a sense of alienness. It wasn't until Glenna said, "It looks odd when it's not all burnt, doesn't it?" that he realised he had only ever seen it in representations, as it was when Poly and Luck disintegrated it: blackened and flat and barren.

"Do you think he knows we're here?" he asked Glenna. "I wouldn't have put it past him to keep an eye on the place, just in case."

"I don't know," she said. "But we've only got half an hour

regardless, so we'd best get started. No, there's no need to do a setup to diminish the effects of the jinx, this time. I rather think we're going to need every unexpected edge we can get."

❧ 13 ❧

Peter wouldn't have dared to grab Glenna's hand when they began joining their magic, so he was glad that she reached out and took his. It wasn't that he felt he simply must hold her hand, but it seemed to make their magic join more swiftly and with greater efficacy, and there was something to be said for a warm hand when a fellow was feeling distinctly cold.

And the magic *did* come out swiftly and strongly: a huge coil of red-tinted yellow magic that was both larger than the two of them and yet somehow, impossibly, fit into the tickerbox's stomach cavity, nestled around the watch-that-was-a-timer.

"That should do nicely," said Peter, nodding in satisfaction. "Do you think we should wait for the next shift to happen when it was planned, or do it ourselves?"

"Whichever way we do it, we should make sure we've got everyone connected, first," Glenna said. "We've only got about ten minutes now, I should think. Not much good doing it ourselves when the tickerbox will only shift us again before we have a chance to do anything about Mordion."

"Good point," Peter said, shuddering. He would hate to

think how much of a head-start it would give Mordion, to be drawn here to the Frozen Battlefield and then left alone to plan a way to outwit Peter and Glenna before they could get back. *If* they could get back after that second shift. "If you start, I might be able to see what you're doing well enough to help."

"I've already started," she said, smiling a little bit grimly. "Perhaps you could use the magic we've gathered to see to the containment spell we're going to need? We could link all the connections we're making to the containment spell as well."

"I've got it," he said; and, starting with the connections that Glenna had begun to make, he wove them into the substance of the containment spell, adding each new connection as she made it, until the whole was a basket, or perhaps a rope, with each connection a strand amidst strands, bound irrevocably together by their joined magic.

He was so busy with the spell that he didn't notice when Glenna finished making connections. It was the heavy whirring of the tickerbox that warned him their allotted time had come to an end, sparking a sudden fear that all their work would again be for nothing. Peter released Glenna's hand and, with shaking fingers, input the connections to be shifted, and the destination-draw for those connections.

The tickerbox seized on it eagerly, with a clicking of its spindly legs, and...*stopped*.

Glenna, rather pale, said, "It's not working. Why isn't it working?"

"There's no pull," Peter said, his mind buzzing. "There should be a pull because we're already connected to them, and I've input that connection as the draw to bring them here. The vacuum should be working."

"Is it no pull, or *too much* pull?" asked Glenna.

"I've already allowed for any versions of us still around," Peter said, feeling the sweat spring up on his brow. "There's too much pull back and forth when the connection is between people, and the army is already strong with Poly's magic, not to mention there's more of them than us."

Glenna's chin firmed. "What if we use co-ordinates for this physical spot?"

"Then we'd need proper co-ordinates for all the people—exactly where each one of them is, not just the interconnectedness of them with us."

"Why can't we be co-ordinates? You linked us to our future selves when we were trying to get back to the future."

"Yes, but I had information for both sides, then. We've only got exact information for us, and we're not a land feature, so—oh."

"I'd rather not be a land feature, thank you very much."

"I know how we can do it," he said. "But I don't think you're going to like it."

She nodded, and to Peter, it seemed as though she did so numbly. Glenna had already grasped what he meant to do.

"Yes, I rather thought so," she said. "It's all or nothing now, though, isn't it?"

"If we're both coded into the tickerbox as well—not as people, but as part of the tickerbox—that should make us into a co-ordinate that we can draw everyone toward."

"Better than making us a co-ordinate in the physical world," she said grimly. "I'd as lief not become a permanent part of the landscape, if it comes to that."

Their eyes met, and Glenna said through her teeth, "Do it."

"It will connect us to the tickerbox forever if something goes wrong again—"

She actually laughed, but Peter wasn't at all sure it was an amused laugh.

"I know."

"And I still haven't fixed the timer—"

"I know."

"And the secondary engine that controls time and interval input—"

"Do it now," said Glenna, her face white. She reached across and grabbed his hand again. "We'll do it together, but we have to do it now."

Peter had never been less sure of himself. It took mere moments to code them both in, limning the connections with that shared magic of theirs and feeling it sink into them. They didn't so much become one with the tickerbox as it became one with them, burrowing deep into the red-and-yellow warmth of their combined magic.

"You'll need to make sure the connections are all there!" panted Peter. "I can't see well enough to do it!"

Glenna reached her hand through the web of connections that stretched out into reality around them, and the tickerbox chirped in surprise as it felt the tug of hundreds of people linking with it from across the country.

"I've got them tight," she said. "But we're going to need more power to get them here. The tickerbox is already working too hard."

So Peter pushed more of that red-tinted yellow power of theirs into the tickerbox, and Glenna pulled, and for the length of the shift, it was hard to differentiate between who was pulling, who was pushing, and where everything was going.

Neither of them lost consciousness this time, either, but between blinking his eyes shut and opening them again, Peter found himself face to face with Mordion.

Behind the man, he saw an army of people with joyful, pitiless faces, each of them gazing forward as if they saw something only they could see: a bright, entrancing, guiding light. Then Glenna squeezed Peter's hand, and he saw her eyes flick down. He looked down, too, and saw the coiling ropes of the containment spell that tangled the feet of the army—theirs and Mordion's by default.

"Ah, Peter Carlisle!" said Mordion. His eyes laughed at Peter as though they shared a joke, and that grated on Peter. "What a shame! I quite thought you'd been trapped in that little bubble you helped me to make. Never mind: I'm afraid you're just a little too late once again! Surrender has been achieved and terms are already set to spellpaper. I admit that I would very much like to know what you did with the Royal Castle, however."

Peter met Glenna's eyes and saw in them the same relief he felt. So Rorkin and the Royal Castle were still safe, were they? Mordion, whatever he had seen, had not seen enough to know about that—or perhaps he had made the wrong conclusions from what he had seen. Peter would dearly have liked to know which one it was.

"You can't have the castle," he said. "It's already beyond your reach."

"I'm sure you thought the same thing about darling little Poly," Mordion said, shrugging. "But here we are, and there you are! I really expected you to try and stop that happening; in fact, I'm curious to know why you didn't do so. A simple blocking spell? How dare you come against me with something so ridiculously ineffective!"

Peter looked into that arrogant, disgusted face and saw his own, younger face reflected back at him. No, not his face: his expression. He swallowed the bitterness that came with the recognition, because it had occurred to him that Mordion did not, in fact, know everything. The man still thought they were here to save Poly, not to patch wounded time by enforcing the stream of events that should have already happened. He had known a little, had guessed a lot, and had guessed wrongly. If he hadn't been so lucky—or if Peter hadn't been so ripe for manipulation—there was a good chance Mordion would have ruined himself.

"I'm curious, too," he said to Mordion. "How did you make it so that we thought we'd arrived before you attacked

Poly? I would have sworn you didn't have that much power—or ability."

"I saw rather a lot of her future as well as yours," said Mordion. "It gave me some rather good ideas about what was possible when you have access to this much magic. My goodness, it was enjoyable watching you follow along behind me—feeding you exactly what I wanted you to know! It's just a shame it didn't trap you properly."

"I've a feeling that's going to be your motif in life," Glenna said.

Mordion smiled at her with all his usual charm. "What exactly do you hope to achieve by drawing us all here? It's already too late: I know all about both of you and your adventures through time to try and stop me. With the kind of magic I've taken on, you'll never be able to hold us here. Even if you somehow manage to bring about the result I saw, you'll only stop me for a moment."

"Is that so?" asked Glenna. "If I were you, I'd look down."

"What nonsense," said Mordion, looking down at the containment magic that had steadily grown up his legs from ankle to calf as they talked. "Do you really think this will hold me? It's not even the right colour: too much has changed. It might hold this rabble for a while, but even if I have to abandon them and start again, I can do it. Now that I know you're here, you won't find it so easy to imprison me again."

"That might have worked on me," Peter said, and tipped his head toward Glenna. "But she's really good when it comes to the Interconnectedness of All Things, and she's also pretty good at knowing when and how to disconnect things that aren't helpful or useful."

"You can't separate a human from all things," Mordion said, his face very white. "You might as well try to kill me."

"It would kill you," Glenna said. "Effectively, that is. You wouldn't be able to connect to the world in any meaningful way, physically or magically. You'd die of hunger or go mad first."

"I've seen the future. It needs me—you need me. I saw the possibility of my absence, and that future unravelled itself first."

"Sometimes the world needs a mad dog," said Peter. "But even if it does, we're going to take your teeth out for a while. And then, one day, one of my friends will put you down for good."

"That was *almost* frightening," Mordion said, recovering his easy demeanour. "Do your worst. You can't disconnect me from everything without setting the world into a spin, and this is at worst a mild inconvenience for me. I'll be back to make trouble, and quite soon, too, I should think."

"We don't need to disconnect you from everything," said Glenna. "Just from a few memories."

Mordion stared at her. "You can't do that."

"The funny thing about saying things like that," Peter said, "is that it doesn't make them true. You might not be able to do it, but Glenna's really good at doing stuff people think she can't do."

"If I had wanted to limit myself to doing only those things that people said I could do, I probably would have died in the womb," Glenna said. "Stand still, please—or don't, just as you like. It won't affect me, but it will probably be very uncomfortable for you."

"I don't actually care if he's uncomfortable," said Peter.

"That's a very good point," said Glenna, and reached out to the connections that, linked as they both were by their magic and the tickerbox, Peter could faintly see.

"Don't touch me!" Mordion said, though his teeth. "You'll regret it!"

"You won't remember this," Peter said, "but you're going to fail again and again. You thought you'd beaten Poly, but she came back. And you'll think you've beaten Glenna, but she'll live. You'll even think you're going to best Annabel for a while, but she'll get you in the end, too. You've only ever been a temporary crimp in people's lives."

"Here we go," said Glenna, her hands outstretched to cup Mordion's temples. He strained away from her, but was held fast by the solid magic that still grew up around his hips, slowly but surely covering every inch of him and absorbing power as it came. "I'd like you all to keep very quiet now; I'd hate to do something unfortunate."

Mordion opened his mouth to speak again, but whatever connections Glenna held delicately in her hands, the touching of them was enough to make him lose consciousness. Glenna didn't bother to catch his head, and Peter, who could still only faintly see the connections that she could obviously see so clearly, hoped that it hadn't jostled anything important loose. Mordion hadn't been entirely wrong: he was necessary to the timeline.

Still, Glenna didn't seem concerned; she spoke only once as she worked, and that was to quietly ask for more feed-through of magic. Peter, with one eye to the trapped army, cautiously sent more in her direction, and for a brief moment felt the utter power of what they had done—could yet do—together. He couldn't have done this by himself; nor could Glenna. She was the one who could see the connections, but without the strength of his magic supplementing her jinx, she wouldn't have been able to reach far enough to touch them. Mordion had been right to try and divide them.

When Glenna at last stood back from her work, delicately loosening her fingers from the connections, Peter asked, hardly daring to breathe, "Can you see the other one? The other connection, I mean?"

"The one from him to them?"

"Yes. I can sort of see it, but I can't see it clearly enough to know. Can you—?"

"I can't disconnect it," she said quietly. "Not without

killing them. They aren't just interconnected; he made them and himself into one living organism. They're not even—I don't think they're even really alive anymore."

The reality of what he could faintly see sank deep into Peter's stomach, churning. "He's the head and they're parts of the body?"

"Yes. He's feeding on their bodies' life-force through Poly's power, using her to connect them all; their souls were gone the first moment he had them under his sway, I expect."

"Even so," protested Peter. "They're people. We can't leave them trapped with him."

"They're not people," said Glenna, her freckles standing out with orange clarity against her pale face. "They're just shells, now—extensions of him. You can't fix that."

"We have to fix it," Peter said, but he knew it wasn't possible, just as much as Glenna did. "We have to—"

"It's not your fault," she said. There was that icy edge to her voice again, but this time Peter knew it wasn't because she was trying to cut at him. She was trying to push away an emotion that would cause her jinx to affect their workings. "Don't you remember what Rorkin said? There are some things that can't be changed, just channelled into a slightly different path. We're here to channel it back where it was before we knocked it out of its course."

"We've done the impossible since we started going back in time," said Peter. "There has to be another way. I'm the one— I'm the one who gave him the power to get where he is. If I hadn't let him manipulate me, he wouldn't have had enough strength to do what he's doing."

"If it wasn't you, it would have been someone else he used," Glenna said. "You've done enough awful things; don't try to blame yourself for someone else's wickedness."

"But—"

"I'm not saying we shouldn't try to stop things, or rechannel them," she added. "That's our responsibility, since he's doing it with insight he was able to get because of us. But it's not going to be terribly useful of us to be always wringing our hands instead of doing something. We can't let Mordion go again, and if we disconnect the army from him it really will kill them—"

"And all the power will go straight back to him," Peter said, rather numbly.

"They're a good part of what's keeping him here: if they weren't, I don't think we could hold him. Besides, if we imprison them, there's hope that someone might be able to help them again one day."

"We know that no-one—"

"I know," she said fiercely. "But do you want to be the one to kill them, right now?"

Peter swallowed. "No."

"All right," she said. "Neither do I."

They didn't strictly have to keep pushing power through the tickerbox and into the containment spell, but Peter kept pushing, anyway. There was a sharp, uncomfortable thought in the back of his mind that said he would much prefer Mordion not to wake up again.

Glenna did the same, and perhaps it was she who began to weave in the threads of Mordion's connection to his army with the containment spell. If so, it was Peter who began to weave in the loose bits of time that no longer quite fit anywhere and had been moving around in the tickerbox's stomach cavity for far too long, in some wholly impossible version of indigestion.

"This might not be quite wise," Glenna said, though she didn't stop.

Peter said, "I know, but I don't want to leave him any loose ends," and he didn't stop, either.

By the time they finished weaving, the red-tinted yellow magic had become smooth and hard and very nearly amber around their captives. Mordion, very nearly neck-deep in it, groaned, his eyes fluttering open.

"Bother," said Glenna, starting back to stand beside Peter.

Mordion stared at her. "Who are you? What have you done to me?"

"We stole your magic and imprisoned you," said Peter, stepping forward a little. "Unfortunately, that's the worst we can do to you right now."

Mordion's eyes rolled back as he tried to see what had become of his army, and a wave of frustration that swept over his face when he caught sight of their rapturous faces through the sheen of glossy amber.

"I'll get out again," he said, through his teeth. He could still move his head, but only just. He did so, stiffly, to look first at Peter and then at Glenna. "I can promise you that."

"Yes, but not before we render you toothless," said Glenna, smiling coldly at him. "I assure you that you won't see me again, so it's not much use trying to remember me."

"I'll...make...the effort," he said, with difficulty; and this time, he looked at Peter.

"You do that," said Peter, as the amber containment magic enveloped Mordion's mouth and then, more swiftly, the rest of his head.

Glenna, shivering, said, "I wish it didn't look like he can still see us."

"He can't," Peter said, even though it was something they both knew. He said it to comfort himself as much as her. Everything should have stopped for Mordion by now— or at least slowed down to the point where he and Glenna would be moving far too quickly to be comprehensible to the man. Trapped in magic and aging and thinking so slowly, he would eventually be the only survivor of the Frozen Battle-field, the power he had stolen slowly drawn out of him by the containment spell through the years. The army, now only husks of people, would turn to dust when the spell failed.

"Once Poly's awake again and starts using her magic, this will all get a lot weaker," he said. "He'll be able to escape."

Glenna sighed; a huge, half-sobbing thing. "I know," she said. "But the amount of evil he can do is already prescribed. We fixed the hole. He won't be able to do more than he's already done."

"I suppose the particles are back to normal," said Peter, trying to smile. He could already tell that the world around them felt as it ought to feel—as Glenna knew it ought to feel. The connection that had been made between them through the tickerbox to draw the army to themselves, as nebulous as it had been when it was first formed, was now stronger than he would have thought possible. He hard rather expected it to fade once the spell was complete.

In the strength of that connection, he could see the seam that their amber containment spell had made not just in reality, but along the edges that had previously trailed off aimlessly into the darkness of an unsure future.

"Yes," said Glenna. "As far as I can tell, anyway. I can do some tests properly when we're not so—so—"

"Yes," agreed Peter. "Later. We'll have to make sure it's going to disintegrate properly for Poly, too. She told me she saw her father when it collapsed, but that might not be an important part of the timeline. Mind you, she also said he was the one who came to see you while we were at the house, so maybe she was joking about that, too."

Glenna went perfectly white, her freckles standing out in her face. "She said that? She said that he's her father?"

"Yes," said Peter, rather cautiously, because Glenna looked as though she had been hit suddenly with something unpleasant. Had Poly not been joking, after all? Had *Glenna* not been joking when she called him her fiancé?

"She must have—oh, she must have been so lonely! Why didn't you tell me?"

"Why should I tell you that?" demanded Peter, defensively.

"After all the things you didn't tell me, it's pretty thick cheek to—"

"You awful little boy!" she flashed. "I told her—I said to her—! Oh Peter! If I'd *known*!"

"What—what did I do *now*?" asked Peter, almost in despair. He could see the filaments of the jinx running along Glenna's fingers, and he could feel them himself. Worse, he could see the tears in her eyes.

She pressed her fingers over her eyes, but Peter saw the paleness of her cheeks between them, and the two icy droplets slid along those fingers. It had never occurred to him before this series of events that he might one day need to think about what he was about to say before he said it. Now that it did, Peter found that he didn't know what he ought to say.

So he kept silent instead.

"Nothing," Glenna said at last. "You did nothing. I did it all—oh, my wretched tongue! Never mind, Peter. It wasn't your fault. It was mine. I was angry and I bit at her, and she took it beautifully. She shouldn't have had to take that, not from me."

Peter didn't know what to say to that, either; he didn't understand her sorrow, or why she said what she said, and it still seemed wiser to stay quiet, though this time he didn't feel constrained by the jinx. He had previously bitterly felt all of the disadvantage of travelling with someone who was affected by every small thing he said, but it occurred to Peter for the first time that he was scarcely less affected by other people than Glenna was. His only advantage had been that, hitherto, dreadful circumstances hadn't been the natural result of that predilection to be affected by other people.

From the start, he had allowed people to manipulate his emotions to their own ends. He had allowed Samuel to goad him into kidnapping Glenna; he had allowed Glenna's forthright criticism of him to prompt him to bullishly push ahead and prove her wrong as often as he could; and then, Mordion…

At least Glenna had mastered her emotions the best she could: she had known herself, and taken all the steps she could to mitigate any bad effects likely to come from her emotions being used against her. She had had, moreover, an actual excuse that came from outside of herself. She hadn't complained about it, and she hadn't blamed other people for it: she had striven to avoid things she knew would cause trouble. She had tried to keep Peter safe as much as she had tried to keep other people safe, by avoiding him as much as possible.

Peter hadn't mastered his emotions because he had never had to suffer the ill effects of them himself. First with Annabel, who had put up with his brash rudeness with all the understanding of a true friend—Annabel, who had never, he now realised with shame, ever had the same regard or kindness from him, or anyone else except Melchior—and then at the university, where his intelligence had bought for him a great deal of licence with regards to rudeness, Peter had never had to consider how his words and actions affected anyone but himself.

He had thought Glenna rude and self-involved: it only now occurred to him with full, devastating impact, that he had been the one, all along, who was rude and self-involved. For all his intelligence, he hadn't been able to see the manipulation of either Samuel or Mordion, and Glenna as well as himself had paid the price for it.

They sat in silence in the amber shadow of the Frozen Battlefield, and Glenna cried orangey tears that didn't quite fall as they should have fallen, while Peter sat beside her and put his arms around her.

At last, against the silence of the containment spell, she said, "I really hate you, you know."

"I know," said Peter wearily. He rather hated himself at the moment, too. "I'm sorry."

"Don't worry," said Glenna, with misery in her tear-glossed eyes and amber-tinged tears still running down her cheeks, "I hate me, too. It's not just you."

Peter meant to laugh, but sobbed instead; and once that first one was out, there was nothing to be done. He cried as much as Glenna had done, if not quite as quietly, and as he'd done for her, Glenna twined her arms around him and let him cry until he'd finished.

Both of them had quite forgotten about the tickerbox and its timer by the time it whirred into life again, but if they'd forgotten about the tickerbox, it certainly had not forgotten about them.

Glenna must have felt it stirring to life, connected as the two of them still were, because she looked up sharply and said, "No, not yet!"

But the tickerbox had already begun, and though Peter made a wild grab for it, it was already too late. With clockwork ticking in his ears and Glenna's hand still clutching his, Peter was flung through time and reality yet again.

❧ 14 ☙

T he shift was short, sharp, and rather explosive. Peter, tumbling free from it, hit his head hard against the amber containment spell that he and Glenna had just solidified, and caught Glenna just before she would have done the same.

A flutter of molten orange burned the edges of his shirt, and Peter frantically batted at it with one hand, expecting to feel the heat and sting of singed material. Instead, he found cool, sticky magic that came away on his fingers and sank silkily into his skin, leaving a momentary sheen of amber.

It wasn't the combined magic he and Glenna had used together, that shone in equal parts cherry red and yellow if you looked at it right. This magic was utterly amber with a deep, glittering core that couldn't be separated into its constituent colours of red and yellow.

And it wasn't just around him, it was *in* him.

His magic.

But Peter had already seen this magic: he had seen it the night someone threw him through a wall and into a broom closet, and he had seen it when the stranger came to visit

Glenna at Poly and Luck's house. That stranger who was Poly's father, or maybe Glenna's fiancé, or—

Peter swallowed, his hand instinctively curling into itself, and somehow his gaze travelled up and away from the very familiar magic, to Glenna's face as she leaned against the hard amber of their containment spell—just the same colour as that magic.

"You've recognised it, then?" she asked. She was smiling, but it was a smile that was tight and rather grim.

"It's my magic!" said Peter, breathing far too quickly. "It was *my* magic!"

"Technically speaking, it's both of our magic," she said. "And a goodly helping of the jinx, too, I should think, after that explosion. I'm not sure what went on with the colour variant; he's never been able to figure it out, either."

"You mean *I* haven't been able to figure it out," Peter said, with the sticky, chest-heavy feeling that he couldn't quite breathe. He didn't know how it was possible, but he was quite certain that it was a years-older version of himself that he had seen both times. A years older version of himself who was—who was—

"I didn't even know it was a combination of our magics until now," Glenna said. She produced a little flare of her own magic, and it flickered along her fingers, glinting amber. "And to think I thought I knew what real interconnected magic looked like! I always assumed that something else happened before I met him that made it like that. It didn't look the same when we combined it, you see."

"Before you met *me*, you mean," said Peter. He wasn't sure why he was so insistent on that point, except that even if he had just figured some things out, Glenna had known those things much earlier and should have told him. "And *actually*—wait. You kissed me!"

Glenna flushed bright red. "I kissed *him*! It has nothing to do with you!"

"It's *me* you're talking about! Stop talking like it's someone else!"

"You're nothing like him," she said, and there was an icy edge to her voice; the old Miss Stoneflange that he had met at the first. "Maybe, if you're very lucky, you'll grow up to be him. I've got my doubts; but then, I've spent more time with you than with him, lately."

"I *am* him!"

"Not yet," Glenna said quietly. "Not by a very long way."

"Wait!" said Peter. "If he's *me*, why were you meeting him? You hate me!"

"Perhaps," Glenna said. "But I don't hate him."

"We're the *same person*!" Forgetting his late resolution to be more careful about what he said to other people in the frustration of the moment, Peter demanded, "Does your jinx make you more irritating, or do you do that as a special favour to me?"

"Funnily enough, that's the same question I often have about you, without having the excuse of a jinx to blame it on. And if we're going to be very technical about things, it's your jinx now, too."

"Oh," said Peter. He hadn't thought about that. He found that he didn't want to think about it, either; there was something far more interesting to talk about. "But then why did you—why would you keep meeting with him after you knew I was him? At the school, at Luck's house—twice, wasn't it?— why would you do that?"

"I suppose I hoped that you actually might turn into him one day."

"You *like* him!" Peter said in astonishment. "I think you're actually in love with him! With me, that is."

"I'm not in love with you," said Glenna. "I'm in love with my fiancé—husband, actually, by the time I met him. He's a you that doesn't exist yet, and might never exist."

Peter wasn't prepared for the wave of heated jealousy that

swept over him. He wasn't prepared for the force of it, or the illogicality of it—or for the fact that he and Glenna's choice of man were one and the same to bear so little weight with her.

Biting back several of the things he would have liked to have said, he said only, "Is that why you were so upset about Poly?"

"Yes," she said quietly. "It's bad enough that she went through everything because we couldn't keep her safe or take her with us. She shouldn't have had to put up with me being snippy at her because I fancied she took my friend away from me."

"Poly's good about things like that," said Peter. He meant it to be comforting, but it gave him a pang on Poly's behalf to say it, because if everything he had learned today was true, the biggest hand in the misfortunes that had befallen Poly was still his. Rather more quietly, he added, "She's used to dealing with me, anyway."

Glenna smiled a little, but became serious almost immediately.

"We'd better get busy, then," she said decidedly. "While everything here is still so bright and new, I mean. We should be able to reach them through the connection in the workings."

"The workings?" Peter had to think about it for far too long before he understood. "You really want to try to talk to Poly again, don't you? By using the interconnectedness of them breaking the spell and us being here at its inception, I mean."

"You said she met her father here," said Glenna, nodding. "And it will certainly fall apart again if she's there to take her own magic that's sunk in. That should be enough on their side to get through if we do it before we shift again. Unless you think you can disconnect us from the tickerbox?"

Peter pulled out the diagnostic, but he fancied he already knew what he was going to see.

It might, perhaps, even have been worse than he'd thought.

"It's melted," he told her quietly. "The wires and the jinx and the magic all in one lot together: I can't get into it physically and I can't get into it magically, either. It looks like the secondary engine for time and interval has blown up again. There's nothing I can do to input what times we'll end up in, and I can't stop the shifts."

"So when the timer catches up, we'll be taken somewhere else—some time else."

"Yes."

"Very well. We can't physically go back to Poly now, can we? To the house, I mean; even if we can find it."

"I don't think so," said Peter. "Now that the future is back where it should be, I think we'll run too much danger of meeting ourselves where we shouldn't."

"All right. We can't go back anywhere that we're likely to meet ourselves. But—"

"Yes, we seem to have gotten around that by sending just one of us to meet the other one, but I don't think it's exactly safe."

Glenna, wrapping her arms around herself, frowned. "Why would we leave Poly alone to start with? I know that we can't change it now—I *know* she's part of the timeline that we're not allowed to change—but why would we do that?"

"Rorkin's socks," said Peter, remembering a conversation they had already had. "He can't travel with anything that isn't already tuned into that original shift, and neither—neither can we."

"We didn't take her with us because we couldn't, at that point," Glenna said slowly. "Just like my shoes. I wonder if that will change?"

Red with shame and sorrow, Peter said, "I'm sorry. If I

hadn't—if I'd at least listened to you when you said not to touch you—"

"Poly didn't seem as though she had any hard feelings toward us," said Glenna. She cleared her throat, and Peter was quite sure she was again on the point of tears. "I told you: I've forgiven the things that happened between us. There's no good looking back at it when we can't change it."

"Then what are we supposed to do?"

"For now, try to at least see Poly again, even if we can't go back to the house."

"All right," said Peter. "She did tell me, ages ago, that she saw her father when she came to the Battlefield; through the amber. Do you think we'll be able to do it now, though?"

"I'm certain we can contact her if we try here, anyway," she said. "You remember I said that Interconnectedness isn't all the pre-set *most likely to succeed* things, don't you? Well, here we have the best of both kinds of Interconnectedness."

"You think we can make a deeper connection here with all the points of connection on both sides."

"That, and the tickerbox," she said. "It's a bit of a mess right now, but at least we're connected to it, and it's connected to the amber. If we pushed a bit more magic into it, do you think we could use it to sort of lever open time enough to get through to them here?"

"I've got a better idea," said Peter, his eyes alight. "And it doesn't involve pushing magic into the tickerbox, either. We'll just get it to shift, like we always have done."

"Won't that—"

"Not a real shift," Peter told her, delighted with his own cleverness. "We can't access enough of the tickerbox to do a real shift on our own terms, and I don't think we could do it safely even if we tried. But if it *thinks* it's going to be shifting and makes the connections between co-ordinates in preparation—"

"We'll have the connection we need to the other time. We

won't even need to know exactly when it is if we target the disintegration of the amber instead of a particular time."

"Exactly!" said Peter.

"We'll need to be able to do it pretty soon," Glenna said warningly. "The next shift is going to be soon enough."

"You find the connections while I set up the tickerbox, then," Peter told her. Truth to tell, there wasn't too much to set up; it was more a matter of trying not to do too much. The tickerbox was already fragile, and he didn't like to think what could go wrong if it wasn't handled carefully. All he needed to use it for was making that Interconnected link: through that link, they could run a simple communication spell along the reflective surface of the amber in front of them.

With the fragility of the tickerbox in mind, Peter was careful to engage the last remaining functional knob on the side of the box as a tempering toggle before he linked it to the connection Glenna had found. It was one more step in the process, but at least it meant he could shut things down before something else exploded.

Some minutes later, the tickerbox was primed and ready for a shift.

Glenna, who was quite well versed now in how the tickerbox worked, reached for it, but Peter pulled it back.

"We have to do it *carefully*," he said.

"Yes," said Glenna, very politely. "I'm aware. Why have you added another function?"

"It's like that new Contraption speaker," said Peter. "Well, sort of: the knob controls how much of a connection we have. If it connects too well, the tickerbox will actually try to shift us and at this point we'll probably end up halfway between here and there. Not enough, and we'll not be able to see Poly. I've got it set quite low, but that should be enough."

He pushed the smallest amount of magic into the box to ignite the process, and imagined that he saw a faint shadow pass across the surface of the amber in front of them.

Glenna reached over to turn the knob rather further, but Peter caught a flicker of real movement in the amber in front of them as well as the dangerous sheen of jinx to her fingers, and he lightly slapped her hand away. Glenna glared at him but then looked up, her eyes brightening as she saw the window-like view of another time that had appeared there.

"It worked! Peter, it worked!"

"I told you it would," said Peter, forgetting himself. He looked into communication spell in the amber to find that Poly's eyes on him: eyes that bore the same old faint amusement and understanding, as well as fondness, though this Poly was younger than he knew her. Perhaps just a year or two older than Glenna, she obviously knew now, as she had known last time they met, that she was his daughter.

Carefully, because he was quite sure that Luck at this point *didn't* know as much, Peter asked, "Do you know who we are?"

She nodded, sharp and short, and Peter fancied she was very carefully not looking at Luck. It was a pity he hadn't known to ask her more about the progression of their relationship when he had been there with them and could have done so. It was also a pity that they didn't know exactly where in Poly's timeline they had met with.

Connected as they were, Peter felt Glenna's urge to say something, and squeezed her hand warningly. "The tickerbox will shift us on again in a bit, but Glenna was certain that we could meet up before it did."

There was confusion there in Poly's eyes along with the recognition. Peter wondered exactly how long ago she'd woken up, and exactly how many of her memories she had regained by now. It made it hard to know exactly what to say, and while he dithered, Glenna said to Poly, "I would have been nicer to you if I'd known."

There was no confusion in Poly's eyes at that; her smile came out, warm and completely unselfconscious, and Peter physically felt the flush of warmth and emotion that came over Glenna through their shared magic.

Awkward in his attempts to be both tactful and circumspect with regards to time, he said, "Sorry, we keep forgetting what part of your timeline we've met with. Are you two already—I mean, is he your husband?"

In a horrified voice that made Peter grin, Poly said, "Good grief, no! He's a wizard who um, rescued me."

"Hallo, Luck," Peter said to the enchanter. "You look even less civilised than usual."

Luck's eyes had been narrow, but now he grinned. "Past or future?"

"Um." Peter polished his glasses to give himself time to think about it—he would really have to do something about the smudginess of them—and with Rorkin's warning in the back of his mind, finally said, "Well, both, I think: we haven't gone far enough to tell, yet. You should see us again soon, actually, only we'll probably be younger then. We'll need somewhere to stay for a while, and we probably won't know who you are."

He said it to Poly more than Luck, but he was watching Luck closely enough to catch the flare of golden magic that wriggled through the Interconnectedness of the amber and tried to sneak through the window of the communication spell and right into the tickerbox as well.

"It won't work you know," he told Luck. "The tickerbox isn't magic; it's clockwork."

"You've made a hole in time. Who are you?"

"That's not allowed. Actually, it's a big kind of Not Allowed. Poly, we've only got a few more minutes before we shift again and I don't know when we'll end up. Once the window dissipates, all the magic trapped inside is going to hit you: I'm afraid there's rather a lot. I had to push a big bunch of it into the tickerbox to solidify the resin in time, and it seems to have leaked through. It might be a bit strong."

The shock on Poly's face sent a stab of shame through Peter once again. "*You* put those people in amber?"

"*We* did," said Glenna, her voice breaking just slightly. Peter wondered if she knew that her hand had tightened around his; if she knew, perhaps, how that hold squeezed his heart almost too much to bear, though he wasn't sure if it was sorrow or perhaps something else. "They would have killed everyone. Or enslaved them. It was all very nasty and we don't want to talk about it."

Perhaps Poly saw the same flicker that Peter saw passing across the resin, because she looked distinctly worried. Hastily, she asked "What happened to you both?"

"Peter pushed too much magic into the tickerbox trying to time travel us," said Glenna. "He does that a lot, as a matter of fact. It burned out one of the baby engines that was regulating –"

Peter, swiftly discovering that he could very possibly both be in love with Glenna and still very much irritated with her at the same time, said with the faintest edge of annoyance to his voice, "It's a *secondary* engine. And it happened to be the one that was controlling time and interval, so we've been ducking in and around all over the place. Mostly we've been going backwards but I'm pretty sure we'll come forward again before too many years. Either that or I've managed to fix it by the time we're older. Anyway, we'll be seeing you."

"No, no, don't go yet!" interrupted Luck. His eyes were bright and excited, his hair sticking out at wrong angles some-where at the back, and he looked very slightly deranged. "There were notes, clues, little bits and pieces in books and such: old ones."

Peter pushed up his glasses and moved almost without thinking to Luck's side of the window. Glenna didn't try to stop him: she drew closer to Poly instead, and he heard her say very quietly to her, "I'm sorry we leave—left, that is— you there. I think anything that wasn't originally tuned to the tickerbox gets left behind. We haven't been able to carry anything with us out of the different times yet. Peter says he'll figure it out, but I suppose we won't, if we left you behind."

"Lady Cimone looked after me," said Poly, but Peter didn't get the chance to hear anything more. Luck, a vibrant, pulsating beacon of power even at a distance of time and space and magic, demanded attention.

He said accusingly, "You've been leaving me clues."

"Yes, you said that. What sort of clues?"

"Ones that led all the way to Poly," said Luck, his green eyes very narrow. "And I would *very much like* to make sure that I still get those clues. If the wrong person gets sent, I'll have to do a lot of very tiresome things to catch up again."

"I don't know where we're going to end up," Peter said warningly. "We can leave clues and that sort of thing if we're being chucked into the past: we've got a pretty good idea of what needs to go on, so if it's just a matter of leaving things whenever we can with a clue here and there—"

"Exactly," said Luck approvingly. "It was bits and pieces of a map that weren't quite in time or in the right place. Little drawings in books that I bought, tiny hints in my house. That's why I got interested. I like puzzles."

"Is that why you like Poly? Because she's a puzzle?"

"You don't like someone for being a puzzle," said Luck. "That's just a delightful bonus."

"Someone else is interested in her too, you know."

"Yes, they tried to blow us up already. I'm not interested in bombs and they're very tiresome—huh. It looks like this is about to collapse. Interesting."

Poly, who seemed to have come to much the same conclusion, drew closer again, her eyes on Peter. It warmed his heart to see her there, safe and whole, when he'd last seen her and Luck in mortal danger.

He grinned at them both and stepped back to grab Glenna's hand. He could feel the tickerbox whirring away, ready to shift them again. "See you soon. Or later. I've lost track."

The tickerbox spat out a very small spark of golden magic that fizzled against the amber, and Peter felt it take hold on himself and Glenna. It shifted them away from the Enchanted Battlefield easily, quietly, and without incident, and they found themselves sitting beside someone's goat byre with the night dark around them and a great many stars in the sky.

"I suppose that's that, then," said Glenna, but her voice didn't sound as miserable as it had sounded earlier. "Goodness, what a smell! What is it? Goats? I knew I didn't like goats!"

Peter tried to open the tickerbox but it resisted, wriggling away to hide in his pocket, and with a feeling of helplessness, he let it. Whatever time they had found themselves in, the suns were already down and he was weary to death. It would likely take years to fix the tickerbox: he could hardly hope to try and fix it tonight, in any event.

He said, "Should we find somewhere to sleep?"

"Perhaps," said Glenna, and her voice was thoughtful enough to worry him. "I think I need to do some thinking first, however."

"What—what sort of thinking?"

"Well, the tickerbox is ruined."

"Yes, I know. I'll try to fix it, but—"

"But we already know you won't be able to," she said. "And if you're not able to fix it, what's the use of my going along with you? I might be forced to shift every time you do, but I don't see why we should have to be together for all of that time. Perhaps I'll go away for a while."

"You can't!" Peter said indignantly. "You already know the future! We're married! We've got a daughter!"

"We don't have anything yet," Glenna told him. "And if you can break time and reality with your tickerbox by showing off, I don't see why I can't do it by refusing to marry you."

"What about the older me? You said you love him—me!"

"I'm still trying to decide if he's worth waiting around for," said Glenna. "If there's anything we know about time and reality, it's that things aren't always set in stone. If I don't think you're likely to turn into him, I don't see why I should wait for him."

"*Wait!*" Peter said fiercely. "Just *wait*, Glenna! I'll prove to you that I'm him!"

"You should prove it to yourself, first," she said. "I don't particularly want you to mould yourself to my idea of what he is, and I certainly don't want you always trying to earn my respect. Try and satisfy yourself that you're a decent person first."

Peter had once thought that he was a reasonably satisfactory person. He had been quite content in the conviction—as he had been in the conviction that he did not make mistakes when it came to logic, magic, or mechanics. The only mistakes he made, as he had thought, were those carefully calculated ones in his experiments.

Perhaps he was more akin to his projects in their experimental stage than the finished product: a series of considered trials and errors that took him ever closer to the finished project—a series of considered trials and errors without which the final product could never exist.

"All right," he said. "All right, it's your choice. Maybe you don't want to travel with me for a while. That's all right, if that's what you want."

"I haven't decided yet," she said. "But don't think I'm going to decide to stay with you just because it's supposed to be our future. You're not even the same age as me!"

"Think yourself lucky!" Peter said, before he could think better of it. "The castle threw Annabel and me back three years into the past—imagine if I'd come to the university at thirteen because I had nothing better to do! You'd have been four years older than me instead of just one."

Glenna closed her eyes briefly, but although her lips were pressed together, Peter was quite sure it was to hide the very small smile he had seen for just a moment.

"You can't tell me that it's worse to have me hanging on your sleeve than to have a thirteen-year-old boy doing it! I was *much* worse at thirteen!"

"I can only imagine," said Glenna, and this time, the smile couldn't be held back. "Oh, for pity's sake, let's find somewhere warm to sleep. I shan't run away from you, at any rate. I'll tell you if I mean to leave."

Relieved to know that much at least, Peter set a small whisp of magic ahead of them to light the way. In that light, some half an hour later, they found a small cottonseed shed by a cow byre. There was just enough cottonseed in it to dig into and make a small, warm hole for themselves without leaving them in danger of being smothered, and Peter found himself grateful for that warmth. Whenever and wherever it was they had arrived, it wouldn't be long before the autumn turned to winter.

When they were curled up together and warm, and the light had been banished altogether, Peter said softly to the back of Glenna's head, "Glenna?"

She hesitated briefly, and Peter almost thought she would pretend to be asleep. Then she sighed and asked, "What is it?"

"When we got to Luck's house again and met Poly and— and the older me…what did I say?"

"You said you were sorry," she said. "And asked me to stay. You said you were sorry I'd had to wait so long, but to please keep waiting a bit longer."

It was too soon to ask her again, but he couldn't help himself. "Are you—are you going to?"

"I still haven't decided yet," she said.

· · ·

The tickerbox must have moved them in their sleep, because they fell asleep in the cottonseed and awoke in someone's garden under shadow of a great, sandstone wall that was part of somebody's grand, New-Civetan-style country-house.

Peter, awakened from a dream of Annabel with the searing, regretful thought that he had never had the opportunity to apologise to her, found Glenna just stirring into wakefulness beside him with an equally dissatisfied expression on her face.

"Do you think we can at least get an idea of the next times the tickerbox is going to take us to?" she asked him, looking around disfavourably at their new surroundings as she sat up. It was still night, wherever they had arrived, but the moon was bright and full, and there was music in the air. "Goodness, there seems to be a party going on. I wonder if we should try to get some food."

"The next shift will be in about twenty minutes," Peter told her, after a quick look at the tickerbox's timer. "Your diagnostic extra still seems to be working quite well, so I don't see why it shouldn't—yes, there we go. I asked it for a prognostication, and it seems happy to do that. In twenty minutes or so, we should be off to the New Civet Capital just a few weeks after the Enchanted Battlefield."

"Wonderful," said Glenna. "Well, I don't think I'll bother trying to get food now, in that case. It seems like a good way to get indigestion. The house looks rather familiar, though, doesn't it?"

"Oh!" said Peter, who had finally realised exactly when and where they were. "This is—I think this is a party I was invited to, back before I went to the university. The Terry's monthly or whatever it was. How odd! It's what I was dreaming about—I kept thinking that there was one more thing I had to do. Well, one more apology to make. Do you suppose the tickerbox brought us here because I dreamed about it?"

"Good heavens," Glenna said. "Who else did you insult so

badly that you dreamed the tickerbox into finding them again?"

"An old friend," he told her. "She put up with me for years; ever since we were kids. I don't think anyone else would have done that. I didn't even—I didn't even know how awful I was to her then, and the way I left her was awful, too. She has her guardian, but I was her friend first, and I should have been better."

"Well then," said Glenna. "You'd better go in, hadn't you?"

"Melchior will probably have me kicked out if he sees me trying to get in," Peter said, rather more to himself than Glenna. He wasn't sure if he was looking for reassurance, or a suggestion that they should just leave. "He always did like Ann better than me."

"Your friend's guardian? What did you do to him?"

"I didn't do anything to him, I insulted Ann."

"I see," said Glenna. To his relief, she seemed mildly amused. "Oh well, I suppose she's got someone behind her, then. She probably needs the support."

"Ann's pretty unflappable," Peter said. "Well, I suppose she had to be; there was Grenna, then me, and even Mordion."

"You're stalling," said Glenna. "I shouldn't try to go through the front doors, if I were you: they really do look like they're on the watch for someone. There's a balcony up there you might be able to get in though, though."

Peter was indignant enough at the accusation of stalling that he made it all the way up onto the balcony in the strength of that indignation, and then into the room under cover of one of the huge potted plants. It occurred to him only then that he was far too untidy to be attending any sort of party, even if Melchior hadn't been grimly on the watch for him. Luckily for him, he spotted Annabel quite quickly. She had obviously seen him climb through the window and was making her way toward him, so he darted toward her and bustled her right out into the hallway before she could object.

Rather breathlessly, she said, "Peter, you horrible boy! What are you doing?"

"Ann," began Peter, frowning, trying to think of the right words.

"What's wrong?" she asked.

Peter laughed, but it was a frustrated laugh. He had had so little practise in apologising. Why had he never thought to learn how to do it? "There's—there's something I have to tell you," he said.

"Is that why you climbed through the window?"

"Yes. That's why I climbed through the window."

"What's wrong?" she asked again.

"I'm sorry."

Annabel blinked at him just like she used to. "What?"

"All right, I know it's not like me," Peter said, trying for dignity. "I'm *sorry*. Lately I've been—Actually, no; I've *always* been awful to you. I didn't know—Well, I suppose I knew, a bit. But you always just took it, and so I forgot to care about whether or not I was hurting your feelings. Anyway, I'm sorry."

There was a gleam of amusement in Annabel's brown eyes. "Is this because Melchior threw you out?"

"What? No. Well, maybe a bit. But someone told me—No, she showed me—"

"She?"

Peter felt himself flush. "Never mind. The point is that I didn't realise how awful I'd been to you, and I'm sorry."

"Who is *she*?" demanded Annabel, her eyes alight.

"Never mind about that," Peter said, hastily. "She's a quick-tempered madwoman, and I should have stayed away from her. Actually, no—That was my fault too, if it comes to that."

"I want to meet her."

"You can't," he said, miserably. "I did something—we did something—and you won't meet her for a bit."

"Peter," she said suspiciously, "have you been playing with your tickerboxes again?"

"Anyway," Peter said, trying not to hunch his shoulders, "I won't see you for a bit, either. I'm sorry about that. And—and about everything else. I didn't understand—I didn't know how it could affect you."

"What's wrong, Peter?" Annabel asked sharply. "Really?"

"I don't have any time," Peter said. "And time is—Well, time is pretty important at the moment. I'm sorry, Ann."

He hugged her for as long as he dared, remembering the timer that was counting down somewhere below the windows, then tried to dash for cover again before anyone saw him. In that, he was only partially successful: certainly no one else seemed to pay attention to him, but as soon as he ducked into the card room to get out through the window there, a complication appeared.

She literally appeared, tweaking the world around them just slightly, and although she looked as though she must be at least twenty-five, he knew her straight away.

It was Glenna.

If he had thought the Glenna he knew was beautiful, this older Glenna was so much more beautiful: confident, quiet, and assured, there was a glow to her that wasn't just in her smile or in the orangey magic that haloed her. Peter, looking at her, almost despaired of the future he hoped for. There was something so terrifying about her certainty, her confidence. This woman was already complete: she didn't need him, didn't have to put up with his nonsense or rely on him for anything.

It was doubtful, in fact, that he could ever hope even to be equal with her.

Peter sat down very suddenly on the loveseat beside him.

"Hello dearest," she said, and came to sit down next to him.

Peter couldn't help the hot flush that surged up his collar and right to the top of his head. "Hello," he said, and cleared his throat.

"I thought I might just manage to catch you here," she said. "I'm afraid that I've been rather unpleasant to you over the last day or two."

It should have made him feel better, but the hot flush Peter felt this time was closer to the flush of tears accumulating. "She—I mean you haven't said or done anything I didn't deserve. You haven't even said or done anything wrong."

"Perhaps not," that older Glenna said, smiling faintly. "But I was punishing you, and that's not quite fair when I said I'd forgiven you. So I thought I'd come and cheer you up. Do you like my shoes?"

Peter gave a surprised laugh. "Are you wearing shoes?"

"Certainly I am!" she said, and lifted her white skirts over the tips of those shoes. "Aren't they lovely? So comfortable, too! One gets used to not wearing shoes after a while, and after that, comfort is so important."

That was his fault, too, and Peter found himself saying, "I'm awfully sorry, you know," though he had already apologised to the younger Glenna.

"Do you know why I love you so much?" she asked.

She asked it casually, lightly; the full importance of what she said didn't hit Peter until several seconds after she'd said it.

"You—wait, you *love* me?"

"That's not the important thing," Glenna said.

Peter tried to take in a breath but found it difficult. "Yes, it is," he said.

She laughed. "Yes, but it's not what I'm trying to say right now. Just for now, try to listen, Peter."

"Sorry," he said.

"Yes," Glenna said. "I know. That's why I love you so

much. If anyone knows what it's like to wrestle with a natural defect, I do. No matter how hard you try, something always goes wrong, and it's much easier to think that it isn't your fault."

"Yours *wasn't* your fault," Peter said. "You didn't ask to be jinxed. With me it's worse; it's sheer, bloody-minded confidence and a refusal to believe I'm in the wrong."

"Yes, but you don't stay the same," said Glenna, smiling at him in such a way that Peter felt he couldn't quite breathe. "You keep growing and changing, and that's where the difference is. Would you mind looking out the window for a moment, dearest?"

Peter did as he was told, and felt the warmth of a kiss pressed into his cheek as well as the brief tickle of Glenna's hair against his ear. He twitched his head around to gaze at her in astonishment, went very red, and looked away again hastily.

Beside him, Glenna sniffed a very small laugh and said, "I keep forgetting how adorable you are when you're younger. You'd best be going, hadn't you? I'll be waiting for you down there, wondering why you're taking so long."

"Right," said Peter, jumping to his feet and very nearly tripping over his own feet. "But what about you—oh—"

He had barely taken his eyes off her, and in that moment, she had vanished, as if she'd never been. As if she didn't have to shift in quite the same way that he and Glenna shifted now, reliant on their tickerbox. As if she hadn't had to depend on a tickerbox at all.

And somewhere deep in his heart, for the first time since the Enchanted Battlefield, Peter felt the stirring of hope.

Glenna was waiting for him when he dropped back onto the grass, and Peter was glad for the darkness and coolness of the outside. He felt that his face hadn't yet returned to its normal colour, and there was a fresh surge of heat to his cheeks when Glenna grabbed him by the arm to stop him overbalancing into the flowerbed.

The tickerbox made a mechanical sort of mumble and danced away onto his shoulder, tangling itself briefly with Glenna's hair while she helped Peter to regain his balance, its sharp feet prickling through his clothes.

"I thought I was going to have to come and get you," Glenna said, the relief clear on her face. "What took you so long?"

The tickerbox nattered at something over Peter's shoulder once again, and he became aware of something soft and fluffy tickling his neck that wasn't Glenna's curls.

He yelped and spun around to find Rorkin standing there with one outstretched hand, in which was a single sock.

"What are you—are you trying to feed *socks* to my tickerbox?"

Rorkin jumped guiltily and put his hands behind his back. "Absolutely not! There was no trying involved: it ate one willingly and came back for seconds."

"Maybe it's trying to learn how to knit," suggested Glenna. She looked as though she were trying not to laugh. "Goodness me, you do seem to turn up at odd times!"

Rorkin turned his jewel-like brown eyes on her. "I tried to bring you a present but I don't think I remembered."

"Why are you here?" asked Peter, in some irritation. "We're just about to go again, anyway."

Rorkin shot him a knowing look. "I know that. *I'm* going soon, if it comes to that! We're all going."

"Rorkin!" said Glenna in delight. "Are you coming with us?"

"We don't know where we're going, you know," said Peter, warningly. "Though we do know when, and for how long. The next jump will only give us a month or so in the weeks just after the Battlefield. What are we supposed to do with a month or two?"

"Treaty," said Rorkin promptly.

"What?"

"Treaty," Rorkin said again. "And laws and that sort of thing. Very boring, but someone has to do it."

Glenna now looked as though she was trying not to cough. "Do you mean *we're* the ones who set up the basis for New Civet's government?"

"I should have known," Peter said. "They're so interconnected that they don't leave any wriggle room. And if I remember rightly, an ancient law will managed to slip through for Luck to take advantage of in a few hundred years."

"That will be the annoying thing," said Glenna. "I don't like leaving things where they'll get in the way."

"Yes, but this is something that's *meant* to happen."

"It's a good thing you're here, then," she said, prompting a small warmth of happiness to burst somewhere in Peter's stomach. "Between the two of us, we should be able to make a very potent mix of deliberate obsolescence and air-tight safety for a few hundred years yet."

"And I'll be there, too," Rorkin said. "You can't forget about me. I shall be very useful. Not yet, but some time soon I shall be *very* useful."

"You're always useful," Glenna told him, patting his arm. She drew in a small, pleased breath and let it out. "Oh *good*! At last we're going to do something fun!"

This time it was Peter who tried not to cough on his indrawn breath. "Arranging a treaty sounds like *fun* to you?"

"Certainly!" said Glenna. "You don't know, then, that I spent most of my early school years learning about law?"

"I suppose you did that for fun, too," said Peter, unsuccessfully trying to hold back a grin. "Well, rather you than me!"

"Yes, I'd gathered that impression. Your older self was the

one who advised me to do it; I have recently realised that you did so for not entirely unselfish reasons."

Glenna must have seen the guiltiness of his face, because she grinned at him.

"No need to look so worried," she said. "I thoroughly enjoyed myself. I had no idea that I was studying something for which I was largely responsible. I did study other countries' laws, but I specialised in New Civetan law."

"I should really start making a list of all these things that I'm supposed to tell you," said Peter.

"Shouldn't bother," said Rorkin. "You can't take it with you, anyway. Do what I do: rely on your memory!"

Peter eyed him askance. "Yes, that's worked out very well for you, hasn't it?"

"Well," said Rorkin at once, "*I* didn't make a giant hole in time and reality!"

Peter, indignantly, replied, "Yes, you did! You already told us so!"

"*I* didn't unravel the future—"

"No, you just ran around in an unravelling castle, making life difficult for me and Annabel!"

"*I* didn't go hugging girls at parties."

Peter looked consciously toward Glenna, who seemed to be trying not to laugh yet again. "Rorkin, you awful beast!"

"*I* didn't—"

"We're not going anywhere with you!"

"Can't help it, can you?"

"We'll see about that," said Peter, because he had remembered something very important. "Just you wait. One day I'll get Glenna some shoes that don't vanish, and we'll see about who can help what!"